Grant Aaronson has been creating fantasy worlds for as long as he can remember. He lives in a deep, dark valley in a windy part of the Pennine Hills, Yorkshire, with his girlfriend and one-eyed cat. When he's not writing or stringing his guitar (Grant was once a touring folk musician), he spends his time painting miniatures and going for afternoon strolls.

For all the people who first inspired me; then kept me from giving up.

A CIP catalogue record for this title is available from the British Library.

ISBN 9781035853250 (Paperback)
ISBN 9781035853267 (ePub e-book)

www.austinmacauley.com

First Published 2025
Austin Macauley Publishers Ltd®
1 Canada Square
Canary Wharf
London
E14 5AA

I would like to thank:

The four people who tolerated my earlier drafts and gave me the feedback I needed.

The British countryside and all it has to offer – which greatly inspired Jack's journey.

The dreadful English weather, without which I would have been unable to stay in most evenings to write the whole thing.

Prologue

A single cauldron burning a pale turquoise flame hung motionless in the centre of the room, a few feet above the floor as though it were standing on an invisible plinth. The men and women of the Warlocks' Council sat about it in a circle, each of them at the ringed table. Their faces were flickering in the dancing shadows of the ethereal fire as they heatedly debated the last bill they had acquired from parliament before the summer dissolution.

"Ladies and Gentlemen, since we are unable to agree on a decision," declared the Chief Warlock, Alayna Strauss, "I suggest we put this to a vote. I shall, of course, abstain; save in the event of a tie." The room went quiet before she gave her council the final command of the session. "For the last time, parliament has voted for a bill in favour of abolishing the levy on black tourmaline." She turned to Eva Valmarque. "Eva, state your case for the opposition and be concise. I think we'd all like to begin summer recess within the hour."

Eva Valmarque stood up with conviction, her flame red hair flashing garishly against the dim turquoise glow. Behind her green eyes was a stare that would have stopped the bravest warrior in his tracks. "My esteemed colleagues," she addressed the room with the commanding yet reassuring tone of a politician, an astute person would have deduced her education was not solely magical. "As we know, the public believes that an amulet of black tourmaline gives them protection from the spells and tricks of those with magic."

Eva paused to look her peers in the eye before continuing: "If it becomes more affordable, it will not be long before all in Talamholean from the King to the beggars are wearing one around their necks. We cannot allow such a thing to happen. For one, while it is prudent to keep the rich and the powerful docile, doing the same to the commoners and the workers could lead to poor craftsmanship, famine or worse. I implore you to keep black tourmaline and other gemstones in the hands of the aristocracy and the merchant classes who need to be kept in check. We have no need to do it to the masses and doing so could lead to moral decline and societal collapse."

She sat down with a flourish. The Warlocks' Council considered themselves above what they deemed common behaviour such as clapping, cheering or booing but a trained eye would have noticed that she was met in equal measure with approving nods and contemptuous scowls.

"Thank you, Eva. Leopold, you may now make the case for, and try to be equally brief. The sun is setting," said the Chief Warlock impatiently.

Leopold Braske chose not the impassioned approach of his colleague, but instead went for mystique and theatre. He stood up as slowly as possible, allowing the scars on his face to flicker in the light. Scars that he could have easily removed or concealed with his magic but seemed to prefer to keep them for the intimidating effect they had on others. He always spoke at a volume that was louder than a whisper but quieter than most speeches when addressing a room full of his colleagues.

"Sirs and Madams," he drawled silkily. "Miss Valmarque is right to point out the risk to morality and productivity our great nation faces if black tourmaline becomes easier to procure. Indeed, many have argued for parliament and the King to make it illegal to own or wear gemstones if one does not possess lands, titles or wealth, but neither monarch nor legislature should be seen openly oppressing the people. Instead, we've always opted for the more subtle approach of making it harder for the poor to achieve higher status." He paused for effect and looked around to see how his colleagues were reacting.

"Before midnight if you please, Braske!" Alayna Strauss said, clearly irked by his exhibition. Braske nodded apologetically while his eyes flashed menacingly.

"I do, however, believe that we are past the point of no return. Now the populus rely more on gunpowder than they do on us. Gone are the days of chivalrous knights and bows and arrows. Wars are now fought with muskets and cannons. A trigger can be pulled faster than magic can be conjured, and it won't be long before the masses catch on."

"If we allow them to keep believing that black tourmaline will keep them safe from our magic, as we have allowed the aristocracy to believe since records began, then they will soon be wearing it round their necks on mass and we will be able to manipulate the commoners as we have the powerful and perhaps return to happier times within less than a century." He finished his speech with a flourish but if he was hoping for applause, it did not come.

"You're a fool if you think you can control everyone, Braske," snapped Quentin Caskill from Eva Valmarque's right. Braske's eyes flashed with anger and he was about to retort with either his wit or his own violent brand of magic.

No one found out which it would be, as Alayna Strauss finally dissolved the situation raising her voice magically to an inhuman roar.

"Enough!" She bellowed so loudly the walls of the Warlocks' Tower shook, making the Graylenmouth skyline come alive for a moment for those outside the tower. "The time has come to vote."

"Those for?" Braske and three others raised their hands.

"Against!" Alayna snapped again. Eva Valmarque answered with three of her own colleagues. A tie.

Alayna Strauss looked contemplative for a moment then shrugged: "The Chief Warlock votes against. The bill to reduce the levy on black tourmaline cannot be allowed royal assent." She held the parchment containing the would-be law in her hand, closed her eyes and concentrated for a few short seconds while caressing the ruby about her neck with the other. The parchment burst into flames then crumbled into ashes and the Chief Warlock's hands were unscorched by the short fire.

Braske's face flashed angrily for a fraction of a second before he brought himself under control, unnoticed by his contemporaries.

"I do believe that is everything," affirmed Alayna triumphantly. "We shall reconvene in September when parliament reopens. Unless anyone has a matter to bring forward." She glared at the other members of the council, daring them to keep everyone in session longer without good reason.

"Well?" Frederick Rundle offered in a hesitant tone. "Off the record, I'm not sure the current relationship between the King and the Prime Minister will survive another session of parliament." Strauss considered him for a moment before she sighed defeatedly.

"You're right, Rundle. We can't put this off any further. What's worse is that they don't even have the decency to keep their animosity private. It seems you can't read the Chronicle these days without seeing that one has publicly insulted the other."

"We can't be seen to take sides; we'll be accused of manipulation and partisanship," cautioned Merion Ridwell.

"We cannot take sides *publicly*," corrected Charlotte Campbell. "Who we side with and what action we take privately is another matter."

"Agreed. I assume," offered Stephen Sparrow, "that we believe it would be better to side with the King? After all, King Wilfrid is young, naïve and easy to manipulate, and monarchs come and go less frequently than Prime Ministers as a matter of circumstance."

The council did not seem to unanimously support Sparrow's claim as he was met with little enthusiasm from his cohorts.

"I may have a third option," piped up Eva Valmarque. Eva was after all the personal and trusted Warlock of the Prime Minister himself, a statement like that quickly brought the room to a stunned silence, everyone hanging on Eva's next word.

"I think, in the long run, it would be in our best interests to replace the King with someone who isn't interested in ruling, someone who would enjoy all the extravagance of being a monarch and would have no time for governance. They would allow parliament to pass whatever legislation they wanted and would probably give royal assent to whatever we put in front of them without reading it."

Braske was not able to mask his anger this time. He hammered his fists so hard on the table and the whole thing shook, all the Warlocks felt it. His scars seemed to be throbbing in anger.

"What you're suggesting is treason, Valmarque! The council and the monarchy have existed longer than the penpushers in parliament. I won't as a member of this council, side with them."

"Control yourself, Braske, and remember where you are," Alayna Strauss commanded.

The Chief Warlock then turned back to Eva. "If I understand correctly, you wish to replace the King with a candidate of our choosing. A candidate that will likely give the Warlocks' Council full control of the executive branch in all but appearance?" Eva nodded in confirmation making Alayna's next question inevitable.

"Who do you have in mind?"

Chapter One

Sunday nights were his favourite times for patrol as nothing generally happened. Jack and his partner, Lyndsey Carter, led their horses by the reins through the cobbled streets of Graylenmouth, following their given patrol route and waiting for a criminal to apprehend or a disturbance to rectify.

The problem was, that there was little opportunity for officers of the Graylenmouth Guard to do either of those things on a Sunday night. The taverns were all closed in accordance with respecting the sabbath. The aristocracy and the merchant classes would occasionally come through the streets on an expensive stallion, or in lavish gilded carriages but they had no need to request the services of the city guardsmen. The criminal classes, both petty and organised, would not risk being seen conducting their activity on quiet Sunday streets where there was little chance for discretion. All of this led to, at least Jack thought, a rather pleasant night to be out at work.

"I'm so bored," Lyndsey grimaced. "Nothing ever happens on a Sunday. I'm not asking for a lifechanging adventure or a dangerous mission, but I wouldn't mind a change from this. We must of circled our patrol route a dozen times and will probably do a dozen more before midnight."

"Must *have,* Lyndsey," retorted Jack with a cheeky smile. "You're moving up in the world and you wouldn't want to embarrass Mr Carter."

"If Mr Carter was constantly correcting my grammar, I wouldn't be Mrs Carter," she retorted with an equally cheeky smile. "That sort of man wouldn't allow me to stay on the front lines of the Guard either."

"True, but I'd be surprised if you make him aware of everything that happens when we're on patrol."

"Not every detail but he knows the important stuff, I try to be—" She broke off as the clanging of a distant warning bell broke the pleasant ambience of the summer evening.

"That's the bell on Gryffyn Street," said Lyndsey. "On a Sunday night? I can't believe anything *that* serious has happened."

They looked at each other and tutted, rolled their eyes, and raised their fists in unison counting "one, two, three."

She drew stone.

He drew scissors.

"Bollocks," Jack hissed. "I'll see what this is about; probably just kids messing around. You stay on patrol and I'll re-join you shortly."

Without another word, he mounted his horse and rode across the cobbles towards Gryffyn Street and the ear-splitting sound of the bell. The citizenry knew that if they needed the help of the guardsmen, they were to come to the barracks or approach them on patrol. That bell was only to be rung in emergencies when time was of the essence and the Guard were nowhere to be found nearby.

He pulled tightly on the left-hand side of the reins to steer his horse down Mermaid Street then broke into a gallop. As the hooves thundered along the cobbles, he felt the clank of splitting metal under the horse's foot. *If my horse requires a reshod, I'll clout the damn bell ringer with the flat of my cutlass.* He thought as he steered his horse around to the right at the bottom of Gryffyn Street and galloped hard towards the ringing bell.

"I'm here, I'm here. Stop ringing the bloody bell before we all go deaf." *A mistake,* he thought, some of the citizenry could be so prudish that even overhearing a guardsman use a minor swear word like *bloody* could land him in hot water with his commanding officer.

As he dismounted and walked towards the no longer clanging bell, he discerned the ringer. Not a group of mischievous children as he had first thought but in fact a grown woman in distress.

"Sergeant, thank god, I didn't know what else to do. He needs to be stopped." Something was off about her. Much of the women of Graylenmouth, regardless of their class, all shared the same modest dress sense be it when in rags, silk or satin. This woman, however, seemed to have ignored the unwritten rules of modesty and in addition, acquired her garments from every single rung of the social ladder.

She was dressed in a whalebone corset so tight, it looked as though her bust might break the laces and rob her of what little humility she had left. There was a short woollen cardigan that draped across her shoulders that barely came down to her middle and could not have afforded her much warmth. Unreasonably baggy pantaloons that could only have belonged to a man and two leather buckled shoes mismatched and different sizes from different pairs. Her auburn hair looked straw-like and windswept as it is likely to when one is in a hurry. Deducing that time was urgent and her need was great, he decided the wise thing to do was make no mention of her appearance and get to the point.

"What's the emergency?" He asked.

"There's a man! He's violent and he's blind drunk. He's got Molly. Molly, my baby sister, at gunpoint and he's not letting her go."

"Where is he?"

"On Unicorn Street at…at…at…"

"At Annabelle's?"

"Yes, Sergeant."

That made sense. Annabelle's was the highest class of brothel Graylenmouth had to offer. Affordable only to the noblest of the aristocracy and the sons of the most successful merchants.

"What's your name?"

"Martha, I'm Martha."

"Martha, I'm going straight to Annabelle's to deal with this. I want you to wait here, count to thirty, then ring the bell again, don't stop until my partner arrives. When she does, tell her what you've told me. Then tell her to load her pistols and head straight for Annabelle's! Can you do that for me, Martha?"

"Yes, Sergeant, thank you."

He was off. Mounting his horse and kicking it into a trot, then a gallop. He had no time to check the mare's shoes. He had to get to Unicorn Street as soon as he could. He did not have time to ask Martha for more details but his instincts told him enough. Molly was most probably a lady of the night and this madman with a gun, was probably a dissatisfied customer. He weaved through the streets until he reached Graylenmouth's red-light district. He knew as much from the oil lamps in this area, which had been painted red on the outside of the glass so that on nights such as this, the streets glowed with a reddish, rather than white hue.

He slowed his horse to a walk when he reached the top of Unicorn Street. Approaching Annabelle's, he dismounted and tied the horse to the hitching post. He checked his side for his cutlass and made sure he could draw it quickly if he needed to. Then he removed his pistols from the saddlebags and placed them in his belt, hoping it made him look more authoritative. In accordance with regulation, they were not loaded with either shot or powder to prevent accidental discharge and he did not have time to load them now.

Accidental discharge, I must be the first man in history to enter a brothel and not be worried about that. He wrapped his knuckles on his breast plate for good luck, then checked the chin strap to his zischagge and walked up the steps to the door of Annabelle's.

The air was thick with the scent of tobacco and opium smoke. Waving his hand around in front of his face to try and achieve better visibility proved to be of little help.

"Officer, Officer Jack Sweep, Sergeant, isn't it? Over here if you please?"

Following the sound of the assertive feminine voice, he walked through the fog where he found an austere middle-aged woman in an equally austere black sequined dress buttoned up with a high collar. Her greyish black hair was pulled into a bun at the back of her head. She could only have been the Madame.

"Are you the owner?" He asked in a baffled tone.

"Yes, I'm Annabelle. Captain Thompson speaks very highly of you, Sergeant," she said discerning his confusion. "I'm glad you're here."

"Where's Molly? Where's this madman?"

"In the drawing room. We must hurry."

"Lead the way."

The drawing room was as smoky as the lobby. About half a dozen girls were sat on the sofas with expressions of terror, some were sobbing. At the head of the room by the fireplace was the unfortunate girl that could only have been Molly, half naked and dishevelled.

The poor girl of about twenty-one was trying to use her arms to modestly cover her breasts. Her petticoat had torn at the midriff and came down just above her knees. She was unable to afford herself more dignity thanks to the brute holding her hostage and standing behind her. His left arm had her neck in a tight grip, Jack hoped she was able to breathe. His right arm was pointing a cocked pistol at her right temple. *If she dies, I'll make sure you suffer a slow and humiliating death, you bastard,* Jack thought to himself.

"You called the Guard? I'll shoot all you whores in the cunts for this, you worthless bitches," he half shouted half slurred. His eyes seemed to flash with malice and glaze with inebriation simultaneously. Nothing in Jack's previous training or experience taught him how to deal with this situation but this was not the time for hesitation.

"What is your grievance, Sir?" He loathed himself for showing politeness to someone so despicable, but for Molly's sake, he decided not to aggravate the man any further.

"My *problem,* you illiterate fuckwit, is that I come for an evening in this brothel with more gold than all these whores have seen in their lifetime and this bitch tells me she won't render the services I require."

The shock that powerful people seemed to suffer when they discovered some people had standards and could not be persuaded with gold never ceased to amaze Jack.

"I am a sergeant in the Guard." Jack hoped his voice did not betray the sense of urgency and desperation that he was using all his strength to banish to the back of his mind. "If you'd like to file a business grievance, I suggest you let the young lady go and we step outside."

"Business grievance," he drawled, rolled his eyes and seemed to shout to the ceiling. "Don't make me laugh. They're whores, not entrepreneurs. And why are you calling this slut *young lady*? Hoping she'll take pity on you and give you a freebee pleb? Ha, your yearly wage probably wouldn't buy you an hour with her. You're no gentleman. I have good money, a good reputation and come from a good family. My father shall hear of this!"

He maliciously whispered something inaudible to Molly while tightening his grip which made her wince and sob. While the brute was lost in his own insane ramblings, Jack took the opportunity to take a few steps closer to them, hoping the smoke-filled room and the brute's own drunkenness would prevent him from noticing. He was now only three feet away. Not knowing what to do next, Jack uttered the first thing to enter his head.

"You're right, Sir, I'm no gentleman. Seeing as you *are*, why don't you point that pistol at me instead of a naked woman?" He risked a little more assertiveness in his voice, hoping it would divert his attention from the fact that the distance between them had just halved.

Seeming to come back to earth after reciting his own vulgar style of poetry, the brute hesitated for a moment then, without releasing his grip on Molly, slowly turned his right arm towards Jack and aimed it at his head. Only a foot from his head. Jack raised his hands.

"Thank you, now why don't you let the young lady go and we'll resolve this as reasonably—"

"She won't fuck you pleb no matter how noble—"

He rolled his eyes while he said it and Jack saw the opportunity. He grabbed the brute's wrist from underneath with both hands, then thrust it upwards as he took several steps forward and bent his arm above his head and backwards in an anatomically impossible position. He felt the man's shoulder pop and dislocate. The brute released Molly but did not scream as most did with the pain of dislocation. The gun went off with a deafening bang. Several of the girls screamed and flecks of plaster fell from the ceiling.

Quickly risking a glance to his right and checking that Molly was safe, he head butted the brute, forgetting he was wearing his zischagge. The brim of the metal helmet caught him in the side of the face, splitting his cheek open. He went down and hit the wooden floorboards with a thud.

Right on cue, the door to the drawing room burst open and Lyndsey and Annabelle ran through. Lyndsey scanned her eyes over the room in a swift pragmatic sweep then lowered her pistol.

"That him?" She nodded towards the brute. "Who is he?"

"No idea, some arsehole. Do you have your irons? I left mine in the saddle bag."

She withdrew a pair of heavy iron manacles on a short chain from her belt and handed them to him. He knelt, turned the brute over and clamped his wrists together behind his back.

"We'd better sit him down and get his wound dressed before taking him to the barracks," Jack said bitterly, that was too kind given what he had just tried to do.

Lyndsey and Jack grabbed him under each arm. Jack could feel his right arm limply moving in the sleeve, not quite connected to the man's torso. Strangely, he continued to seethe with malice but showed no signs of pained injury.

"Annabelle, do you have any bandages or stitching? We need to see to his wound. Then we'll get the scumbag out of here."

"No need," replied Annabelle embracing Molly in a maternal fashion. "I have a…Warlock who can heal minor natural injuries. Girls fetch Olivia, will you."

The brute was starting to find his words again. "You'll hang for this, Guardsman," he seethed at Jack. "My father is in the cabinet. He'll see to it that you lose your rank, reputation and miserable excuse for a life."

"…but until then you're in our custody." Lyndsey frowned unperturbed. "Now, show a little grace. I'm going to pop your shoulder back in on the count of three. One, two, three." There was a soft clicking sound as the man's arm slid back into its socket.

Just as he had shown no signs of pain upon dislocation, he showed none when it was reconnected. Lyndsey somehow had a knack for popping shoulders back into place, though how she was able to do it with the man's hands chained behind his back, Jack never knew. Perhaps being the wife of a physician had afforded her skills that other guardsmen did not possess. Lyndsey looked triumphant, gave a self-satisfied smile and brushed her long brown hair out of her eyes. Then she bashfully looked around the room almost hoping to be congratulated on a job well done.

The brute opened his mouth again, clearly about to offer Lyndsey some of his trademark politeness when the door opened. Olivia came through. Jack had never met her but by the way she was dressed, he knew she could only be a Warlock. She wore a long bright orange satin dress which, unlike Annabelle's, stopped just below the shoulders. Her strawberry blonde hair cascaded down her back all the way to her waist. Around her neck was an amulet of aquamarine on a leather chord. Like all Warlocks, she wore no shoes or socks.

Without a word or a look to anyone, she walked straight to the brute squatted down opposite him and looked at his wound. She fixed him with a stare, not a threatening one but a calm and serene gaze. The brute's eyes glazed over but not with further drunkenness. He was now swaying slightly with a look of calm elation on his face as though he'd just smoked half a crop of opium. Jack reminded himself to ever be wary of Warlocks and their tricks.

Olivia placed her hand on the brute's cheek then closed her eyes and concentrated for a moment. When she removed her hand, the gash was gone, leaving no scars and only dried and smeared blood. Olivia looked up at them and smiled.

"He will be in his trance for the next hour or so."

"Can he walk?"

"Not far."

"Ok, we'll get him on the horse. Lyndsey, you better return to patrol. Help me get him out of here, will you?"

"Shouldn't we take statements?"

He sighed empathetically. "I doubt they'll want to." Prostitution was illegal throughout Talamholean but due to the powerful having a fondness for it, the authorities always turned a blind eye, meaning that any prostitute willing to give a statement risked arrest and prosecution herself. *That's why this twat was surprised when I turned up here. Thompson's going to remove my sergeant's stripes and have me cleaning the latrines all year when he finds out I responded to a whore's call for help.*

It was not easy getting him to the horse. He dragged his feet constantly and drooled on Lyndsey at one point, leaving his high-born saliva all down her shoulder. Eventually, they had him bent over the rump of Jack's horse. He comically swayed side to side face down, staring at the stone cobbled streets with his hands chained behind his back.

"Ok, what's troubling you now?" Lyndsey asked as they led their horses to the top of Unicorn Street. Jack could be prone to bouts of silent thoughtfulness that would often irritate his closest friend.

"Madam Annabelle knew who I was. I've never met her; she said Captain Thompson speaks highly of me."

"Captain Thompson's the fourth son of a silk merchant. Make's sense that he'd frequent the fanciest brothel in the capital I suppose."

"I don't doubt that, but the Captain rarely speaks highly of anyone and hasn't ever shown me anything but frustration and resentment. Besides, I had my zischagge on and I've never had my portrait painted, it's not as though there's anything unique about my appearance from that of another guardsman."

They said goodbye to each other at the top of Unicorn Street. Lyndsey mounted her own mare and trotted back towards the patrol route. Jack made his way through the streets of the capital towards the City Centre and the barracks of the Graylenmouth Guard.

The building was white in colour with an ancient design. Its angular roof slanted upwards from each side and met in the middle to form a point. There were stone cylindrical pillars supporting the roof that cropped out from the front of the building. He tied his horse up at the foot of the steps, put the brute on his feet and led him with difficulty towards the front door.

"Evening, Jack. Thought you and Carter would be enjoying a quiet patrol," came the familiar tone of Captain Johnston, officer of the night watch. "Who's this? Had a bit too much drink, have we, young man?"

"He has, but that's not why he's away with the fairies right now. A Warlock put him in a trance to heal his wound."

"Wound?"

"I cut his cheek open with my helmet, in self-defence of course."

"Busy Sunday you've had, Jack." He got up from the desk and walked over to the brute examining his cheek.

"Incredible! Not a scar nor scratch, and both parliament and the mayor claim we don't need our own Warlock for injured guardsmen." He tutted and shook his head.

"Guessing we won't get much from him in this state. I'll stick him in the cells and process him later. What's the charge?"

Assault, Jack thought, *attempted murder, kidnapping and possibly rape.* He hesitated, knowing he could not get any of that to stick without statements. Statements that would have to come from Annabelle and Molly who would be unlikely to cooperate.

"Drunk and disorderly," Jack said after a moment's pause.

Johnston tutted and rolled his eyes. "It seems the wealthy don't need a tavern to get pissed like the rest of us. Thanks, Jack. You better get back to patrol before Thompson catches you and accuses you of malingering."

*

A few moments later, he was walking side by side with Lyndsey again, leading their horses by the reins. They circuited their patrol route a few more times until the bells tolled midnight and they made their way back to the barracks.

They did not enter through the front door this time but round the back as they needed to see to their horses.

"Jack, Lyndsey," Aaron, the stable hand, greeted them with a friendly nod. Lyndsey smiled and returned the nod.

"You're not going to be happy, Aaron; I think I've snapped a horseshoe." Aaron groaned. "I'll take a look in the morning."

They removed their saddlebags and handed their reins to Aaron. Lyndsey did not stay at the barracks anymore since she became a married woman last year and had taken up residence with her husband. They bid each other goodnight and went their separate ways.

When he reached his room, he was exhausted. He got undressed and went straight to bed, blowing out the candle once he was comfortable.

He did not know how long he had been asleep but it could not have been long. It was not yet dawn when the door to his room burst open and in pranced

Captain Thompson, looking both angry and pleased with himself in equal measure. He was accompanied by two burly guardsmen on either side of him.

"Sergeant!" He declared in a menacing voice as his thin moustache quivered in anger. "You're under arrest. These men will escort you to the cells. Come quietly!"

He glared at Jack almost daring him to make a scene and *not come quietly*. Bleary eyed and semi-conscious at having just been awoken, Jack rubbed his eyes and returned the glare.

"On what charge, Sir?" He replied with just a modicum of defiance to avoid appearing insubordinate.

"For assaulting the son and heir of the Home Secretary." Jack was escorted to the barracks' cells; uncertain if he was experiencing a bad dream.

Chapter Two

The windowless cell swam in the light from a candle in the middle of the room. Jack relieved himself into the bucket in the corner then sat on the sheetless straw mattress. On the short trip back from the 'toilet', he stubbed his toe on a loose brick and swore loudly into the dim gloom of the cell. *This is where I die,* he thought bitterly. *In a windowless room underneath the Guard House.* He knew that there were better cells free. Ones with at least a window but Captain Thompson probably took great delight in detaining Jack in the lower cells.

These were usually reserved for the most dangerous type of violent offender, or career criminals and condemned men awaiting the firing squad. That last thought made Jack shudder.

He would think of his family and what his execution would mean to them. He *would* think of his family if he had any, none that he knew of anyway besides Lyndsey. Jack's earliest memories were of the cotton mills. He had been told that he was left there as a baby.

When he was old enough to hold a broom, they had him earning his room and board sweeping the excess cotton from under the machines. He had to do this as quickly as he could before the loom contracted and crushed many a young sweeper as it was known to do.

At the age of eight, a recruiting officer from the Guard came to the factory with promises of an education and a life of excitement. They were not even concerned that an eight-year-old might be too young to join. The Mayor of Graylenmouth at the time had decided that recruiting the guardsmen from the ranks of the very young and very disadvantaged was the best way to clean up the city streets.

"You won't be on the streets until you're fourteen, laddie," the plump recruiting officer had said. "You'll spend the next six years learning to read and write, how to ride a horse, how to load and fire a gun and how to fight with a cutlass." To an eight-year-old, the idea of handling a pistol and a sword was far more enticing than learning his letters, but he was now far more grateful for the latter.

On the first day, he had met Lyndsey, and as the two youngest recruits, they befriended each other immediately. Which was good as Lyndsey had been the daughter of a fur trapper and could load and fire a pistol with admirable speed and frightening accuracy for an eight-year-old. Had it not been for her, he would never have passed his firearms training.

Since completing a guardsman's education eight years ago, he owed them two more years of service and then he would be free. To do what, he did not know, *and I never will now,* he thought bitterly. *I should have just killed that posh arsehole and thrown his body in the river.*

He sighed deeply at the realisation the law did not seem to apply to the sons of politicians and lay down on the cold hard bed, hoping that his situation might look more promising when he awoke. It was not easy to sleep without a blanket but eventually, his tiredness took over his anxiety and he drifted into an uneasy sleep.

The door to the cell burst open. "Get up please, Sergeant. Captain Thompson wants to see you." It felt like he had only just closed his eyes, but at a glance, he saw that the candle had now burnt nearly to its bottom and he knew a few hours had passed.

They led him down the corridor and up the stairs of the detention area by lamp into the higher levels and into Captain Thompson's office. The commander of the Graylenmouth Guard was sitting behind his desk, nose-deep in his administrative duties, signing paper after paper with his quill.

"We've brought him as you requested, Captain," said one of the burly men who had just led Jack from the cell.

"Thank you, wait outside both of you until I call you in," the Captain ordered brusquely, and the guards obeyed.

"Sir, what's going on? Why have I been—" The Captain raised a hand swiftly and commandingly ordering Jack to silence without removing his eyes from the desk. He heard the guards close the office door and waited in uneasy silence.

The bastard's enjoying this. He's going to eke out as much vindictive pleasure as he can before he sends me to the firing squad. Well, I'll give him a fight. I'll defy and I'll state my innocence, but I won't beg. I won't give him that pleasure.

24

The Captain added his signature to one last document, set down his quill, then after what seemed like an eternity, slowly raised his head towards Jack and fixed him with a stare. Jack stood to attention, knowing the Captain would not order him at ease any time soon, if at all.

"Well, *Sweep*!" His commander would often make a point of emphasising Jack's surname as though trying to remind him of the cotton mill where he came from and pontificating his own wealthy background as a means of superiority. "The Home Secretary is prepared to forgive you in return for a small matter. You must appear at his residence this evening to apologise to both him and his son for your mistake. Tell them that you had been drinking on duty and entered the establishment hoping to avail yourself of a lady of the night."

"You then came across the son of the right honourable Lord Pluff, a noble man who was trying to steer you from sin, you saw it as your duty to beat this man and arrest him unlawfully."

"Excuse me, Sir!" He said astounded. "Is that the version of events the man I arrested gave you?"

"The man you arrested was released within an hour of you bringing him here. When I realised you had arrested the son of the Guard's most vocal supporter, I discharged him and escorted him home myself having to grovel before Lord Gregory thanks to you." He seethed. "Fortunately, I assured him that I would deal with the matter personally. That is, deal with *you*. So, you will do as I ordered and apologise to the young man and his father."

"The young man's version of events is very different to what happened."

"I don't care. You have nearly caused a political scandal, and if you have any sense of duty, you will apologise to the family. We need to clear this up now before Bernard Crenshaw finds out."

Jack thought Bernard Crenshaw would probably take more offence at the young man's release but decided not to bring that up. "So politics trumps justice, does it, Sir?" He said instead.

The Captain smirked. "Can you prove your version of events in a court martial?"

I can, there's the testimony of Molly, of Annabelle, of all the girls that were in the room at the time. Even Lyndsey. But his heart sank. He could not ask those girls to testify for him and he did not want to drag Lyndsey's reputation into a political scandal.

"No, Sir." He sighed. The Captain's smirk seemed to broaden.

25

"Then, you shall do as I ordered and make your apologies," he sneered triumphantly.

"In fact, Sir, I won't. I have the right to a court martial and I would prefer to see justice done." The Captain's eyes flashed and now he was angry. Jack could not help but allow himself the small victory. There was no way a court martial would find him innocent with lack of evidence but at least it would make it harder for the Captain and the Home Secretary to keep the Annabelle's incident out of the press' hands. There was a chance, though a slim one, the Home Secretary may drop the charges out of fear for his family's reputation.

"Guards!" The Captain barked and they entered the room obediently. "Escort Sergeant *Sweep* back to his cell. It appears he still has much contemplation to do."

A few minutes later, Jack was massaging his bruised stomach and wincing. On return to his cell, he had reminded the guards that he had the right to a visitor and legal representation and demanded they contact Lyndsey. After too many reminders, one of the prison guards had responded to his request with a blow to the abdomen which winded Jack sorely and put an end to his notions of any rights. It was becoming clear that habeas corpus did not apply to men who had fallen out with the establishment.

In theory, they have a week, Jack thought to himself. *A week to either charge me or let me go. I doubt either of those things will happen though. Before a week goes by, I'll be before the firing squad on the hush-hush.* He needed to think quickly if he wanted to escape his fate.

Even the fastest of thinkers could not have found a way out of this predicament. There was only one entrance to this cell and even if he could outwit or overpower the guards, he still had to escape the barracks, and then what? He could not just waltz out of the city gates as a wanted man, and the only place there was to hide would be Lyndsey and her husband's, which would be the first place they searched.

"I'm well and truly fucked!" He cursed aloud in the darkness with his head raised to the heavens. *Sleep seems to cure stress.* He thought in a vain attempt to reassure himself. *Maybe things will seem clearer after some sleep.* Though he doubted it very much.

*

The next day seemed to pass slowly. Or at least, what he thought was a day. It was hard to gauge a twenty-four-hour cycle when shut away from the world.

He ate, he pissed, he shat, he watched the candle burn lower and lower until it burnt out again. He tried to make conversation with his guard but he did not seem to be a talkative man. He had dared to ask him if there would be any butter to go with his scarce meals of bread and water that were brought to him periodically. The guard ignored him, pretending not to hear anything.

The next two days followed much the same and he was beginning to wonder if he would spend much more time like this before the firing squad. He imagined that Thompson probably wanted him worn down, broken and showing minimal defiance. He would then meet his execution with resignation. That was beginning to seem the amiable option. Jack could not help but admit that to himself after what felt like three days in the cell with no possible hope of escape.

On what he imagined to be the fourth day brought an unexpected but bitterly welcoming break to the routine. The burly prison guard entered but not with food. He was carrying a black strip of material and a rope. Realising it was time, he showed no resistance when the Guard commanded him to face the wall. The rope was used to tie his hands behind his back, the material was his blindfold before the Guard turned him around and frogmarched him out of his cell.

Something's not right! He thought immediately. *They're not taking me to the yard.* He was right, blindfolded or not, he knew the barracks. To go to the yard where the firing squad would be, one would have to turn left out of the cell. Even with a blindfold on, he knew they had turned right. This route led out through the gantry and onto the streets, where there was often a wagon waiting to carry many a condemned man to his death. This made no sense to him.

Surely they were not going to hang him like a severe criminal or burn him like a witch in public. There would be no way to keep the Home Secretary and his son out of the papers without discretion.

The cool summer breeze on his face told him they had just left the building. The dark material of his blindfold did not brighten. It was night-time. As he stood there, he could feel the two guards on either side of him, hear them breathing, and hear them tutting and clicking their heels impatiently. *They're waiting for someone or something. I could make a break for it now.* He thought desperately before realising it was pointless to attempt to outrun two guards at night with his hand bound behind his back and without the ability to see. A desperate escape indeed but at this point, what choice did he have?

He would never find out whether he would be successful in his escape attempt as just then he heard a carriage come down the street and slow down to a stop. The strong smell of horses and the loud sound of neighing told him it had halted right in front of him. He heard someone, presumably the driver, leap down, open the door and open up the steps. Though he did not hear anyone descend.

"The Captain has released Sergeant Sweep to you as requested, my lady," said the Guard to his left in a monotone voice.

"Thank you, boys," replied a woman in an enchanting yet stark voice. "Bring him in, will you?"

He felt a hand on each shoulder forcefully drive him forward and up the stairs into the carriage. Then, with little grace, the same hands turned him around and forced him on to the seat. A luxurious bench with a cushion that provided him with great comfort after three days in a cell. Not the hard wooden ones he would sit in when being transported around by the Guard. He knew immediately he was now in the custody of a powerful woman but what he was doing here he had not yet discerned.

He heard the woman knock twice on the side of the carriage and he lurched forward ever so slightly as the horses began to pull it forward. He took a moment to straighten and balance himself as the box on wheels faltered and quivered slightly on the cobbles.

"Tell me," said the woman. "Are you a man of honour, Sergeant Sweep?"

He wavered for a moment, not knowing what his answer would lead to.

"It depends, my lady, I suppose, on whether or not I'm being asked something dishonourable?"

"Very interesting." The woman chuckled. "Could it be considered moral to only answer honour with honour and dishonour with dishonour? That is one for the philosophers I suppose, so I'll get to the point. Are you an honourable man who will give me his word that he will not attack me or try to run off if I untie him? I have a lot to explain before we arrive at our destination, and I like to make eye contact with people, which right now makes you the wrong sort of captive audience. So do I have your word?"

He hesitated before answering. His hopes of escape were thinner now than they had been a moment ago on the street; but not impossible. Wherever he was going, it was not to be executed. High-born women in carriages do not take condemned men into custody. He decided that his present situation was probably a safer one than if he were an unarmed and wanted fugitive on the streets.

"I will neither attack you nor will I run away, my lady," Jack gave his word reluctantly.

He heard her fingers snap and within an instant, the knots in both his blindfold and the rope around his wrists unravelled and fell to the floor in a lifeless flop. He squinted and rubbed his eyes as they adjusted to the lamp light of the carriage on a late summer evening.

The red velvet décor of the plush transport came into view as well as the woman sitting opposite him. A woman, who he knew could only be a Warlock by the way she was dressed. Even if she had not just freed him with the click of a finger, you could always distinguish a female Warlock from their attire. Unlike Olivia, the Warlock from Annabelle's, this one had a fondness for the colour black.

Her black wide-brimmed hat with a Scarlett band to match her strikingly scarlet hair, covered much of her face, giving her beauty a mysterious and somewhat threatening look. She wore a tight black bodice giving her a busty look which was embroidered with red and gold stitching into the shape of two unicorns facing each other and a flowing black skirt. She was fingering an amulet of amethyst around her neck, which a moment ago had been dangling tauntingly over her cleavage.

The more powerful and higher-status female Warlocks often dressed immodestly as it helped with their allure and often got them what they wanted with the opposite sex. It was rumoured that when a lady warlock served a powerful man, she would be the one who really held the power. Regardless of whether the man she served was aware.

Finally cementing her appearance as one of the magically gifted were her shoes, or in fact the lack of any. It was known across all the climates of Talamholean and regardless of the weather that all Warlocks went about their daily business barefoot. It was said that this was due to the fact that they drew their magic from the earth and footwear made them less powerful.

"It appears that my word was irrelevant, my lady, as I have no magical powers of my own. I'd wager I'm no more a danger to you now than when I was tied up." He couldn't help but be astonished with the pomposity of his own syntax. He had never been alone with a member of the gentry before and it seemed to be having an effect on his manner. Her posture alone made him check that he was not slouching.

She smiled and raised her eyebrows, impressed. "You flatter me, Sergeant, and it's good to know that your powers of perception make you neither naïve nor ignorant. I assume my barefootedness gave me away?"

"That, and the amulet."

"You don't have to be Magical to wear an amulet. Many wear them for protection."

"But not an amethyst. That has powers a Warlock can channel but doesn't grant any protection unless I'm mistaken." The sudden realisation of exactly what powers amethysts granted a Warlock made him freeze in fear momentarily.

"Fear not, Sergeant." She laughed again, almost reading his mind. "I have no need to use this," she said, referring to her amulet. "After all, you gave me your word. I'm glad to say I think I made the right choice picking you. It seems you're a rather well-read commoner. Though, of course, unlike your colleagues, you spend much of your free time in the city library rather than the taverns."

"It seems you know a great deal about me though I don't even know your name."

She smirked, eyeing him shrewdly. "I am Eva Valmarque, member of the Warlocks' Council and personal advisor to the Prime Minister."

He would have tripped, were he not sitting down. If she was the Prime Minister's Warlock, it could only mean he had been taken from the cells at his orders and the Prime Minister himself needed him; but why?

Lord Crandon was a wealthy man and could afford the best of the best for his personal bodyguard or the most ruthless assassin for his more sinister needs. What did he want with a sergeant in the Graylenmouth Guard?

"Am I on my way to meet the Prime Minister then?" He asked uncertainly.

"Eventually," she replied. "He has need of you. We're on our way to his mansion now."

"Need of me?" So he wasn't going to be executed.

"Yes, but that will be explained on the morrow. Tonight, I shall make sure that you are well treated. You will be fed, and you will be allowed to bathe and take some rest. The Prime Minister will receive you at dinner time tomorrow."

It was not long before the carriage came to a slow stop. The coachman dismounted from the driver's bench and unfolded the steps for them; upon exiting into the street, he saw it. The Prime Minister's mansion that could have billeted the entirety of the Graylenmouth Guard three times over.

A lime-white building in parliament square that during the day must have almost leered over the citizens of the capital. It was five stories high with ornate gargoyles and pillars adorning the front. Each window had its own stained-glass work of art depicting Lord Crandon's political career; the man must have wished his achievements immortalised to all his successors.

As the coach drew away, Eva ascended the large semi-circular steps to the front door and beckoned Jack to follow. There was a servant waiting to greet them. He was dressed in livery finer than that of the wealthiest merchant.

"Cecil will show you to your room and see to your needs, Sergeant," Eva declared, "and I need your word on one more matter. You will be meeting the Prime Minister after dinner tomorrow, until then, you are not to leave the mansion. I can of course make sure that you won't." She glanced down towards her cleavage and the amethyst. It seemed to glow with a purple auror in the candlelight. "But it would be more amiable for both of us if I didn't have to."

"You have my word," he said this time without hesitation, not wanting Eva to use her gem and put him at the mercy of a more disturbing kind of sorcery.

"I take my leave of you then. Until tomorrow, Sergeant."

"Until tomorrow, my lady."

She smiled playfully and departed. She clearly took delight in being called 'my lady' even though she was not one. Jack did not recall her introducing herself with the title of duchess, countess or another aristocratic station. Eva seemed to carry herself in a manner that made people address her as such unwittingly.

Cecil, the proud servant, led him up the stairs and to his room, then stood there at the door awkwardly. Realising Jack had to dismiss him, he did so, and then he entered the bedroom.

He suddenly realised, for the first time in his life, that he had missed out on a great deal. The room was lit by many candles within a chandelier. The walls, ceiling and carpet were all a shade of golden cream. There was an oaken writing desk, numerous chairs and a four-poster bed.

He noticed an adjoining room with a bathtub. He wanted to wash but did not want to recall Cecil, so he decided to change into the night clothes left on the bed and go to sleep. Despite the knowledge that he was as much a prisoner here as he was in his cell, he fell asleep immediately, overcome by the fatigue he had suffered in the last few days.

Cecil awoke him with a knock at the door and a tray of bacon and eggs the next day. "Will you be requiring coffee, Sir?" Cecil enquired.

"Why not." He had smelt the aroma of the new and fashionable hot drink when passing coffee houses on patrol but never wanted to spend his hard earnt wages on something that seemed frivolous. This time, however, it would not be at his expense.

"Oh, and, Cecil, if it's not too much trouble, do you mind running me a bath?" Cecil faltered for a second, apparently shocked to have received an order delivered so humbly and uncertainly.

"It's no trouble at all, Sir." He smiled bemusedly. "Will sir also require a shaving kit?" *Cheeky bastard,* thought Jack and he was unable to stifle a laugh.

"Yes, I suppose I will. It wouldn't be polite to meet the Prime Minister unshaven."

A few moments later, he entered the bath that Cecil had drawn. The warm water seemed to cure all the aches that three nights in a cell had given him. He soaped as slowly as possible wanting to relish in the comfort of the warm bath. After drying and shaving himself, he returned to the room where Cecil had laid out some clothes on the bed with a note, 'To be worn today by request of Miss Valmarque'.

Thinking of the amethyst, he dressed himself in the long undercoat, a lavish green doublet, white britches and leather buckled shoes. He felt rather odd and out of place in a rich man's clothes.

"Err, Cecil, have I done this right?" He said a moment later in the corridor gesturing to his attire.

"Yes, Sir, very good, Sir." Believing him but still feeling very awkward, he went downstairs.

He decided to while away the hours before dinner in the library. He had never seen one so big. He took his pick of histories, philosophies and the sciences, rubbing his eyes periodically as they strained in the candlelight. He enquired if he could take his meals in there and Cecil obliged. He only saw Cecil when he brought food as he found it awkward to have him standing around, so he dismissed him. He seemed happy to be given time off.

At six o'clock, Eva entered the library dressed more modestly than last night, though still barefoot and with the same amethyst around her neck. She was now in a black gown that laced up to the front. Having finished his meal, she beckoned him to follow her to the drawing room and they walked down the corridor together.

The drawing room had a cosy-looking ambience with oak panel walls and a red embroidered rug upon the floorboards. A man sat with the proud poise and posture of an aristocrat by the tall roaring fireplace, one hand resting on a cane the other supporting a pipe he was smoking thoughtfully.

"Sergeant Jack Sweep of the Graylenmouth Guard, as promised, my lord," announced Eva as they entered the drawing room.

"Thank you, Miss Valmarque," replied the man in the maroon armchair by the fireplace. "Please have a seat, Sergeant," gesturing to an identical armchair opposite. He did as he was bidden to. Eva stood between the Prime Minister and the fireplace, resting her elbow upon the mantlepiece.

The Prime Minister was wearing a blue silk shirt and a gold-coloured doublet which flashed in the roaring fire, his shoes and pantaloons looked as though they were worth more than all of Jack's wages combined, from both his time in the Guard and the textile mill.

"Do you know why I've brought you here, Sergeant?" The Prime Minister asked before taking a long inhalation on his pipe.

"I'm told you have need of me, my lord," replied Jack.

"True enough, but before we get to that, tell me what you know of our nation and government?"

Jack thought for a moment, gathering his words and phrasing before answering. He would have to speak plainly. He judged that the Prime Minister was a proud man who might send Jack back to his cell and the mercy of Captain Thompson if he offended him.

"Talamholean has operated as a constitutional monarchy ever since the unification. In general, the balance of power is held between the monarch and parliament. One holds legislative power, the other executive."

"…and what do you suppose the executive responsibility encompasses?"

"I don't, my lord."

"I thought as much." He smirked. "The ability to read will not give a sweeper from the textile mills the ability to understand. The executive chiefly deals with foreign relations, command of our armies and navies, and the ability to veto legislation from the parliament. In living memory, the first two have become unnecessary. Do you know why?"

33

"The army and navy are scarcely needed and have been reduced to the bare minimum of servicemen and ships as Talamholean has not seen a battle since before the unification. Our nearest foreign nation, the country of Marailia, has become a great trading partner; war between the two of us is mutually unbeneficial and as our relations depend on trade it is a relationship largely handled by parliament," he answered quickly, not wanting to give the Prime Minister the further satisfaction of another smirk.

Nevertheless, the smirk came. It seemed the Prime Minister did not have much respect for those who could not vote. "Very good, no doubt recited verbatim from a Chronicle article, but very good," he replied with an air of arrogance and pomposity before continuing. "What do you know of current affairs?"

"Not a lot, my lord," he lied. "My guardsman's duties don't bring me into affairs of state, and I spent the last three days in a prison cell before coming here yesterday," he finished, assuming that pleading ignorance may be the best way not to upset the Prime Minister.

"It is no secret that King Wilfrid and I despise each other. If we manage to pass a bill, he vetoes it whether it's a legislation of my design, or the opposition's. In our weekly meetings, my advice falls on deaf ears and he gives no satisfactory reason for opposing me when he gives his opinion to the journalists. The King, in short, is a petty man with no power but that of a veto quill, which he will exercise for no reason other than to irk his parliament for attention. Have you now worked out why I've brought you here, Sergeant?"

"Yes," he said, so shocked and appalled that he forgot to add a 'my lord'. "But I'm afraid you've asked the wrong person. I'm a guardsman who enforces the law, I draw the line at assassination. I've no love or admiration for the King but I will not commit murder, regicide or otherwise. I'm sorry, Prime Minister, you'll have to send me back to the barracks to face court martial."

The Prime Minister snorted menacingly and choked on his pipe. Though he was being mocked, Jack internally revelled in the satisfaction of making the Prime Minister, whom he was beginning to dislike, choke on his tobacco. He finished his coughing fit, steadied himself and began to reassure Jack.

"I'm not asking you to assassinate anyone, I simply want you to deliver a message."

"A message?"

"Yes, you are to travel up the Graylen to Wylclyst and deliver a message to Lady Alice of Wylclyst Manor. Once delivered, you are to follow her instructions. If you have gained her favour, I shall see to it that you are pardoned for this debacle you have landed yourself in with the Home Secretary. Do you accept?"

"I accept, my lord. When do I leave?" He needed no time for deliberation. He could handle himself on the road as a guardsman trained to fight with a sword and pistol. He had never left Graylenmouth and the opportunity to go beyond the city walls for the first time filled him with excitement. It seemed a fair trade for a pardon.

"Excellent; you will leave tomorrow at nightfall. Miss Valmarque, the message if you please?"

Jack looked up at Eva into her green eyes, expecting her to produce a wax sealed envelope with the Prime Minister's signet.

The Warlock produced nothing. She began to smirk as broadly as the Prime Minister had been a moment ago. "This won't be pleasant, Prime Minister; you may wish to leave. I'll call you back in when the message is complete." The Prime Minister frowned and left promptly.

Jack thought to make for the door but knew it was hopeless as Eva began to gently caress her amethyst and fixed him with an ominous stare. *"Stand up!"* The commanding voice was not his, but Eva's. She was speaking to him without moving her lips. Her voice seemed to be emanating from the amethyst around her neck in a buzzing tone as the gemstone pulsated in the firelight.

He stood up involuntarily despite his resistance. Unable to move, she ignored him as she produced a goose feather quill, seemingly from thin air. The quill seemed to have a nib like a scalpel, razor-sharp and made of steel. He gulped, now incapable of screaming and incapable of running.

"Remove your doublet and shirt. Lie face down on the table," buzzed Eva's voice from the amethyst. He removed the articles of clothing, then slowly walked over to the wooden dinner table, unable to do anything else. As he began to lie down, he half knew what was about to happen, but the confirming of his suspicions did not soften the pain of the experience.

A searing pain cut into his back without warning. Had he been able to move his jaw, he would have certainly bitten his own tongue clean off. He felt the cold metal of the quill nib cut into his back between the shoulder blades. Short cuts. Shallow cuts. Swift cuts.

The pain did not ease with each incision and his inability to scream somehow made it worse. The fire crackled and combined itself with the sound of a blade going in and out of his flesh.

She called the Prime Minister back and the cutting stopped. He heard Lord Crandon affirm Eva's message before leaving the room a second time. Then he felt her hand on his back, outstretched and pressing hard. The pain worsened as though salt had just been sprinkled into his new wounds. Then it stopped.

He could move again. He sat up promptly, and immediately felt his back awkwardly with both hands over his shoulders. There was nothing there. No blood, no wounds and no scarring. Eva was wiping blood off her hands with a rag.

"Lady Alice's Warlock will be able to reveal that with ease," she said.

"Do you normally send messages in such a barbaric fashion?" He glared, knowing that was all he could get away with in his current plight.

"If you're captured, we can't risk the message falling into the wrong hands." She shrugged. "Now get some rest, you leave tomorrow at sunset."

*

The following evening, he was back in the carriage with Eva, being taken from the Prime Minister's residence to a place beyond the city walls. He went through his provisions and equipment one last time. Two pistols, better than the ones he carried in the Guard, made by a master craftsman no doubt, with powder charges and two dozen lead shots for ammunition. A rapier, more flimsy and less reliable than his cutlass but if he were to pass himself off as a vagabond on the road, it would make sense to be carrying more common and civilian weaponry. He was also given a hunting knife, good for skinning hares and any other game he may be able to feed himself with.

Along with all this, the Prime Minister had 'loaned' him a pouch of fifty gold sovereigns which he accepted bitterly at the realisation that even if he did make it back successfully with a pardon, as he had been promised, he would probably soon be facing the prospect of debtor's prison.

"There's one more thing, Sweep," said Eva as he carefully placed all but the rapier and the hunting knife into his backpack. "This is from me," she said producing a small black gemstone on a thin silvery chain.

Jack gasped and recoiled as he sheathed the hunting knife and slid it into his boot. He had no desire to accept any gifts, magical or otherwise, from the Warlock after her recent behaviour. He would never forget the pain and humiliation he had suffered at her hands and was beginning to think that Warlocks were no less immoral than the witches they burn in the town square.

"It's black tourmaline; it will protect you from sorcery should you fall foul of any less scrupulous magicians."

"Is that likely? Especially when the Warlocks' Council claim to hold the moral authority on magic and burn all those who misuse it."

He thought he saw her face contort into a vengeful scowl. If he did, she composed herself in the passing of a second and bore her green eyes into his, in a piercing stare.

"No, it's not likely but isn't a good guardsman prepared for anything," she asserted, and he knew he was not going to win this argument.

He reluctantly outstretched his arm and opened his hand, expecting her to place the jewellery in his palm. Instead, she placed the chain on his wrist. Without warning, the two ends of the chain coiled around and joined on the other side, before chain and gemstone, seemingly conscious, coiled and rolled its way up his forearm. He fell to the floor writhing in panic, trying to remove the chain with his free hand as it travelled towards his elbow. He tugged but the chain tightened into his skin making him gasp and flinch. Eva smirked and chuckled mercilessly as the chain came to a halt past his elbow and halfway up his upper arm.

"It will sit there comfortably as long as you don't try to take it off. Relax, Sergeant. It's for your own good. If you make it back alive, I might consider removing it." She was clearly enjoying the misfortune she had caused him in the last twenty-four hours. Sighing with resignation, Jack stood up and went through the equipment in his pack again, he made sure the black powder was stored in a manner that would keep it dry.

The carriage continued beyond the city walls for another ten miles before it came to a slow stop. Jack hung the rapier at his belt and donned a leather trench coat over his rough spun woollen clothes. The clothes of a nomad. He shouldered his pack then opened the carriage door and jumped on to the road, not waiting for the coachmen to roll out the steps.

"It is the twenty-ninth of June; Parliament dissolves tomorrow and does not reconvene until September the seventh. This means you have just over two months to deliver your message to Lady Alice and return to Graylenmouth," she said to him, while peering down at him through the carriage's open window. "Oh, and one more thing, Sergeant." She reached through the window and mussed her hand in his blonde hair and smiled sarcastically. "There," she declared. "Much more the look of a windswept traveller." She knocked on the carriage roof and departed.

Jack looked around into the green fields of the farmland that surrounded the River Graylen near the capital and started to make his way north, keeping the Graylen on his left-hand side, or to his west. Despite all that he had suffered in the last few days, he could not help allowing himself a small, albeit somewhat hollow smile. He was on his way somewhere, for the first time in his life.

Chapter Three

"Lady Atherton, young wife to Lord Atherton and the daughter of Defence Secretary Lord Norcrock, will undoubtedly be the belle of this weekend's disillusionment ball. The esteemed Lady is rarely seen out an about without wearing the finest silk, the most fashionable accessories, or her entourage of equally gorgeous and adoring serving maids. This writer will be sure to get to the bottom of how she always looks so damn gorgeous. Even if I have to break into her house and rifle through…"

Victoria Lionsgate paused from dictating her newest article to her secretary, sipped her coffee and sighed. Surely that would be enough for the gossip column for tomorrow's Chronicle. The grandfather clock by the door chimed, realising the time she dismissed her secretary for the day.

She entered the lobby of Lionsgate Hall, pulled on her coat and hat, and then entered out onto the street where her coach awaited. Her trusted serving maid, Daisy, greeted her with an enthusiastic smile. Without direction or instruction, the coachman whipped the horses and took them to the offices of the Graylenmouth Chronicle where Lord Bolingbroke awaited her. A short moment later, they arrived.

"You go on ahead in the coach, Daisy, I'll meet you there." Daisy nodded and bid her employer farewell as the coach departed. Victoria brushed out the creases in her white and gold frock with her hands, straightened her hat and burst through the doors to the Chronicle headquarters.

"Lord Bolingbroke is expecting me. I'll head on through," she proclaimed like a woman on a mission without stopping or slowing her gait, ignoring the protests from the reception staff as she twisted the handle on the door to his office and burst through.

Lord Bolingbroke was clearly taken by surprise. He was sitting back in his chair, trouserless with his shoes wide apart upon the desk. Between his legs were the soft brown curls of a serving girl, currently providing him his lunchtime recreation. He opened his eyes at the sound of the door. The girl withdrew her mouth from his genitals, looked around, then promptly stood up bashfully before being hastily dismissed. Looking flustered, the editor of the Chronicle edged his chair towards the desk, concealing his bare-legged lower half.

"Please don't get up, my lord." Victoria grinned. "I wouldn't want to embarrass you further."

Bolingbroke panted and narrowed his eyes. "You're early, Lionsgate, our appointment wasn't for another half an hour."

"Your message was to discuss my contract of employment. If you mean to let me go, I'd like to know as soon as possible."

Bolingbroke eyed her shrewdly and it told her all she needed to know. He was intending to dismiss her. However, as the manner in which she had entered his office afforded her no small amount of negotiating power, he was clearly considering his next move. Victoria, having raised a son and a daughter who were both prone to mischief in their infancy, was more than comfortable with a long and awkward silence and waited patiently for his retort.

"There's political unrest of late," he responded after the silence became too much for him to bear. "The King and the Prime Minister are locked in a battle, and one must give way eventually. I cannot devote more column inches to gossip and frivolity. The dross you write is of no relevance and import to the reader."

Victoria considered him for a moment without betraying the uncomfortable notion that she had to agree, her articles were indeed dross. Nevertheless, she could not break her facade, not now, not when she had been working towards it for so long. She had to keep playing the role of the ditzy gossip columnist who wrote asinine drivel. So much depended on it.

"Let's just ignore the fact, shall we, that I could sell an article to the Gazette, which would love to hear how the editor of their biggest competitor likes to receive fellatio from a serving maid half his age who is younger than his own daughter. No, my lord, instead of that allow me to draw your attention as to how the female readership of this paper would turn tale and flock to the Gazette if I were to offer my precious column inches to them. I know my lord's income is entirely dependent on sales of this paper and I wouldn't want to rob him of his fine wines, fine foods and finer serving girls."

She had him and she knew it; the look of anger on his face was the same frustrated look all aristocrats showed on the rare occasions they were forced to experience powerlessness. He sighed heavily and rolled his eyes, accepting defeat.

"I'll get the secretary to renew your contract. It will be posted to your house within the next few days."

"I'll be sure to read it thoroughly. If I may impress upon my lord further? I require the use of his carriage. I have a high society event to report on at the social club and I'm sure my lord doesn't wish one of his most valued reporters to be late."

He nodded indignantly and she departed with a graceful yet patronising curtsey, leaving the offices at the back entrance and entering Lord Bolingbroke's coach. The driver set off.

She seemed to make her next appointment a lot quicker than her first, the people in the streets always took less time to clear the way for a lord's coach. She checked into the club. Daisy was waiting for them in a private booth.

"He has arrived," Daisy revealed as she greeted Victoria. "Shall I tell the waitress we're ready to receive him?"

"Not yet," said Victoria, pulling a black veil and shawl from her handbag. She draped the shawl about her shoulders then unravelled the veil over her hat, masking herself completely. She slouched a little, adopting the posture of an older weather-beaten woman. She then nodded to Daisy who went to fetch their invited guest.

Daisy returned a moment later with him. Under the veil, Victoria gave Daisy a slow and knowing nod to dismiss her, then gestured to her guest to sit down. He looked bewildered. Though Victoria could not blame him due to the secrecy of their meeting, there was something else as well. Despite the privacy afforded by the booth, the man seemed on edge, looking over his shoulder constantly as if being watched. He was dressed like a wealthy man, though Victoria knew that was Daisy's doing to give him an inconspicuous appearance.

The clothes would not fool anyone, however, due to the fact that he did not carry himself in the manner of an aristocrat. He slouched, his head was bowed to stare at his shoes and his dark hair was not cut or styled in the manner of one who could afford a barber.

Those eyes as well, thought Victoria, *far too fearful and watery to be a member of the nobility.* Taking pity on him and wanting to ease his apprehension, Victoria got straight to business.

"I believe you have some information for me regarding suspicious activity at the palace?" Victoria croaked, disguising her voice as though to sound like that of a woman thirty years her senior.

"Yes, Ma'am," said the man in a fearful whisper looking over his shoulder for what seemed like the dozenth time.

"You have nothing to fear, this is a private booth and I have taken precautions to ensure no one will be listening at the door. Tell me everything, but first confirm to me your credentials so I may corroborate your story, young man." A flattering addition as he was at least forty, but if one good thing came from being a gossip columnist, it was the realisation that people were much more at ease and forthcoming with information when complimented.

"I'm footman to the Trade Secretary, Lord Murray," began the man. "Have been for the last five years, including the last three when he was first appointed. He's not a bad bloke for an aristocrat, or a politician. He paid for my daughter's tutor when he found out I couldn't afford her schooling. So I've always gone beyond the boundaries of a normal servant's remit. Anyway, last Friday, my lord was very pleased with himself having finally secured the votes in parliament to pass his trade bill."

"The parliamentary session overran so I said I'd deliver it to the palace myself. I have often delivered messages to the King from the cabinet and was only happy to do so. I left it with the rest of the bills that were awaiting King Wilfrid's signature in the palace's gatehouse."

"And do you know why the King vetoed your master's bill?" Victoria was suspecting she may be about to discover she was on a wild goose chase. The King vetoed bills all the time, be it out of concern or spite. It was hardly the evidence of political corruption Daisy had informed her about.

"That's just the thing, Ma'am. The King never received it! Had it been vetoed, it would appear in the parliamentary records, and I've checked them, there's evidence to suggest it's not the only bill. Very occasionally, maybe once every two years, there's a record of a bill that neither received the King's signature nor his veto. I informed Lord Murray and he recommended that we pursue the matter with caution and discretion, that's when your servant found me."

"Do you have a copy of the bill and the parliamentary records?" Victoria croaked, struggling to disguise her voice or hide her feigned lumbago. Her interest was rising from the low expectations she had had a moment ago.

"Yes, Ma'am, but not about my person."

"No bother," said Victoria, who would send Daisy to Lord Murray's residence to fetch them tomorrow.

*

Victoria and Daisy were in the carriage returning to Lionsgate Hall an hour later. Victoria informed Daisy that her 'theatrical duties' would no longer be required today. At this, Daisy removed her wig of long brown curly hair, revealing her black bob underneath. She then took a silk handkerchief from her pocket and began to scrub off the freckles she had painted on her cheeks earlier that day. Finally, Daisy removed a pair of spectacles from her smock and put them on.

"If I may be so bold, I'm not sure all this discretion is necessary, Ma'am, but I'm not complaining, it's fun being your sidekick."

"You may be so bold, and I'm glad you enjoy it." Victoria smiled realising she should check her books and see if she could give Daisy the raise she had earned. "You did well finding the footman. Where *did* you find him?"

She shrugged. "He was outside the offices of one of the private investigation firms screaming about treason and treachery. I informed him I could arrange a meeting with someone who would investigate thoroughly and free of charge. What do you think this is, Ma'am?"

"At the very best incompetence, at the very worst corruption, and by someone high up in the government. Either way, it's worth looking into."

The carriage pulled up to Lionsgate Hall and a few moments later, Victoria found herself back in the drawing room. She dismissed Daisy for the day, then informed her secretary she would not be needed. She had no desire to write any more gossip today.

Just then, the doorbell rang and realising she had dismissed Daisy, went to answer it herself.

A mousy-haired girl was at the door and Victoria invited her in and beckoned her into the study, poured her some water and sat down. She bid the young girl to do the same. Then she reached into her desk drawer and withdrew a leather pouch containing fifteen gold sovereigns. She then withdrew another three from her purse and added it to the pouch before handing it to the young servant.

"I asked a lot of you, Francesca, and you couldn't have had Lord Bolingbroke in a more compromising position, which made things a lot easier for me. That's why I've given you an extra three." Francesca received the gold with the same bashful look she had had when Victoria caught her with her lips on Lord Bolingbroke's member.

"Thank you, Mrs Lionsgate."

"Please spend the money wisely," Victoria pleaded, almost maternally, not wanting the young girl to be in the service of the grotesque editor of the Chronicle until her looks faded.

Chapter Four

Lyndsey Carter spent disillusionment day on a crowd control assignment amongst two dozen other officers of the Graylenmouth Guard. It had not escaped her attention that Jack was nowhere to be seen.

The public was often worked up in a mixture of rage and excitement at witch burnings, and for this reason, she sat atop her mare in full uniform, her deep brown hair tucked up into her zischagge which was fastened under her chin and had the three-pronged visor over her eyes.

Her breastplate was strapped over her brown leather jerkin. Her matching brown britches and riding boots, with her feet in the stirrups, made sure she was ready to ride into any fracas at a moment's notice. Her cutlass dangled threateningly at her left side, at her belt were two pistols, loaded and at half-cock. One with shot, another only with powder. Firing the shotless pistol into the air as a warning was often enough to make an angry mob think twice. The smell of black powder and a thick shroud of white smoke often gave the most furious men pause for thought.

The official, a young man in a tricorn hat with a crisp and untarnished military-style uniform of maroon, stepped onto the wooden dais beside the bonfire. There were three people tied to stakes that protruded upwards from the large kindling. They writhed in their bonds and screamed through their gagged mouths.

All around the bonfire were the public, congregating in a ring about ten yards out from the pyre. Lyndsey and her colleagues, on their mounts, occupied the space between the two. The crowd was numbered to at least four hundred. She knew it would soon thin out when the shrieks started. They always dispersed when they heard the condemned feel the heat of their execution.

"You have been found guilty of treason against the Warlocks' Council for performing unapproved sorcery beyond the boundaries of moral responsibility and are to be burnt as witches until dead," the official boomed with an air of pomposity. "May your ashes be scattered on the wind and trampled underfoot."

The condemned, two women and a man, inaudibly pleaded through the material binding their mouths, helplessly praying for mercy that they were not about to receive.

Lyndsey observed Alayna Strauss, the Chief Warlock, ascend the steps to the dais in a magenta gown and flowing blond hair. She was wearing an amulet with a large ruby as she knelt then grasped the kindling at the bottom of the pyre and concentrated. The edge of the bonfire burst ablaze in equally ruby coloured flames, unnatural and not the usual orange flames of a woodfire. Lyndsey knew this was a magical flame that burnt hotter, yet somehow slower, than a natural one. Such was the cruelty of the Warlocks.

"They helped a tavernkeeper keep the rats out of his cellar with a couple of spells. How is that treason? Meanwhile, there are thieves and pickpockets who don't even get an afternoon in the stocks," Lyndsey heard an old man say to his wife in the crowd.

"Aye," his wife replied sardonically, "help the rich and you're a respectable Warlock worthy of admiration. Help the likes of us and you're a filthy witch and must burn to death."

I'm supposed to take their names and report them for being grossly offensive, Lyndsey thought as the ruby-red flames made it to halfway up the pyre, *but none of my colleagues heard it and I can't discipline everyone just for having an opinion.*

Though a good ten yards away, Lyndsey was starting to feel the heat from the magical fire. Ash was starting to drift down from above, making Lyndsey grateful for her zischagge. Her mare whinnied and she stroked its plume reassuringly. The crowd took a few steps back feeling scorched from the heat. The worst had not yet come.

The flames reached the top of the pyre, to the stakes, and the pained squeals began, high-pitched and ringing shrilly with torment. The crowd collectively seethed and winced.

Lyndsey was grateful for the small amount of dignity provided by her helmet, ensuring her own opinions on witch burning would not be betrayed to the nearby members of the public. The screams were long and bone-chilling. Lyndsey was grateful that, unlike those with magic, guardsmen who fall from grace usually meet the firing squad rather than the funeral pyre. At that, she thought of Jack.

You'd better have met the firing squad. I've not seen you since our last patrol and then you disappear without a trace, without a farewell. I thought we were friends!

The screaming ended and the three bodies hung limp and lifeless, wreathed in the magical flame. Alayna Strauss ascended the dais once more and addressed the crowd in a long lecture about the immorality of those who practised sorcery without the approval of the Warlocks' Council. The members of the crowd, who did not depart when the screams started, now began to disperse, rarely keen to be lectured to. Lyndsey tuned out her dulcet tones and observed the departing crowd.

Only a few remained either to listen to the Chief Warlock or to watch the corpses slowly wither and char into ash. When it reached a safe number, she and her colleagues dismounted and made their way back to the barracks.

Aaron, the stable hand, greeted her when she arrived and asked if she had seen Jack. It seemed he wanted to lecture him about not working his horse so hard so he did not have to spend his time begging the blacksmith for another horseshoe. Lyndsey assured Aaron that she would pass on his bollocking, along with her own, when she next saw him.

Her shift had finished but she did not go home. She had her own independent investigation to do. She went back into the barracks and to the secretary's office and knocked on the door, where Katie welcomed her with a smile.

"Hello, Lyndsey, what can I do for you?" The kindly secretary of the Guard said, looking up from her desk and smiling at her over her spectacles that were on the end of her nose. She seemed grateful for some female company; the majority of the Guard were overwhelmingly men and so the secretary took a liking to the few and far between female guardsmen such as Lyndsey.

"Hi, Katie, do you have a copy of the duty roster for this week and last week?"

Without protest or inquisition, Katie went over to the drawers in the corner of the room and returned promptly with two pieces of parchment. Lyndsey was relieved; what she was doing was not illegal or immoral but she had the impression her own investigations might raise an eyebrow from Captain Thompson.

A cursory look at the roster told her that Jack had not been on duty since Sunday when they had dealt with the incident at Annabelle's, nor had he been rostered for patrol at any time this week. Five days without being put on patrol was not a common occurrence.

"Has Jack put in a request for leave?" Lyndsey asked quizzically.

"No, and the Captain doesn't generally grant leave around this time of year when parliament dissolves and the witch burnings begin," replied Katie without looking up, immersed once more in her administrative duties.

"Is he in the infirmary?"

"Infirmary's empty."

Not wanting to arouse suspicion, she thanked Katie for her time and went to the armoury to return her weapons and equipment, but she still did not return home. She went straight to Jack's room in the billets and found something even more strange. Not only was Jack not there but neither were any of his belongings. The bed had even been stripped of its sheets as though the servants considered the room unoccupied. Jack had not only disappeared without a word to her but somehow the servants were aware.

Now concerned, she determinedly doubled back and went towards the centre of the barracks and along the long corridor on the ground floor until she reached the door to the office at its end. The office of Captain Thompson. She wrapped her knuckles on the door aggressively.

"Enter!" The irritated voice of Captain Thompson barked. His aggression did not deter Lyndsey, who opened the door before his growl reached the second syllable.

"What is it, Carter?" The Captain shouted, fixing her with his trademark glare and clearly hoping to intimidate her.

"It's Jack, Sir, he disappeared and I'm asking for permission to investigate his whereabouts."

"Sergeant Sweep has failed to report for duty since Sunday. When he inevitably comes round from his drink-fuelled stupor and leaves the ha'penny whorehouse he's no doubt enjoying, he'll be looking at an afternoon in the stocks. If he's lucky." Thompson smirked in a manner that was common in richer folk when they offered their opinions on those they considered to be the lower classes.

"Sir, he's disappeared without a trace or a word to anyone. Including me!" She left out the part about Jack's room being ready to accommodate a new guardsman as well as the fact that someone had *conveniently* neglected to slate him for duty. It would be foolish to reveal to the Captain what she had recently discovered. For all she knew, the Captain might be feigning ignorance on the matter and it would be wise for her to do the same. At least for now.

"The fact that he said nothing to you is not evidence. If he has any dignity, he'll be discreet when using the whorehouse. If you have any substantial proof, please let me know. Otherwise stop wasting my time, Carter, and get out."

She left promptly, knowing that further protest would get her nowhere. She knew the Captain would not be forthcoming with information, but he *had* told her something. She had not mentioned Jack's empty room. If Jack was languishing in a whorehouse, and she knew him well enough to know that that was not likely, then his room would be as he left it.

A guardsman's quarters were not usually emptied of its contents until his death or resignation had been confirmed. Only the Captain could order a room clearance, which meant that Thompson knew something. Something he would not easily divulge to Lyndsey.

She was certain Jack was not dead either. All the cadavers in Graylenmouth were kept at the barracks' mortuary until the relatives could identify them. She had escorted a grieving family through the same mortuary that very morning and she had, mercifully, not seen an unidentified corpse that resembled Jack.

Walking home as the lunchtime rush began in the streets of the capital, Lyndsey spun and dodged her way from the paths of horses, coaches, would-be suitors and market traders trying to sell her all manner of aphrodisiacs and fertility treatments. It was almost second nature to her, for she knew the streets of the capital well and avoiding the lunchtime commotion effectively was like a reflex. As she reached the front door of the townhouse she shared with her husband, a thought struck her. A thought she kicked herself for not having before.

"Annabelle!" She cried aloud making a nearby flower girl jump.

Annabelle had recognised Jack and mentioned Captain Thompson to him. Jack had told her that very night. Jack had mentioned how funny it was that she recognised a man she had never met. It was not as if Jack was a monarch whose portrait was everywhere. How did she know Jack was on patrol that night? Hanging her coat up, she made her way to the kitchen to see what she could prepare for lunch, resolving that it would be a good idea to pay another visit to Annabelle in the near future.

Chapter Five

His legs were sore and beginning to seize up. Several days of hiking with little rest would do that to a man. In some ways, it irked him more than Eva Valmarque's trinket. He could still feel her silver chained black stone on his arm. He had not tried to remove it and true to her promise, it had not tightened or caused him pain and discomfort, but the gentle sensation of the silver chain against his skin was a shameful reminder of her cruelty, and it made him feel like a dog on a leash.

Jack had spent the last two days ambling up the east bank of the Graylen from dawn until sunset. He slept in the wild by night. That was another problem. His back ached from sleeping on the ground. No one had warned him that sleeping rough would not be the glamorous adventure he had been led to believe.

He had covered perhaps twenty miles in total. He drank the water provided by the river and ate the molluscs he had managed to find at the riverbanks, roasting them on a crudely constructed campfire by night. The Graylen's water tasted sweet enough, especially after a long day's hike, but the small invertebrates provided little sustenance, and without substantial food portions, his stomach was beginning to pang.

Jack awoke at first light on the morning of his third day of travel. The bright summer sunrise pried his eyes open. Ignoring the pain and loud rumble provided by his stomach, he arose from the beech tree he had been sleeping under and grudgingly scraped away the wet layer of dew that had positioned itself between him and his leather trench coat, which he had been using as a blanket. He poured the remains of the previous night's water on the smouldering embers of the dying fire, gathered his things and made the short way back to the pathway by the Graylen's bank.

The river looked majestic in the crimson morning hue. The sunlight was dancing off the calm and slow-moving surface of the water delicately. He had never known it so serene. In the capital, where the river met the sea, it was always roaring and aggressive as it turned the grinding wheels of the few remaining preindustrial corn mills. Here, thirty miles north of the city in the flat and fertile farmlands that fed the entire capital and at least half the nation, the river was calm, slow-moving and filling the surrounding area with a tranquil ambience which boosted Jack's morale a little.

Jack removed his boots, rolled up his trousers and waded into the Graylen on the shallow east bank. The water was cool, giving a calming contrast to the warm summer's morning. Placing his wineskin into the water to collect his ration for that day, he then returned to the grassy bank. He put his boots back on and set off on his journey for another day's walk. He hoped he could cover a good amount of ground before his belly gave him no choice but to stop and forage for his breakfast.

Blackberries sometimes grew near riverbanks and that was an encouraging thought. Fruit would be a welcome change from small animals, though it would not be enough to sustain him. He needed a square meal.

A few miles north of where he had started today's journey, he came upon a bush that bore fruit, unfortunately, it was not one that produced blackberries. He could not identify the variety, which was small, red and firm. His better judgement told him that consumption would probably cause him worse digestive problems than hunger and he groaned in frustration.

He stopped and checked the map. At this, his spirits lightened. A short way north of here there was a footbridge, and the footbridge led to a village. There might be an inn, and an inn meant food and a bed for the night. He had hoped to return from his quest without spending a penny of the Prime Minister's 'loan' but avoiding debt was not a preferable alternative to starvation.

Staying at an inn for the night, long before sundown, felt like wasting time, but even if he found food now, he'd have to start a fire which would slow him down in equal measure. If his quest was to be halted, it would be best if he got some proper food and rest.

He returned the map to his pack and set off in a fast walk, almost a run; his eyes were fixed as far ahead as his sight would allow, to the eastern edge of the river, hoping the bridge would come into view any moment now.

Half an hour later, he saw it and his heart leapt. He broke into a run in the direction of the bridge, thinking only of food and rest. He could see white walls with black wooden beams and thatched rooves making up the many buildings on the other side and knew he would abate his hunger soon.

Upon reaching the edge of the stone bridge, he began to cross. His thoughts only on his hunger. He was nearly surprised by the three men on the other side who escaped his notice. They had seen him first and without delay, rose from their small fire and alighted the footbridge standing three abreast, barring his way to the west bank.

Jack cursed himself internally. While he had never been trained to move silently and unseen like a spy, he could have employed a little more subtlety upon his entry to the village. Now three men, two of them a foot taller and wider than he was, and who looked like they had survived many a fight, were standing between him and recreation. They smiled menacingly and flashed their teeth, several of which were missing. The crazed look of a brutal killer behind each of their eyes.

The third man, short, slender and weaselly-faced, stood between his larger companions. He tilted his head back to afford him a sneer down his long thin nose and addressed Jack.

"State your business!" he said, glaring down his nose at Jack. Jack immediately knew he would soon have to defend himself.

Whatever these people were after, it was not something amicable or a fair business deal. These men were undoubtedly brigands. There was nothing official about them.

"I'm a farmhand, I travel the land as and where my skills are needed. I'm travelling north to the fertile plains. I thought I might stay at your inn for some rest and recreation before heading off at first light tomorrow?" Jack had rehearsed this story in his head during his travels of the last two days. He knew someone would ask him eventually, so he had practised the lie with the diligence of a thespian learning his lines for the theatre. Actually saying it aloud with conviction made Jack feel both astonished and absurd. He hoped his face was betraying neither at this moment in time.

"You may come to our village. You may stay at our inn, but there's a toll. A toll for crossing the bridge and a protection fee," the weaselly-faced man answered as the heavy-set men on either side of him chuckled through their sparse sets of teeth.

Jack's suspicions were confirmed. He began to make a display of caressing his sword hilt as though doing it in an absent-minded manner. Hopefully, this would give them the impression that he would not cower to their intimidation.

He was not scared of a fight. He had been trained to hold his own against opponents larger and stronger than him and he had done so many a time on patrol. This, however, was three against one and Lyndsey was not at his side.

He would also have to avoid killing. Jack had not killed before but that was not why he was eager to be merciful. He had no moral quandaries with taking another life, providing it was in self-defence and his opponent gave him no alternative, as was likely the case with these men. Unfortunately, their deaths would raise suspicion and he would find himself in a dungeon, awaiting the local magistrate for judgement.

When the fighting started, he would have to subdue them, as well as keep them alive. He did not have time to sit in prison or endure a murder trial. He would have to be quick. He would have to be clever.

"Protection from who?" Jack asked quizzically, already knowing the answer.

"From my boys and me." The weaselly-faced man sneered and his muscular goons chuckled along, displaying their unsettling teeth.

"How much is the toll and the protection fee?" Jack asked having no intention of paying it and surreptitiously eyeing each goon, trying to anticipate which one would attack first and how he would best defend himself.

His pistols were unusable, concealed in his pack and not loaded. He had his rapier but he would have to use it sparingly if he was not intending to end a life.

"Three shillings to cross the bridge and another shilling for each day you're in our village. If you can't afford it, I'm sure a handsome blond boy like you can repay us in other ways." His eyes flashed malevolently during the last sentence and Jack had no intention of finding out what he meant by that.

He decided to give them a chance to back down before the brawl started. "I'm not paying that, not by coin or any other means, but I'm coming into the village and I'm crossing this bridge. If you step aside and let me pass, we can forget this conversation and let each other be. Now, get out of my way!"

The three men looked almost stunned for a moment as though they had fully expected Jack to pay up or beg for mercy. The weaselly-faced man turned to the goon on his left and gave him an instruction before stepping backwards to the other side of the river. "All yours, Frank."

Frank swung his fist in Jack's direction, his arm fully outstretched. A punch Jack imagined would have knocked him clean out had he been on the receiving end, but Jack was quick. He swivelled clockwise in a half turn to the right and aimed a well-placed kick between Frank's legs. Admittedly, one of the most dishonourable tricks one could use in a fight, but since they were trying to rob him, Jack surmised that codes of honour would not serve him here. Frank exhaled breathlessly and slumped to the ground clutching his privates and wincing uncontrollably.

The other heavy-set man drew a knife and stepped towards Jack. He swiped sideways through the air, left to right, and Jack dodged stepping back just in time. The second man seemed as strong as Frank and having now seen what Jack was capable of, would probably not be taken down so easily. Jack kept ducking and weaving the man's attacks, watching for a sign of weakness. He had forced the fight off the bridge and back to the east bank.

Jack's hunger was starting to take its toll on him now; he was beginning to tire and it would not be long before he was overcome with dizziness. He knew he had to end this fight and end it fast.

Fortuitously, Jack had spotted a flaw in his opponent's aggressive fighting style. The man had inhuman levels of speed and strength but did not know how to balance himself. Jack knew then that his moment to attack would be when he made his next thrust. The man swiped; Jack dodged. He swiped again and Jack answered with another dodge. *Come on, attack me with the point, not the edge,* Jack thought impatiently and the heavy-set man obliged, as though reading his mind and acknowledging Jack's request.

He thrust forward towards Jack's face from his right shoulder. Jack watched the cold steel of the knife glint in the morning sun as it came towards him. He swiftly moved to the man's right, the knife point missing his face by a few inches. Jack saw in an instant that the man had put all his immense weight onto the balls of his feet. Instinctively, Jack grabbed the man's fully extended knife arm above the elbow and pulled with all his strength while shifting his own weight to his left foot and aiming his right shin in a sweeping kick just above his opponent's knees.

The man seemed to comically hover in the air for a second before he fell to the ground. He was still tightly clutching the knife. Not wanting to give him a chance to attack again, Jack brought his bootheel down on the man's hand with all the strength he could muster. He winced as he felt the bones crunch. The ensuing scream was almost as bad.

When Jack returned to the bridge, the weaselly-faced man had drawn a blunderbuss from beside the fire then pointed it at his head. "Stay back!" He squealed nervously.

Jack drew his rapier and rounded on the man with a wrathful look on his face. When only four feet stood between them, the weaselly-faced man dropped the gun and ran. It fell to the floor without going off. Just as Jack had suspected, there had been no flint in the hammer.

He sheathed his sword, finished crossing the bridge to the west bank, and made his way between the buildings of the village, looking out for the sign of an Inn. Having no luck, he went down a narrow back street, hoping it would lead to a scent of roast meat and vegetables that he longed for torturously.

His hunger was now mixing with the adrenaline from the fight and the narrow street was beginning to swim and waver before him. "Hey, you! Hey, I saw you fighting, turn around damn it!" He heard a man cry from behind him urgently. Jack drew his rapier and pivoted instantly.

He thought he saw a bearded and dishevelled man in rough spun clothes and a leather apron. He could not be sure; a second later, he was collapsing into the dirt, a lack of decent food and rest finally overcoming him.

Chapter Six

The sun had set when he awoke. He was lying on a bed in a dark room. A warm summer breeze was gently fluttering at the curtains by the open window above him. The work bench in the centre of the room was supporting his backpack and sword. There were no bars or anything that gave this room the look of a prison cell which told him he had probably not been arrested. He tried to stand up but his stomach was now aching with hunger to the point where he could not do much more than grimace and seethe in pain. He called out for help and cursed himself silently as a man in an apron entered, carrying a tankard and a plate of food.

He could not recall ever eating at such a fast pace. He consumed the two slices of bread and the block of cheese so quickly that it could have given him indigestion. Crumbs were flying everywhere and missing the plate but he did not care. This was sustenance like he had never experienced before. It was not the most flavoursome meal but his hunger made that irrelevant.

The man in the apron sat down on the chair in the corner of the room and considered Jack. "You've been out all afternoon. Horace and his gang are in fits, they've never lost face in a fight like that. It's the talk of the town. They're out for your blood."

Jack took a moment to bring himself back to reality. He assumed Horace was the weaselly-faced man from the bridge, whose courage had quickly left him when his cronies went down.

"He's got more of his men searching the taverns and the inns, looking for you," the man continued. "Best lie low here for a few days 'til they get bored." Jack was coming to his senses and beginning to recall the events that took place on the bridge.

"Who are they?" He replied eventually.

"A bored bunch of criminals who like to run this town while the authorities turn a blind eye! A blind eye they willingly turn while Horace and his gang pay them a generous fraction of the money they extort from the townspeople." Jack was beginning to feel sick again. The Graylenmouth Guard was far from a paragon of virtue, especially with people like Captain Thompson in charge, but they never took bribes from criminals and bullies to look the other way at the expense of the masses.

"What are you doing here and why did you come to Ulston anyway?" The man in the apron said. Jack took a moment, still in a slight daze, to remember his rehearsed story.

"My name is—"

"No!" The man interrupted. "Let's not exchange names if you don't mind. Given who you've angered, it's best if I don't know too much about you."

Jack paused. He assumed that he had been dealing with a gang of chancers earlier, trying to rob someone on a whim. Had he realised he had walked into a village in the grip of organised crime, then he would have fought to kill back on the bridge.

"I'm a farmhand. I'm travelling up from the farmlands near the capital to the fertile plains looking for work."

The man in the apron sighed and bowed his head. His shaggy black hair and wiry salt and pepper beard illuminated in the candlelight. "This village's income is dependent on hospitality towards travellers. If Horace and his gang insist on intimidating all our visitors, it won't be long before they stop coming altogether and Ulston is reduced to a ghost town."

"Is Horace the man who ran off earlier? Is he the leader?" Jack asked.

"Yes, he's taken all he can from the craftsmen and shopkeepers, so now he waits at the bridge with his two scariest henchmen hounding strangers. I'm a blacksmith but I had to close my forge a month ago. No one can afford my services anymore, thanks to Horace."

"How many henchmen does he have? I've taken care of two of them, they won't be able to intimidate anyone for a while." Jack had no time to deal with Ulston's predicament. He was on a quest of his own and was not a guardsman at present, but he could not help looking for a solution to help the towns people for all they had suffered from Horace and his gang.

"There's at least a dozen more. You're a good fighter, I saw you, but you can't face down that many, you'll be killed, and slowly. They'll want to make an example of you to anyone else who has notions of standing up to them. We may be defenceless but it's not your job to save us."

Jack begrudgingly resigned himself to the blacksmith's wisdom. He did not like it but he was powerless to make a change here and he had a message to deliver. "What's the quickest way back to the bridge from here?" He asked defeatedly.

"Left out the door and to the end of this street. But they'll be watching the bridge. Leave the town to the north and stay on the west bank. There's a ford five miles north of here. You can cross back over to the east bank there."

"Thank you. I'll impress upon your hospitality a few hours longer if you don't mind, I need more rest. I'll be gone before sunrise. Thank you for hiding me at great risk to yourself," Jack said.

"You can't leave anytime soon." said the blacksmith incredulously, disbelief spreading across his illuminated face as he shook his shaggy black mane. "They're still enraged. If they find you, they'll do worse than give you a beating."

"I have appointments to keep and a long way to travel, I can't delay longer than I have to."

The blacksmith grumbled something about the rashness of youth before taking his leave. Jack fell asleep almost instantly. A full stomach and a bed were all that he needed.

*

He was awoken a few hours later with breakfast. It was still dark outside. He would have preferred to have slept longer, though felt rested enough. He ate, got dressed and loaded his pistols before putting his pack on and attaching his sword belt. He secured the pistols to his belt so that they sat concealed behind him under his coat. He hoped this would avoid any unwanted attention from any who saw him.

Knowing the blacksmith would be too proud to accept money, he left one of the Prime Minister's gold sovereigns under the breakfast tray before departing out the back door. He kept to the shadows and headed north.

The streets were deserted as many settlements were early in the morning. A pale mist was rising from the ground and hovering ominously in the dark. *Just a few more yards to the edge of the town, then I can relax. Then I'm free,* he thought to himself. Once out in the open countryside and a good distance from the village, he should be safe. He made his way through the winding paths to the northern corner of Ulston, where the riverbank was once again visible and made his way in the shrouded mist of the morning gloom.

"Oi!" An angry yell came from behind him which he wilfully ignored hoping to himself it had been meant for another. "Oi, farmhand. Turnaround!" Not knowing how to proceed, he chanced a cursory glance over his left shoulder. What he saw then made him turnabout.

Horace was there, sitting on a destrier surrounded by at least ten large cronies on foot, armed with clubs and flaming torches. "You owe me compensation for injuring my men and the bridge toll. You can forget the protection money though, farmhand. That's something you won't get from us now."

Shit! thought Jack. *Too many of them. My pistols might take care of two of them, but I doubt even a master swordsman could handle the rest alone.*

Horace and his men would be ruthless, as the blacksmith had warned, they would feel they needed to take vengeance on Jack in order to salvage their reputation.

Jack resigned himself to his fate and hoped he made his voice sound intimidating. "Why don't you see if your horse gives you the edge this time Horace?" He shouted. "Maybe then you won't have to run and piss yourself."

Now he was in trouble. Horace, without another word, charged his destrier towards Jack and his men ran after him, clubs and torches brandished aloft. Jack knew victory was impossible, but he could at least relieve the town's people of Horace.

His right hand moved towards his first pistol behind his back, waiting for Horace and his horse to come close enough. Pistols only obeyed a man's aim accurately within a range of ten paces, Jack was not going to risk missing.

Twenty paces, he withdrew the pistol and fully cocked the hammer.

Fifteen paces, he aimed down the barrel and at the criminal's head.

Ten paces, he pulled the trigger and Horace's skull spat blood from its back as he fell to the ground. The destrier neighed fearfully and turned tail racing back towards the town.

He dropped the pistol and withdrew his second with his left-hand, cocking then aiming it at the large man with the club who was nearest him.

He fired. He missed! *Fuck,* he thought. Lyndsey had always berated him for favouring his stronger right hand during target practise. He had never had to fire two pistols in quick succession before and never thought he would have to rely on his left.

Despite his mistake, the leaderless gang members stalled and slowed in their advance. They had clearly not expected to be facing a man with guns. Jack placed his hands behind his back once more, feigning the existence of another pistol and hoping it would slow them.

It did not work. When the man he had missed a few moments earlier came within striking distance, Jack drew his sword and swiped left to right in one swift motion before his short club could be brought into the fight. His sword point made contact with his attacker's neck. The man clutched his throat as he fell into the grass.

He ducked the swing of a jackhammer from another man as he thrust the point of the rapier into his chest. He had been told in his training that killing with a thrust was a bad idea when facing multiple opponents, he soon discovered why. It took too long to withdraw the weapon from the man's ribcage as he turned to face his next opponent.

Not having the time to prepare himself for the next fight, he left his torso exposed as he steadied the blade that he had unwittingly brought too far to his right. His body unguarded, the man's club caught him in the belly.

Winded, the sword fell from his hand as he bent double and fell to his knees. *Make it quick,* he thought as the man raised his club for a killing blow and his comrades drew nearer.

A large rock caught the goon in the temple and he went down. Blood trickled down the side of his face. All around his friends were dropping their crude weapons and raising their hands in surrender.

Still nursing his belly and unable to get up, the townspeople were now threatening the gang members with pitchforks. The remaining men were rounded up and marched back towards the village. It was not long before the blacksmith and another man, who was leading Horace's destrier, greeted Jack and pulled him to his feet. Jack wanted to thank them but was not quite able to speak yet.

"This man runs the stables; he'd like to give you this horse as a thank you," said the blacksmith.

"Thank you. What will you do with the captured men?" Jack wheezed, hoping his breath would return soon.

"We are not vigilantes but they can't stay here," replied the blacksmith. "If there's any money left from the gang's exploits, we'll have them return it to the townsfolk before we banish them. This town may now be able to thrive again.

You'll always have our gratitude for that." Jack nodded graciously knowing what would be said next.

"While we're grateful," said the stabler, "the provosts will come here when the earl doesn't get his monthly bribe. We'll have to tell him what happened here and tell him where you went. I'm sorry but the townsfolk must appear blameless in Horace's death or face the earl's wrath. For your own sake, take this horse and ride north as far as you can, put as much distance as you can between you and Ulston."

Jack understood, thanked them, then took the reins. After fetching his sword and pistols, he mounted the destrier and rode hard along the path by the western bank until he reached the shallow ford. He dismounted and reluctantly sent the destrier free. It was far too grand for a travelling farmhand, or even a sergeant of the Graylenmouth Guard.

He sighed and decided not to take sleep. The sun would be up in a few hours, and he had already enjoyed some bed rest at the blacksmith's. More rest in the wild would drive his morale down. If he set off now, he could cover more ground on his long journey to Wylclyst before the next night. He crossed the shallow ford on foot and headed northwards once more.

Chapter Seven

Lyndsey's Monday morning had been a dull affair in comparison to Jack's, but eventful nonetheless.

Not being on duty today, she got dressed after her husband left for his practice. She put on a loose cream frock and left her dark brown hair down. Not the rags of a pauper, nor the lavish garments of one to whom money was no object. A dress that betrayed her station as the wife of a physician or as the press called it, 'the middling sort'. As commerce had grown steadily over the last century in Talamholean, the old aristocracy had not known how to label this new emerging class of merchants and skilled practitioners who held a decent income but not extravagant wealth or titles and the ever-blurring class boundaries tended to befuddle them.

Lyndsey did, however, see an advantage to women's clothes even if they were more restricted in movement than a guardsman's uniform. A pair of pistols were easier to conceal. She was hardly expecting a fight from Annabelle but did not want to go in unarmed either and had managed to seamlessly store two of her derringers in her bodice. Small pistols, but deadly enough.

She made her way through the streets of Graylenmouth, her eyes watering at the smell. The dustcarts had not come at the weekend due to all the disillusionment celebrations and the smell of excrement that the citizenry flung from their windows into the streets was potent. Raising a handkerchief to her nose and mouth, she quickened her pace through the cobbled streets and brick buildings until she reached Annabelle's and hammered on the oak door. A young woman with no sense of modesty led her into the lobby and she asked to see Annabelle, who appeared shortly afterwards, looking as austere as ever in one of her high buttoned gowns and tight bun.

"Sergeant Carter!" Annabelle declared not trying to mask her amusement. "I judge by your attire, you're not here on Guard business but if this is a social call, I don't think my staff can see to your *needs*. Or are you here to, as they say, 'experiment'!" Annabelle was stifling an amused giggle that Lyndsey had no time for. She got straight to the point.

"I'm here to talk about the events that took place here the Sunday before last, Madam. I can do it now in a civilian capacity or I can come back when I'm next on duty and treat it as 'Guard business'. Which would you prefer?" Lyndsey made her tone clear that she was not in the mood for jokes. Annabelle dropped her mischievous persona and promptly invited Lyndsey into her office for some privacy.

The office was a garish dim red, with maroon velvet curtains and red lamps that illuminated the red-painted oak panelled walls. "I'll assume your time is precious. So is mine. I'll get straight to the point. How did you know and recognise my colleague, Sergeant Sweep – know him, I'll add – by his first name – and recognise him when he had his helmet fastened?"

Annabelle looked aghast, clearly not expecting the young investigator to be so abrupt. Unsurprisingly, she attempted a thinly veiled threat, trying to divert the conversation instead of answering Lyndsey's question.

"Is Captain Thompson aware you're here? He's a frequent client of ours! I wonder how difficult your life would become if I mentioned in passing to him that you'd come here harassing me and my staff." Annabelle glared, hoping that Lyndsey would squirm and cower. She would not.

"He could, but seeing as you've now admitted to me that my commanding officer is a client of yours, I think he'd be reluctant to pursue the matter, as with that information I can make life equally difficult for him." Lyndsey would never debase herself with something as low as blackmail, even towards someone as reprehensible as the Captain, but neither Annabelle nor Thompson himself knew that.

Annabelle accepted defeat. "She told me the two of you would be on duty in this area and I should send someone to ring the bell." Annabelle offered grudgingly as she withdrew a long opium pipe from her desk drawer, lit it, and began to inhale. It filled the room with a foul smoky smell. "I knew one or both of you would arrive here. I was supposed to make sure you did your job and arrested him; she assured me you would. She said you both had more sympathy for people like my girls than the average guardsman."

"She?" Lyndsey said, now knowing for sure that Jack was not in a brothel as Captain Thompson had speculated the other day.

"The woman from the government, red hair and dressed like one of my girls when they're working. Not that she's ever done that work. You could tell from her accent and posture, she's never had to do a hard day's graft on her back like the rest of us. She said there'd be a need for me to call the Guard on Sunday night and I was to send someone to ring the bell and then to expect the two of you."

Something was not right, Lyndsey knew. This woman whom Annabelle spoke of had somehow orchestrated a man to have a violent outburst at the right time during their patrol. Not exactly understanding the full picture, Lyndsey was certain it was linked to Jack's sudden disappearance.

"Did this woman from the government give a name?"

"Never to me, but she had a long conversation with Molly the morning after you were here last, no idea what they spoke about. They were in Molly's room for over an hour." Lyndsey opened her mouth but Annabelle had guessed her next question and answered it immediately. "You can't speak to Molly, that's out of the question. She's my best girl and I won't have your investigations upsetting her!"

Lyndsey rolled her eyes and attempted an appeal to Annabelle's softer nature and hoped that the sympathy she had just shown to Molly was not purely for financial reasons.

"Are you aware that Jack is missing? He's not been seen since the night we made the arrest here, an arrest he made at great risk to himself. If you recall, we did not insist on forcing statements from your staff, knowing it would put them in danger. Jack arrested a man without evidence out of respect for their safety. I'm here to try and determine where he is and why he's missing. Are you willing to help me, and more importantly, is Molly? Is she aware that the man who risked his life to save her might be in danger?"

If Annabelle was moved by her words, her face did not betray it. Without change to her expression, she took a few more puffs on her pipe, then said: "Come back on Wednesday first thing. Molly's not working then, and you can have a word with her. I'll talk to her in the meantime and tell her what you've told me." She then paused for a moment and gave Lyndsey a sympathetic look. "I liked Jack. I liked Jack and I like you. You didn't speak down to my girls and put their safety before yours when that man was in his stupor."

"When that woman from the government came with a bag of gold and a bizarre request I didn't know it was to stitch up Jack and possibly you as well. If

I did, I'd probably have still taken it, but having met you both since, I deeply regret that now. I'm sorry."

Lyndsey left Annabelle's with her handkerchief to her face once more. Her head was spinning as she tried to ignore the faeces that scented the air. Things now seemed less clear than when she had awoken that morning. She had naively assumed that a chat with Annabelle would tie up all the loose ends and point her in Jack's direction. Now there were more loose ends than there had been before, and she was no closer to finding Jack. Not going home as she had planned, she went straight to the barracks. Having to do that on her day off was not usually enjoyable but she needed to know.

She went in through the front entrance and Captain Johnston greeted her with a surprised smile, shaking her hand and grinning emphatically.

"Good to see you, Barry. Just needed to chase up the paperwork on an arrest and I wanted to make sure it's all there before Thompson gets the satisfaction of giving me a grilling," she lied, not wanting to reveal the true purpose of her investigations.

"Fair point. I don't think I'd be able to enjoy my day off either knowing I might be giving satisfaction to the Captain," he replied knowingly and Lyndsey knew her intentions were safely hidden.

"The drunk that Jack brought in the Sunday before last, what was his name?"

"Don't know, he was too out of it to give his name at the time and some important people came to release him before he came around," mused Barry.

"Important people?"

"Yeah, men from the civil service, you know, dressed like the army but in maroon uniforms and tricorn hats. They said that he shouldn't be here and if we don't forget about it, we'll have the full force of the home office to deal with. Oh, and get this, the Home Secretary himself signed the release papers."

Lyndsey was lost for words. What would Lord Pluff want with the average bordello customer? "Do you think he was a relative?" Lyndsey asked not sure if that was the right enquiry to pursue but had no better ideas at present.

"Or a close friend? That's exactly what *I* thought," Barry offered. "Why else would a cabinet minister interfere to release someone on a drunk and disorderly charge?"

She thanked Barry for his help, then made her way home, realising she needed a bigger handkerchief.

She was annoyed that Jack had arrested this seemingly important assailant with just a drunk and disorderly charge. She knew they could not get anything more to stick but perhaps a rape or assault charge may have made the man think twice before behaving like that in the future. A man she realised she now needed to speak to urgently, but how? She had no name, no address and know idea if he was even a resident of Graylenmouth. Only that he was somehow important to the Home Secretary. She would have to pay him a visit then.

Her next patrol would take her near Parliament Street where the city residences of all the cabinet could be found. People might be more forthcoming if she was in her guardsman's uniform. Thompson wouldn't authorise it, but he didn't have to know!

The thought of bending the ethical boundaries of being in the Guard did not fill her with much admiration for herself, but Jack was her family. They had known each other since the age of eight and were siblings in all but blood. Family came before career. Afterall, had she drawn paper that night and gone to the brothel first, she may be the one missing now.

Missing without a trace or even lying dead in a ditch somewhere. That thought was too much to bear and she shook it out of her mind immediately. She returned home promptly, desperate to escape the smell of the city's atmosphere.

*

Not long after the grandmother clock at the Carter Residence chimed six, Michael Carter returned home from work. Having been trained well by his wife, he hung his coat and hat on the stand by the door, then removed his boots before greeting Lyndsey with an affectionate kiss.

"How was work?" She asked, after returning his kiss with equal affection.

"More cases of gout to deal with. I swear these rich people get it on purpose just to show off their status."

Lyndsey rolled her eyes. As a guardsman, she was no stranger to the fact that many among the gentry and nobility seemed to lack in brain cells what they had in gold and a taste for the finer things.

"Any sign of Jack?" He asked. "I hope you gave him a good grilling for going AWOL."

"No, and I don't think he's gone AWOL." She proceeded to tell her husband all she had discovered that day, including her planned visit to the Home Secretary under false pretences. Michael listened patiently until she got to the end then embraced her, then kissed her passionately, to which Lyndsey responded with a knowing grin.

"If I ever go missing, I have nothing to fear," he said, and Lyndsey giggled. They made their way up to the bedroom for an early night, deciding to forgo dinner.

Chapter Eight

Jack was sat in the corner near a window of an inn as the sun began to set. He was enjoying a tankard of stout and a plate of steak and potatoes. He had never had steak before, but after coming close to death in Ulston three days ago, Jack thought now would be a good time to sample the finer things.

Two men, one with a fiddle, the other a concertina, were sat at the table by the door, singing a bawdy song about a rich man who had lost his wealth and reputation after his mistress betrayed him. *Not bad*, Jack thought. This was the sort of music the upper classes considered below them, but as far as Jack was concerned, he would have this over the pompous orchestral noises they usually preferred to hear in their opera houses. That music was non-existent this far from Graylenmouth and there were fewer of those who preferred it, an improvement that Jack was now beginning to appreciate.

The innkeeper was frequently finding excuses to check up with Jack every so often and see if he needed anything else, clearly desperate for another gold sovereign Jack had presumed, unable to withhold his admiration for the old man's cheekiness despite his constant hounding.

Since Ulston, Jack had returned to his old ways and spent another three days of eating foraged food and sleeping under the sky. The hot meal, the ambience of the inn and the thought of a mattress tonight were beginning to abate his discomfort. He would have to return to a nomadic life first thing tomorrow, *but that's tomorrow, tonight is a separate matter entirely*, he reassured himself as he grinned at a petite blonde bar maid and she returned it with a nervous giggle.

Just then, a fierce-looking man, bald, with scars upon his face and a bulky sword at his side, strode in pompously. Jack's right arm twitched in surprise, Eva Valmarque's jewellery vibrated gently, not causing him pain, but the shock had been unexpected. After wearing it for nearly a week, he had begun to barely notice it.

The bald man scanned the inn in a single motion of his neck then walked in Jack's direction slowly. The chain on his upper arm vibrated rhythmically at his approach.

"May I sit here?" The man said in a silky voice, gesturing to the chair opposite Jack. "Conversation is sorely missed when one travels long distances," he said.

Jack had no choice but to offer him the seat. He could have declined but did not think it would be wise to offend this man who seemed to exude a kind of menacing subtlety. He could have thought up a convincing lie to refuse this man's company but that would have meant showing hesitation. A man like this would notice that and find a way to exploit it.

"My name is Braske. I'm a wool merchant travelling north on business from the capital up to Wylclyst." Jack's eyes widened, and it took all his strength not to gasp. *He knows!* Jack thought. "How about you? What leads you up the Graylen?"

"I'm a farmhand…" and Jack went on with his well-rehearsed story, trying to ignore the tones of panic his voice was now betraying. When he finished, Braske frowned. Jack returned his attention to his hot meal, trying to appear nonchalant. Before he could finish eating, the scarred man grabbed his hand and turned it over, holding it palm upwards and observing the marks on his fingertips and under his fingernails.

"Very well equipped for a farmhand. Tell me, what game have you been hunting on your journey northwards?" The man's voice was almost threatening and confrontational as though he was daring Jack to plug the gaping hole he had just discovered in the lie. Jack knew what Braske was referring to. He had spotted the black powder marks on Jack's hands. The ones he had acquired firing his pistols three days ago in Ulston. Soap had been a rarity and washing his hands thoroughly was not an option in the wild. The powder marks had remained and were now giving Braske the advantage in this battle of wits. He had made one mistake though; he'd provided Jack with a means of further explanation.

"Rabbits, and the occasional squirrel when I come across a wooded area." Braske smiled maliciously and Jack knew his story had not been believed.

"Funny, there are no wooded areas by the riverbanks on my map, at least not between here and the capital, but perhaps my map is out of date?" Jack nodded in agreement and Braske seemed amused. He guessed that the best way to deal with this man was to say as little as possible. There was something else as well;

the silver chain on Jack's arm was now vibrating and pulsing with such an energy that he was sure Braske might hear it.

"Anyhow, it's good that you're well-armed in these dangerous parts and in dangerous times. I only rode up from Ulston this morning; have you heard of it? Very charming little riverbank village. Anyway, it seems there was a scuffle there just three days ago. Some vicious brigand appeared in town and slaughtered the appointed law enforcement before stealing a horse and making his way northwards. Did you hear?"

He knows! thought Jack trying to control his temper at Braske's version of events. *He knows and he's trying to goad me.*

Whether Braske wanted to fight or to see if he would let something slip in anger was something Jack had no intention of waiting to find out. He had to get away from him and get away quickly. He could not attack him, not in a crowded place with witnesses which would give him the appearance of a murderer and Jack only had the knife in his boot. He had foolishly thought he would not need his sword or pistols and left them in his room. It would undoubtedly require further weaponry to stand up to someone like Braske who did not seem the type of opponent to go down easily. He might even have magic. Perhaps that was what the vibrating trinket was trying to tell him.

"If you'll excuse me, Sir. I've had a long day's travel and need to retire before doing the same tomorrow. I take my leave," Jack said hastily before getting up to leave his half-eaten steak.

"Of course," said Braske, who's sneer told Jack that he was enjoying the absence of an answer to his query regarding Ulston. "I'm riding north tomorrow as well. Perhaps we can have breakfast together then set off as travelling companions?"

"Perhaps," replied Jack having no intention of doing such a thing. He stood up, bid Braske goodnight, then walked around the bar and up the stairs to his room.

He allowed himself a quick sigh of relief before retrieving his pistols and loading them. He left them at half-cock upon the bedside table before closing the window and sitting up on the bed, keeping his eyes on the door. *Another uneasy night's sleep,* Jack thought bitterly, wondering if he would be lucky to get any at all. At least he was not in the wild again and was grateful for that.

The whole encounter had come and gone so quickly as he replayed it in his mind. How did Braske know about Ulston? He had noticed the powder burns as well but a man couldn't notice those by accident. He had to be looking for them specifically.

And what was going on with the tourmaline, Jack suddenly thought. The bauble on his arm had settled now but it seemed to come alive in the presence of Braske. Eva had said it would provide him with protection from magic. So, was Braske a Warlock? Is that what Eva had meant? That the stone and chain would vibrate and provide him with a warning in the presence of those with magic?

The most recent events of the past evening had given Jack a myriad of concerns and questions and he could not believe that less than an hour ago, his most pressing concern was how to successfully woo the bar maid. Unsure how best to proceed with his new predicament, Jack's eyes slowly began to feel heavy and he fell into a reluctant sleep.

His dreams were as unsettling as his present situation. Horace and his cronies, one with his throat cut open, the other with a deep chest wound, were standing around him on the bridge to Ulston. The back half of Horace's head was missing. They were pointing at him and groaning eerily. The looks in their eyes were not threatening. They had more of an accusatory notion about them and Jack protested to his imagined spectres. "I had no choice!" Jack asserted to his accusers. "It was kill or be killed. I'm no murderer!" The spectres ignored him and continued to groan.

*

Jack awoke long before sunrise. He had requested an early wake-up from the innkeeper long before Braske had arrived, thinking it would be prudent to set off before dawn unnoticed. He was glad of that now. He declined breakfast; the idea of missing out on bacon, eggs and black pudding before another long day's travel frustrated him, but if Braske was sniffing around, he had best not linger.

He paid the innkeeper for some bread and cold meat for the road, then made his way out of the inn and up the river. It was still dark, there was a bright full moon in a cloudless sky. Another clear summer's day was ahead and that lifted Jack's spirits a little.

Jack noticed the Graylen's waters by the east bank were only around six inches deep here. He waded in up to the ankle, his walking boots keeping his feet dry, and walked north for as long as the river would allow. After a mile or so, they deepened again and Jack returned to the riverbank. If Braske knew how to track, and Jack assumed that he probably did, then the disappearance of his footfall a mile south of here might cause him to give up, or at the very least delay him in pursuit.

As the vast open fields of Talamholean's wild country began to give way to the mining communities in the county of Ailshyre, the riverbank's footpath turned into a cobbled road: a single man on foot would leave no track, which was better news for Jack.

The appearance of a well-constructed road, however, did not give haste to his quest. He was now having to weave his way in and out of travellers who were clogging up the road and stand aside entirely so that carriages and wagon trains could pass. They would not exactly stop for a lone traveller on foot, so Jack was forced to give way.

At midday, Jack came to a fork in the road. The single cobbled carriageway now split into two. One continued northwards up the riverbank and to the source of the Graylen, where Lady Alice was presumably expecting him in Wylclyst. The other broke off and to the northeast pointing to a town called Ailsby.

Jack checked his map. Continuing northwards was the faster route, but he still had nearly two months to reach Wylclyst, perhaps a diversion through an unassuming mining town would be an unlikely course of action and not something a pursuer would expect. If Braske was indeed giving chase, then he may take the north road. He had told Jack he had been heading that way last night. Jack did not believe Braske's travel story any more than he believed him to be a wool merchant, but if Braske reached the fork without any tracks to follow, he would probably assume Jack had taken the north road.

On further inspection of the map, he saw that to the northeast of Ailsby was a woodland named 'Frostholme Forest'; it had a small track leading through it which re-joined the riverbank shortly after its northwest border. *A track too narrow and too treacherous for a horse no doubt. It would be hard to follow me through there,* thought Jack and his mind was made up. He returned the map to his pack and took a moment to gaze southwards as far as his eyes would allow. He decided he could not see anyone in pursuit but that did not reassure him. He set off to the north-east, in the direction of Ailsby.

The afternoon's walk was a slower affair than he had hoped. Jack was still a day and a half's hike from the mining town and now a larger abundance of tradesmen and merchants were travelling up and down the great road in heavily laden wagons which bounced along the cobbles. Jack would stand aside to let them pass. If though the driver did not look too threatening, he would stick his thumb out to try and hitch a ride if they were travelling in his direction. He had no luck with that. At best, they ignored him. At worst, they offered him expletives which Jack found more amusing than offensive.

As sunset was approaching, Jack's thoughts turned towards finding what the lands of Ailshyre had to offer in terms of a bed for the night. He knew he would have to leave the road. He hoped he had done enough to make sure that Braske was not following him now, but that did not change the fact that thieves and pickpockets were likely to emerge from the darkness at night. He had no desire to awake tomorrow morning and find all his belongings missing.

Jack noticed wagon tracks in the grass that had veered off from the cobbles to the right. Two lines made by wagon wheels, roughly six feet apart, Jack had never learned how to track but knew enough to realise that these were fresh tracks. The grass had recently been flattened. Five yards ahead of him, Jack saw the tracks of a second wagon trampling the grass in a similar way before joining the trail of the first. Checking the map for a second time today, Jack noticed that nothing was nearby. Perhaps there was a popular campsite or rest stop that was a trade secret among the frequent travellers of this road. Not having a better option, Jack followed the tracks.

After nearly an hour's walk, he came to an ancient ring of stones. Three feet high, and each four feet apart from one another, they encircled a fire at the centre. Two wagons with tattered canvases and two horses were secured and tied up outside of the stone ring. The huge circle was at least twenty feet in diameter. He could smell roast chicken and almost salivated. He could hear a campfire song being sung.

Not wanting to cause alarm, he held his hands up in the air and slowly made his way towards the fire. He wondered if he was being foolish not to load his pistols first but resolved he should not let the events of last night cause him to lose faith in others.

The campfire song ceased when a young boy, who did not look too far from adulthood, spotted him and shushed his companions before standing up and aiming a musket squarely at Jack's head. Jack halted immediately, wondering if the only reason all older men appeared cynical was perhaps because those who were not rarely reached middle age.

"What do you want?" The teenage boy barked as he cocked the musket. Jack could tell by the boy's posture and the way he closed one eye to aim that he was no amateur. He knew how to use that gun despite his youth.

"My name's—" he hesitated, recalling what the blacksmith had said to him in Ulston, he decided that his real name should remain a secret. At least until he made it to Wylclyst. "My name's Michael…" said Jack borrowing the name of Lyndsey's husband before launching into his well-rehearsed farmhand story for the second day in a row.

"You're going the wrong way if you're heading to the fertile plains, you should have taken the north fork in the road ten miles ago and carried on up the river," said the youth.

"I've been foraging for food and living off the land for a week now. I thought I would take a detour to Ailsby to resupply. I assume there's a butcher or a greengrocer there?"

At that statement, the boy's travelling companions laughed a loud acerbic laugh. Jack's tenseness turned to embarrassment for a moment. It was more of a half-truth than a lie. He had been fed at the inn last night but that made his hunger for proper food worse. If he could not even tell a partial lie convincingly, his quest would be hopeless.

"That there is," grinned a black-haired man in his early twenties, "but not much else apart from the mine."

"Don't forget the inn, 'The Weary Traveller', and the whorehouse? The men of Ailsby spend their time walking between the mine shaft and one of those two places. But if I lived in that town, I'd do the same, so who can blame 'em," added a mousy-haired woman of a similar age wearing an engagement ring. Her attention turned back to a chicken skewered on a spit that she was rotating on the fire. "Take a seat, Michael, and put that sodding gun down, Simon. He's harmless, and if he's not, there's three of us."

Jack had never known such affable company from a group of strangers. He ate roast chicken. He drank strong ale, though not too much as he wished to face tomorrow's walk with a clear head. They exchanged stories and it appeared their quest seemed to mirror his. The black-haired man, called Lucas, was Simon's older brother. He and his fiancé, Holly, were travelling down to the capital. They were silk traders from the eastern regions. Jack knew from his infancy in the textile mill that silk fetched the highest prices in the capital where high society was as abundant as it was ostentatious. Afterwards, they were to get married and Simon was to be the best man.

Jack gave them his story too. He stuck to his farmhand story but he was sure to give it the same sense of desperation and urgency. He replaced the detail about Eva's back message with a part about carrying a letter of import from the head of the agricultural guild to some important official. His whole adventure in Ulston was trimmed to an argument he had had with three muggers and their randy horse, at which Holly laughed so heartily, that he spilt half his ale nervously on the grass. Mercifully, no one noticed.

As the fire was dying, the three travelling companions returned to their wagons for sleep and shelter for the night. The three of them it seemed were all sleeping together in the second smaller wagon, the first laden with all their expensive silk.

Jack bid them goodnight and pulled his trench coat over himself and laid his head upon his backpack as a makeshift pillow. The pack still contained his pistols and Jack at last concluded he had made the right decision not to load them.

He dreamed a peaceful sleep that night, free of the nightmare he had suffered at the inn the previous evening. He and Holly were travelling the cobbled road and sat side by side at the front of one of their wagons, he had her arm around her and the horse's reins in the other. She was laughing at all of his jokes and gazing up at him to affectionately kiss his cheek. "But what about Lucas? This isn't fair on him!" Jack would protest weakly as she would laugh and look at him more affectionately.

Holly screamed and Jack had heard that scream before. The scream of the fearful when they were cornered by sinister men on the streets of the capital. The same scream Molly had given the night she had been held captive at Annabelle's. Jack awoke and was glad to have left his rapier by his side as he drew it and leapt to his feet. The wagon containing the silk was ablaze.

"Stop screaming and follow Lucas to get water. I'll try and save the silk!" Simon shouted over the roaring flames. The smell of woodsmoke and burning fabric filled the air.

Simon had not noticed that Holly was not screaming at the fire, but at the bald man with a scarred face and a black leather buff coat who was emerging from the darkness brandishing his sword. He cut down Holly with a swift blow to the head and she writhed on the grass spasmodically. Simon turned away and ran, perhaps to retrieve his musket when Braske's sword went through his lower back. He gasped breathlessly as he took hold of the sword blade that emerged from his belly. Braske withdrew the blade and Simon flopped to the floor lifelessly.

Jack charged at the attacker in a rage. Braske ran his fingertips along the length of the sword blade, now dripping with Simon's blood, and it began to glow white hot.

Jack brought his rapier down on Braske with all his strength and the bald man parried upwards. The clang of steel pierced the air and he nearly lost his footing. Braske had parried his attack with such ease that Jack knew his opponent would be near unbeatable. That did not instil a fear in him. All that mattered now was making Braske pay or dying in the attempt.

Jack attacked again and Braske parried with little effort. He was solely focussed on defence, willingly refusing himself a counter riposte which only increased Jack's anger. On Jack's third attack, Braske's parry cleaved his sword asunder, giving way to the superior metal and the intense heat the backsword was now emanating. Triumphant, Braske held him at sword point and Jack reluctantly raised his hands in defeat.

"Hurry up!" Jack shouted in frustration, not wanting to savour his demise or Holly's murder.

"Don't be so eager, Sergeant, I have one more of your friends to deal with. Then you'll have your turn," sneered Braske along the length of his sword.

With his sword free hand, he stroked the ruby about his neck and concentrated. Jack shuddered as he recalled Eva and her amethyst. A ring of ruby-red flames, six feet in diameter, rose up around them and the wagons, horses and stone circle disappeared from view. Braske smirked victoriously before turning about and disappearing through the flames unharmed.

Jack cursed aloud in rage and sorrow, kicking himself for not finding a place to sleep alone. Simon and Holly were now dead, and when Lucas returned, he would certainly be dead too. It was Jack's fault. If he had not followed their tracks here and introduced himself, they would still be alive. They would still be laughing and joking on their journey to the capital and planning their wedding.

He knew there was no escape from the fiery prison Braske had created for him. He had not paralysed him like Eva had, like he'd been expecting, there was no need. The flames were six feet high and he could not jump them. He could attempt to go through. This was no ordinary fire which might be quenched by a vigorous roll on the grass. This was a Warlock's fire and hotter than anything natural.

Though he could not see, he forced himself to listen as Lucas returned. He heard the grieving scream that could only come from a man upon realising he had just lost his beloved and his little brother in the same moment. He heard musket fire, but it clearly had not been of any help as Lucas gave another scream which quickly ceased. Not seeing a way out and not wanting one, Jack removed his hunting knife from his boot and secreted it up his sleeve, determined to do whatever damage he could to Braske. He was not expecting a quick death and thought he probably did not deserve one.

The fire went out in an instant and Braske returned, wiping the blood from his sword with a rag. A rag torn from Holly's dress. Jack raged internally as Braske began to speak in his silky tones. "That was very clever. Leaving the inn unnoticed and, I assume, using the river to mask your tracks? But I'm afraid Miss Valmarque's gift makes it impossible to hide from people like me."

That revelation was irrelevant to Jack now. He did not run as he knew it was probably hopeless. He waited for Braske to get closer. He waited for his moment. He knew he had to be patient. "Our mutual friend, Miss Valmarque, gave you a message on your back for Lady Alice which I would very much like to read. Be compliant and I'll give you a swift death. Explain to me the method in which she inscribed the message. A queer-looking goose feather quill and an amethyst I assume?"

Exactly that, thought Jack, though he said nothing. Remaining in a silent rage and struggling to understand how a man who had just killed three people in cold blood could conduct a conversation as though discussing the weather.

Braske shrugged. "Very well." With another caress of his ruby, the flames engulfed them again. This time in a smaller ring, Jack knew if he outstretched his arms, he would burn his hands, but it did not matter. He stood rigid on the spot as Braske made his sword glow for a second time then moved towards him. He held the backsword inches from Jack's face, and he felt the heat irradiate his cheeks. Braske then gently pulled the sword back and moved it towards the floor before gently placing it on Jack's outer left shin. Jack screamed as he forced himself not to recoil into the nearby flames.

Braske withdrew the blade after what felt like an age and then bore his eyes at Jack. "Feeling like cooperating now? No? Perhaps you'll feel more collaborative when the next one goes on your scalp, or your face or maybe even your—" as Braske's gaze was fixed on Jack's groin, he saw his opportunity. The knife, which was already unsheathed and in his hand, came up, then went forward. He thrust it into Braske's chest with full force causing him to yelp and cower. It would not be enough to kill him.

Jack knew his buff coat was too thick for that, but the scream Braske made gave him a great deal of satisfaction. He twisted the knife as much as the thick leather would allow and Braske yelped again. He brought up his other hand and ripped the ruby amulet from his neck, then with all his might, pushed Braske away. He stumbled and fell to the ground as the knife slid out of the leather, a quarter of an inch to the point covered in blood.

The fiery circle went out in an instant. Intuition told him his next move. He threw the ruby to the ground and crushed it with the heel of his uninjured right leg. Braske cursed and Jack knew he had made the right move. He then picked up his broken rapier at the hilt. Braske had left it with a foot-long jagged blade but that was all Jack needed now as he rounded on the Warlock with wrath and revenge in his thoughts. With the look of a condemned man on his way to the gallows, Braske fumbled in his pockets and pulled out a lump of pyrite.

Your sorcery won't save you now, you murderous cunt! Jack thought to himself. Braske grasped his pyrite, screwed up his face in concentration then became transparent for a moment. He vanished as Jack attempted his killing blow, thrusting his sword stump into the space where Braske's throat had been a moment before. He cursed loudly into the darkness, screaming until his breath went out and his throat went hoarse.

Jack knew that his first duty was to tend to his wound but that would have to wait. Three people were now dead, dead because of him and his recklessness. Eva's ornament had warned him that Braske might be magical the previous night. He had been foolish to think that a few diversionary tactics had thrown him off his trail and made him safe. Had he found his own camping spot, Holly, Lucas, and Simon would still be alive. They deserved a proper funeral, or at least the best he could provide.

He went to Holly's corpse first and discovered she had not yet become one. Braske's sword had given her a deep gash in the side of her head but not killed her instantly. Her eyes were rolling in the back of her head as she convulsed on the ground by the burning wagon. He knew she did not have much time. He knew that he was the only one who could let her die painlessly and with dignity and he hated himself for having to do it.

He put his arm around the back of Holly's head and pressed it in tightly to his chest. He felt her breath quicken and she ceased to convulse. *I will make sure you suffer twice as hard for what you've made me do, Braske.* It was almost an oath. The self-loathing he now possessed for being forced to give Holly a merciful death would soon be unleashed on Braske.

He found Lucas' body a few yards away from the wagons with a musket lying next to him. Braske had at least shown him more mercy than his fiancé seeing as he had been stabbed through the heart. Almost an instant death, though Jack doubted that compassion had been Braske's intention.

He dragged their corpses to the unburnt wagon and hoisted them in. They were heavy and cumbersome, but Jack did not mind. The difficulty of the task felt like only a modest punishment given that he held himself responsible for their fate. Not having a spade, he had no choice but to give them a cremation. Jack was not sure if that would have been their preference but doubted they had ever given it much thought due to their youth, he hoped it was enough.

He wrapped each of their bodies in some of their fine silk that Simon had managed to retrieve from the other wagon. Then, he laid them side by side before fetching a hot brand from the dying fire in the stone circle and touching it to the wagon's canvas, which set ablaze and spread quickly.

"I'm sorry. You offered me nothing but kindness and hospitality which I repaid with your deaths. Simon, I should have turned tail and retreated when you drew your musket, then maybe you'd all still live." He kicked himself at his pathetic attempt at a eulogy as the flames rose higher. The smell of wood smoke now mixed with that of burning flesh, but he did not flinch or look away. He stood vigil over their funeral pyre, a solitary figure illuminated in the blaze. A single tear slid down his cheek but he allowed himself no more. He was to blame for all they had suffered and would not disrespect them by allowing himself any more catharsis.

When the sun rose, he gathered his things and went to the horses. He set the larger one loose then climbed on to the smaller mare and drove it slowly back to the road. *I'm a sergeant in the Graylenmouth Guard. I'm supposed to protect the innocent. Now three innocent people are dead thanks to me, and to top it all, I'm also a horse thief.*

He would not finish grieving for a long time, but he had to force that same grief to the back of his mind for now. Not for his quest. Not for duty. Certainly not for honour. No, for Holly, and for Lucas, and for Simon. Braske was out there and he knew he would find him again. When he did, Jack would take his revenge, for them, he swore to himself.

Chapter Nine

Members of high society were prancing to the rhythm as an orchestra played classical music in the corner of the great hall. Victoria sat with Daisy on a table at the edge of the dancefloor and was applying the unusually proud posture she used when in her gossip columnist persona. Her wide-brimmed hat askance and her gloved left hand resting on a wooden cane with a white pommel. Her right hand, also gloved, delicately held a glass of merlot which she would take frequent fake sips of as she whispered instructions to her serving maid.

Every member of parliament who served in the cabinet had attended, along with those of the shadow cabinet. Lords and their ladies from all the oldest and most noble houses in Talamholean were also at the King's Disillusionment Ball, which made King Wilfrid the Second's absence all the more recognisable. The Queen and the young Princes were missing as well. This had not escaped Victoria's notice.

In attendance with the higher members of the aristocracy were some of the wealthiest merchants. Those whom the nobility would sneer at privately while fawning over in public, their immense wealth making them an unwise candidate for an enemy.

These were the most successful silk and cotton traders or the new and emerging industrialists, hoping to marry their sons or daughters to the child of a lord. Half the room had money but no status. The other had status but less money. Marriage between two such families would be a mutually beneficial business deal between two kinds of very different though equally egomaniacal people, Victoria surmised.

Whenda, the King's great-grandmother and the first monarch of a united Talamholean, had abolished serfdom ninety years ago. The historians would assert that this had led to the current social and economic change. As now, those who had once been serfs were free to pursue their own interests and make a success of their life. As far as Victoria was concerned, the only difference between the current system and the old was that the masses were now beholden to two ruling classes, where before there had been one.

If change were to come about this century, then those very same masses would have to take action. Not a war or a revolution, Victoria knew enough history to be aware that tearing down entire governments only to replace them with new ones at the drop of a hat rarely led to progress where liberty was concerned.

What was needed was a constitution, an official written document that clearly defined the remit and responsibilities of both the monarch and the parliament. Recorded history in Talamholean reached just beyond a thousand years and the system of governance they now had was shown to have been cobbled together slowly over that period.

The world was changing and the rulers were not adapting, trade now replaced war in most cases. War generally meant higher taxes and rebellion of the merchant classes who tended to finance the lifestyle of the nobility. With little threat of conflict coming from in or outside of the kingdom, parliament and the King had entered into a strained relationship. Both considered their first duty to be defence of the realm. With little of that to do, they had begun to squabble like petulant children.

The problem was, when the children squabbling were the most powerful men in the land, everyone else suffered too. If there was a constitution curbing their powers and keeping them in check, the suffering of the masses could be alleviated. Victoria believed this with great passion, and it irked her to have to act ignorant of political matters in public.

"I don't think we're going to learn much tonight, Ma'am," said Daisy through her wig and painted-on freckles. "They're all avoiding you; they don't want their conversations turning up in your column." It was true, since the doorman had checked their invitation and welcomed them to the palace, no one had said a word to them. A dancing couple would stray towards them from time to time, then they would conveniently stray in the opposite direction upon noticing Victoria.

"Just keep taking note of what I tell you, and note anything odd you happen to notice too," said Victoria without looking in Daisy's direction as she stayed in character.

"Yes, Ma'am." Daisy blushed through her fake freckles as she always did when her employer valued her observations.

Victoria had not expected to learn much from any of the attendees. Her own reputation had seen to that. She and Daisy had come to the ball as observers, but for once, not of the rich and infamous.

"By my count, there's seven," said Victoria from behind her glass as she feigned a gulp of her wine.

"There's definitely seven, that's what the handsome one told me in the cloakroom," grinned Daisy.

"I wish you had told me that earlier. That confirms it then. Let's go." She discreetly poured her undrunk merlot into a floral centrepiece and made her way to the exit with Daisy.

"Mrs Lionsgate, a moment of your time please?" Victoria was shocked. She had not expected anyone to approach her, given her reputation.

She turned around to find the Prime Minister's own Warlock, Eva Valmarque, looking resplendent in a black gown with a plunging neckline. Only a Warlock could get away with dressing so immodestly at an official state event.

Victoria trusted the Warlocks least amongst all the powerful. They claimed their role in government to be solely advisory. Victoria was certain that if that were true, they would not be opposed to the notion of more transparency. To this day, not a single member of the public or press had been granted entry to the Warlocks' Tower.

"How may I be of service, Miss Valmarque? It is a great honour to be addressed by one of your kind. Truly a story to tell my grandchildren one day." Victoria took a long and deep curtsey as her role required it.

"You flatter me. May we talk somewhere more private?" Victoria had no choice but to agree. Being alone with a powerful magic user was foolish but she could not let the public's perception of her falter. If she had refused an audience with a woman who served one of the most powerful men in the country, people would become suspicious. They always did. Victoria nodded and Eva led her and Daisy through the hall to a small antechamber.

The room was dark. Eva waved her hand across several candles that were on the table while caressing a ruby amulet and the room illuminated with a magical orange glow.

"Thank you for agreeing to see me. If your maid could wait outside?" Victoria had no choice but to dismiss Daisy. She did not want to, but refusing a Warlock was not a good idea. Daisy left, allowing the music of the orchestra to refill the room for a moment before the door closed again.

"I've read your column, it's mostly vapid, but you're a perceptive woman. That much is apparent." Victoria did not disagree but neither did she have to stay in character to appear offended.

Her columns *were* vapid, but who in their right mind would start a conversation with an insult? "Your penmanship affords you more power than people give you credit for," Eva continued. "We, and by we, I mean the council, have need of your skills."

Eva Valmarque was as hasty with her requests as she was with her insults. She was beginning to form a low opinion of the Warlock and her disregard for first impressions, but she knew this might be too good of an opportunity for a journalist to turn down.

"My interests are piqued but I need more information," said Victoria. "What do you want from little old me?" She added a pout as she knew that was what people expected of her.

"It probably didn't escape your attention that only eight members of the Warlocks' Council are in attendance tonight," said Eva.

"I noticed that Leopold Braske is not here but I assumed he is tending to our dear sick King," said Victoria, knowing very well that the King was not in ill health.

"Sick?"

"That's what one of the footmen told me," lied Victoria, knowing full well why the King was not present here tonight.

"The King is not here because he refuses to be seen publicly with the Prime Minister, protocol forced him to invite the highest member of parliament but not to attend himself."

This was not new knowledge to Victoria but she feigned surprise all the same.

"So I assume Braske withheld his attendance out of loyalty?" She knew that was not correct but the question fitted her ditzy persona well. Leopold Braske was after all the King's personal Warlock and by all reports, fiercely devoted.

"No, Leopold Braske resigned from the council, and with it, the King's service, shortly after parliament dissolved. He has since disappeared. If he ever resurfaces, he will be tried and burnt as a witch. When that happens, we need to make it appear that his fall from grace is also his just desserts. Do you see your role here, Mrs Lionsgate?"

"A smear campaign, I like it!" That was not exactly true. In recent years, even in her tasteless column, she had stuck clear of anything that could be considered serious reputational destruction. She poked fun yes, but never made the objects of her writing out to be corrupt or immoral individuals. It was difficult to cast aspersions on one's moral character when you were commenting on the dress they wore or the coach they rode in.

Nevertheless, she had no respect for a member of the Warlocks' Council and would have no qualms smearing one such as Braske. She also saw another opportunity. "What will you give me in return, Miss Valmarque?" Victoria said raising her eyebrows.

Eva had clearly been expecting this; in politics, no one got a favour without receiving one in return. Even the Warlocks were not above this.

"What can I give you?" Eva said with a hint of defeatism.

"An interview with Alayna Strauss. It seems only fair that the most powerful woman in the government should meet the most powerful woman in the press." She took care to compliment the head of the Council with adulation rather than disdain. "I shall be alone in a private room at Madam Centaur's Coffee Shop on Wednesday, from midday to two o'clock. If Miss Strauss joins me for at least an hour of that time, you'll get your column inches defaming Braske. Good evening." She turned and left without waiting for Eva's response, terrified that Miss Valmarque may set her alight as she had done with the candle, she headed to the door, maintaining character with all her strength.

*

As the coachmen took them back to Lionsgate Hall, Victoria was vomiting into her hat: her skin the tone of a white linen sheet.

"What did she do to you?" Daisy gasped affectionately while patting her employer on the back.

"Nothing, she just wanted a favour, but I genuinely thought I was a goner when I walked out without her dismissal," said Victoria in a gap between her retches.

"Do you think Miss Straus will show up on Wednesday?" Daisy asked.

Victoria sighed. "I doubt it but it was worth a try. I'll have to think of a way to ask her important questions without breaking character, just in case. Anyway, leave me, Daisy, I'm fine. Get out your sketchbook and start drawing."

Daisy was gifted with an exceptional memory when it came to faces. All the same, it was best if she got to work now. They had both noticed seven footmen earlier, and Daisy's liaison with one of them in the cloakroom had confirmed it. Seven footmen in purple military-style uniforms who worked at the palace. She was now sketching their likenesses onto paper. Only one of them could have opportunely *lost* the trade secretary's bill!

Chapter Ten

"Our rulers, be it in an official capacity, or the more sinister one held by the wealthy merchant lobbyists were all in attendance at the annual ball last night. A lavish soiree in accordance with tradition during the first week of parliament's summer recess and held at the royal palace. The invitees of such a grandiose event feasted on a seven-course dinner: consisting of roast duck, chicken, pork, beef and lamb. They drank the finest wines imported overseas from Marailia. I do not blame you if that makes you baulk, seeing as the rest of us are lucky if we consume meat once a week. (Though they can keep their wine for all I care.)"

"Did our esteemed leaders discuss a means of helping the rest of us? No, dear reader, they discussed how to make life easier for themselves and their own interests. If you need further proof of how meaningless the whole event was, then you should know that famous air head and insult to writers everywhere Victoria Lionsgate was present at this very ball. Sleuthing her way among the gentry and the industrialists, being more concerned with what they were wearing and who they were sleeping with rather than the plight of the common people from whence she came, and on whom she has now turned her back."

"To add further insult to injury, where do you suppose the funding for such an event came from? The deep pockets of the merchants and the industrialists perhaps? From the considerable (and tax exempt) revenue the King and the aristocracy make from their estates? No, dear reader, it came from the coffers of the state treasury. The money they rob (sorry, tax) from us, which they claim is needed to maintain the military for our own safety. Well, how do you feel about your well-earned money being used by those richer than you to fatten their bellies and drink wine you could never afford, even if it does taste like piss and no sensible tavern owner would ever stock it."

"It is clear to me that their corruption knows no boundaries and must be kept in check. I hereby call on you, dear reader, that it the duty of us all to demand of our rulers the drafting of a const..."

The voice of the young academic, who was standing on a soapbox in parliament square as he read Bernard Crenshaw's latest article to a large crowd that gathered to listen, faded as Lyndsey carried on with her afternoon patrol.

"We should turn around and arrest him for gross offence," demanded Matthew, Lyndsey's new partner and in her opinion, a sycophant.

"The legal term is 'grossly offensive', and it's not against the law to have an opinion you don't share."

"*Sorry,*" replied Matthew in a sarcastic tone that told Lyndsey he had just taken gross offence of his own.

The sticklers are always overly sensitive. Jack wouldn't have reacted like that. Lyndsey's irritation at her new partner almost seemed to sharpen her resolve for finding Jack. When the city bells chimed two o' clock, she and Matthew took a break for lunch. She told him she would meet him on the corner of Sorceress Street in an hour to continue patrol. To her relief, he did not seem perplexed or offended that she did not wish to spend lunch with him.

Lyndsey mounted her horse and then made her way to Parliament Street. She dismounted and led the mount by the reins until they reached number thirteen. The Home Secretary's official state residence. She tied up her horse before knocking on the door and an elderly housekeeper answered a few moments later.

"Yes?"

"There's a crowd in the square listening to protest speeches on political dissent. All fans of the elusive Bernard Crenshaw it seems. They look harmless enough but I'm just here to warn the cabinet and check if they need my protection. Just in case they turn riotous." Lyndsey had thought a story like this would be the best cover for gaining entry to the house. The crowd in the square had given her the means to lie with conviction.

"Thank you for letting us know. I shall inform his Lordship. Good day!" She closed the door quickly, but Lyndsey's well-trained reflexes made sure she had one of her boots in the door before it could slam.

"My apologies, Madam, but regulations insist that I speak directly to the Home Secretary himself so I can confirm he received the warning." That part was at least true, even if her reason for being here was not. The servant hesitated for a moment, almost as though she was not sure what she was to do next.

"You had better come in then," she eventually wheezed. "The Home Secretary may be busy at work, but a member of his household could speak to you. Would that be appropriate, Sergeant?"

"It would," Lyndsey replied reluctantly not knowing how to get around the issue and not being able to turn back now. She would have to think of a way to speak to the man once indoors.

The elderly housekeeper led Lyndsey into the drawing room where she was given a seat and offered tea, which she refused. She sat in the high-ceilinged and mahogany-panelled room; it reminded her of how the other side lived. There was a fire roaring in the hearth. Unnecessary in Lyndsey's estimation. It was early July and even high-ceilinged rooms were not exactly open to a draft in the summer. The rugs were immaculate and must have been cleaned by a team of servants daily. Lyndsey was beginning to wonder if Bernard Crenshaw might have a point.

"I believe you have some important information for me, Sergeant. A matter of protocol the housekeeper tells me?" A familiar voice came from behind her that made Lyndsey double-take. She turned around and saw the young man whom she and Jack had arrested that night at Annabelle's. The eyes that had glazed over at Olivia's stare and the right arm she had popped back in were plain to see. Strangely, the man was looking at Lyndsey as though greeting a stranger whom he had met today for the first time.

Lyndsey seethed internally; she could not lose her temper. That would mean being thrown out of the house before discovering anything and possible dismissal from the Guard for abuse of power. Lyndsey felt at her left side for her cutlass unthreateningly and surreptitiously checked her breast plate was fastened. She had to be careful, but at the same time, this was her best opportunity to find out more.

"Hello again, young man, I hope you're feeling better than when we last met." She used the tone of a concerned friend rather than that of an arresting officer.

"I'm sorry, have we met?" The young man replied. "I do not recall, Madam."

"You had, shall we say, a disagreement with my partner at Annabelle's the Sunday before last?"

"Annabelle's! Is that where I'd spent the evening? Good grief!"

"Annabelle's and the cells at the barracks; you honestly don't remember?" Lyndsey asked disbelievingly. He was in a drunken state when she and Jack encountered him but she would not have said he was blind drunk enough to forget the whole ordeal.

"I don't remember anything that day from four o'clock onwards," said the man abashed. Lyndsey did not think the man they had arrested that night would be capable of such humility. "My father set up a meeting for me with the Prime Minister. He wants me to go into politics like him and thought setting me up with a job in the highest parliamentary office was a good first step. I get to his house only for this woman to tell me he's been called away on urgent business. She invites me in for coffee, that's the last thing I remember. Next thing I knew, I was back in bed here with a sore head and a scolding lecture from my father about squandered opportunities."

"A woman? A servant?" Lyndsey's head was swimming with a million questions, but this seemed the most pertinent right now.

"I don't think so. She was dressed in a lady's finery and spoke like a lady too. She looked like a King's mistress by the low cut of her dress."

A Warlock, Lyndsey knew instantly but could confirm it with one more question.

"What colour was her hair?"

"Red I think."

Definitely a Warlock, and the Prime Minister's own. The cartoonists in the Gazette and the Chronicle often sketched the Prime Minister looking docile with his red-headed Warlock sat on his shoulder whispering orders. The woman who had paid off Annabelle to go along with her scheme no doubt. She could not recall her name at this time but it was plain to see that this was who the young man had encountered that night. That would explain why he remembered nothing.

"Is your father in? I'd like to speak to him about the matter if I may?" Perhaps the Home Secretary was involved?

"No, he's gone to the family estate out in his constituency for the summer," he said, looking ashamed now. "Am I in trouble?"

"No, but I would like a clearer picture of that night. I'd like to interview you properly if I may. May we have another meeting?" Eager as Lyndsey was to know more, she would have to return to patrol before Matthew grew suspicious.

"I suppose, may I ask something about that night?" He replied looking both nervous and pained. "Did I hurt anyone? I don't remember anything, and I don't think I could live with that knowledge if I had." Lyndsey had developed a sixth sense for spotting liars. It was common in most guardsmen when they ceased to be rookies. She could tell that this man was an honest man. She not only believed his story but also believed that his encounter with Molly, and later Jack, did not come by chance. Someone had played them all for fools, not realising or caring how many innocents like Molly got in their way.

"What's your name, young man?" Lyndsey asked.

"Adam," he replied.

"Adam, as far as I'm aware, a few people were shaken at your behaviour but no one was done any lasting damage. You should also be aware that I do not believe you were acting of your own freewill that night. Furthermore, I believe that you, me, and my partner have become pawns in a game being played by the powerful. Do you trust your servants?" Adam looked shocked at all the information she had just given him, clearly processing it all before replying.

"They're loyal to the family but not to me individually. My father is still the head of the household."

"Then I best say no more for now," Lyndsey answered. "Can you meet me at the Unicorn Inn by the west gate tomorrow night? The wealthy don't frequent it and it's always noisy so we can be assured no one is listening."

"I'll be there," Adam said.

She cautioned Adam not to share the information they had discussed. It seemed the wisest course of action for now. She bid Adam farewell then returned outside to her horse and set off to find Matthew. She did not have time to eat now, and the rest of her shift would be difficult on an empty stomach, but it had been worth it.

So the Prime Minister's own Warlock had used her magic to make sure Adam who, now she had met him in his right mind seemed incapable of behaving as he had that Sunday night, would cause a disturbance at Annabelle's. A disturbance she and Jack would surely answer. All to make Jack disappear without a trace, but why? Jack was more or less her brother and she thought highly of him, but he was not important or powerful. What did the establishment want with a lowly sergeant in the Graylenmouth Guard?

Was the Prime Minister himself involved too? Lyndsey had to consider that or was his Warlock serving her own interests as the cartoonists and journalists liked to claim.

Today was Tuesday and she had taken care to make sure that she would not be slated for patrol tomorrow. She was due to speak with Molly at Annabelle's first thing. Learning what she just had from Adam, she would have to rethink her interview strategy tonight, but there was time. She also had another appointment with Adam at the Unicorn Inn.

Lyndsey sighed in frustration as she made her way back towards Sorceress Street and her irritating partner. The puzzle may look clearer now than it had done a few days ago but she was no nearer to finding Jack than she had been from the start.

Chapter Eleven

Jack had almost ridden without stopping since his encounter with Braske. When he did, it was more for the horse's sake than his own. Though he was weary and in need of sleep, he was unable to do so. He was constantly alert, knowing Braske would find him again thanks to Eva's tourmaline. Yet, he was not afraid. He knew, thanks to Miss Valmarque and her trinket, that another encounter with the monster was inevitable and he was determined to settle the score.

The setting sun was an hour from disappearing over the horizon as Jack passed a signpost on the northeast road stating that Ailsby was one mile away and Jack knew it was time. He made his way off the cobbles and travelled due north until he came to the ancient and famous oak tree he had spotted on the map earlier. According to the histories, this mighty tree was almost as old as Talamholean itself, being noted as the sight of one of the greatest folk and fairy tales in the nation's history.

Children were told that it was in the shade of this very tree that the trickster Mischievous Morris had promised the Troll Emperor the head of the Fairy King in return for half his people's wealth. The Emperor, disliking the King more than he loved riches, agreed to the terms and Morris told him he would return three days hence with the King's severed head but the gold had to be handed over now. Morris then bid the regal troll farewell, departing on a huge fleet of wagons full of gold, but he never returned.

Eagerly awaiting on Morris in this very spot, the Emperor was not able to comprehend the idea that he had been duped. He died at the foot of the oak tree once starvation took hold and his remains still provide the great oak sustenance to this day, or so the story goes.

Jack knew that Morris and the troll were both an invention designed to teach children not to be too trusting of strangers with promises too good to be true. Nevertheless, the great oak tree would serve for what he had planned tonight. He removed his pistols from his pack. He then took a twenty-foot length of slim rope and tied a knot at the front of one of the trigger guards. He walked the rope around the circumference of the tree trunk then back through the guard, carefully feeding the remaining length of the rope between the front of the trigger and the guard itself.

The pistol was hanging off the rope two feet up the trunk like a wall ornament. He took great care to pour in the powder charge for the suspended pistol before closing the pan and pulling the hammer to full cock. He loaded his other pistol with both powder and shot, put this one at half-cock and placed it in his belt. Then, he took the other end of the rope in his teeth and climbed up to a sturdy branch. He sat and shimmied along, as far as his weight would allow. Now in place, maybe ten yards from the oak's trunk, he pulled the slack in on the rope, took the other pistol in his belt and pulled it to full cock. He waited.

Certain that Braske would be making his appearance soon and hoping the tourmaline bracelet would not give away his precise location, Jack waited patiently as the lifeless faces of Holly, Simon, and Lucas were ever-present in his mind's eye.

The wood of the oak was beginning to numb his behind and his back and legs began to ache as a result of the awkward position he had been forced to hold to keep his balance on the branch, but he continued to endure. Justice, or as Jack saw it revenge, had to be served. The sun was now set and had been replaced by the darkness of night.

Then, in the moonlight, Jack saw a bald man with a glowing white-hot backsword in hand making his way across the field towards the oak. Not forgetting his plan, Jack waited patiently as Braske drew closer. He could not panic and act too quickly. Braske was the better of them with a sword and he no longer had his own to counter. If Jack was as handy with a pistol as Lyndsey, he would have attempted a headshot when that scarred face came with in twenty paces but he was not going to risk that after he had failed to hit the ruffian back in Ulston. Jack's chief weapon against his opponent were his wits and he was going to use them.

Braske reached a point when he was ten yards from the oak's trunk, then stopped and scanned the area in the gloom. Jack could have sworn his eyes passed over the branch where he was sitting; but did not linger there, much to his relief. Eventually, his eyes stopped. Fixed at the foot of the tree where Jack's backpack had been left. He had taken the bait. Jack allowed himself a second of silent celebration but remained focussed.

"You disappoint me, Sergeant Sweep! A famous oak tree is not the best place to hide regardless of whether you're facing a Warlock." Braske continued to stare at the pack but did not move. He was trying to tempt Jack out of hiding and he saw his chance. He gave the rope a short and sharp tug and the shotless pistol he had left hanging on the trunk went off in a cloud of white smoke. Above him, he heard the rapid beating of wings as a flock of birds were fleeing the oak tree's shelter at the sound of gunpowder breaking the silence.

"Be sure to use your second shot more wisely," Braske sneered and marched towards the foot of the trunk. *Don't worry, I will.* Thought Jack taking aim and waiting for the right moment.

His second pistol went off with as loud a bang as the first and Jack heard a scream. When the smoke cleared, he saw Braske on the ground, yelling in pain and clutching his knee. The ball had landed in the side of his kneecap as Jack had intended but he had no time to celebrate. He leapt from the branch and ran towards the Warlock, picking up the sword that had ceased to glow white hot when he dropped it and held it to Braske's throat.

Jack had been aiming his pistol at the man's knee for two reasons. The first, he needed information, and the second, he wanted him to suffer.

"Very cunning, Sergeant." Braske begrudgingly winced in pain through gritted teeth. His arms swiftly moved to the pyrite stone around his neck. Jack saw what he was doing before he could get his hands there and removed the fool's gold before throwing it into the grass six feet away. Jack wanted to taunt him, wanted him to feel as helpless as he had made him feel at the ring of stones but knew his time was short.

"You're finished, Braske. Answer my questions and I'll see to it that you have a quick death. Which is a fate too good for you!" Braske said nothing. He only seethed and glared. "Why are you following me and why are you trying to stop me from reaching Wylclyst?" Jack began.

Braske continued to silently glare. Expecting this, Jack placed the ball of his foot onto the side of his kneecap where the bullet had entered and began to shift his weight until Braske howled.

"Lady Alice! You can't be allowed to reach her, it's treason. The King has the divine right to rule."

"I thought the Warlock's plan was for me to deliver this message. Are you not a Warlock?" Jack was becoming impatient as he sought clarification.

"I *was* a member of the council until three days ago when I resigned, thanks to that bitch Valmarque and her machinations. She's using you in her game." Jack had more or less worked the last part out, it seemed obvious now that Eva Valmarque had somehow been involved with all the events that had occurred that night at Annabelle's. Whether she was taking advantage of an opportunity she saw or orchestrating everything like a chess grandmaster, he was not sure, but she was definitely the chief schemer and responsible for all that had occurred to Jack since that night. Jack would have liked more information on this matter but decided his time was short. He needed other information.

"How does the black tourmaline allow you to track me? Valmarque said it would protect me from magic." He knew there would be a technical explanation of how gemstones had certain ethereal qualities that those with magic could manipulate but that was not what he was looking for.

"Ha!" Braske's familiar silky tones were now becoming hollow as the blood drained from his face. "That's what we've been telling the powerful for centuries so they feel more comfortable around us. In truth, they reveal the wearer's location and lend us an ear to all their endeavours as well as give us insight to their thoughts. It helps us keep them meek. Haven't you wondered why black tourmaline is about the only gemstone you never see a Warlock wearing?"

He had not, but in truth, Jack had never spoken to a Warlock before meeting Eva. He was hoping he would not speak to many more in the future. Eva, and presumably the other Warlocks, were using his newly acquired jewellery to spy on him and perhaps even influence his thoughts. That made sense, why else would you have to force someone to wear something they had been told to believe would protect them?

"One more question, Braske, and think carefully if you can. This one depends on whether you get a painless death. Why did you kill those three innocents two nights ago? They bore you no threat and you were powerful enough to capture me without harming them. I was sleeping when you attacked, you didn't even need to wake them!" Jack did not think he was going to like his answer, whatever it may be, but he had to know.

Braske did not hesitate to respond. "You needed to know I was serious and wouldn't accept any tricks or games from you. It was nothing personal, I just wanted you to know I don't waste my time and it would be best for you to cooperate." He returned to his pained glaring and Jack was right. He did not like the answer.

So Holly, Simon, and Lucas, who had all done nothing to Braske, were killed so he could assert a point. Jack thought of Holly's spasmodic convulsions before he had been forced to kill her, then slowly dug the point of Braske's own sword into his belly, making sure to twist the blade sharply before withdrawing it.

A fatal wound, but not one a man was known to die quickly from. Braske's hollow tones switched to pleading ones almost immediately. "Please! End it. End it please?" He was gasping as blood began to emerge from his mouth and nostrils which trickled down the side of his face. Jack was no longer paying attention. He returned to the oak's trunk and gathered his second pistol, before returning his belongings to his pack.

Flint and powder had left a scorch mark upon the trunk in the place where he had hung the pistol. A tribute to another tale beneath the Great Troll's Oak that none save Jack and the tree would ever know. Soon Braske's remains would feed the tree roots just as the Troll Emperor's had. At that thought, he stretched out his hand to touch the trunk.

"I'm sorry," he said, "to feed you something so rotten, the Troll Emperor probably tasted better."

Braske was now begging as he passed him on his way to the horse. "Sergeant Sweep, Jack, Jack Sweep, mercy please. Surely as a guardsman, you won't let me die this way?" Jack did not react to his pleas and treated them like the leaves of the oak that he could now hear rustling in the night breeze.

Upon returning to where he had hitched the horse, Jack had every intention of heading to Ailsby on horseback but an idea had stricken him. He took Braske's sword out of his belt and looked at the blade one more time. The blade was pure ferramus. This was a rare metal that could only be found in one mine in the whole of Talamholean. The common people had only heard of it. The middling sort might be lucky enough to have it in the form of an alloy. Only the gentry, nobility and other landowners would see it in its pure form and in this quantity.

This metal was almost indestructible and a sword could not be made from anything finer. It was edged on one side and well weighted for quick blows. In addition, it had a finely crafted basket hilt that would protect his hand in combat.

The sword would not likely glow white hot for him as it had for Braske as Jack had no magic, but it should serve his needs for what he was planning. He rolled up his right sleeve and slid the blade under the silver chain containing the tourmaline stone. With the hilt in his left hand, he thrust the point down into the ground and then steadied it with the edge of his right foot. He pulled his right arm away from the sword and towards him with all his strength.

Once again, the chain had a mind of its own. It shrunk and dug its way so tightly into Jack's skin that it drew a few drops of blood, but it would give no more resistance. The chain snapped with a feeble ping before landing ahead of him in the grass. Jack picked up the chain and placed it into the horse's saddlebag. He wondered if the Warlocks already knew that he had freed himself, or would they deduce that in a day or so? When would they realise he was travelling in the wrong direction, thinking only of hay and fresh water?

"You're the second one I've had to set free in less than a week. It'll be a shame to continue on foot, but I don't want Eva knowing where I am at all times," he admitted to himself as he whacked the horse's rump and it thundered off into the night.

The horse he had set free after the events in Ulston was far swifter and grander though parting with this one hurt him more. This one reminded him of the three silk traders he had met recently. Braske's death had bought him a sense of justice but not assuaged his guilt. Jack watched the horse disappear into the darkness then turned south towards the northeast road. He'd be in Ailsby in a day. He would not stop long; he would resupply and then head northwest towards the forest.

"A dense forest is not ideal when on horseback," Jack conceded to himself, "but letting that one go is the worst thing I've done tonight by far."

Chapter Twelve

Lyndsey had returned to Annabelle's at sunrise the following morning, back in civilian livery. She thought her guardsman's uniform would be too intimidating and she did not want to put Molly in distress unnecessarily. Molly was sitting opposite Lyndsey with her sister, Martha, the girl who had rung the bell that night, her hand tightly clasped in her sibling's for reassurance.

"You're not in trouble, Molly, and I'm not here as a guardsman. I'm investigating this matter independently and I need your help. Your sister is welcome to stay if you wish." Molly nodded nervously in understanding. "I know it's difficult so please take your time if you need to. What happened with the man on the night he held you hostage?" She decided not to mention Adam by name. It was best for everyone's safety if she divulged as little information as possible for now.

"Don't answer anything, Molly," snapped Martha quickly before Molly could get a word out, "and don't trust her. She's here to make an arrest so the Guard can look good. They've always sneered at our type." While Martha's tenderness towards her sister was admirable, Lyndsey struggled to conceal a frustrated exhale. It was true that much of the Guard held Molly, Martha, Annabelle and others like them with little regard, but Lyndsey did not. They were citizens. Citizens that she had taken an oath to protect upon becoming a guardsman. She reassured Martha of what she hoped would be the last time taking care not to make her frustration explicit.

"As you can see, not only am I out of uniform, I am also not taking statements. If I were to report what Molly tells me, I would have no evidence making the charges flimsy at best. Annabelle will tell you that my commanding officer is a prolific customer here, meaning that even if I wanted to make a report, it would soon be quietly forgotten." She gave Martha an understanding look while she observed her own explanation process itself behind Martha's eyes.

"It's OK, Martha, I want to help, that man saved my life and if I can do anything to return the favour, I will," Molly finally said in one quick breath with a hint of steely determination diluting the nervousness in her voice.

"Thank you, Molly, please continue," said Lyndsey.

"I was told to expect a well-paying and high-status client. That wasn't strange as those tend to be a lot of our customers. When he knocked on my door and I told him to come in, you could tell he'd been drinking. He was slurring and had a mad look in his eye, but a lot of them do when they've hit the bottle and are feeling horny. I only got scared when he told me to…to…to…"

"It's OK, you can skip over that detail if you wish," said Lyndsey, not wanting to make Molly feel uncomfortable.

"I told him I wouldn't do that and most likely none of the other girls would either. Annabelle's good to us, she checks what we're all willing to do and not do when she hires us and makes sure we have clients who won't force us to do what we don't want," Molly continued, showing relief and finding her voice again. Lyndsey nodded, urging her to go on and not sure if kind was the right word to describe Annabelle who was essentially a pimp. "When I refused, he pulled out a gun and held me hostage before dragging me into the lobby."

"That's when Annabelle sent me to ring the bell," Martha finished for her sister.

"Thank you," Lyndsey bid them both. "I only have a few more questions for you, Molly. Was there anything about this man's behaviour that seemed out of the ordinary? Aside from drunkenness and lust." She had not planned on asking this question before meeting Adam yesterday, but the new information he had given her had made it necessary.

"Well," Molly looked puzzled, "I'd only say it was a type of drunkenness I'd never seen before. Many men come here inebriated. Their look and behaviour is more or less the same for every man. There was something about this one though, it was like he had access to a stronger wine than anyone else."

A magical trance, it must be! thought Lyndsey who now needed to ask about the second matter. "Annabelle has told me of a woman with red hair who came to see you the morning after. What did she say?" Lyndsey was now on the edge of her seat as she knew this was the pivotal information she needed and perhaps the key to finding Jack.

"We spoke for a long time me and her. She said she was a Warlock and could heal any wounds in return for me keeping quiet. I told her I didn't really have any, save a few mild bruises which Olivia was able to heal, so she gave me a bag of gold for my silence."

"A silence you're now betraying, Molly," said Martha, fear more than apparent in her voice.

"Molly," said Lyndsey, ignoring Martha, "You don't have to continue if you don't want to, but I assure you, I will handle everything you tell me with great care and secrecy." She meant it; as much as she loved Jack, she would not sacrifice the lives of innocents to find him. If Jack were here, he would insist upon that.

Molly seemed to need no time dismissing her sister's council before finishing her story. "She somehow knew that the man hadn't paid up before you arrested him. Then she said I'd done a great service for the Prime Minister. I didn't really understand what she meant or how she seemed to know everything."

"Did she give a name?" Lyndsey said who was now almost certain who this woman was.

"No," replied Molly, "but I guessed she was someone powerful by the way she spoke and carried herself." Lyndsey's heart was beginning to sink at the thought of declaring war against the Warlocks' Council.

"Thank you for your time, Molly, you've been very helpful. When I find Jack, I know he'll appreciate that."

Molly returned her thanks and Lyndsey took her leave, intent on returning home before meeting Adam at The Unicorn tonight. Michael was not working today either and the thought of an afternoon in her husband's company seemed rather pleasant right now. She knew she should be diverting her attention to finding Jack, but she had done all she could at present.

She also had to process the fact that her worst fears had been confirmed. Eva Valmarque was behind the events that had befallen her and Jack that night. The red-headed and determined member of the Warlocks' Council who was also in the service of the Prime Minister. If the papers were to be believed, she made all his decisions for him. Whatever she was really like, the thought of facing her made Lyndsey shiver with fear. This woman was more powerful than Lyndsey, both physically and in terms of political influence.

Lyndsey was now more eager than ever to spend some time at home relaxing with Michael before an inevitably exhausting night interviewing Adam in a busy pub, but a plan was beginning to formulate in her head. An exhausting and improbable plan, but perhaps an effective one. Lyndsey stopped in her tracks. She resolved not to return home and instead headed towards Parliament Street.

She would not knock on the door and enquire as she had done so with the Home Secretary. She was out of uniform and even if she were attired as such, that would not fool the Warlock, but Lyndsey was well versed in another and more subtle form of enquiry.

*

A few hours later, Lyndsey was across the street from the Prime Minister's residence and sat on a public bench with a copy of the Chronicle in her hands. She was not reading it, though many who saw her there would have been forgiven for thinking so.

She tilted her head towards the open paper on her lap, but her eyes were gazing upwards. Upwards towards the building across the street, where the Prime Minister of all Talamholean lived for as long as he held that office. She had been waiting for hours now and she would have to depart soon to meet Adam, but she willed herself to stay on the bench.

Parliament was dissolved until September, as was the Council. The Warlock would no doubt be within that building advising and influencing the Prime Minister. She had nearly two months to put the ideas she wanted in his head before the legislature reopened.

The door across the street opened and it was as though Lyndsey had summoned the Warlock and brought her forth with a single thought. She saw a red-headed woman, dressed in a black gown traverse the threshold and descend the elegant marble steps to the street. Upon reaching the bottom of the lavish staircase, the woman checked around her for any would-be pursuers.

Lyndsey did not want to waste the opportunity that had just presented itself. She had only seen sketches of Eva Valmarque in the papers. While they were not a flattering or accurate likeness, this woman had been dressed in the same manner she was often sketched. A black hat and showing more cleavage than modesty would allow for other women. It had to be her.

Lyndsey allowed the Warlock a decent head start before beginning her chase. She trailed her target at a safe distance and always made sure there were many members of the public between the two of them. That way, it would not be hard for Lyndsey to melt into the crowd if the red head suspected she was being followed and looked back.

To Lyndsey's relief, she seemed confident of her secrecy. She seemed to be in a hurry, which Lyndsey hoped would yield good results for her pursuit. After being led on a short walk through the streets of Graylenmouth, Eva slowed her pace. Stopping, she entered a fanciful coffee shop on Siddle Street, 'Madam Centaur's'. Lyndsey counted to ten and followed her inside, wishing she had a hood or a hat to disguise herself.

"Mrs Lionsgate will receive you in room fourteen, Madam," she heard the maître'd say before a wave of red hair made its way through the public seating area towards the private rooms, reserved for the higher-status residents of the city that could afford it. Lyndsey knew this was where her chase ended as she would not be able to enter room fourteen without revealing herself.

"Can I help you?" The impatient maître'd barked, who seemed to be wondering why Lyndsey was standing there.

"Err, I need a job, are you looking to hire a waitress?" She said, thinking fast and hoping the man had not noticed her at the times she had been on patrol.

"We have a full complement of staff thank you. Good day!" He snapped.

Lyndsey turned and left, relieved she did not have to spend the next hour being interviewed for a job she did not need and feeling better than she had done a moment ago on the bench.

That brief pursuit had not been fruitless. Eva was meeting Victoria Lionsgate. The gossip columnist who wrote vulgar stories that poked fun at how people dressed.

When guardsmen were in the barracks getting ready to start patrol, her articles were read aloud and passed around as a means of amusement. Lyndsey had no idea how the peculiar Mrs Lionsgate was involved in this. She only knew that she would be enquiring after her as well in the near future.

Chapter Thirteen

"She might be here soon, Daisy, you'd better make yourself scarce. I don't think she'll be very forthcoming unless I'm alone," Victoria said to her servant as she made herself comfortable on one of the armchairs in room fourteen at Madam Centaur's.

"I can't leave you alone with the head of the Warlocks' Council, Ma'am. What if she threatens you, or worse?" Daisy said worryingly and no doubt out of concern for the employer she greatly respected.

Victoria was grateful for her loyalty but could not risk losing the opportunity she had. She was not exactly sure that Alayna Strauss would make an appearance, but she had a good feeling, given how Eva Valmarque had been desperate for Victoria's help at the ball.

"Go on, take the afternoon off. If the Chief Warlock wishes me harm, your presence will not do much to stop her. She'll hurt you as well and I won't have that on my conscience!" Daisy looked at her mistress with a mixture of admiration and offence but obediently said nothing and left the room. Victoria opened her note pad where she had spent the last day and a half carefully crafting interview questions. Questions posed such that the answers would reveal much but phrased in a way that appeared unsubstantial and would not reveal the deep cover she had cultivated for herself over the years.

Victoria had been a young girl of eighteen, barely a woman when she married Edward Lionsgate, a young barrister. As the daughter of a tavern owner, many in the middle and upper echelons of their town had sneered at Edward for marrying so far below his station. Edward was unbothered by this and she had loved him, and still loved him, all the more for it. That still did not quash her anger at the judgement she had received.

They had kept their revulsion at Edward behind his back, but they had been more overt in their disdain for Victoria. Shunning her at gatherings and making snide comments about her education when passing in the street. They had moved to the capital shortly after their wedding to seek Edward's fortune and the people of Graylenmouth had proved just as snobbish as those in her hometown. Never having told them of her beginnings, the gentry would always somehow deduce it. In her youth, Victoria had not mastered the art of speaking or carrying herself like those of the upper class.

As Edward's talent for legal work led to a higher fortune and reputation so too did their bitterness seem to rise proportionately. By the age of twenty-three, Victoria had had enough. She had picked up many a dark secret about the people who offered her nothing but snide comments and passive aggressiveness from their servants. Victoria would often socialise with them. She found their company less judgemental. While it was never her plan, this had armed her with the knowledge of who her enemies were sleeping with outside of their marriages, or who was not being entirely truthful when keeping the books on their households' finances and other such pearls of wisdom.

Victoria began to write down what she had heard and anonymously sent it to the Chronicle. This continued for eleven more years until Edward's tragic death in a smallpox epidemic. Mourning her husband but no longer needing to protect his reputation, she threw off Cynthia Baron, her pseudonym, and revealed herself.

The enjoyment had gone out of her job since then. Now as a person to be feared, she had not received any more sneering comments. Her previous enemies, having departed Graylenmouth in disgrace long before she revealed herself, were no longer around. Even if they were, they would be reluctant to cause her offence. She was now aged forty-two and while her previous achievements filled her with pride, her job no longer did.

There was nobody left in high society that knew of her humble beginnings, and as a person to be apprehensive of there was no one worthy of her ire. Not wanting to destroy people who had done her no wrong, she had turned her penmanship to the material, writing about clothes and social activities. She would playfully satirise anyone who seemed ridiculous but never go out of her way to destroy them. The meaningless articles she had been churning out in the eight years since Edward's death were essential to her secrecy, and for income. Five years ago, she had decided her talents could be put to better use. That was when she had recruited Daisy to her staff.

There was a knock at the door which brought Victoria out of her wistfulness and she called them to enter. It was not Alayna Strauss as she had hoped but Eva

Valmarque once again. Eva did not greet her, instead, she sat herself down on the comfy leather armchair opposite. She said nothing, eyeing Victoria with a curiosity that made her feel uneasy until she eventually broke the silence.

"Am I to assume that Miss Strauss won't be joining us?" Victoria said.

"You are," replied the Warlock with a sneer.

"Then I'm afraid you won't get the articles you requested, that was the deal. If that will be all?" Victoria got up to leave hoping her abruptness would not cause Eva to become wrathful, but it appeared that she had something to add.

"We no longer need your help regarding Braske, it appears that the problem has sorted itself out. He died alone with no witnesses early this morning not far from Ailsby," Eva said.

Victoria knew she had only shared that information to make her feel uneasy. If a man died as far away as Ailsby, the news would not reach Graylenmouth on the same day, unless you were a Warlock. Victoria did not want to ask the next question but could not break character.

"How do you know this?" Victoria asked as Eva sneered triumphantly.

"We had a man under surveillance, we were tracking him. Braske picked a fight with him and lost shortly before our man freed himself of our supervision."

Victoria was not going to ask a follow-up question, though she wished to. Victoria Lionsgate, the gossip columnist, had to appear uninterested in these matters, unlike the real Victoria, a person who was known only to herself and Daisy.

"Are you here to gloat, Miss Valmarque? If that will be all, I'll bid you good day." Victoria got up to leave but it appeared that gloating was not Eva's only intention.

"I have another offer for you from the council which may be of interest," said Eva, which Victoria considered momentarily before sitting back down.

"Go on."

"We're asking the same again, a smear campaign, only this time of a different person. Bernard Crenshaw," said Eva.

What does she know? thought Victoria momentarily gripped with fear before controlling herself in an instant and ready to deny anything at the drop of a hat.

"Who?" She said with as much innocence as possible causing Eva to roll her eyes and sneer for a second time. Despite the Warlock's condescension, Victoria was relieved.

"Bernard Crenshaw is the writer and publisher of many a pamphlet that criticises the government with reckless abandon. He's causing a stir among the people. Are you willing to help us? As for your reward, we will *consider* giving you an interview with Miss Strauss but only once Crenshaw's reputation is lying in the gutter," said the Warlock as though she was addressing a naïve child.

"It's tempting. Where does he live and what does he look like?" Victoria said, assuming that would be the logical question for an ignorant person.

"Nobody knows. If the council knew, we'd be able to deal with him without your help." Victoria knew what she was implying and at last, saw a way out of the web she was about to become tangled in.

"No, I'm sorry, I know my column isn't exactly pleasant to the people I write about but I've never made things up. If I did, I'd be open to libel." That was true, none of the people she wrote about had ever sued her. Even in her earlier career, she could be visceral with her opinions but had never twisted or changed the facts.

"We suspect that Mr Crenshaw will be more concerned with maintaining his anonymity than taking you to civil court. Think it over, Mrs Lionsgate, I will meet you here in a week's time for your answer." This time, Eva was the one who left abruptly before Victoria could say another word. She grasped the pyrite amulet around her neck, became briefly transparent then disappeared. Victoria wondered if it was moral to smear a man who had never done her a single bad deed and had in fact brought her nothing but joy, happiness and a sense of purpose into her life.

*

An hour later, at Lionsgate Hall, Victoria was explaining the afternoon's events to Daisy. Daisy, it seemed, was more reluctant to accept Eva's offer which Victoria was at least considering.

"It goes against everything we stand for and everything we're working towards Ma'am; you can't accept no matter what she offers you!" Daisy had a fieriness about her when she believed in something that Victoria could not help but admire, even when they disagreed.

"You're right on principle, Daisy, but agreeing to the Warlock's request will help keep our cover; sometimes you have to dabble in immoral practices for the greater good!"

Daisy opened her mouth and inhaled, about to offer her own counter argument when the doorbell sounded and she went to answer. She returned shortly with a street urchin holding a copy of one of Daisy's sketches of a palace footman. This was about the trade bill. Victoria had almost forgotten about her other investigations in light of today's events.

"Daisy, fetch the young man some food. Would you like some water too, young man?" She asked the lad who did not seem much older than twelve and offered him a seat. He nodded and Daisy disappeared in the direction of the kitchen. "Are you bringing me that drawing because you've seen that man?" The boy nodded. "Where have you seen him?"

"Outside the Warlocks' Tower, m'Lady. He sometimes appears there with papers concealed in his purple jacket that he hands to the servants once they answer," replied the boy quickly as though he did not want to mess up his words.

"He never goes in?" Victoria said, although that was no surprise. The Warlocks were famously secretive.

"No, my begging patch is by Warlocks' Tower, there's always rich folk there. I never actually see anyone go in and out except the Warlocks." The boy spoke again licking his lips as Daisy returned with a glass of water and a plate of bread and ham.

"Is he always delivering papers?" Victoria asked.

"Always papers, usually from his pocket and neatly rolled up, then someone hands him a pouch, it's gold. I asked for money from him once and he gave me a whole gold sovereign from the pouch. I'd never seen one before; me and my brothers ate well for the next two days."

"He actually gave you one?" Palace footmen were known to be as tight fisted as the royal masters they served.

"Yes, m'Lady, I was quite surprised too as he looked very snobbish, people like that tend not to give people like me any of their time. I was just trying my luck but was quite amazed. I think he thought it was the quickest way to get rid of me."

That made sense, shouting at the boy would have caused a scene and drawn attention to himself. If Victoria's hunch was correct, the man did not want to do that as she suspected he was not doing something legal.

The young boy finished the food and drank his water, then Daisy saw him out. Upon returning to the drawing room, they continued their discussion. This time, Daisy did not argue in light of the new information the boy had provided.

"I have to accept Eva's offer. The Warlocks are involved and I need to gain their trust," Victoria declared. "That footman you were flirting with at the ball, is this him?" She asked, holding up the sketch and Daisy shook her head. "Do you think you could meet with your friend and get this man's name?" She finished. Daisy nodded in agreement. She would not argue once Victoria had made her mind up. There was no point.

Chapter Fourteen

Lyndsey's pursuit of Eva that afternoon had not left her much time with Michael but she was grateful for his company and cherished the short moments they could find together. At seven o'clock, as the sun began to set, she bid Michael farewell and told him not to stay up late for her. She was investigating and she did not want her husband to lose sleep. Michael understood but still did not like the idea of his beloved wife going to one of the rowdiest pubs in the capital alone.

Lyndsey was flattered that Michael cared for her as she cared for him but was even more respectful of the fact that he did not insist on accompanying her or forbid her from going altogether as other husbands were known to do with their wives. The fact that neither thought even seemed to occur to him made her give him a longer kiss before she put on her cloak and left. She would have loved to have an evening out with Michael but an extra person might have intimidated Adam and she did not want to scare him away.

She made her way westward to the Unicorn. When she arrived, she paid the barman for a drink and then chose an empty table by the door. The pub was not yet packed, the toll workers at the nearby gatehouse usually filled this place out when they finished their shift. That was when things generally became noisy.

Lyndsey had discarded her uniform in favour of civilian clothes again but in a pub like the Unicorn, it was not wise for a woman to sit alone at night, married or otherwise, unless she dressed modestly and sternly, Lyndsey had done both. She was wearing a pair of riding boots with a long knife concealed in the left. She was not expecting a fight to break out but it made her feel safer all the same. She would have preferred a pistol but that was too big to conceal and guns on one's belt tended to invite challengers.

She wore loose-fitting cotton britches and an equally loose-fitting shirt of red linen, over which was a sleeveless leather jerkin. Her dark brown hair was done up at the back in a tight bun. She had stolen this trick from Annabelle, noting before that it had given her a stern appearance. Lyndsey did not want to frighten

Adam, but she did not want to give others the appearance that she could be intimidated herself.

Her attire seemed to have done the trick. People would occasionally glance at her but their stares never lingered. She sat with a proud posture while sipping her ale sparingly. The heat of the old fire filled the high wooden beamed ceiling of the capital's noisiest pub as the toll collectors came off duty and slowly filled the place. The newly arrived clientele had almost tripled the occupancy of the inn as men in black uniforms and tricorn hats ordered drinks from the bar, speaking to the bar staff in a familial manner.

"Sorry, love. This seat taken?" A man smiled gesturing to the seat opposite Lyndsey by the window.

"I'm afraid I'm waiting on a friend who'll be joining me shortly." Lyndsey smiled back at the man, though she took care to keep a commanding tone in her voice. She had found, professionally, that keeping an air of authority about oneself in public generally kept her safe from unwanted attention or unnecessary violence. The trick was to appear as though you were not to be messed around but make it clear to others that you had no intention of doing the same to them, so they did not feel threatened in turn. Her success in this was proven as the man smiled back at her and wished her a good evening before going to join his friends and their loud conversation about a difficult customer who had refused to pay the toll earlier that day.

When Adam walked through the front door, she hastily beckoned him to her table and gestured to one of the bar staff to bring a drink. It had not occurred to her to tell him to dress down. She thought it had been obvious but he was attracting quizzical looks from the patrons. In his top hat, long frock coat, ruffled shirt and mahogany cane, he looked out of place in a pub frequented by commoners. The little lordling seemed to be realising his mistake as she paid the waiter for a drink and passed it to Adam.

The waiter lingered at the table for a while, gawping at the man in expensive clothes expecting to maybe become wealthy by proximity before Lyndsey dismissed him with a generous tip which she thought she might ask Adam to reimburse her for later.

"Thank you for coming," she said getting straight to business and not wanting to waste any more time while Adam was unwittingly attracting unwanted gazes. Lyndsey withdrew a parchment quill and inkpot. "Please go over the events of Sunday before last. Everything you remember, or don't remember?"

Adam's explanation did not give Lyndsey any more insight than when she had last spoken to him, except one. Eva Valmarque had been wearing both a topaz and a garnet when she let him into the Prime Minister's residence. As Lyndsey understood it, one was for amnesia, the other for manipulating naïve men; she was more or less certain of Adam's innocence by now based on her instincts, but judges did not accept instincts as irrefutable evidence in court.

Court, that's wishful thinking, thought Lyndsey. At no point in history had a Warlock been dragged before a judge. They seemed to escape the rule of law more often than royalty and aristocracy.

"I just have one more question before we finish. Have you ever met or spoken to Victoria Lionsgate?" Lyndsey was not sure why she asked that question, or if it would bring her any revelatory information. Right now, she was willing to fire her pistol in all directions in the hope of hitting an elusive target.

"The gossip columnist?" Adam replied curiously. "I've heard of her and read the occasional article, but I've never met her. Father forbids me from attending social events in case I do something stupid in front of someone like her and end up in the papers."

Adam had just put the bare bones of a plan into Lyndsey's head. She thought carefully before phrasing her next question. She had to be tactful.

"Would you be willing to be the object of one of her articles, Adam? If it might mean solving this mystery we've all become involved in."

Before Adam could answer, a drunken tollkeeper waded up to their table through the crowded pub with hatred behind his eyes. Lyndsey braced herself for a fight. She hoped she could try and diffuse whatever situation was about to occur peacefully. The tollkeeper must be taking exception to someone of Adam's ilk in a pub meant for the commoners. It seemed class mixing was despised at all ends of the social spectrum in Graylenmouth.

Lyndsey knew it would take all her skills training and experience to resolve this amicably and without bloodshed. Causing a violent scene, even unintentionally and in self-defence, could cause her the loss of her guardsman's commission as well as a stint in prison, and if she were forced to kill, hanging. She would not make a widower of Michael.

When the tollkeeper stopped at their table, he slammed his tankard down and soiled the wood in a river of ale. He frowned at Adam before, to her surprise, rounding on Lyndsey.

"You!" He said with an intrusive and accusatory finger jabbed furiously into Lyndsey's personal space. "You arrested my brother-in-law for corruption, now you're on our turf taking bribes from the rich folk." He gestured to Adam. "It seems you'll look the other way if the price is high enough, will you, Carter?" He glared into Lyndsey's eyes as he blinked. Occasionally, his posture would falter.

Lyndsey had not recalled the man prima facie but she recognised him now. It was Stephen Dickinson, who's sister was married to Bruce Harris, the infamous 'Graylenmouth Grifter'. Lyndsey and Jack had arrested Harris three years ago when he and his henchmen had infiltrated the tollkeepers and started charging an extra two shillings to the capital's visitors and pocketing the profits. They had bribed city officials, as well as the other tollkeepers to turn a blind eye, to the point where Harris's latest scheme became Graylenmouth's worst-kept secret.

Inevitably, the scheme had to crumble due to their hubris. Like all great criminal schemers, Harris became arrogant and drunk on his own success. The conmen had, at first, taken care not to add the two-shilling charge to the most powerful and wealthiest of people. This changed on the day when the infamously snobbish Lady Sybill, one of the Queen Consort's ladies in waiting, was returning to the capital after a visit home. She had decided to show Harris, who was working at the east gate, the same disdain she showed for everyone she considered 'common'.

Harris would not let her insults slide. He considered himself a criminal mastermind and, therefore, a higher status than everybody else. He demanded not only the two shillings from Lady Sybill, but also the gold ornaments from her coach and the jewellery about her person.

When Lady Sybill arrived at the palace in a fluster and relieved of her jewels, orders reached the barracks within the hour. Captain Thompson pulled Jack and Lyndsey off patrol and ordered them to arrest Harris, Dickinson and any tollkeepers suspected of corruption, which was nearly all of them. Harris was now in the lowest dungeon of Graylenmouth's harbour prison and would be for another ten years, but it seemed Dickinson had managed to keep his hands clean and plea enough ignorance. He had been let off with an afternoon in the stocks and it seemed had somehow been able to re-join the tollkeepers despite his previous malfeasance.

"I'm not taking bribes, Mr Dickinson. This man is helping me with another corruption investigation which involves more powerful people than any of us. I chose to meet him here where none of their spies would likely be nearby."

Underneath the table, and unseen by Dickinson, Lyndsey brought her booted foot containing the knife towards her so she could draw it at a moment's notice. She hoped she would not need to.

"It's one rule for us and another for them. That's the rule the Guard abide by, isn't it, Carter?" He said again jabbing his finger furiously and ignoring what she had just told him.

Lyndsey was losing patience but she kept calm. Both of which seemed to work to her advantage as she took the real risk. She stood up quickly but did not move towards Dickinson, who flinched but did not move to fight.

I have him. She knew as she raised herself to full posture, glowered firmly into his eyes, put her hands on her hips and declared: "You and your brother-in-law were quite happy to abide by that rule when you were going out of your way to beggar farmers and craftsmen from their hard-earned coin but ignored those with real power. If Harris had kept his cool and let Lady Sybill pass that day, you would still be bankrupting your fellow man while high society turned the other cheek." Dickinson faltered, clearly the altercation was not going the way he had hoped.

Lyndsey defeated him with her last statement. "In fact, it's very troubling that they let you re-join the tollkeepers given your past offences. Perhaps I should stop by the gatehouse on my next patrol for a thorough search of your books and coffers. I assume you're at the west gate these days due to its close proximity to this pub?"

There were now a few other tollkeepers nearby looking at Lyndsey with a curious eye. The looks of shock on some of their faces told Lyndsey that perhaps they were not aware of his past offences. Realising he had bitten off more than he could chew, Dickinson cowered back into the crowd mumbling something about getting another drink. Lyndsey wanted nothing more than to leave but knew she had to show she could not appear to have been intimidated so sat back down opposite Adam who was now gazing at Lyndsey with the awe of a theatre patron alone with his favourite actress.

"I'll do it!" Adam said with unmistakeable adulation in his voice.

"What?" Lyndsey said, not sure what Adam was agreeing to. The situation with Dickinson had brought her out of her investigations for a moment.

"Whatever your plan is for me to be humiliated by Victoria Lionsgate."

This was clearly a new experience for the young man who was fast acquiring an addiction for it.

When they finished their ales, they left the Unicorn. Lyndsey, being grateful for Adam's help, offered to walk him home. She feared for his safety walking through the rougher parts of the capital dressed in expensive clothes and probably carrying a few expensive possessions as well. Adam's face betrayed a hint of shame at having to be safely escorted home by a woman but he did not refuse the offer.

"How did you know he would back down?" Adam said. "I thought we were goners when he started pointing his finger at you like that."

Lyndsey shrugged. "Dickinson's all bark and no bite. I remember from when I arrested him that his tough man act tends to buckle under pressure," said Lyndsey as they reached Adam's house on Parliament Street. She bid Adam goodnight then turned about and made her way home. Her thoughts were reminiscing about the first time she had encountered Stephen Dickinson.

She had chased him that day down the street and through the markets before apprehending him with a diving tackle. He had been the only one who had managed to flee the gatehouse when they turned up to raid it. Having lost the usual game of scissors paper stone to Jack on that occasion, she raced after him until he was subdued. *Me and Jack will have a good old laugh when I tell him I ran into Dickinson again,* Lyndsey kept reassuring herself as she reached her front door.

When she got upstairs, Michael was already asleep. She thought he looked so peaceful there and did not want to wake him. She was desperate to share the evening's events and watch her husband gasp in awe as he often did when she shared her work with him, but they both had to be up early tomorrow, and Lyndsey did not want to keep them up unnecessarily. She could tell him in the morning. She got into bed after changing, cuddled up to her husband and put an arm around him. He purred peacefully and put and arm around her in return but did not wake. His embrace was all she needed as she fell asleep almost instantly.

Chapter Fifteen

He had not planned to sleep when he lay by the side of the road and stretched himself out upon the ground. He just needed a little rest after his encounter with Braske the previous night. In truth, all the events that had occurred since the night at the stone circle had taken a toll on him, both physically and mentally, and his body refused to go on. He was hungry, he was tired, the burn wound Braske had branded him upon their first encounter was beginning to heal but it pained him all the same.

The warm evening sun and the pleasant warm breeze only helped incentivise Jack to lie near the cobbles for a while. In his exhaustion, he drifted into sleep almost instantly as he gazed at the clouds.

The spectres of Horace and his cronies were now replaced with those of Holly, Simon, and Lucas. What made him shiver most was the fact that Holly's head wound was clear as day and she continued to convulse in fits as she made her accusations at him. This time, they spoke, though not in any voices that matched their own as Jack could recall.

"There are pistols in here, well-made ones and all, and enough powder and shot to bring down an entire cavalry detachment," said Simon, clutching his belly wound before adding "…and look at this, gold! More than I've ever seen. This bloke must be a more hardened criminal than us."

"Or a spy," said Lucas nervously, also in a voice not his own. He was clutching his chest. "Let's get out of here before he wakes up!"

Holly said nothing but continued to convulse and pointed at Jack's side, to his sword. Braske's sword. He wanted to apologise for now using the weapon that had killed her and for his role in her death. He needed a blade and had none of his own anymore. He swore to himself and now to Holly's spectre that he would use it more honourably and justly than Braske ever had.

"In a minute," said Simon again. "You get the horses ready. I wanna get my hands on that fancy steel of his."

Jack awoke suddenly, a man with terrible breath and a hook nose was crouching beside him, at Jack's left side, with his hands upon the sword hilt. He was carefully removing it from Jack's belt with such concentration that he did not notice Jack awaken. Jack took full advantage and swiftly brought his right hand across and landed a punch on the thief's nose with full force. The thief squawked, swore, and rose to his feet taking several paces back. He clutched his nose with both hands, blood oozing between his fingers.

Jack leapt from his sleeping position and drew the rest of his sword. The thief glared at him through his fingers and Jack challenged the man by gesturing towards himself with his sword free hand. Daring him to attack him if he could. The thief, it seemed, lost his appetite for a crime once faced with a broken nose and an alert opponent armed with a ferramus sword.

He turned about and ran back to the northeast road where his partner in crime awaited him atop a horse while leading another by the reins. Jack was still ten feet away in pursuit when the bloody faced man leapt onto his mount. The two men made haste down the cobbled road with his pack, which contained all his possessions save his sword.

Jack cursed louder than the thief when he had broken his nose as he stopped and hopelessly watched the horses make their way towards the horizon. Everything had been in that pack, his pistols and ammunition, the map, his gold. If Eva and the Warlocks were still able to track and observe him, they would surely be planning to abduct another guardsman right now.

It was almost dark; he had slept too long. Jack had no choice but to turn about and head to Ailsby. He would be there within the hour. He could not track, and even if he could, the horses had stuck to the cobbles leaving nothing for a pursuer to observe. On foot, swift pursuit would be equally impossible. His only choice was to head to the mining town and hope that food, rest and shelter would be available there. He would also be hoping for charity as he was unlikely to find any of those without coin. Jack cursed himself for not being able to banish his exhaustion until he had reached the town.

*

Night-time had arrived in full by the time he reached Ailsby. He knew then that Holly, Simon, and Lucas had not been hyperbolic in their description of the town. The cobbled streets were well-maintained but that was about it. There was residential housing but little in the way of shops which were all closed now. Even if they were open, he had no money to spend. The only places thriving with people were the inn and the whorehouse as he had been warned.

He tried his luck at the inn. He did not try to beg or barter for a bed free of charge. Instead, he went to enquire if there was a priest or a monastery nearby, the sort of people who would provide sanctuary and philanthropy to a starving traveller with nothing to offer in return. The innkeeper answered Jack with a grimace and a lecture about godless times and a godless world which led Jack out on to the streets again, alone at night with no food, no money and no hope of warmth.

He decided to visit the mine. He did not think it would provide him with food and recreation but he had tried everything else, it seemed his only option now, albeit a hopeless one. He made his way through the streets, following the signs, until he approached a vast open mine shaft with a sign above the opening reading the words 'Ailsby Coal Mine'. The words were etched in coal dust, it seemed to be the only resource the town had in abundance.

Knowing that lingering by the bleak mineshaft was not likely to bring him fortune or joy, he decided to leave the town and head northwest immediately towards Frostholme Forest. There would no doubt be plants and animals there to forage and hunt for, though he had no idea how he could hunt anything without his pistols. Lyndsey had grown up as a fur trapper before joining the Guard and knew a few tricks about hunting in the wild. He cursed himself once again for never asking her more about it.

If she'd lost the scissors paper stone game that night, she would probably be having an easier time than me. Though it was meant as a complement, he kicked himself for almost wishing all he had suffered on his friend. As far as he knew, Lyndsey was safely back in Graylenmouth with her husband, still going about her guardsman's duties and living her best life no doubt. He was glad of that.

Jack gave the grim place one final look then turned to depart. Just as he was turning to leave, he heard something. Something that clanked and squeaked. It was coming from the shaft itself, echoing up the passageway out into the air. It was getting louder. *Who would be in the mine this late at night?* Something was amiss.

He knew he should not remain but his curiosity got the better of him. He crouched to the side of the shaft's opening behind a disused mine cart and waited. The squeaks and metallic clanks were getting louder and now there were voices.

Two men at least. Their loud and strained discourse muffled by the echo of the passageway.

Jack's knees were starting to ache, and he realised he had hidden sooner than he needed to. They were closer now. Not more than thirty feet by the sound of the screeching mine cart.

Eventually, two burly men with mischievous facial expressions emerged from the opening. Straining and bent double, behind a mine cart nearly overflowing in a heap of coal.

"I told you we should have taken the horses in to pull the cart. I'm fucking drained. I need to rest," wheezed a red-headed man with arms the size of tree trunks. He had a musket slung over his right shoulder. Jack could see it was at full cock and probably loaded.

"It's not safe for horses down there. If they'd died, we'd have to wheel this whole damn thing back to Frostholme ourselves!" A black-haired man with a bushy beard panted, standing up straight and looking elated to finally do so. He was carrying a long wooden pike with a sharp metal point.

Frostholme! They're heading the same way, thought Jack, wondering how risky it would be to reveal himself to these two. It seemed to him that they were stealing coal from the mine but they looked harmless. He did not have the shivers he would feel and still felt at the thought of Horace or Braske.

"We could have used Barney's horse. He doesn't need it anymore. If that had failed, then we could have continued on foot," protested the red-headed man also stretching after what Jack deduced to be a long and arduous journey with the mine cart.

"Barney's dead, his horse and belongings are to go straight to Rosie upon our return. Remember, we own nothing as individuals. You know the rules, we're responsible for that horse until we return it. If it dies because we were reckless, Rosie might have us branded and banished!" The black-haired man spoke in such a matter-of-fact tone as though what he had just told his companion was common knowledge, but Jack was not sure he followed.

The men were now finished resting and began to load the coal into large sacks. "Might have to hide some of this and come back later," said the black-haired man. "We can't take it all with just the two of us. We'll have to make a second trip. This was supposed to be a three-man job."

"If we have to take Barney's horse back with us, can't the horse take some of the coal?" The red-haired man replied.

"It could, but if we come across any sheriffs and have to make a run for it, we'd lose the horse and the coal. I don't want to explain that to Rosie."

"Curse Barney for falling off his horse. If he hadn't died, the job would be done by now."

Jack decided to reveal himself at this very moment. He still was not sure what to make of them, but he now believed that making their acquaintance would be mutually beneficial. "Excuse me, I couldn't help overhear your conversation," he said as he walked around the back of the cart slowly and with his hands halfway up, not wishing to appear threatening.

The men jumped and the red-headed man unshouldered the musket to point it at Jack's head immediately. The black-haired man grabbed his pike and held it to its full length, wanting to keep Jack at the end of the long pole. Jack kept calm and continued to keep his arms up, hoping this was still the best way to avoid danger.

"What are you doing here?" The red-haired man said, his musket shaking.

"Who are you?" The black-haired man added, his pike quivering in unison with the other man's musket.

"I believe we're both in a difficult situation and we can help each other. It seems you have three horses but only two riders, and a great deal of cargo." He gestured to the coal in the mine cart. "I will happily be your third rider and return the horse to you when you reach your destination. All I ask as payment is that I may share what food and provisions you have and be shown passage through Frostholme Forest?" Jack took care to keep both his hands visible and his tone unthreatening.

He guessed by the way they were shaking that they had never used those weapons before. In some ways, that made them more dangerous than experienced fighters, so he took care to stay calm and try to put them at ease.

Jack could tell that his offer was being considered. The two men exchanged glances furtively, not wanting to take their eyes off Jack for too long.

"My name is Jack." He added, making an effort to gain their trust. "What are yours?"

"Oliver." Said the red-haired man, lowering his musket slightly. "This is Peter." He added with a tilt of the head towards the black-haired and bearded man. "What are you doing at the mine on your own at this time of night?"

"I arrived in Ailsby shortly after night fall. My money was stolen from me as I slept by the side of the road. I thought I'd visit the mine before making my way through the forest." Jack hoped that by sharing his recent humiliation with them they might find some common ground and be more willing to trust him.

"Sounds like we've both suffered misfortune," said Peter, lowering his pike slightly but not taking his eyes off the ferramus sword which was more than visible hanging at Jack's side. "Why do you want to travel through the forest?"

"I'm on my way to the fertile plains, it's the quickest way," Jack said quickly, now returning to his well-rehearsed farmhand story.

Oliver glanced at Jack's sword. "You know how to fight?"

"Yes," Jack replied.

"...and you know how to ride a horse?" Peter added.

"Yes, I can ride."

"...and if you're on your way to the fertile planes, does that mean you know about farming?"

"A little bit," Jack said telling only his second lie of the night. The first being the now familiar story about travelling to the fertile planes. On balance, Jack thought this was the most honest he had been to someone else since the start of his journey.

Peter and Oliver now lowered their weapons fully but gave no indication that they had accepted Jack's offer, so he remained at pike's length with his hands up. He knew that any kind of sudden or unexpected movement would frighten them and that was not what he wanted now. If they were to be his new travelling companions until he reached the far edge of the forest, then they had to trust him. For his safety and for theirs. Jack did not want to kill again if he did not have to, and he certainly did not want to be responsible for someone else's death again.

"He's skilled," said Peter, "and we'll need a new acolyte to replace Barney." He finished, seemingly out of the corner of his mouth, trying and failing to conceal his speech from Jack.

"Rosie may not accept him," replied Oliver. "She's quite picky with who she allows in, and she says it's not just about skills and abilities, it's about loyalty too."

"So we make use of him to get the coal back and if Rosie doesn't like the look of him, we send him on his way or slit his throat!" Jack did not like the sound of that but could tell by the way they had both shaken a moment ago, that they likely lacked the ruthlessness to commit such an act.

They resolved their discussion and both looked towards him. "Your word that you won't double-cross us or try to run off before we've reached our destination?" Peter said.

"You have it. Do I have yours that you will respect my person and property, what little I have left, while we travel together?" Jack said, not being able to shake off what Peter had said about slitting his throat.

"Aye!" They replied in unison.

"Help us fill these sacks with coal," said Peter. "We should get six in total then we'll walk them to the horses, they're tied up a mile from here. Two to each horse and we should reach the rendezvous on time!"

Jack did as Peter bid. It did not take long to load the cloth sacks with coal but their weight grew with each lump. As the three of them walked their loot to their mounts, it felt like longer than a mile. They each tied their sacks to the front of the saddle and rode off towards the forest. Jack was not sure what awaited him at the rendezvous and was even less sure what to make of this Rosie, whom the two men seemed to have spoken about with a mixture of fear and admiration.

All he did know was that having aided two coal thieves, who were clearly part of a larger gang, fully put his former life as a guardsman now behind him. If he ever saw Lyndsey again, he wondered what she would make of the fact that he had been forced into a life of thievery by the very men who claimed to uphold the King's laws. Jack was not sure if that was a comical or depressing predicament.

Chapter Sixteen

"Bernard Crenshaw, a man who has exercised no restraint telling his readers what he thinks of me (and if you're unaware, dear reader, his opinions on yours truly are not pleasant) has been telling many of us not to trust those who govern, be they Parliamentarian, Monarch or Warlock—"

"Remove any mention of the Warlocks please!" Eva said looking up from the parchment as she read it aloud. "I don't want the readers of the Chronicle to make any associations. It's better if we're not mentioned at all."

"As you wish, Miss Valmarque," Victoria said with affected sweetness and a grudging thought. Then with her quill, crossed out all references to the Warlocks on her copy that she would take to the printing press after the meeting.

"Otherwise, I think it's rather good for the first article. Make sure you increase your scathing tones steadily in each successive publication so it's not obvious we're trying to smear him," the Warlock ordered.

"Indeed, I shall," smiled Victoria, wanting to pick up the inkpot and throw the bottle and contents all at Eva's face to correct that smug expression. "I'll take it to the printing press now if you're happy. It should make tomorrow's Chronicle."

"Very good," replied Eva with a triumphant expression getting up to leave.

"About my payment, Miss Valmarque?" Victoria started.

"All in good time, Mrs Lionsgate," Eva interrupted before she could continue. "Let's see how successful this smear campaign of ours is. Then we shall discuss payment."

She grasped the pyrite around her neck, quickly became transparent and disappeared. Victoria knew this was done as a demonstration of power. Eva was no doubt returning to the Warlocks' Tower to report on their meeting to the Council which was only a short walk from Madam Centaur's. Using magic was rumoured to be draining for a Warlock and a short walk would be preferable.

Unless you wanted to make a point. Like most powerful people, Eva Valmarque chose to say more with a gesture than with a phrase.

*

Victoria stopped at the offices of the Chronicle on her way home to drop off her amended article to the men at the printing press. A marvellous achievement in engineering that allowed many copies of many people's writing to be all over the city in less than a day. To the middle and upper classes, this was world changing. Victoria knew if the commoners could read it would be more beneficial for them than anyone else. Although in the case of her gossip columns, she bitterly wondered if it was perhaps a godsend that most paupers were illiterate.

She wondered if her actions would ever become public knowledge, now or to future historians. *If they did, would future generations understand and forgive me for what I'm doing? Would they understand I endured these necessary evils for my own protection or would they think me a coward?*

The young man working the printing press stared at Victoria quizzically as she handed over a copy of her column for tomorrow's edition. The one that Eva had approved. In her reverie, it had appeared to the other man as though Victoria's vacant stare and brief detachment from her surroundings may have been some sort of serious illness. She made an excuse and an apology to the young man, claiming lack of sleep, then made her way home to see if Daisy had had more luck with her task that day.

*

When she returned, Daisy awaited her in the drawing room, out of disguise and enjoying a glass of wine.

"Well?" Victoria quizzed her.

"His name is Neil Monks," said Daisy triumphantly. "I showed his colleague the drawing; he was more than obliging to give up the information once I'd paid for it. He wasn't half bad either…for a virgin." She grinned. "Though that does explain his eagerness I suppose." She finished with a giggle and took a gulp of her wine.

Victoria was always grateful for the sacrifices Daisy would make for their cause, although Victoria doubted if Daisy viewed them as 'sacrifices'. Victoria was of a different generation and could not understand. Perhaps she had spent too long in the world on her own and she could not comprehend how people from other walks of life lived.

Daisy had been an out of work and destitute actor when she came to Victoria. During the last plague in Graylenmouth, she had been cast out by the theatre after it went bankrupt. Victoria had employed her on the basis that her theatrical skills would be put to better use in her service than on the stage.

"Did you find out where he likes to go? When he isn't working or making sinister trips to the Warlocks' Tower that is," Victoria asked her trusted servant after being consumed by a daydream for the second time that day.

"He wasn't working today, that's what his colleague said. I know where the servants leave and enter the palace though. I'll stand there tomorrow and the next few days in disguise and wait for him to leave. Then I'll tail him," she said in a nonchalant tone explaining the surveillance operation as though discussing the weather.

"Use a different one from today when you questioned his friend and a different one from when we attended the ball. We must be careful nothing can be traced back here," Victoria ordered to Daisy who nodded in agreement.

She spent the afternoon in her study writing. Not gossip columns but more important thoughts. Her own thoughts and philosophies and also a partial memoir on all she was undertaking and how the events of her private life fully contradicted those in her public one. Maybe one day, people would read it, and future generations would know who she truly was and all she had sacrificed.

Before teatime, there was a knock at the door. She returned to the drawing room and bid a now tipsy Daisy to see who it was. Daisy stood up and straightened herself to appear sober with a giggle. As she went to answer the door, Victoria wondered if she should have a word with her servant about watching how much she drank.

"It's a handsome young man to see you, Ma'am," slurred Daisy a moment later.

"What?" Victoria said. "I'm not expecting anyone."

"Shall I send him through, he says it's important." She hiccupped at the end of the sentence.

125

"Yes, I suppose," Victoria said, somewhat curious. "Then go to the kitchen and make yourself a strong coffee, Daisy!" Daisy blushed and appeared with the young man a moment later before making her way to the kitchen.

The man was in his early twenties. He had a mop of curly blonde hair and expensive clothes to match. She knew she had not met this man before, yet she recognised him all the same. She invited him to sit down opposite, and he did as he was bid. In all the confusion she was now feeling, she hastily adopted her proud and pompous persona of Victoria Lionsgate, the gossip columnist.

"How can I help you?" She said as he took his seat.

"I'd like to inform you of possible material for your next column," the man replied looking nervous. "The subject is one Adam Pluff, the son of the Home Secretary."

"He's high status enough to write about for sure. Though I would need some proof that what you're about to tell me is true. I can't risk being taken to court for libel."

"How about my word that I won't take legal action for what you print about me, Mrs Lionsgate?" The man said more nervously than when he had first spoken. "I've done some terrible things and I need to atone for them. I shall give an interview, exclusively to you, free of charge. Nothing will be off the record; you may print everything I tell you."

Victoria was stunned. Ever since she had cast off her pseudonym, gossipy rich folks were always knocking on Victoria's door. Usually, though it was to inform on others rather than themselves and usually in return for a favour. A favour which came in the form of a sack of gold. The fact that Adam was not settling a score with someone or after money made Victoria suspicious.

"What's the catch?" She said sharply. "You don't want gold and you're not taking revenge on another. This all seems too good to be true."

"There's no catch, I simply have a guilty conscience and wish to confess," he said sincerely in a manner which Victoria noticed was rather uncommon in men of Adam's station.

"Then find a priest or hand yourself into the Graylenmouth Guard. I deal in gossip, not moral and legal matters."

"I'm afraid if I were to do either of those things, it would find its way back to my father who would use his influence to cover things up. As my story will no doubt prove," Adam said. Victoria had no idea what to make of him.

Victoria considered him, both her fake and real personas had enough on their plate with Eva Valmarque and now, Neil Monks. She doubted this would be worth her time but perhaps becoming more familiar with the son of a cabinet minister would aid her political endeavours in the long run.

"One meeting to start with," agreed Victoria after some consternation. "Give me an hour of your time now, and then I'll see if there's any point in meeting you again or publishing your story."

She went over to the desk and withdrew a quill an inkpot and a roll of parchment. She then sat herself down and dipped the quill into the ink before turning back to Adam. "Well, young man, start at the beginning."

Chapter Seventeen

Jack had travelled a fair distance with Peter and Oliver when he reached the borders of Frostholme Forest. It had not been an unpleasant experience. Though he was tired from a day and a night's ride, the two men had kept their promise and shared their food with him. Jack was thinking now of sleep and guessing that their rendezvous must be nearby. They had worked the horses hard and it seemed both beast and rider would benefit from some rest.

"We'll slow to a walk and head in for a mile before the trees get too dense," said Peter. "We should make the rendezvous point by nightfall. That's where they'll meet us in the morning," he finished with a furtive glance at Jack before exchanging an apprehensive one with Oliver.

Jack could tell that their decision to let him help transport the stolen coal had seemed like a good idea back at the mineshaft. It had made the task ahead seem endurable. Now nearing their job's completion, they would have to explain his presence, as well as the loss of their original companion, to this elusive 'Rosie'. It was making them nervous.

He thought he might slip away quietly in the night once they slept, but he knew they would probably be able to track him through a forest that they knew better than he did. He also knew he was not likely to get far without a map and a compass. A compass was essential here, without road signs or landmarks. His best chance was to see what awaited him at the rendezvous tomorrow morning.

There were now sparse pine trees all around them, they did not seem to be travelling a well-beaten track, but his companions seemed to know where they were going. Peter kept checking a compass and a crude hand-drawn map while declaring the occasional "This way!" or "Over here!" to Jack and Oliver.

As darkness gathered, they reached a small clearing containing the remnants of a campsite. Presumably once accommodated by Oliver, Peter or one of their contemporaries. There was a dead fire, encircled with small stones cutting a black and charred image among the bed of decomposing pine needles. The long since burnt wood had become charcoal dust as Oliver swept it aside with his boot then disappeared into the darkness among the trees to gather more fuel. Jack did the same as Peter began to prepare the rabbits Jack had shot with their musket that afternoon.

At least that may have gained me their trust. Maybe this Rosie won't be suspicious of me when she hears I helped feed her men.

Earlier today, they had stopped for a break and Oliver mentioned it would be nice to have some meat. Jack said that he was a reasonably good shot and could probably get a rabbit or two with the musket if Oliver would lend it to him.

It took a great deal of persuasion before he was handed the gun but the promise of spit roast rabbit for tea proved too much for his companions in the end. Under heavy supervision from his new and untrusting travelling companions, Jack had acquired a pair of rabbits twenty minutes later. The fact that he was responsible for their dinner and had not tried to misuse the musket, he hoped would work in his favour.

Jack was still unsure of Peter and Oliver. They were criminals but so was Jack now. He had aided them in their theft of the coal, not to mention he had recently lost what remained of the Prime Minister's gold to those two robbers, which would soon guarantee him a long stay in debtors prison upon his return to the capital.

They were not; however, the sort of criminal Jack had been used to dealing with as a guardsman. In Graylenmouth, the criminals were hardened professionals at worst, or minor first-time petty offenders at best. Most were driven to criminal activity out of economic necessity or because they were sick in the head. That applied to neither of his companions. They were practical men, skilled men, they could find honest work if they wanted to. They were not sick in the head either. Those types of men do not let you travel with them for a night and a day and let you live.

Jack returned to the campsite with some small twigs and moss for kindling as well as some larger logs for the slow burn. He arranged them accordingly and added Oliver's haul to the assembly upon his arrival. He then asked Oliver for the musket again, assuring him he did not require powder or shot. Oliver obliged and Jack held the musket over the newly built fire, lengthways and parallel to the ground. He brought it to full cock and pulled the trigger with some kindling placed between the hammer and the pan. The flint struck the dried moss which began to burn, he used his coat to fan the smoke. It was not long before the fire was roaring.

"How do you know so much?" Oliver said a few hours later as Peter was turning the skinned rabbits on a spit. "We would have been here for hours trying to get that fire going if you weren't here."

"I travel around the farmlands between harvests each year," Jack lied, not wanting to betray the fact that he had received the extensive training of the Graylenmouth Guard. "You pick these things up the more you travel."

Peter took his attention off the rabbits for a moment and eyed him shrewdly before saying, "You can take a rabbit's head off with a musket, you can ride a horse as swiftly as anyone, you can start a fire quicker than most and judging by that fancy sword you carry, you know how to use one of those too. A bit too knowledgeable for a mere farmhand?"

"I can't skin and cook rabbits though, where did you learn to do that?" Jack said hoping a bit of flattery would disguise the fact he was trying to change the subject.

Peter did not press his suspicions on Jack further, but Jack thought he caught him eyeing him suspiciously on occasion as they each ate their food.

They bid each other goodnight shortly after eating, being too tired to do much else. Jack's instincts told him he should not lower his vigilance. He had not known them long and it would be unwise to trust them. He had no desire to wake up with even fewer belongings than when he last slept. The warm fire, his now full belly and the fact that he had ridden all day made him ignore those same instincts as he closed his eyes and drifted into a dreamless sleep.

*

It was morning when he awoke to the sound of his companions pouring water on the dying embers of the fire and gathering their things. Jack would have done the same, were it not for the fact that two robbers had taken everything but the clothes he wore and the sword on his belt.

"Here," said Oliver, handing Jack some bread and a flask of water. "Not the best breakfast but there's not much travelling left to do. They'll be here soon and you don't want to meet Rosie on an empty stomach. It'll take all your effort for her to like you."

Jack thanked Oliver before eating and drinking quickly and soon enough, the others arrived. Half a dozen other men as burly as Oliver and Peter, armed mostly with clubs and pikes, save for two who had muskets.

Their leader, a middle-aged man with a black receding hairline and a salt and pepper beard, approached Oliver.

"Do you have it?" He said stroking his beard with a quizzical look at Jack.

"Enough to keep the forges going for a couple of months plus a little more," answered Oliver gesturing to the sacks of stolen coal. "All thanks to our new…'friend'," he finished with a nod towards Jack, answering the man's quizzical look.

"Where's Barney?" He said hovering his eyes over Jack before ignoring him again.

"He pushed his horse too far and it threw him," said Oliver. "We bumped into Jack in Ailsby and he offered his help. We wouldn't normally have accepted but with Barney gone, we needed it. We'll also need someone to fill Barney's shoes and Jack's pretty handy."

"You are telling me the truth, aren't you, Peter, about Barney and how you met this 'Jack'? Rosie will know if you're lying and it's best to be honest now," said the middle-aged man.

"It's all true," said Peter with a grim look on his face. "Oliver will confirm it and we'll say the same to Rosie when she asks."

Without further inquiry, the middle-aged man walked over to Jack. Finally focussing his attention his way and eyed him up before finally speaking. "Peter's a good man and so is Oliver, I believe what they've told me and you have my thanks," he said with a sense of gratefulness and pragmatism that Jack could not help but have respect for. "Sadly, my thanks will count for little if Rosie judges differently. I'm afraid you must hand over your sword. If Rosie deems you worthy, you'll get it back."

Jack did not want to give up the sword. It was the only fine thing he had ever owned, and it had begun to serve him as a talisman to remind him of all that he had suffered, as well as a reminder of Holly's death. That was something he must never forget if he was to avoid repeating his past mistakes.

Outnumbered and with nowhere to run, however, Jack nodded in agreement and reluctantly handed his sword over. The middle-aged man thanked Jack and then made a gesture towards one of his men. The next thing he knew, a bag of roughhewn cloth was placed over his head and his hand was being placed on someone's shoulder before he was led off, in which direction Jack had no idea. He could still feel the pine needles underfoot but that was no indicator of location now. Not in lands unfamiliar to him.

Jack felt as helpless as he had the night he had been taken from his cell and made Eva Valmarque's acquaintance. He shivered at the thought of the red-headed Warlock and the message she had carved into his back. Wondering if a similar or worse fate awaited him now.

Chapter Eighteen

The provision of street lighting in the capital was a frequent and continuing source of humour to the locals. One of the mayor's many predecessors had decided to implement it thirty years ago. True to his election promises, every major street in Graylenmouth had been enhanced with the addition of oil lamps to afford better visibility at night-time. They now lined each street on either side and fifteen yards apart. Less true to his election promises, was their height. They mostly stood at eye level, providing the locals with a dazzling glare that many had found more tiresome than having to find their way in the dark.

Both the Chronicle and the Gazette had ridiculed the mayor without mercy for his grave error but both gave different reasons for his incompetence.

The Chronicle had blamed the mishap on ineptitude. The metal for the lampposts themselves had to be brought in from outside the city, as there were no iron mines near Graylenmouth. Allegedly, the civil servants in charge of the scheme had not taken the time to plan it properly and ordered an insufficient amount of steel.

The Gazette had reported a different version of events and claimed that the mayor had crumpled when his rich benefactors had complained that street lights outside their bedroom windows would disturb their sleep. Torn between fulfilling an election promise and keeping his creditors happy, he had built them at a third of the height he originally planned.

Whatever the reason for eye-level street lighting, Lyndsey was glad of it. She wore a long and black cloak of wool over her frock that evening. She stood around the corner from Lionsgate Hall and appeared partially concealed in the shadows between the low streetlamps who's light covered little ground. She did not want to attract attention after the events that had transpired at the Unicorn. A cloak was also the easiest way to conceal a loaded pair of pistols which were now at her belt.

She knew being dressed like this on a warm summer's night appeared suspicious, but the streets of the capital could be dangerous after dusk and she knew it would be unwise to walk the streets unarmed. She had been waiting there an hour when Adam made his way to their meeting spot through the evening gloom and greeted her.

"Well?" she said, lacking the patience for pleasantries that Adam's class would insist were always mandatory. "What happened? Did she take the bait?"

"She wants to see me again so I think so," Adam said, seeming slightly shocked at Lyndsey's rapidity.

"And you were sure not to mention Eva and the Warlocks? It's too dangerous to let that on until we know what she's up to!" She said anxiously.

"No, I just mentioned that I must have had too much to drink that night and I don't know what came over me," said Adam looking abashed. A look that was becoming a regular one for him.

Lyndsey went over everything Adam had just told the gossip columnist, hoping she would not find anything she considered to be out of place. She could not think of anything so instead asked one more question.

"When are you meeting her again?"

"On Saturday; she said to enter through the servant's entrance."

That was strange; why would she want to keep a visit from the son of the Home Secretary a secret? Regular meetings with someone close to a prominent cabinet minister could only cause more gossip and speculation that women like Victoria Lionsgate thrived off. Her need for discretion was confusing to Lyndsey. It only intensified her eagerness.

"Are your servants' faces well known to the public and press?" She asked after a certain amount of deliberation.

"Only the housekeeper and the butler, they came highly recommended by one of father's friends."

"...but not the maids or the footmen?" She asked again as she began to formulate a plan for dealing with the gossip columnist.

"No," replied Adam.

"Okay, I'll go with you next time and pretend to be one of your maids. We'll form a cover story before then." She appreciated Adam's help but doubted he possessed the skills to get the truth out of someone like Victoria Lionsgate. If she were to find out what was going on, she would have to be in there with him.

Adam agreed and Lyndsey walked him home for the second time since they had met. She then made her way gloomily back to her own house. She knew Michael would be working tonight. One of his higher paying clients had a wife expecting to give birth any day now. As a respectable physician, he would have to stay with the client from now until the baby was delivered. Given that she had not started labour when Michael left this morning, Lyndsey knew it could be several days before she saw her husband again.

Still, if Michael's presence gave the newborn a chance of knowing it's mother, Lyndsey would be glad. Lyndsey's own mother had died giving birth to her. Her kindly father had not resented her for it, nor had he assigned any blame to Lyndsey, but the burden of knowing her mother died because of her could sometimes weigh on the mind.

With no mother to care for her, her father would take Lyndsey into the wild with him as soon as she was old enough. She would assist him in his profession as a fur trapper. By the age of six, she could load and fire a pistol in the dark and by the age of eight, she was a crack shot. Soon after her eighth birthday and their umpteenth and last excursion into the wild, her father caught dysentery and died on the return journey to the capital.

Distraught and with nowhere to go, Lyndsey sold their furs at the market and joined the Guard as a recruit. If she had not met Jack then, her life may have fallen apart. It was not unheard of for women to be in the Guard but it was rare. Her instructors and fellow recruits, save Jack, would not hesitate to point that out to her and make her feel unwanted.

It irked many when she came top of her class in firearms training. She was less adept with a cutlass, but Jack had excelled at that. They used their strengths to assist each other with their weaknesses and eventually became qualified guardsmen.

Jack had requested Lyndsey as his partner upon beginning active duty. If he had not, they would have moved her into a tedious admin role. He had always claimed he did it for his sake as much as hers. Her skill with a pistol was second to none and he would be foolish not to want her at his side when facing down a dangerous criminal, but she was still grateful to him.

She let herself into her small townhouse, which now seemed larger and emptier without Michael. She decided to go to bed after making dinner as she knew nothing interesting would come from a late night. She hoped her husband was having a more exciting night delivering a baby.

Her plans for the evening would not come to fruition. After finishing her meal, she stood up and the room began to shake. The lamps began to flicker in and out as the transparent outline of a red-headed and green-eyed woman in a small black dress appeared in the centre of the small living room, standing on the rug between the armchair and the sofa. Lyndsey stood by her table and checked that her pistol was still at her side. She instinctively cocked it as Eva Valmarque became solid.

"Please take a seat, Sergeant Carter," said the Warlock, gesturing to Lyndsey's own sofa and taking a seat in the armchair opposite, "*and leave your pistol on the table*," she added without moving her lips and fingering the amethyst around her neck. Lyndsey had no intention of being parted from her weapon but felt herself putting it on the table involuntarily before going to sit down.

"I'll assume you know who I am, but do you know why I'm here, Mrs Carter?" The Warlock said. Lyndsey was certain she knew the answer but she was not going to let that on to the woman. She decided playing ignorance would be her best chance of surviving this encounter.

"Who are you? Other than a Warlock," said Lyndsey not wanting to overplay the stupid card. "Why have you invaded my home?" Lyndsey was not sure if that had been too defiant, as well as foolish, but if she were about to face torture and humiliation, or something worse, she would let her distaste for the woman be known while she was still able to. Lyndsey felt her arms and her legs begin to shiver with fear. She corrected herself and stiffened her limbs immediately before Eva could notice.

Eva considered Lyndsey with a sarcastic smile before replying as though she could not decide whether Lyndsey's boldness was something to be respected or reviled. Then she sighed with and air of impatience.

"My name is Eva Valmarque," she said, "member of the Warlocks' Council and personal advisor to the Prime Minister, but you knew that. I'm also quite certain that you and young Adam Pluff have been poking around in affairs of state. That is why I'm here to speak with you. As you no doubt have worked out."

Lyndsey's face said nothing but her mind was racing. She had been so careful, meeting Adam in the Unicorn, making enquiries under the cover of guardsman's duty and keeping to the shadows when out in public. Lyndsey felt that she only had one card to play.

"If the Prime Minister is displeased with the work I have been doing, then he can summon me to his residence or visit me himself. Is he aware that since I own half this house, I have the vote? If he wishes to count on it, he should not hide behind his Warlock," Lyndsey said, knowing with near certainty that Eva was probably acting out of her own interests at this moment and not the Prime Minister's.

"I'm not here on the Prime Minister's behalf," she confirmed. "I'm here to put a stop to your meddling."

"What meddling? I'm a guardsman, I arrest criminals and gather evidence. How is that any concern of yours? I thought the Warlocks had more pressing business than pickpockets and brawlers." Continuing to show rudeness to the Warlock would not end well for her, but if she were going to die, she would do it with defiance on her breath. She was determined not to grovel, no matter what this woman had in store for her.

"I wonder what it would take for you to cease falsehoods, Sergeant?" The Warlock said stroking the amethyst about her neck. "Perhaps pain? I could command you to make a roaring fire then walk on to it and stand there for as long as I desired! Perhaps disgrace? I could order you to strip naked and walk the streets in the red-light district until the sun came up." Eva paused and smirked as though she was savouring the power she could wield over Lyndsey. "Alas, my time is precious. *Stand up straight!*"

Just as involuntarily as she had been parted from her pistol, Lyndsey did as Eva commanded. She was now standing as rigid as a statue with the posture of a high-born, in front of Eva Valmarque who was caressing her amethyst and smirking triumphantly. *"Come here,"* said the Warlock without moving her mouth and Lyndsey immediately walked towards her, unable to resist the command of the woman who had now claimed the role of Lyndsey's controller.

"On your knees!" Lyndsey dropped to the hard wooden floor so quickly, she knew she would have bruises, though she doubted she would live to confirm it. *"Keep still!"* Her body went rigid, and she was not sure if she would be able to breathe for much longer.

Eva's green eyes were boring into her as Lyndsey knelt before her like a condemned man, helpless before a corrupt judge who was about to delight in passing and unfair and vengeful sentence.

She had to escape. Not in the physical sense, which was impossible, but if she tried hard enough, she knew she could die with happier memories in her head. Lyndsey refused to face death in fear and despair and would not give the Warlock anything that would no doubt bring her satisfaction.

She thought and reminisced with all her strength. It was all that mattered now. She thought of her father, laughing and telling stories by the campfire while the two of them carefully skinned the dead animals of their expensive pelts. She thought of the day she met Michael at a winter fayre and how her heart had raced when he asked her to dance. She thought of all the meaningless yet entertaining conversations she and Jack would share when they were on patrol and how it helped whittle down the hours on boring shifts.

She thought of the day, and the night, she married Michael and how that night he had made her feel a kind of joy she did not know could be experienced.

Then Lyndsey felt all the muscles in her body relax suddenly. Unseen by both of them and within her boot, Lyndsey moved her toes. Eva's face was unresponsive, she had not meant to return control of her body to her, nor had she noticed her newly acquired freedom. Lyndsey stayed in a kneeling position on the floor. She had no weapon and did not think it would be wise to reveal to Eva that she had somehow broken free.

"*Why did you follow me into Madam Centaur's the other day?*" Eva commanded wordlessly.

"I *was* following you," said Lyndsey. "But you weren't my quarry. That was Victoria Lionsgate." Lyndsey was relieved to see that she also had the ability to lie. "An informant of mine at the Chronicle told me she was meeting a Warlock, I assumed it was you, but I didn't know where, so I sat outside the Prime Minister's residence and tailed you. She's got damning information on a client of mine and I went to investigate. I take on private work outside of my guardsman's duty. When I discovered you were meeting privately, I backed off as I knew I wouldn't get very far."

Eva had clearly not been expecting this answer and looked stunned for a moment. It seemed to be to her satisfaction as Eva did not question her further, on that matter at least.

"*You've been seen meeting Adam Pluff on three separate occasions. Why?*"

"He's the one who hired me. I'd met Adam before when my partner arrested him unlawfully." It pained her to slander Jack but she would be of no use to him if the Warlock killed her. "I went to his residence to apologise, that's when he mentioned that his father was in trouble, and I offered to meet him in the Unicorn to discuss business. I told him to speak with Victoria tonight as a cover to see if he could find out what information she had on the Home Secretary." If there had not been a well-rehearsed lie behind Adam's meeting with Victoria tonight, Lyndsey wondered if she would have been able to make up the rest so easily.

Eva paused for a long time. "It appears I misjudged you, Mrs Carter," she said at last, this time her lips did move but nothing sounded sincere about her apparent misjudgement. *"You can move again half an hour after I've left,"* she commanded wordlessly and magically. "Spend that time thinking about what an inconvenience your meddling has caused me," she spoke without the aid of the amethyst before returning once more to the gemstone. *"Tell no one I was here, tell no one we met and tell no one what we spoke of!"*

The Warlock rose to her feet and walked into the hallway. A few seconds later Lyndsey heard her own front door open and close.

She arose immediately in a fluster. She took several low and deep breaths, almost unable to believe she had just escaped an encounter with a Warlock through sheer luck and strength of will.

Lyndsey was not sure of the logic behind it, or even if logic was the right word to use. It seemed she had freed herself from the Warlock's control when she had fully removed herself mentally from her predicament. Perhaps by creating a situation where one was too detached from the moment to succumb to fear, their magic could no longer control you. Lyndsey would be sure to recall at least one happy memory a day from now on in case she encountered Eva again.

She also thought it would be a good idea to conceal a derringer up her sleeve, and maybe an extra one in her bodice at all times for good measure. Had she done that tonight, she may have been able to pay Eva back in kind.

Eva had also betrayed another weakness in the powers of a Warlock – who liked to proclaim their magic was of a supreme divinity and without flaw. When ordering Lyndsey to *do* something, she had used her telepathic voice, channelling the power the amethyst gave her. On the one occasion she had ordered Lyndsey to *think about* something, she had spoken with her physical voice, clearly and plainly as one man speaks to another. This, Lyndsey surmised, meant that the mind control powers, which instilled the non-magical majority with more fear than any other aspect of a Warlock's abilities, did not extend to controlling a person's thoughts. Only their actions.

The fact that she had commanded Lyndsey not to speak of the meeting to anyone, instead of telling her to forget it, had altogether confirmed this. They may be able to erase entire evenings from one's memory as she had clearly done to Adam, but it seemed that erasing a specific event or action from a human mind was too complex, even for a Warlock.

Despite Lyndsey's shock at coming close to death at the hands of a Warlock, she was grateful for the experience. Knowing an opponent's weaknesses made them easier to defeat.

Chapter Nineteen

He had been walking all day and most of the night. That much he knew; it was all he could be sure of. They had stopped a few times but had not allowed him to remove the bag from his head. He had sat there on each occasion as morsels of bread and flasks of water were thrust into his hand and he awkwardly fed himself. He had tried to listen to the sounds of nature when he could. This opportunity was not a prevalent one as the sound of nine men's footsteps and their conversation tended to drown everything out more often than not, but Jack could have sworn he had heard the sound of a stream a few times, as well as birdsong, though that told him nothing.

As night had fallen, Jack was led to a tree where he sat down and rested his back against the trunk. It felt hard but some rest was a welcoming thought, bag or no bag, he may fall asleep in an instant. A day's walk through rough terrain tended to give one that feeling. Though he knew sleep would not be probable, even if it would come so easily to him.

He was being taken to meet Rosie, their leader. Someone who they all seemed to respect and fear in equal measure and Jack had no idea either how to behave or what to say when he met her. She was evidently a clever and shrewd commander for insisting on all the secrecy he had experienced. Hopefully, she was just too. Leaders who are neither just nor clever tended not to inspire the loyalty she was receiving from these men.

She was possibly ruthless as well. He remembered the way the moustached man spoke of her before the bag had been placed over his head. He knew from the look in his eye that Rosie was not someone you wanted to anger, or the consequences could be dire.

Jack heard footsteps heading in his direction and then heard the soft creak of pine needles as someone sat down beside him. Maybe three feet away by Jack's estimation. He had no idea why. No one had really spoken to him in the last twenty-four hours except to bark directions or tell him it was time to eat.

"Don't look up and try not to look like we're conversing. If you can hear me, cough loudly." Jack heard the voice of their leader, the man with the moustache. Jack neither moved his hand up to his mouth nor adjusted his neck as he gave a loud deep cough.

"Oliver and Peter haven't changed a single detail in their story, that's good," started the man. "For them at least, they talk very highly of you, that's not exactly a negative in your account but it won't matter to Rosie very much. Nevertheless, you have my thanks, Jack."

Jack did not think he would be able to say anything, even if he knew what to say, as that would betray that their leader and the prisoner were communicating, and he guessed the man was speaking to him at great risk to himself.

Fortunately, there was no need as the man continued without waiting for much of a response. "Barney's dead, which might mean Rosie can find a use for you. We already know you can ride, and Peter and Oliver tell me you know about farming; we know you don't seem to have any moral quandary about thieving. Can you do anything else? Can you work at a forge? Do you know anything about building or drainage? Think about what skills you have. It will help you when you meet Rosie."

The man did not wait for a response from Jack, nor did he ask for a cough to show that he had understood. As Jack heard him stand up to leave, he risked some speech. "Why?" Jack said keeping his head still and making sure not to gesticulate. "Why help me?" Jack said clearly, but not too loudly from under his bag.

"There are only two possible outcomes that await you when we meet Rosie. She'll be passing judgement where your fate's concerned," said the man. "Only one of those outcomes will be something you want to happen, but I've said too much. I'm very grateful that you helped us out of a tight spot back in Ailsby and I'll do what I can to return the favour. Think about how useful you can be."

Without another word, the moustached man walked away and Jack heard the footsteps getting fainter. Then someone else, a heavier man Jack had judged by the sound of his footsteps, walked nearer. He heard a musket cock which told him he was under armed guard for the night.

*

The next morning, Jack was treated to more bread and water before setting off again. Not for long this time. He felt the pine needles give way to something harder and manmade, and the roaring of a river told him he was being led over a rickety wooden bridge and then to a well-trodden path. About a mile north of the bridge, he was guided off to the left onto more uneven ground where he could feel twigs and tree roots underfoot.

At around midday, his journey came to an end. The natural sounds of a forest gave way to the sounds of civilisation. He heard the bustling chatter of hundreds of people going about their daily business. Had it not been for the previous events of the last two days, he would have sworn he was back in the capital on market day.

Discovery of who these people were would have to wait. Now there were arms on his shoulders as he was being steered quickly on what felt like a different pathway. The sudden absence of the breeze told him he had been moved indoors somewhere as he felt himself being sat on a chair. He heard footsteps on floorboards getting fainter, then heard the leader say, "Rosie will see you shortly, wait patiently. Don't take the bag off." A door clicked shut nearby and he was left in silence, save for the muted sound of a nearby crowd.

Jack sat there hearing the muffled sounds of people moving around, laughing and chatting outside. He tried to process everything he had just experienced. He had spent enough time in the crowded capital to be able to judge the size of crowds by sound alone. There were at least a hundred people in the area he had just been. Jack had not had a chance to look at a map since he was robbed on the northeast road, but he remembered enough to know that this was a vast forest. He had walked long enough, and even without his sight, he knew he must be deep within it.

How could a community of this size sustain itself this far from farmland, roads or other necessary amenities? Jack remembered that Peter and Oliver had travelled far to steal a large amount of coal and now their behaviour in Ailsby made much more sense to him.

None of this made him feel any better, nor did it shed any light on his current situation. Why was he here? The man had said there were two outcomes and only one of them would be good. In his opinion, Jack did not think either of these outcomes was likely to be amiable, given the luck he had had on his quest so far. He was now defenceless and outnumbered in the middle of nowhere without sight, sword or pistol. He could have easily removed the bag and restored his sight, but the man had told him that would not work in his favour.

Rosie, whoever she was, would soon interrogate him and he had no negotiating power and no means of defence. He would have spent this time trying to think up a strategy for when he would be questioned, but that would be no use. It was hard to establish a means of defence when what you are defending yourself from is uncertain.

He was alive at least. Largely thanks to someone called Barney. Barney who had been Peter and Oliver's original partner in crime before he had met an unfortunate fate at the disobedience of his own horse. It seemed that Barney's death had created some sort of vacancy. A vacancy which perhaps Jack could be allowed to fill, even though he had no desire to.

Was that what the moustached leader had meant when he spoke of the more fortuitous outcome, and if so, what was the lesser? Death and torture? Jack was beginning to wish he had stayed in the cell at the barracks and faced a hopeless court martial. That would have been preferable to anything he was beginning to assume he would receive here.

Before Jack could dwell any further on the possibility of meeting a sour fate, the door to the building opened. He heard footsteps again, those of a single person, gentle and getting louder before they stopped. He heard the scraping of wood. His interrogator had pulled up another chair and he heard them sit down. Jack said nothing but sat up straight, with his back against the chair and feeling ridiculous that he was showing acknowledgement to a person he could not see.

"Are you comfortable?" A calm yet authoritative female voice came from the space in front of him. The voice of Rosie no doubt.

"No!" Jack said so abruptly that he felt even more ridiculous than he already did speaking to someone with a bag on his head. He was not lying but he had no idea why he had shown impoliteness. That was unwise, given what he had been told of Rosie he did not think she would tolerate brutal honesty. To his relief, however, the woman questioner only laughed but did not speak a second time, leaving an awkward silence when her laughter finished.

The silence remained for a time. It felt like a decade which forced Jack to speak again, knowing it was unwise but unable to bear the quiet. "Can I take this bag off?"

"Not yet; soon enough if I like what I hear," replied Rosie's calm voice. Jack could tell that she had not found the silence unbearable. "I have a few more questions and if you pass the first of my tests, you may have your sight. Peter and Oliver tell me you're a farmhand. Is that true?"

"No, I'm a sergeant in the Graylenmouth Guard." Jack could have kicked himself. The answer came out as hastily as his first and again, he had no idea why. He had his well-rehearsed farmhand story, which he had told to all whom he had encountered since Ulston. Which he had now abandoned so flippantly and with no good reason.

The woman laughed again. It was not a hollow laugh or a condescending one. It sounded more like the laugh he would hear from Lyndsey when they were out on patrol, and he had told a joke. Though he was not trying to be funny and had no idea why Rosie found him so hilarious. "Well, Sergeant, I'm told you came across my acolytes in Ailsby. What brought you there? That's many leagues beyond a guardsman's jurisdiction, wouldn't you say?"

Jack paused before answering that particular question. It seemed to him that Rosie had removed his ability to lie. *She must be a Warlock!* He realised. That explained why he was advised not to remove the bag, so he would not see the gemstone around her neck that she was using to force the truth from his answers. He remembered that her footsteps had been unnaturally soft when entering the room and it dawned on him that she must be without shoes. Jack could not reveal his true quest to her; he doubted she would show aid or sympathy. Neither would he be able to lie to her.

"I'm afraid," he said after some hesitation, "I cannot answer that." Jack hoped that that would be enough to sidestep the magic. It had been an honest answer, but probably not the one Rosie was hoping for.

Rosie sighed in resignation. "You're clever, I'll give you that. You may remove the bag, Sergeant." Jack did as she bid, and it took some time for his eyes to adjust. The room was gloomy as the afternoon sun poured its light through the windows. It seemed very minimalist in here compared with what he had heard outside. Though a large room, it was empty, save for the two crooked chairs they were sitting on. It had old unvarnished and semi-rotten floorboards with walls that seemed to be assembled out of cobb in a poor and uneven fashion.

When his eyes finally did acclimatise, Rosie came into view. Before he had removed the bag, he knew instantly why the men he had travelled with spoke of Rosie with an anxious fear. Now, he could tell just as instantly why they held her with respect in equal measure.

She dressed and carried herself just as authoritatively as she spoke. She wore a modest dress that revealed little, rare for a Warlock, green dyed and with gold embroidery that flowed to the floor. There was little left bare at the top as the dress ended where her neck began. Her face was soft and feminine; she had the clear alabaster skin that only magical women seemed to be able to achieve unaided by cosmetics. Her copper-brown curly hair reached her shoulders and her darker brown eyes bore into Jack, quizzically and curiously. She wore an amulet of rose quartz about her neck.

"It only works when the person doesn't know they're being subjected to magic," she said, holding up the rose quartz, revealing to Jack the reason he had been unable to lie just now. "Like most magic, it's nothing more than a parlour trick, but parlour tricks have their uses I suppose." She looked thoughtfully at the rose quartz. There was something philosophical in her tone that made Jack wonder if she was addressing him or a non-existent audience.

She turned her attention back to him with a determined look. "Nevertheless, I still have questions for you, Sergeant Jack. Be aware that while you may be able to lie, this is a small community, not the capital, lies are hard to sustain here. Do you understand?"

"Yes!"

"Our food and resources are finite here. If a new acolyte wishes to join," she gestured to Jack, "he must prove himself worthy. Do you follow?"

Jack nodded, not sure if it would be wise to tell Rosie that he had no intention of joining. He did not know what to make of all this but his life was not here in the middle of the forest. His life was in Graylenmouth, if he would ever be allowed to resume it.

"As we do not wish to be overpopulated, we don't usually recruit new acolytes until one of us dies," Rosie went on.

Jack did not want to know what happened when someone simply wanted to leave, given the precautions the men had taken to make sure he did not know the way here he guessed it would not be a pleasant answer.

"Fortunately, for you, one of us *did die* on the journey to Ailsby. I'm told you had no hand in that but that's of no matter to me now. I have a vacant space in the commune and a man who may be able to fill it. I'm going to find out if you're worthy of that space."

Rosie may have dressed differently to Eva Valmarque but she shared her taste for the theatrics. She was now leaving another lingering silence. A tactic she no doubt applied to make Jack feel ill at ease before her interrogation resumed.

"Do you actually know anything about farming? Seeing as you're not a farmhand," she asked.

"No," said Jack, understanding what Rosie had meant about being able to sustain a lie. Had he lied, it would not be long before he found himself betraying his falsehood in front of the occupants and showing to all he was not a farmer in any way.

"Can you work a forge?"

"No."

"Do you have any knowledge of building or engineering?"

"No!" Jack was beginning to feel more useless than when he had the bag on his head.

"What *can* you do, Sergeant Jack?" She was sounding exasperated now.

"I can fight," he said which prompted another laugh from Rosie which he found annoying.

"I have an abundance of men who can fight, Sergeant, as you well know from the manner in which you arrived here. I need skilled men. Men who can build, grow, and make things. Another fighter won't help me feed this commune or give it decent shelter," she said, now in a more serious tone that dared Jack to challenge the argument.

"From what I can gather, the man who fell from his horse had the same skill set as me. It seems I would be the perfect replacement?" Jack pressed her reluctantly. He wanted to finish his mission, not become an acolyte but something told him if he showed his reluctance to join, she would not send him on his way with a map and a week's worth of food.

"True enough," she said, "but even with Barney's death, I still have fighting men in great quantity. It would be far wiser to have one less mouth to feed than it would to fill his space with an unnecessary acolyte."

She was philosophising again. Jack knew her mind was almost made up regarding his fate and fought for his life with a desperate plea. "I'm better than most with a pistol and there's not many in the Guard who can fight with a sword like me." A boast but not a hyperbolic one. In his recruitment training, he had excelled at beating all in his class. Much to the chagrin of his peers, save Lyndsey. While not the best shot, he hit his targets, with his right hand more than he missed and he uncertainly assumed that did make him 'better than most'.

"Is that so?" Rosie said. Now rounding on him with a fierce curiosity that Jack didn't like. He knew he had said the wrong thing. "Perhaps you can prove your skill with that sword of yours."

Jack hesitated but did not see what else he could say. "If I have too," he said defiantly.

Rosie put her index fingers to her mouth and whistled a long and atonal high-pitched sound. Two guards with muskets slung over their shoulders entered the room immediately and stood rigid, awaiting her orders. "Our guest thinks he's a better fighter than you, boys, escort him to the arena and return that fancy sword to him. He can fight another for his place here."

Jack had not had time to imagine what Rosie was planning for him when she whistled for the guards, but he knew that nothing he could have imagined would have been worse than what she had decided. As the guards escorted him to the arena, he wished he had not been so boastful. He would now pay the price for his hubris. He would either die fighting someone or be forced to kill a stranger against his will. Neither outcome was pleasing to Jack; either outcome would doubtless be pleasing to Rosie as she would soon be liberated of another mouth to feed.

He caught glimpses of the community as the guards forced him along at gunpoint with his hands in the air. The pathways were cut entirely by the footfall of the commune and not well-made and maintained tracks. The smell of decaying faeces made him realise why Rosie and the leader had been eager to ask him about drainage and engineering.

The buildings were constructed entirely out of wood and cobb containing neither bricks nor mortar and Jack could tell at first sight, not assembled by a carpenter or a builder. They looked as though arbitrary planks and tree cuttings had been nailed and tied together like a child's approximation of how a dwelling should be built. Jack wondered why anyone would be desperate to join such a community.

When Jack arrived at the arena, his imagination had failed him again. He had been expecting a grand amphitheatre that he had seen illustrations of in history books about the ancient civilisations. Instead, he would be fighting for his life at a clearing in the forest. A clearing that had been extended by the addition of around fifty tree stumps for the spectators to sit on.

He stood there, silent and defiant, at gunpoint with his hands up. It was not long before the audience began to arrive and take their seats on the stumps.

Eventually, the crowd filled up and Rosie entered the centre where he was standing with the guards. By her side was the man with the moustache.

She raised her hands and the audience chatter ceased instantaneously. Jack could tell she had not done this with magic but with the respect she garnered from her acolytes.

"This man, who has lied to us, for he is not a farmer, he is no more skilled than any of you, has claimed he could best our best fighter in sword combat. I have always taught you, my acolytes, that arrogance like that must be proved before the people. For boastful men who go unchallenged will leave cracks in the foundations of our society. Cracks, that if ignored, will destroy the very culture and way of life we have tried to build here."

She gestured to a man in the crowd and he entered the ring carrying the ferramus backsword that Jack had acquired at the Troll's Oak. He held it out and Jack grasped the hilt reluctantly, knowing he could not say or do anything that would free him from his imminent duel.

"Jack, the challenger, will now face our finest swordsmen. Oliver!" There was a roar of cheers and thunderous applause as Oliver stepped into the ring with his own sword.

The ear-splitting roars became a faint buzz to Jack as he realised, he would be fighting the young man who he had met in Ailsby not long ago. They had shared bread together, rode together, and conversed together. Oliver had given Jack no reason to dislike him, and he had no desire to either kill or be killed by someone who he had shared companionship with. Rosie raised her hands; the crowd went silent once more.

Oliver looked terrified, offering his gaze in every direction but Jack's. Jack was equally frightened but not for himself. He remembered the way in which Oliver had trembled when he held the musket and had no desire to kill a man who was equally reluctant to do so.

"Eamon and I will take our seats and you will duel when I give the order." She did not wait for a sign of confirmation from either of them as she and the middle-aged moustached man turned about and made their way to the tree stumps. The guards went to the edge of the ring, which in reality, was just the area of forest floor where they would be duelling.

Not knowing what to do, Jack raised his sword and brought the flat of the blade to a stop just in front of his face. A salute, he had been taught to do this long ago in fencing class as it was deemed less barbaric to show your opponent respect. Oliver did the same, though Jack noticed his sword was shaking as he did it.

Rosie gave the order to begin and he took a fighting stance, putting his right foot ahead of him and facing his opponent. His left foot was behind him, driving his weight forward for when he needed to attack. Oliver seemed never to have been taught this as he charged towards Jack with reckless abandon, screaming a crazed war cry with his sword held above his head and exposing his torso entirely. Jack could end Oliver with one blow if he wanted to.

He stepped aside quickly and smacked Oliver on the back with the flat of his sword as he passed. There was a loud crack as the blade made contact. He knew he had hurt and probably bruised him, but at least not given him a fatal wound.

This knowledge did not make Jack feel any better as Oliver released an ear-splitting howl, appearing to never have experienced pain that great before. The crowd laughed. He spun on the spot immediately to face Jack again. There starting positions now reversed, he was seething through his gritted teeth and looking at Jack murderously.

Jack had no intention of humiliating the man as he had just done but he did not want either of them to die. Until he could think of a solution that did not involve either of their deaths, he had no choice but to prolong the fight for as long as possible.

Perhaps humbled by his failed attack, Oliver edged towards him slowly this time. Jack despaired at his opponent's poor technique as he came closer, both feet pointing forward and pacing one after the other. In his training, recruits had to master the fencing stance before they were even given swords to hold. Right foot forward, left foot behind and pointing sideways. The stance that Jack was now adopting as if it were a reflex. This allowed the swordsman to both attack and evade attacks swiftly. Oliver's muscular physique may have made him the commune's best close quarters fighter, but Jack's fencing knowledge made him the swifter duellist.

Now within striking distance, Oliver brought his sword down from above with another war cry. Jack took a step back. Oliver's sword briefly hovered two feet above the ground, occupying the space where Jack had just been standing. Jack parried to the side with full force and his opponent's sword spun out of his hand and landed on the hard ground with a clang.

Jack took three paces back and pointed towards Oliver's sword with his own. He would not kill an unarmed man. Oliver's shakes were now more out of anger than fear. Jack wanted to explain that he was not humiliating him for his own or anyone else's entertainment. He waited patiently as Oliver knelt beside his fallen sword but kept his eyes on Jack, feeling around until he found the hilt.

When Oliver was on his feet again with the blade in hand, he seemed to change tactics. He began to circle Jack, side-stepping in a six-foot radius. Not wanting to become dizzy, Jack countered his movements and they circled each other. Jack could hear, and see, Oliver's heavy breathing, his shoulders rhythmically rising and falling as he tried to control his respiration against the glare he now fixed on Jack. Regardless of his anger, it seemed that Oliver was quite happy to stay in this repetitive dance while he thought on his next move.

If I don't end this soon, he'll hurt himself, Jack thought. *I need to finish this and do it without harming him.*

Jack had no idea what Rosie would do when he defeated Oliver but refused to kill him. She had hoped Jack would rid her of one of her many irksome fighting men. This vulgar display of amusement was a means of absolving herself of the blame and making Jack the scapegoat.

Resolving that he would rather face execution than kill for Rosie's scheming, he stepped towards Oliver, shifting his weight front to back between his feet. Oliver swiped across, hopelessly and further than he needed to. Jack ducked the attack, then sprang up, parried as Oliver brought his sword back across and kicked him hard in his unguarded belly.

Oliver dropped his sword and fell to his knees as he clutched his stomach and exhaled, winded as Jack knew he would be. He kicked Oliver's sword away then held him at the point of his own.

The crowd erupted in a mixture of boos and cheers. Jack could not tell which was louder and he did not care. Oliver was looking at Jack with anger and sorrow, appearing as though he was deciding whether he should taunt Jack to finish him or beg him for mercy.

Over the noise of the crowd, Jack did not hear Rosie walking up to his right-hand side to speak to him. "Kill him!" She ordered. "Take your place as an acolyte and prove your claim as our finest swordsman."

Jack did not hesitate with his reply. "No!"

"No?" Rosie was clearly not used to hearing that word.

"I will not kill a man for entertainment, or because you order me to!"

Rosie seemed astonished and Jack thought he saw a brief flash of anger across her face. She raised her hands a final time and the crowd went silent. "He has passed the first test," she said addressing her acolytes. "His skills do not make him immoral. But can he join us? We shall see." Her ability to lie so convincingly on a whim and to so many people at once unnerved Jack.

The crowd began to thin out and head back to the main area of the commune as Oliver recovered from his blow and got to his feet. Jack tried to speak with him but he seemed to be using all his effort to pretend he could not hear him. Jack watched as the crowd made their way back to the place where he had seen the poorly made wooden shacks. Only he and Rosie remained now.

"You are of no use to me, and your mercy makes you more dangerous than useful," she declared and Jack thought it was taking a great deal of effort to suppress her anger.

"What would you have done if I had killed Oliver?" Jack said, ignoring her restrained wrathfulness and feeling a little sick with the fact that he had just been made to fight someone to the death.

"I'd have claimed you cheated and ordered the guards to shoot you," she replied, remorselessly as an executioner.

"You would have let Oliver die just to rid yourself of me?" He said thinking he would throw up soon.

"I told you, I have too many fighting men and a lot of mouths to feed. Resources are scarce."

Jack was now unsure why he was not vomiting at the realisation that Rosie had hoped to reduce the numbers of her community by using Jack to execute Oliver under the guise of gladiatorial combat. She was clever, yet ruthless and Jack knew escaping from here would not be easy.

"Are you going to kill me?" He asked, gripping his sword tightly and ready to fight.

"I'm not sure," she said. "I made a mistake in having you fight. If I kill you now, my acolytes may grow suspicious of me."

Jack would start thinking of an escape plan once he had calmed down.

He did not follow Rosie straight back to the commune and he did not wish to be in her company a second longer. He stood staring at the space where Oliver had been kneeling. Kneeling with the same look in his eyes that Leopold Braske had that night beneath the Troll's Oak, just before Jack had skewered him with his own sword. The look of a man who was expecting his life would be about to end imminently. Jack was glad he had no reason to hold Oliver responsible for Holly's death.

Rosie seemed to be of the opinion that economics was a justifiable enough reason to kill a man in a barbaric fashion, especially if you could dupe another into doing the deed for you. Her mistake had been in getting Jack to perform said deed, as grief was the only thing that would make him do that.

Chapter Twenty

"You make your servants wear *this?*" Lyndsey proclaimed in disgust as she tried to pull the short skirt of her disguise down below her knees, to no avail. She was hoping to conceal a derringer or a dagger about herself as she had resolved to do so after her meeting with Eva, but the maid's uniform Adam had given her did not provide her with such an opportunity.

"It's not my fault! Father insists on it for all the girls. He says it's the only way we can be sure the staff aren't stealing from us," Adam said blushingly with his back to Lyndsey as she struggled to breathe in the tight black sleeveless dress she was wearing, along with sandals instead of shoes.

"How old is your eldest maid?" Lyndsey asked curiously, recalling that the elderly house keeper she had encountered was not dressed in such a fashion.

"I'm not sure," said Adam. "Perhaps twenty-five?"

Lyndsey silently cursed Adam's perverted father and pitied his mother if she believed thievery was the Home Secretary's only reason for making his chambermaid's dress in such a fashion.

Lyndsey passionately disliked her new attire, yet they had no choice but to continue as planned. She had heard the numerous rumours that Lord Pluff insisted on such a uniform in his household, to dress differently now would surely elicit suspicion. She resolved that if it came to a fight, she would be more than a match for a gossip columnist in hand-to-hand combat.

The coach passed Lionsgate Hall, not stopping at the front entrance and turning a corner as it made its way towards the rear of the building.

When the coach eventually slowed to a stop, Adam made for the carriage door. "Adam, I'm supposed to be your servant remember," said Lyndsey, trying to hide her exasperation. After all, he was new to this sort of lifestyle. "I don't think you should be exiting the carriage before me," she finished, now dreading going out onto the street in the clothes Adam had provided. Lyndsey could recall some of the whores at Annabelle's who had dressed in a more dignified manner.

Adam gave Lyndsey another bashful nod in agreement and she opened the door before exiting into the street.

The servant's entrance was around the back of the vast building on a quieter back street but that did not make Lyndsey feel any less self-conscious. She rolled out the carriage's steps for Adam to descend as quickly as she could, before they both hurried to the small wooden door. A servant with a bob of black hair let them in which Lyndsey was all too eager to do before someone she knew might have spotted her.

She had been suspicious as well as curious as to why Victoria Lionsgate did not want Adam entering through the front door for all to see. That would have attracted gossip among the people of Graylenmouth. Gossip which she no doubt needed for income as well as reputation. She was grateful for it for now though as it gave her some privacy when dressed in these ridiculous clothes. The servant girl was looking at Lyndsey with a curious eye. Lyndsey knew she was no doubt silently thanking her own employer for not making her dress in such a way.

I hope no one noticed me out there and tells Michael they've seen me dressed like this. Lyndsey allowed herself that last negative thought before pushing her anxieties to a desolate corner of her mind and bringing her focus into the present, to the mission. Hopefully, Adam would ask the questions she had told him to. If not, she had other plans and other strategies.

Daisy led them both through the servant's quarters and then up a long spiral staircase where they reached a long corridor before showing them to the drawing room. She stopped before opening the door. "You can go in, Master Pluff," she addressed Adam. "But I'm afraid your servant will have to wait outside. Mrs Lionsgate was not expecting you to be accompanied."

Adam hesitated. Lyndsey knew he was thinking of the correct line. They had spent the week rehearsing potential scenarios such as this, as well as the best thing Adam could say to avoid them. Fortunately, he did not hesitate for too long.

"I really must insist on Belinda's presence," he asserted. "She has the most incredible memory you see and serves me as a sort of de facto secretary." Lyndsey mentally sighed with relief. He had done well. He said the line almost verbatim but sounded natural enough. He had even used the rehearsed name they had agreed upon, 'Belinda'.

Daisy was about to offer further protest before a middle-aged woman's voice came through the door. "Let him bring his servant. If she's part of his household, I'm sure she'll keep the meeting a secret for his sake." Daisy nodded in acknowledgement to her unseen employer before opening the door with a curtsey.

"Good to see you again, Master Pluff. Please have a seat," said the gossip columnist before turning to Lyndsey. "My, aren't you a pretty young thing. I can see why the young man wants to keep you so close. I don't think I was ever as pretty as you, even in my youth, though I never had the confidence to dress like *that*! Would you be so kind as to give me a twirl so I can take in your youthful figure?" Victoria said. Lyndsey knew when she was being patronised and this was undoubtedly one of those moments.

In character, Lyndsey looked at Adam and he nodded, ordering his pretend servant to do as the gossip columnist had bid. She did not resent him for it. She had told him to be as accommodating to Mrs Lionsgate as possible in order to gain her trust, but that did not make her feel any less awkward as she held onto her already short skirt and began to gracefully turn on the spot for the amusement of the woman. Despite her lack of clothes, Lyndsey could feel herself getting warmer with embarrassment and hoped her face was not getting redder.

She did not know how many times she had turned around before the gossip columnist began to squeal and clap in the same sickly-sweet way that a governess might encourage a shy four-year-old.

"Bravo, Bravo, such elegance. I pray you stop now, my dear, before Daisy and I are overcome with jealousy." Lyndsey stopped and slowly turned the rest of the way around so she could see all three of them.

Victoria and Adam were facing each other and sat in the armchairs, Daisy was standing by Victoria's left-hand side with paper and quill, taking notes for her mistress. Lyndsey thought she saw the black-haired servant send a smirk in her direction before returning her attention to the paper.

She had had little respect for Victoria Lionsgate before meeting her today. Now she had none. As far as Lyndsey was concerned, she was nothing more than a bully. The only difference being that she had managed to eke out a living from her harassment of others. In addition, the fact that she was in league with someone like Eva Valmarque made her even more vulgar in Lyndsey's eyes.

After the recent humiliation the woman had just forced Lyndsey to suffer, she now loathed her with every fibre of her being. Lyndsey, with great exertion, pushed away those feelings. Being angry would make her lose focus and inevitably miss something. She needed to keep herself in the present, for Jack's sake.

"It's good to see you again, Young Master," said Victoria, now turning her attention to Adam. "I have good news!"

"Yes?" Adam enquired with interest.

"Since our last meeting, I have done some research, and I think what you have told me may be worth more than a column or two, perhaps I can make a book of it. Or even a series of books," Victoria declared triumphantly.

"I'm happy for you," said Adam. "I'm to assume then that you and I are to have many meetings such as this?"

"We shall, but first, I just want a short bit of information on another matter. Tell me what you know of Lord Murray?"

"The Trade Secretary?" Adam replied sounding as confused as Lyndsey felt. "Never met him; Father's not particularly fond of him either. Thinks he concerns himself with the plight of the common man too often."

"Very well, worth a try," said Victoria. For a fleeting moment, Lyndsey could be sure she had spotted genuine disappointment on the gossip columnists face.

Victoria Lionsgate now began to grill Adam about his exploits and how he had found himself in a daze the fateful night he had attended the brothel. Lyndsey was beginning to feel useless. She was of no use here and Adam was doing a good job of keeping the vile harpy occupied.

She could be of better use elsewhere perhaps. She must have an office, a place where she kept important records and documents. Lyndsey might be able to learn something if she could find anything like that. She had suspected that being present for Adam's interview might not shed any light on why Victoria had been dealing with Eva Valmarque. Despite making a living off writing dross, she doubted Victoria Lionsgate was as stupid or naïve as she behaved.

There were certainly sinister intentions behind her meetings with the redhead and Lyndsey was not going to discover what they were standing silently and listening to this conversation. She had hoped that by getting Adam to talk about the encounter with Eva which had led to his arrest at Jack's hands, she might let something slip about her associations with the sorceress but her face betrayed nothing as she listened intently to Adam and checked Daisy's notes.

Fortunately, she and Adam had prepared for this eventuality. "Master Adam Sir, sorry to interrupt but may I be excused?" Lyndsey said coyly. Adam paused in his story and looked around at Lyndsey. She could see the fear spread across his face for a moment as he knew what this meant.

"Medical issues again, is it, Belinda? You poor thing. Of course, you may."
Playing his part well, he then turned to Mrs Lionsgate. "My servant needs to use
your facilities if she may. She has an unfortunate condition, about which you
would probably rather not hear." Adam had rehearsed his lines well and clearly
took this seriously. Lyndsey was grateful at this and did not care about the public
humiliation she was being made to suffer for a second time this afternoon.

"Of course," said Victoria, looking a little concerned. "There's one next door
to my study, up the stairs second door on the left." Lyndsey could have jumped
in joy. Victoria Lionsgate had just revealed the location of her study, where she
no doubt did most of her work, and more importantly, kept most of her secrets.

Lyndsey left the room with the speed of someone who required the use of a
bathroom imminently and raced up the stairs, being sure to go through the first
door on the left and not the second.

Chapter Twenty-One

Victoria was beginning to wonder if there was any point in taking an interest in young Adam Pluff. He had sparked a certain curiosity in her upon their first meeting as not only had she viewed this as a possible way to infiltrate the cabinet, but his nature was also in stark contrast to most young men of his status. He seemed humble and empathetic. Most wealthy young men tended to be brash and arrogant.

Despite his difference in temperament, however, he seemed just as ignorant as his peers, he was only more self-aware.

She was beginning to regret commenting a moment ago about writing a whole book and seeing more of Adam. It had been a ploy, an appeal to his piousness to see if he could shed any light on the situation with the trade bill. Now Victoria had to sit through a meeting and listen to him drone on about his foibles. Once they were finished, she would produce an excuse not to see him again and that would be that. She was busy enough with Eva Valmarque and Bernard Crenshaw and she did not have time for this overprivileged young lord who loved the sound of his own voice too much.

...and the way he makes that poor chambermaid dress, thought Victoria in disgust as she nodded occasionally to give the illusion that she found his rhetoric interesting. She felt terrible for making the young girl blush like that and for making her do that humiliating twirl, but caution had forced her to do so.

The way he had insisted on bringing her into the room, her skimpy outfit and the fact that she was wearing sandals that made her practically barefooted had forced Victoria to believe she was a Warlock. If she had let one of them into the house, she would be taking a great risk. By getting her to twirl around several times, Victoria could check for gemstones. None were concealed about her person. It was easy to tell in a uniform that tight.

Victoria shuddered again at the guilt of what she had put that poor young girl through when Daisy brought her out of her trance.

"We're wasting time; you need to make an excuse and get rid of him."

The words were inked on Daisy's paper. She had just this second shown the message to her mistress under the pretext of checking spelling. Victoria nodded at her servant in agreement. "Yes, well done, Daisy, it definitely has two L's," she added for good measure before addressing Adam. "Another half hour and we shall break for lunch. Is that agreeable, Master Pluff?" Adam agreed. She would offer him lunch and then think of a pretext to get rid of him. Daisy was right. She had more pressing matters.

There was an almighty crash from upstairs! The smashing of glass so loud, it brought all three of them to stunned silence.

"That came from upstairs!" Daisy gasped, hiding her face from Adam and betraying a look of concern to Victoria.

The chambermaid; perhaps she's not as innocent as she appears, thought Victoria, stunned at the revelation that she may have just looked upon youth and beauty with the same level of underestimation as a man.

"Please check the bathroom and see that young Belinda is alright?" She said to Daisy before whispering to her servant. "Then check the study."

Her servant left the room swiftly and Victoria turned back to Adam, whom she noticed had an equally concerned look on his face. The same one Daisy had given her a moment ago. Perhaps he was not as stupid as he appeared either.

Chapter Twenty-Two

Upon reaching the top of the stairs, Lyndsey immediately tried the door to the study. It was locked but she had suspected this. Victoria Lionsgate clearly was no fool. It was not an issue, the bathroom she had sent her to was next door and Lyndsey knew what could be done. She carried on one door further, turned the polished brass handle and went through into the bathroom.

As a full-time salaried guardsman and the wife of a rising physician, Lyndsey had not considered herself among the poorest of the city. Upon seeing just one of the many bathrooms in Lionsgate Hall, she now began to feel as though she was. There was not only a lavatory, which was a rich person's luxury unlike the outhouses used by the middle and working classes, but there was also a bidet, a sink, and a huge bath big enough for six people. The bath and sink were also complete with taps.

She had only ever seen the huge pumps on street corners and had used them herself as those who were not affluent had to do when acquiring water. These, however, were small and ornate. The kind most people only hear about or read of in one of Victoria's columns.

Lyndsey had no more time to seethe at the way the wealthy lived. She made her way straight across the room to the large window on the far side. She twisted the handle and pulled it open while keeping a tight grip on the frame. She then put her head out and looked to the left. To her relief, the ledge went all the way along to the next window; to Victoria's study.

She carefully crawled onto the two feet thick window ledge before grabbing hold of a stone gargoyle and pulling herself up. She sidled along, hoping the people on the busy street below would not think to look up. She would have cut an odd figure in this ridiculous costume balancing here. She prayed that only being one story up would be enough to not give passers-by a good view up her short dress.

Upon reaching the study, she carefully returned to all fours and started to work at the outside of the window. It was locked. There was no way to open it without tools from this side. This did not please Lyndsey but she knew there was not much else she could do. She could not force an entry as that would be a hard thing to explain to Victoria Lionsgate. She crawled back along the window ledge then carefully stood up again and re-entered the bathroom.

There was an almighty crash. Lyndsey had not been able to steady the window upon her re-entry, she had needed to outstretch both arms in order to keep her balance. As she jumped off the ledge and into the bathroom, her outstretched right hand collided with the windowpane, which in its frame swivelled all the way around and slammed behind her into the wall.

The glass shattered and spread itself over the floor in almost infinite pieces. Lyndsey was sorry to be wearing sandals but fortunately, only had a shallow cut on the top of her foot where a stray piece of glass had caught her. Her guardsman's reflexes had ensured she was clear of most of the broken glass before it could do her serious harm.

Almost instantaneously, there was a thundering of footsteps followed by an equally thundering knock on the bathroom door. "Are you alright? Is everything OK, Belinda?" Daisy's voice came from the corridor outside.

Lyndsey composed herself then went to the door and opened it. "I...I...opened the window f-for some air, it must have swung around in the breeze. I'm sorry." The stutter was not completely affected, the adrenaline rush she had gained from investigating on the ledge had somewhat influenced her speech pattern.

Daisy did not appear convinced but mercifully did not press the matter further. "You're bleeding," she said, "Let me dress that up for you."

*

Twenty minutes later, Daisy was escorting Lyndsey downstairs and back to the drawing room. The cut she had gained on her foot stung but did not force her to limp. Lyndsey was grateful as she had no desire to explain to either Michael or Captain Thompson why she was hobbling had she acquired such a problem.

"Oh dear, oh dear!" Victoria Lionsgate exclaimed. "I think we may have to finish early, Adam. I have to see to my broken window and I suggest you discipline your clumsy chambermaid."

"Fear not, Madam, I shall," said Adam, with a rather convincing fake frown in Lyndsey's direction.

*

As the coach pulled away from Lionsgate Hall shortly afterwards, Lyndsey was beginning to wonder if Victoria Lionsgate deserved the same fate she had promised would befall Eva Valmarque.

Chapter Twenty-Three

"It was no accident; she broke the window coming back in," said Daisy, sweeping the loose shards of glass into a pile underneath the broken window.

"Coming back in? You mean she was out there for some time?" Victoria said in disbelief.

"There're footprints and handprints on the window ledge. Going in both directions. She was trying to get into your study!" Daisy confirmed.

Victoria did not like the sound of that. Young girls dressed like harlots snooping around her house was as unsettling as having to slander Bernard Crenshaw for the Warlocks' Council.

"Did she get in?" She said nervously.

"It doesn't look like it. That window can't be opened from the outside and the door's still locked. There's no sign of a forced entry."

Victoria breathed a long sigh of relief. The thought of anyone other than her or Daisy gaining entry to the study could potentially result in the undoing of everything they had been working towards for the last five years.

She could not believe she had been so naïve. A young aristocrat with a youthful servant who he had managed to pass off as an unassuming bimbo had infiltrated her house and nearly exposed her work. Things could have been a lot worse, but had she been vigilant this could have been avoided altogether. The seemingly moronic Master Pluff had managed to fool her when all this time she had assumed she could fool him in order to infiltrate the cabinet.

Daisy finished sweeping and the two of them went next door as she unlocked her study. One of the two most important desk drawers was the third one down, the bottom most drawer. It contained the records and memoirs of all that she and Daisy had been investigating for the past five years. Victoria gave the drawer a gentle tug and it did not open, telling her it was still locked. She doubted Daisy was mistaken about the young hussy not gaining entry, but she had to be sure.

The second most important drawer was more of a secret compartment. The carpenter who made the desk had used cedar wood for the top, eight inches thick. Victoria had made sure in her own time to hollow out a section at the front where the corner could discreetly be removed. She now slid off the right-hand front corner. The most recent and essential articles she had written and stored there in the previous week still remained, much to her relief. They could still be published.

They returned to the corridor after checking the study for other possible signs of entry. They found none but Victoria decided it would probably be a good idea to put a stronger lock on the window soon. She would contact a locksmith as soon as it was convenient.

"I've taken my eye off the ball, Daisy," she said. "I was so obsessed with the idea that Adam might be an entry point into the government because of his family connections. It didn't occur to me that he might be the one manipulating me," she conceded.

"I never liked him, but I didn't exactly have him sussed out from the start, Ma'am. I had him for an idiot but it seems he's quite clever. Why do you think he's got his servants snooping around after you?"

"I probably wrote an article about one of his relatives some years ago and he's out for revenge," Victoria hoped. She had no reason to believe his motives were anything beyond the petty and the personal. She hoped with even more fervour that he was not in league with the Warlocks', that would mean his motives were of a more sinister nature. She had no evidence to believe that and did not want to worry Daisy unnecessarily if she could avoid it. Regardless, both Victoria and Daisy decided they would not be meeting with Adam and his spying servant again.

Chapter Twenty-Four

"I can't believe we got away with that. They had no idea that you were looking around," said Adam excitedly as the coach made its way to Parliament Street along the cobbles of Graylenmouth.

"They know!" Lyndsey grimaced. "They just couldn't prove it, but they're not stupid, that was a flimsy excuse I gave for breaking the window. If you weren't the son of the Home Secretary, they would have probably made a citizen's arrest and summoned the Guard." Lyndsey was glad it had not come to that. It would have been tricky to explain to her colleagues. "Turn around, Adam, I want to get changed."

Adam turned his back but was still eager to talk about the events they had just experienced. "How are we going to play it next time?" Adam said, whose first experience in information gathering had given him an excited demeanour.

"There's not going to *be* a next time, Adam, they won't invite us. They can't risk accusing us of burglary due to your station but we won't be seeing them again. They won't risk us snooping around a second time, especially as she's definitely hiding something." Of that, Lyndsey was sure. She had searched many a house when on duty and had not yet come across one who locked the window to their study, or even kept the windows closed on a warm summer afternoon.

"What if I keep insisting on another meeting?" Adam said sounding a little disappointed. Lyndsey finally removed the maid's uniform after a third sharp tug over her head and the liberation of her ribcage felt almost euphoric.

"She'll keep giving you excuses about how she's too busy until you eventually give up," said Lyndsey after taking the first deep breaths she had experienced since donning the disguise.

"But you said yourself you need to investigate. How are you going to do that now?"

He had a point. She was now more eager than ever to find out what the gossip columnist was up to but her mistake with the bathroom window had lost her a cover story. Adam's servant could hardly turn up to Lionsgate Hall on her own. That would look more suspicious than breaking the window as well as confirm any suspicions that Victoria Lionsgate undoubtedly now had.

As Lyndsey finished getting dressed in her civilian clothes, the coach arrived at Parliament Street. She finally concealed a derringer in her bodice and a dagger up her sleeve as she had planned. She said goodbye to a now deflated Adam and upon jumping into the street made her way back to her own house.

She was now feeling grim about her next move. Adam had been right, there was no further way to investigate Victoria Lionsgate save one, and she did not like it. She would have to break into the study and have a look around. Either at night or during the day when Victoria was not in. She shuddered at the thought. Breaking and entering was the work of a common criminal and Lyndsey had taken the guardsman's oath to apprehend and arrest people like that, not act like them.

She also wanted to find Jack but was now almost as eager to discover why the Warlocks were in cahoots with a gossip columnist. Perhaps uncovering that would give her enough information on the Warlocks to extort them into telling her where Jack was. She knew that was an optimistic thought as she doubted a Warlock could ever be coerced or blackmailed. Her previous meeting with Eva Valmarque had betrayed a weakness in their magic to Lyndsey, but Lyndsey knew that one's ability and one's pride were separate issues entirely, and many people would rather die before succumbing to extortion.

She climbed the steps to her own front door and let herself in. There was a noise in the kitchen. Lyndsey carefully removed her shoes, not wanting to reveal any loud footsteps. She then removed her derringer from her bodice and cocked it. She tiptoed to the kitchen. Slowly. Whoever was in there had not heard Lyndsey, to her relief.

She slowly made her way along the hallway, pistol in hand. She knew she would not need to use the dagger against the intruder. She rarely missed with a gun.

She was close now and the burglar was making no effort to keep quiet. *If it's a Warlock, I have to act quickly. I can't let them touch their gemstone. I shouldn't even give them a warning before I shoot.* That was a reprehensible thought to Lyndsey but she doubted someone like Eva Valmarque would offer her any kind of warning in return.

She kicked open the kitchen door as loudly as possible. Experience told her that this was the best way to catch the intruder off guard.

"Put your hands up!" She boomed, entering the kitchen and hoping that that would be enough to stop the assailant.

She breathed a sigh of relief. Michael Carter had leapt into the air when his wife entered the kitchen brandishing a firearm. He dropped his sandwich and wheeled around before seeing the fear and then the relief on his wife's face. Lyndsey laughed uncontrollably before casting her weapon aside and racing towards her husband. At his embrace, she burst into tears.

"Are you OK?" Michael said returning his wife's tight squeeze.

"Yes." She sobbed. "Sorry, I've had a stressful day and didn't expect you to be in. I thought we were being burgled. Sorry," said Lyndsey, distraught at the fact she had nearly shot her husband.

"Quite alright, we all have bad days," said Michael in an understanding yet confused tone. "Can I make you some food perhaps?"

"No, let's go upstairs. To bed." Lyndsey had had an awful day and just wanted Michael. When the two of them were together, time stood still. Nothing else mattered, she needed that now. Michael did not protest.

Chapter Twenty-Five

The commune looked rather picturesque in the afternoon sun, he had begrudgingly admitted that to himself. It had been a week since his duel with Oliver and Rosie had given him permission to stay, for now at least.

Everyone here spoke to him as though it was a privilege to live and work among this secret community. Other than the natural beauty of the area, he was still to see evidence of the perceived paradise of which the acolytes would boast.

Rosie's claim of how skilled men were needed here was perhaps the only thing on which he could agree with her. He had slept worse here than in the wild. While he had not expected a feather bed, he had thought he would have more comfort than the hard ground in a crude shelter that gave no protection from the draft. Had it been raining; he would have certainly been drenched. He was grateful it was summer.

Without dustcarts or organised sanitation, the smell was worse than the roughest slums in the capital. The people of the commune had decided that once you had wandered far enough out of sight beyond the treeline, that any patch of ground you saw could be the privy. It was almost impossible to avoid the smell at any point on the redwood clearing. That odour was not the result of keeping livestock as he had first thought. The residents said he would get used to it but after a week he doubted that.

What little food there was, was not well prepared in the absence of a good butcher or a good cook. The only food source was the forest's wild flora and fauna which was hunted and gathered by those who were given that role. Having no farmers to speak of and being unable to cultivate the land for growing, men would leave the redwood enclosure once a month and return with whatever they could. He had heard the hunters talk of how they had to go further and deeper into the forest to acquire their game. The food sources had been more abundant once, but it seemed their own poor organisation had depleted it. Jack did not want to be around when it had depleted completely.

He was beginning to assume that Rosie had bewitched them all into believing this was paradise. The people had been fooled, perhaps by magical means, and they believed that this meagre existence was somehow superior to any other way of living.

He had been thinking of escape but no solution had yet presented itself. There were no walls or guards stopping him from leaving the enclosure but without a map or a compass, he had no idea in which direction he should travel. He had hoped to observe the sun rises and sunsets so that he could at least glean an idea of east and west, but the tall trees made it hard to determine the exact points where it rose and fell.

There was a stream that ran close to the enclosure. Jack had guessed, without certainty, that this may be a tributary of the Graylen and following its current might lead him back to the river, but that could take weeks.

Until he could think of a plan, he had no choice but to play his part and pretend to be an active participant in the community. Rosie had allowed him to keep his ferramus sword, which had now become the only possession he really owned. Many of the commune's inhabitants had been impressed with his skills against Oliver in the swordfight so he had decided to make use of himself as a fencing teacher. Using broken branches, he would teach men and women of all ages the footwork, stances and actions of good sword fighting.

Rosie had not spoken to him since his duel but she almost certainly disapproved. She was not fond of fighting men and thought she had them in surplus, but he had to occupy himself somehow. There was little to do here and if Jack did not keep himself busy, he would just wander round aimlessly with nothing to do like many others here did. He surmised it was for the best that no one, including himself, knew how to brew or distil alcohol or the commune's demise would be coming a lot sooner than he thought.

While Rosie's management of the place was not efficient or effective, she was not naïve. He now knew why she had been so eager to thin out the population on his arrival here. While she had not been dishonest in her reasons, he had not quite expected anything quite this bleak.

He would have to take the risk and make a desperate escape soon. It seemed mad, though still less mad than waiting on Rosie's decision which would no doubt end in his death, or someone else's at his expense as she had tried to do for Oliver, who had now become a morose and reclusive individual. He was not the least bit like his former self whom Jack had first met in Ailsby.

Jack had offered to give Oliver the same sword fighting lessons he was giving to the others. At least he would have, but speaking to Oliver had become impossible as he was now avoiding him, which was very hard in a small community of people trapped in an enclosure. He would turn about and walk the other way whenever he saw Jack. The look on his face was always a bizarre mix of fear and loathing. Jack had not dwelt on this much as he knew Oliver would be reluctant to forgive him and he had to prioritise his own safety.

*

Jack's fortunes were to change one Sunday afternoon when an opportunity to leave the commune arose. He had been teaching a group the fencing stance and getting them to step forward and back appropriately in accordance with proper technique, when something hard hit him in the back of the head. It was hard and small. Like a stone. It did not render him unconscious, but he felt the back of his head tenderly as his eyes streamed and the would-be sword fighters around him swam in and out of focus.

He slowly adjusted to his dizziness. He heard and soon felt fast and heavy footsteps quickening in his direction, thundering across the hard ground.

He pivoted to face his attacker, but he was not quick enough. He was being tackled to the ground and he fell immediately. He had not been able to anchor his balance after receiving a blow to the back of his head. He felt his own sword being taken from his side and saw it being pointed at his throat. The blurry outline of a red-headed man was standing over him, sword in hand.

"Apologise for toying with me and I won't toy with you before I kill you!" Oliver's voice came as the blurry figure stood before him in the foreground, the tops of the redwoods framing his background against the blue summer sky.

"I had no choice. It was either that or kill you as Rosie was hoping." It seemed a foolish response but when a man had abandoned the rule of law, his assurances gave you no guarantee he would follow through on them. In Jack's estimation, Oliver's temper and brutish behaviour told him that an apology would be no guarantee of keeping his life.

"Liar!" Oliver declared. "She loves me, or at least she would, had you not humiliated me. You should have just killed me."

Jack had had enough and not for the first time since he arrived here. He would not apologise for sparing someone. As his vision was coming back to him, he noticed once more that Oliver's lack of training had not taught him how to hold a sword properly. Without a second thought, Jack grabbed the blunt edge of his backsword, wrenched it away, and kicked Oliver with full force.

He had been aiming for his gut again but his dizziness affected his aim. The heel of Jack's boot landed with immense pressure between Oliver's legs. This was not the first time Jack had kicked a man there. Unlike the ruffian in Ulston, Jack had not done it intentionally this time, though he surmised that Oliver was just as deserving. He was a young and naïve man, lovesick for Rosie and her way of life and Jack had punished him for his ignorance.

Unfortunately, he had also just given her an excuse to kill him and he would have to make his escape more imminently than he had first thought.

Oliver's reaction, however, was not what one would expect of a man who had just received such a blow. He did not try to cover or caress the affected area, he did not make any sounds of pain, his facial expression and body language betrayed no signs of recent trauma either, he just continued to seethe and glare.

Jack was suddenly reminded of the ruffian he had arrested at Annabelle's that fateful night. At the time, he had put the man's behaviour down to drunkenness but he was now struck by the anger behind Oliver's eyes. It was identical to that of the man who had taken Molly hostage. The uncontrollable rage. Jack was so struck by the similarities, that he could not recall witnessing it before, outside of this occasion and the other.

Oliver seethed a few more times before his eyes rolled into his skull and he collapsed. Jack went over to check he was OK. He was fine, a little bruised and unconscious but no lasting damage. He had no desire to check the wound he had given Oliver himself but would ask someone else to do so in due course.

"Step away from him please, Jack, and come with me." Jack looked up to see Eamon staring curiously at him. He had arrived on the seen with eerily quick timing seeing as Oliver had collapsed less than a minute ago. "Step away and come with me, Rosie wants to see you."

Of course, she does. The last time I encountered a man behaving exactly like this, I encountered a Warlock shortly after and things only got worse for me.

Jack followed Eamon across the enclosure to the building where he had first met Rosie. He looked back to see crowds of people were now congregating around the spot where Oliver had fallen and he sighed. He knew it would not be long before false rumours began to spread about him trying to kill Oliver, then Rosie would have her excuse. She may run her community very differently from the government in the capital, but she employed the same dirty political tactics.

He was certain that she had bewitched Oliver with her magic and manipulated him into a bloodlust. She was now going to sentence him to death or something worse in order to rid herself of him. If there was one silver lining, she had sent Eamon to apprehend him too soon and he had not killed Oliver as she had probably hoped.

His thoughts then turned back to the man he had apprehended in Annabelle's in what seemed like an age ago now. His behaviour was the same, he had the same glazed look in his eye as Oliver had. It was not intoxication. It was magic. Had Eva Valmarque or someone else in the Warlocks' Council orchestrated the events of that night? The night that had changed his present, probably shortened his future and sealed his fate as a criminal in exile seeking redemption.

Eamon escorted him into the building where Rosie was waiting and thoughts of Eva escaped his mind. Rosie did not seem angry. She did not even seem smug, neither was she disappointed nor exasperated. He had been expecting at least one of these emotions from the leader of the commune. She instead seemed as philosophical as she had the day they had first met. She was standing by the window in her golden-green dress, barefooted as expected, with a topaz and an amethyst about her neck. Her right hand was supporting her head as she gazed out the window, her left was absently caressing the gemstones which Jack noticed with apprehension.

"Thank you, Eamon," she said. "You may leave us." Eamon bowed low, showing his loyalty to his chief before departing. Rosie looked out the window as though lost in a moral conundrum for a moment before saying, "I'm not a Warlock. I'm a witch."

"Sorry?" He said. He had been expecting a painful execution or something worse, not a meaningless declaration from the sorceress.

"When you first arrived here, you called me a Warlock. I'm not, I'm a witch. Do you know the difference?" She turned her gaze from the window and her brown eyes bore into Jack as she seemingly brought her focus back to the present.

"Warlocks are legal, witches are not," he said uncertainly. He had not really given the matter a great deal of thought until now.

"Who do you think determines which magic users are Warlocks and witches?" She asked him like a teacher trying to coax the correct answer out of a confused student. He hesitated and thought for a while, not wishing to spend his final moments being led to conclusions.

"I know what you're getting at. You're saying the Warlocks' Council have too much say on the proper use of magic. You do not like or associate with the Warlocks' Council and therefore consider yourself a witch. As they would, you." Jack said impatiently. If she was going to kill him, he wanted her to get on with it.

She did not lose her temper as he had feared. Instead, she nodded approvingly. "Just so, do you know why the nine members of the council seek to regulate magic so vigorously?"

He wondered why he had not given the matter much thought until now. He had spent his entire life in Graylenmouth and the Warlocks' Tower had probably passed in and out of his field of vision at least once a day in all those years. He never had much love for the Warlocks, even before he met Eva. It was a constant topic of conversation in the city, and the press, that the Warlocks were secretly running everything behind the scenes but most people wrote that off as a conspiracy.

The idea that the Warlocks, who commanded powerful magics, needed to control and influence things behind the scenes seemed ridiculous to most. Juxtaposing this with his recent encounters with magic, he arrived at an answer to her question.

"They're not as powerful as they want us to believe. If they don't keep an eye on other magic users, they may lose that secret, and all the power it allows them." He was almost certain he had solved the mystery. Before his quest began, he believed Warlocks and witches to be the omnipresent and near divine entities they purported themselves to be.

Other revelations now came to him as well. He had been able to defeat Leopold Braske twice in single combat. Something that was reported in stories and accounts to be as likely as slaying a deity. Eva Valmarque had caused him great humiliation and pain with that amethyst of hers rather than just teleport or fly him to Wylclyst. Now he thought of it, it seemed convoluted to just carve a message into his back and send him on his way. He now was recalling Rosie referring to magic as parlour tricks when he first met her. Suddenly, things were becoming clearer to him.

"Exactly," confirmed Rosie. "They want us to believe they're gods. Omnipotent and untouchable. They make us believe they have the power to move mountains which is believed by both commoners and aristocrats. While we avoid them in fear, they use their tricks to influence the King and the parliament. Which brings me to the problem of you, Sergeant." That almost shocked Jack, he had momentarily forgotten why she had summoned him here.

"What do you mean?" He said, now not sure how her enthusiasm to discuss the Warlocks' Council was relevant.

"You're on a mission for them. Don't deny it, I sensed the mark of their magic on you the day you arrived. I don't know the details and I don't want to know. You do, however, leave me in a dilemma which I believe I have now solved with help from Oliver." She caressed the stones around her neck again and Jack checked his sword was at his belt and ready to draw.

"Fear not," she said, letting go of the gemstones. "I will not be using magic on you now. The Yellow stone was necessary on Oliver or he would never have attacked you." She noticed his quizzical look and explained further. "A topaz will amplify feelings of lust or love, making them more suggestible to the one they have infatuation for. Oliver loves me as many here do, it was easy to suggest he attack you once the topaz worked its magic." Jack finally understood why female Warlocks tended to dress in revealing clothes.

"The amethyst," she continued, "would have been for you. I hoped Oliver's rage would make it hard for you to avoid killing him this time. I was going to make you wander off into exile in despair, but it appears you subdued him before I could get that far." She spoke about her sinister plans so calmly that Jack felt he would have been less afraid if she had said them in anger.

"I should kill you and be done with it, but I could have Alayna Strauss and the council coming after me, so you will leave this place tonight. I will provide you with provisions and equipment. Food is already in short supply here; I hope you appreciate the risk I'm taking to send you away," she continued, perhaps anticipating his anger.

Jack knew nothing of governance but he knew these people soon would descend into starvation under her leadership. There was little to eat and what little there was would soon be gone, not to mention the poor standard of living she had forced upon these people.

The tyranny they unknowingly suffered at the hands of both her magic and her ruthlessness was not enough to sustain a society. While the government of Talamholean was neither honourable nor considerate of the average man, the people still retained their freewill. Jack would choose that and all its foibles over this place at any time. He just hoped he would be able to resume his place there one day.

Despite being beyond his jurisdiction as a guardsman, Jack wanted to help these people too. Jack could not cite a legal reason for Rosie's immorality, but he knew she was corrupt. He wanted to save these people and free them from her.

He wanted to, but he reluctantly conceded that he could not. He had no idea how to break her magic. Even if he killed her, which he would not do in cold blood, he could not be sure that it would break her hold over these people. There was also the logistical aspect of leading hundreds of wayward acolytes through the forest and back into society. Jack had no choice but to accept her exile and return to his mission, but he did make a promise to himself.

If he ever made it back to Graylenmouth, he would one day return here. He would do what he could for the people she had subjugated and liberate them. With or without Rosie's consent.

Jack was now more eager than ever to reach Wylclyst.

*

When night had fallen, Eamon escorted Jack beyond the redwoods. Rosie had at least taken Jack at his word that he would leave without a fuss, which was no doubt the reason Eamon escorted him alone, though he was still being led away in the manner he had arrived, with a cloth bag over his head. The exact location of this place would still be a mystery to him. Perhaps Rosie suspected his desire to return one day.

They had walked for an hour or two when Eamon allowed him to take the bag off. In the darkness of the night and surrounded by pine trees once more, Jack was not sure if there was anything to see for a moment before his eyes adjusted.

"There are no paths between here and the forest's edge," said Eamon. "You need to keep heading exactly sixty degrees northwest at all times; you should reach the road to Wylclyst in a day or two." He finished handing Jack the map and compass.

Jack was grateful. Despite Rosie's scheming, Eamon had done him no wrong and Jack was now beginning to remember all the rationality he had shown when

176

they first met. Perhaps he was one of the few whom Rosie had not manipulated with her magic.

"Eamon?" Jack said cautiously after thanking him. "Why do you remain there and take orders from her?"

To Jack's relief, he did not seem affronted at being asked this. If anything, he appeared relieved to finally be questioned. "It's not ideal," he said gazing into the distance. "But it's a purpose and an existence nonetheless."

"You know it can't last. The food's running out and if starvation doesn't take hold, dysentery and disease soon will," he said, knowing Eamon had probably worked this all out himself already. He nodded in agreement but did not offer a reply. Jack continued hoping that Rosie's magic did not have the same hold on him as it had on Oliver earlier that day. "You need to lead them out of there. Even without Rosie in charge, there are not enough skilled people to run the place."

"I have tried to recruit skilled folk; builders, farmers and so forth. She won't accept them unless she's able to ensnare them. She's not fond of disagreement," he said, at last, the tones of glumness in his voice unmistakeable. "I fear I'm unable to break her hold over them, nor could I lead them all away from her safely and discreetly."

It was not glumness; it was despair. Now Jack sympathised with Eamon more than he did himself the night Eva had carved her message into his back. Here was an honourable man torn between watching his community slowly descend into collapse and risking treason or desertion. He viewed neither as a practical option but seemed unable to bring himself to leave alone.

"Are there any others among the acolytes like you?" Jack said hoping he would know what he meant.

"I'm not the only one she hasn't ensnared but we're a minority. Less than twenty of us at my guess," he replied curiously.

"Talk to them, do whatever you can to keep those people alive for as long as you can. When I can, I'll return here and do what I can to help you all," he said not knowing what that would be, or how he would achieve it.

Jack could tell Eamon did not believe he was capable of helping, or perhaps had no idea how he was to keep the acolytes alive but gave him his thanks all the same before they departed.

Chapter Twenty-Six

Dear reader, I feel that it is ever my duty to tell you once more about the sordid affairs of that so-called freedom writer Bernard Crenshaw. I now have several accounts from various sources who understandably wish to remain anonymous, that the man is a notorious sodomite and frequent user of the services of male prostitutes...

Lyndsey threw the Chronicle aside in disgust, not wanting to know the finer details of Victoria Lionsgate's latest article or caring what Bernard Crenshaw did in his spare time. She was feeling satisfied and refreshed this morning and the gossip columnist would not spoil that for her. Michael was still asleep and snoozing peacefully after they had provided each other with a night of tender ecstasy. In the morning light, she thought him more handsome than ever. He looked so peaceful, she could not bear to wake him yet as she tiptoed out of the bedroom and downstairs to the kitchen to make herself breakfast.

She had patrol duty this afternoon. The last time Lyndsey had patrolled on a Sunday, it had ended up being the last time she had seen Jack. Lyndsey did not like where that thought may lead her and she cast it out of her mind.

She finished her meal and then made some for Michael before returning upstairs. She gently shook her husband by the shoulder then handed him his breakfast as he sat up, rubbed his eyes and came to. "Don't get used to this," she joked. "I happened to be up before you and thought you deserved a reward for last night," she finished with a wry smile.

"Thanks," said Michael, returning her smile and making a start on his porridge. "You didn't seem in much of a talkative mood last night. Is everything OK? I hope you're not worried about something."

Lyndsey hesitated, she yearned to tell her husband every detail of the last few weeks. How Eva Valmarque had been in their house and she had had a battle of wits with the cruel Warlock. How she had been working with the man Jack had arrested and he was not as he first seemed. How she was thinking about breaking into the house of Talamholean's wealthiest and most influential writer and that if she did, she would be breaking the law, and if she were caught, she would be facing at least a decade in prison with many a violent criminal whom she had placed there.

Lyndsey could not tell him. Not because she thought him untrustworthy. Michael had her trust more than anyone and the manner in which they had spent last night proved that. Neither did she believe her husband would try to talk her out of her plans. Michael always deferred to his wife on matters of legality, her occupation provided her with more expertise on the matter. Lyndsey would always defer to him on matters of medicine.

Lyndsey could not tell Michael anything, not yet at least as a matter of personal responsibility. Knowing what she had discovered had made her vulnerable to the Warlocks and possibly others in positions of power. Sharing her newly acquired knowledge would make others vulnerable. She had to keep it a secret, for now at least. It pained her to keep him in the dark but she knew it would pain her more to put him in danger unnecessarily.

"I've had a stressful week; I can't switch off after patrol sometimes. I was a bit shaken, but you did your husbandly duty last night and now I feel much better." She smiled and winked at her husband. The last sentence had at least been honest.

She kissed Michael goodbye and made her way to the barracks early. Lyndsey wanted to visit the shooting range as that often helped clear her head before patrol. The sun baked the cobbles of Graylenmouth with a warm glow. The smell of bacon and eggs coming from the market made her wish she had not already had breakfast.

The Sunday ambience was often a pleasant one in the streets of the capital. She had recalled that she had complained to Jack about a quiet patrol when she last saw him. She could not help but smirk hollowly at the irony of complaining about a quiet patrol which subsequently turned into the situation at Annabelle's.

She arrived at the barracks and greeted Captain Barry Johnstone who was working on the desk once again. She got changed into her uniform and riding boots. It felt good to dress appropriately after being forced to wear that humiliating uniform only yesterday. Attired in her jerkin, britches and boots, she made her way to the armoury and retrieved her pistols, as well as a decent amount of powder and shot, but not her cutlass, helmet and breastplate. She would not need them yet; her patrol was not due to start for another two hours.

She went back to the front desk and asked Barry for the key to the shooting range, which he handed over with a flattering quip about how if all guardsmen spent as much time there as she did, they would not need to be jealous of her shooting skills. Lyndsey returned his flattery with a humble smile and a thanks then made her way to the range.

It was only a little longer than twenty paces. Pistols were not accurate at any further distance so there would be no use in extending the single narrow corridor. A musket could perhaps reach a range of forty to fifty paces but the Guard had no use for muskets. When you rode horses and engaged in close combat, pistols and cutlasses served one's requirements best.

The floor ceiling and walls were covered with six inches of feather stuffed material like a badly made mattress, save for a few areas on the wall where oil lamps had been affixed, this was to prevent the spherical shots from ricocheting when one spectacularly missed.

There was a circular target at one end to aim at and a small table at the other where one could keep their spare pistols and ammunition. It was in short, a rather gloomy and windowless corner of the barracks. But windows were not useful in a shooting range to anyone.

Lyndsey lit the six oil lamps. There were three on either side of the corridor. Two where she would stand, two halfway up the corridor and another two by the target. She returned to the other end and loaded her pistols. She poured powder into the pan and closed it and pulled the hammer all the way back until it clicked satisfyingly. She raised the barrel and dropped the lead ball-shot in, followed by the remaining powder from the charge bag.

Pulling out the ram rod, she compacted the shot and powder down into the barrel as far as it would go, remembering to remove the ram rod and place it back into the holder beneath the barrel. She had been the only recruit in firearms training not to forget to remove the ramrod and discharge it when shooting. She had smiled with pride when Jack and the other recruits had to hang their heads in shame and coyly walk over to the targets to retrieve them.

She repeated the process of loading with her second pistol. Her father had taught her all the necessary skills and procedures of handling and firing a gun when she was a child. It came to her easier than most things. She took the first pistol and aimed it at the bullseye of the target, looking down the sight and lining it up. She slowed her breath. In. out. In, then out again and squeezed the trigger. Smoke filled her end of the corridor with a bang, and without a window for ventilation, she coughed aggressively as the white smoke sparked by the black powder filled her lungs.

She waded through the smoke, waving her hands around to avoid further retching and approached the target. A bullseye, almost a perfect one. It was slightly off-centre and to the left. This was good enough for her firearms instructor all those years ago. "A hit's a hit and a kill's a kill!" He was famous for saying but it was not good enough for Lyndsey.

True enough, a shot landed on a would-be attacker's head would guarantee a defeat over him, regardless of which part of the skull it had entered, but the conditions of the shooting range were not the same as that of a real fight. She had taken at least fifteen seconds aiming before she fired. Fifteen seconds could mean the difference between life and death in a real fight. Enough time for your opponent to shoot you first or charge you. Firearms instructors always lectured one on technique but never on the heat of battle.

Mercifully, situations where one needed to use a pistol on an attacker were few and far between for civilians and guardsmen alike, but Lyndsey tried her best to recreate them with her second shot, allowing herself no more than ten seconds lining up the sights before pulling the trigger.

The shot was as good as the last, only this time it was off-centre to the right, leaving a peculiar overlapping circle shape in the centre of the target. She reloaded her pistols and repeated the process trying to bring the time she spent lining up the shot to no longer than three seconds.

No matter how good you are, that doesn't mean there's no room for improvement, her father used to say to her when he carved targets onto tree trunks for an infantile Lyndsey to practise on. Not long after meeting Michael, he had told her that he shared her philosophy in his approach to medicine and she had fallen for him soon after. That philosophy they shared was what drove her now. Being the finest shot in the Guard did not count for much if you gave your attacker enough time to charge you and break your neck.

She reloaded her pistols, then fired them again and repeated the process many times until she had lost count. Time stood still when she practised shooting just as it did when she was alone with her husband. She had managed to get her aiming time down to around six seconds when Barry knocked on the door and poked his head inside coughing loudly at the thick powder smoke that now engulfed the corridor.

"Sorry to interrupt, Lyndsey, but there's a woman here to see you," he said nervously. Lyndsey had a reputation at the barracks for being semi-wrathful to anyone who interrupted her when she was using the range.

"To see '*me*'? Who is it?" Her stomach panged with fear at the thought of Victoria Lionsgate or her inquisitive dark-haired servant finding out she was a guardsman; or worse, Eva Valmarque now coming to threaten her at her place of work.

"A young woman, harlot I think, she seems quite scared," Barry replied nonchalantly. That ruled out the three women she feared at least, and Lyndsey was relieved and now somewhat curious.

"...and she's asking for me personally?" Lyndsey enquired.

"That's right."

Lyndsey left her pistols as she followed Barry and returned to the front desk to greet her mystery enquirer.

It was Molly. The prostitute from Annabelle's whom she had interviewed before and who she and Jack had met on that unlucky Sunday night.

"How can I help you?" She said sympathetically and now intrigued.

"Sergeant, thank god!" She said. "There's been another incident at...where I work. Please come."

Lyndsey knew they would have to leave immediately, lingering here any longer would look suspicious; she would inevitably have to explain to Captain Thompson why a whore was in the barracks asking for her personally.

"Allow me a moment to acquire my weapons and armour and we'll head there immediately," Lyndsey resolved. "You can tell me what's happened on the way," she said, wondering if Adam or another unfortunate had been magically manipulated again.

"I'm sorry, Sergeant, but there's no time. We must leave now before it's too late." Lyndsey knew it was against her better instincts, as well as protocol to follow Molly alone, unarmed and unarmoured into an unknown situation.

She was about to tell Molly that she needed to wait patiently while she retrieved her pistols and requested back up, or she would have. At that moment, Molly turned away from Barry's view and gave Lyndsey a smile and a knowing wink.

She was more than intrigued now. Molly wanted to get Lyndsey on her own and had created a false danger to do so. But why? Lyndsey resolved that she may have information that would aid her investigations. She turned to Barry. "Captain, I'm starting duty early today."

Barry shrugged. "Thompson won't give you extra pay roll for it you know."

"Don't I just," she acknowledged rolling her eyes and heading out the front door with Molly.

Despite the lack of apparent danger, Molly was eager to make haste back to Annabelle's. "What's going on, Molly?" Lyndsey said with a vigorous gait as she struggled to keep up with Molly's determined strides.

"We've got a client, he's there now. Annabelle thought you might like to question him but we don't have much time."

Lyndsey had suspected a harmless situation when Molly seemed at ease with her being unarmed. That is at least unarmed in the official sense. Lyndsey had not had time to retrieve her pistols from the shooting range. Even if she had, it would have been hard to load them while making her way to Annabelle's in a near sprint. She had, however, stuck to the promise she had made to herself of always being armed. The promise she made after her encounter with Eva Valmarque. She had managed to conceal a knife in her boot.

She may yet have need of it as well. It seemed that Molly and Annabelle had a client who might be able to help them with this mystery. Unarmed men were often possessed by a kind of uncontrolled ferocity when cornered. Lyndsey hypothesised that an unarmed, as well as naked man would doubtless become even more ferocious. Even the most educated men could become animalistic when robbed of their dignity with nothing else to lose.

"Who's the client?" Lyndsey asked at a near dash, her thoughts now turning to interrogation and questioning methods.

"Annabelle said not to talk about it out here in the open, she said it would be best explained when you get there," said Molly with a glance over her shoulder as they crossed the street.

The quick pace in which they made their way to the red-light district did not afford either of them much grace or dignity. They had to dodge and weave their way around members of the public in an impatient and jerky dance.

Annabelle did not greet her with the mischievous antics she had been expecting, instead adopting a more serious and professional manner. "Thank you, Molly. Good morning, Sergeant. Would both of you step into my office please?" It was more an order than a request as she turned about. She made no gesture to beckon either of them as though she knew they would do as instructed without needing confirmation.

Lyndsey did not like being ordered around. Especially by a civilian when on duty. On this occasion, however, her curiosity trumped her pride, and she followed Annabelle. Her office was unchanged since her last visit and was still every inch the garish image of a brothelkeepers place of business. Annabelle's usual austere dress sense stood out equally garishly in a room full of deep maroons and purple velvets.

"Thank you for coming, Sergeant," she said dropping her professional persona. "I'm sorry for the secrecy but it's crucial for the safety of my girls that as few people as possible are aware of this." Lyndsey understood, she had had enough experiences since Jack disappeared to know that Annabelle had done the right thing to keep their client a secret.

"Who do you have here?" Lyndsey had every intention of being polite and respectful to Annabelle and Molly, but in her enthusiasm, the question came out of her so quickly it was a wonder her diction did not falter. Only the rich and the powerful could afford the services Annabelle and her establishment provided. That tended to exclusively mean the men who ran the government and those who provided those men with funding in return for favours.

"He's upstairs. All in good time, Lyndsey, I need certain assurances from you first." Annabelle was frowning at Lyndsey as though she was a petulant child. Lyndsey composed herself.

"I'm listening," said Lyndsey. She did not like the idea that Annabelle had the power to set the terms of the interrogation. Nevertheless, it seemed she may have done Lyndsey a great favour and she decided to hear what she had to say.

Before asking after these assurances, Annabelle checked her windows were bolted shut before going back to the door and opening it. She stepped outside and looked around as though checking to see if someone was listening at the door before returning to the office, closing the door and bolting it. Lyndsey was wondering if the King himself might be in the room upstairs given the extra care Annabelle was taking to guard against potential eavesdroppers. Or perhaps…

"The man upstairs in Molly's chamber is the Prime Minister," she said in the tone of a near whisper in case someone else might still be eavesdropping.

"Don't worry, he's not going anywhere," added Molly seemingly reading Lyndsey's frown. "He has certain *tastes* which make it easy to detain him,"

Molly finished with a giggle. Lyndsey was relieved but whatever the Prime Minister's tastes were was the one thing she had no interest in.

She held no cards to speak of when it came to negotiating with Annabelle, but that would not stop her from arguing if she thought anything was unfair. Lyndsey fixed Annabelle in the steeliest stare she could muster. "What assurances do you need?" Lyndsey said, hoping that Annabelle was not going to try and ask for money or dignity from Lyndsey.

"Thanks to Molly, we have an advantage. You will be able to question him without betraying your name or appearance or without even revealing that you're a guardsman."

Lyndsey thought that sounded too good to be true and was about to ask how an earth they were able to achieve that but Annabelle cut her off. "Furthermore, the safety of my girls and this establishment is paramount, I shall accompany you to make sure you do not compromise that." Lyndsey felt patronised and opened her mouth, attempting a protest but Annabelle spoke once more. "Don't be offended, Sergeant, I know you have no intention of harming my girls but people make mistakes. I shall be a silent as the grave. If you say anything I don't like, then I shall give you a signal." None of this was ideal for Lyndsey but she did not deem it unreasonable either, it would have to suffice.

"Finally, the Prime Minister cannot know he is being interrogated. He believes and must continue to believe that he is enjoying the company of his favourite whore…" She made a gesture towards Molly. "…and her colleague." She nodded at Lyndsey and momentarily allowed herself a smirk.

"No! Absolutely not." Lyndsey did not bother asking Annabelle how she hoped to accomplish a seemingly impossible feat and did not care. She was a married woman. Undercover work was one thing, but going so deep undercover that she had to lie with another man was too much.

She wanted to resolve her investigations. She wanted to find Jack and she wanted to make Eva pay for her part in this and all she had made her suffer, but not at any cost. The ends did not justify the means and doing it at the expense of her principles, along with her marriage vows, was not something she was willing to do. She would find another way.

Before Annabelle could persuade Lyndsey, Molly gently placed a hand on her forearm. Lyndsey looked up. Despite a lifetime of serving men in such a way, Molly possessed an inner strength behind the eyes that most in her profession did not. There was only determination there. "You don't have to do anything. I'll do that. Just ask your questions, put on a playful voice and giggle every so often," Molly reassured.

Lyndsey thought it over. She still was not sure how any of this could be done, but now trusted Molly and was thankful to her. Ethically, Molly's proposal seemed to be a fair one and she slowly nodded in agreement, realising her newfound admiration for the young girl. Molly smiled encouragingly. "Your name is Lydia," she said opening one of Annabelle's desk drawers and taking a riding crop. Lyndsey was confused for a moment before she realised Molly had just given her an alias and nodded again in confirmation.

It was a short walk up the stairway to Molly's boudoir; this was not the living space in which Lyndsey had previously interviewed her. It appeared that whores more than anyone took the time-honoured adage of 'don't shit where you eat' quite literally. There were as many rich maroons and purples as there had been in Annabelle's office, along with red and orange lamps against velvet sheets draped over the four-poster bed. There was no duvet on the mattress itself. Instead, there was a politician, the most recognisable of all the members of parliament.

Lyndsey had never met the man but recognised him without difficulty. The cartoonists in both the Chronicle and the Gazette had made a good likeness of him despite the exaggerated facial features they had sketched him with as their profession required.

His wrists and ankles were tied individually to each of the bed posts by a short length of rope as he lay flat on his back with a blissful smile on his face. Were he not blindfolded with one of Molly's silk scarves, Lyndsey imagined his eyes would be glazed over in an equal measure of elation. Lyndsey had come across many men with peculiar interests when on duty, but this one was certainly new to her.

Now Lyndsey understood why Annabelle had opted for a more subtle approach to the interrogation. Robbed of his sight and his movement, Lyndsey would be able to get information from him without revealing who she was or why she was there. It was obvious that the Prime Minister had found himself in his current plight willingly. He was not a muscular man, but Molly was a petite and lean young woman. She would not have been able to bind the Prime Minister without his consent.

Annabelle stood in the corner, folded her arms, and leaned gently against the wall. A silent observer. Molly knelt next to the helpless Prime Minister on the bed.

"I hope you've not been misbehaving since I went away, my lord," said Molly in a mockingly stern voice that was not her own. "If you have, I'd have to punish you." She gave a sickly-sweet giggle and gently scraped the riding crop up his leg.

"Please, my queen, I'm a good man. Don't punish me," The Prime Minister playfully begged, turning his head to look in her general direction through the blindfold and grinning profusely, making his pleas even more unbelievable than the tones of mockery in his voice. Lyndsey wondered for a moment if she was watching a poorly acted play at the theatre.

Suddenly, Lyndsey had an idea, she had no inkling as to whether it would work, but it was a way in and she resolved to try it.

"*Queen?*" Lyndsey said in an equally severe tone that made her look so disgusted at herself that she was glad the Prime Minister was blindfolded. Molly looked shocked, she had clearly not planned on introducing Lyndsey yet, but thankfully, did not betray this sudden change in the proceedings. "*Queen!*" She repeated. "There's only one 'queen' in all of Talamholean, my lord, and that's the Queen Consort, Queen Winifred, wife to the King. To suggest that anyone other than her has that title is treason." She paused and looked at Molly. She had no idea if what she was doing would work and shrugged, hoping for a sign of encouragement or approval.

Fortunately, Molly grinned and gave her a thumbs up before mouthing the words 'go on'. That was all Lyndsey needed.

"Perhaps your treason deserves further punishment?"

The man seemed unsure of what was happening for a moment as he looked in Lyndsey's general direction. Perhaps her sickly-sweet voice was just as good as Molly's and he had wondered how she had moved around the bed so quickly and without the sound of a single footstep.

"This is my friend, Lydia," said Molly, rectifying his apparent confusion. "As you can see, she's twice as strict as I am. Which is just as well as you seem twice as naughty today, my lord."

"I beg forgiveness, my queen, but 'you' will always be 'my queen', that hag will not. Though I beg Lady Lydia's forgiveness."

She had hit the right mark and she knew it. The Prime Minister and the royal family were less than fond of each other, it was no secret. While he had continued to play his sordid sex game, he had not been able to suppress his personal grudges. Lyndsey knew this was the correct line of questioning to pursue.

"You are not forgiven, Prime Minister. I, Lady Lydia, am a royalist. You are a lowly advisor, a privy councillor. You are a peasant compared to royalty and not fit to lick the real queen's boots. Though you would be lucky to," Lyndsey said with a flourish causing the Prime Minister to look pained momentarily and it did not seem to be part of the sex game. It was as though he was withholding information he did not want to be concealed from his fake captors.

"The Queen Consort," he said after some hesitation and with a certain amount of trepidation. "Will not hold that title much longer. My Warlock has seen to it," he finished with the knowing smile of a powerful man.

Lyndsey held in a gasp and gave Molly and Annabelle a commanding stare, instructing them to do the same. The information was revelatory but she had to remain calm. Men were known for being hyperbolic or altogether full of falsehoods in the company of women whom they lusted after. Lyndsey had no idea how to proceed.

Fortunately, Molly seemed to know exactly how to confirm the recent information and took the perfect line of questioning. "If you're telling the truth, I'll reward you," said Molly gently caressing the Prime Minister's genitals through his undergarments. Lyndsey turned away and withheld a dry retch as she noticed the area start to bulge. "...but if you're lying to me, your real queen, I'll punish you as a monarch punishes insubordination."

With that declaration, Molly brought her right hand down upon the Prime Minister's cheek with such force that he howled with pleasurable pain as her slap echoed off the walls of the boudoir. It left a visible red handprint on there so obvious that Lyndsey wondered how he would explain it to his wife if it had not faded when the time came for him to return to her.

"I'm not lying, my queen. My Warlock had the idea to overthrow the King and replace him with another, Lady Alice."

"Liar!" Lyndsey hissed bringing the riding crop down on the man's chest making him howl in pleasure and pain once again. "You lie to your queen just to make yourself seem powerful. How on earth can you hope to pull off such an act of treason when Lady Alice is a hundred miles from here and parliament is not even in session." Neither of those would in fact make what he suggested unrealistic, it only seemed the best way to coax more information from the man.

Lyndsey had no admiration or respect for the Prime Minister but that did not give her any pleasure in inflicting pain on the man. He may have consented to the act but Lyndsey did not feel as though she was consenting herself. The fact that the Prime Minister seemed to enjoy his contact with the riding crop somehow made it worse for Lyndsey.

"I would never lie to you, my queen," pleaded the Prime Minister and answering Lyndsey's question but looking towards Molly. "Miss Valmarque planned the whole thing. She arranged for a guardsman to be disgraced in the line of duty with his commanding officer. We used that as leverage for him to travel to Wylclyst and deliver a message to Lady Alice. We expect her response any day now."

It took all the strength Lyndsey had not to beat the Prime Minister to death with the riding crop. She stood there frozen in a rage, battling internally with logical reason and reckless abandon before Annabelle saved her. She crept up to Lyndsey's side and gave her a silent maternal embrace. At least Lyndsey imagined that's what a maternal hug would have felt like, her own mother not having lived long enough to provide her with such.

Without a word, Annabelle led Lyndsey out of the boudoir and back to her office while Molly continued to taunt and mock the Prime Minister.

*

"How long has he been paying for these services?" Lyndsey enquired a few minutes later over a mug of coffee in Annabelle's office.

"Since he first arrived in the capital to take his seat in parliament. That was a long time ago before Molly was working here and when he was a young backbencher, but his tastes haven't changed." Annabelle was speaking about his sordid interests as if she were discussing her books to an accountant. This was something Lyndsey had trouble understanding, but she assumed that Annabelle had seen much and more in her line of work.

"So he's been indulging in this practise for well over a decade and not a single journalist or political rival has tried to expose him?" Lyndsey struggled with that more than she did with Annabelle's indifference.

Annabelle shrugged. "The only people with the power and influence to expose him have equally embarrassing secrets of their own. Bernard Crenshaw would tell you that the powerful are united in their obsessions with money and influence and he's mostly right, but he left out a third obsession and that's their perversions," Annabelle finished with a mild air of exasperation. Lyndsey could tell this was old knowledge to her and not the thing she wanted to discuss before she took a long sip of coffee. "Do you think he was telling the truth? About overthrowing the King and replacing him with Lady Alice?"

Lyndsey had not had long to think about that but she was certain the Prime Minister had spoken in honesty. The involvement of Eva Valmarque, the same Warlock's recent appearance in her house and the fact that Adam had met her on the night he uncharacteristically caused a scene in this very establishment, as well as the fact that Jack had been missing without a trace. There was no conceivable possibility that what he had said was boasting alone, it tied all these events together in a single explanation.

To make matters worse, it seemed that Captain Thompson, the commander of the Graylenmouth Guard, had played a part in this too. Lyndsey had never liked him but had always written him off as arrogant and incompetent rather than corrupt. When she had evidence, Lyndsey would ensure that he would be sharing a gaol cell with Victoria Lionsgate.

"Yes, it's too convenient not to be," she said and Annabelle nodded in agreement.

"I have to go soon but I need a couple of favours if I may?" Annabelle was silent, Lyndsey was not sure how to interpret that so continued. "Are men often that willing to divulge information in this establishment?"

"Oh yes, we provide services to a lot of rich men, and they like to show off to the girls how powerful they are." Lyndsey had suspected such an answer. Though not a pleasant revelation, it would serve her needs.

"What Molly has just achieved with the Prime Minister." She paused, not sure how to articulate what she wanted to say. "It was spectacular, thank her for me, will you, and when she next has an appointment with Julius Thompson, could you ask her to try the same again?" Annabelle understood what Lyndsey was getting at and nodded in agreement.

"Also, I need a small crowbar. Do you have one?" The fact that Annabelle found her the short metal implement without asking a single question regarding her intentions proved that she had been the right person to ask.

There was still one mysterious loose thread. Its name was Victoria Lionsgate and Lyndsey was determined to find out how she was a part of all this. When night fell and Michael was asleep, she would return to the window ledge outside her study.

Chapter Twenty-Seven

For the first time at night since departing the capital, Jack felt safe, or at least as safe as one can in the wild. A few miles from the northern border of Frostholme Forest, Jack lay by the roaring fire wrapped in a fur cloak. A parting gift from Rosie and seemingly one of the few finer things the acolytes had to give. Jack knew this had not been given in kindness. Rosie could not have been sure that Jack would not betray the existence of the commune to the Warlocks' Council one day, even if he did not know the exact location, and if he did, she would want to have been seen to have helped him on his way.

Jack allowed himself a smirk at the thought of pitting Rosie and Eva against each other in a battle of wits and magic. *A fitting end for all you've both put me through.*

The cloak was now one of the two fancy things he owned. Lying on the ground, his sword was at his side and ready to be used in the unlikely event that someone was nearby to attack him. This was doubtful due to the fact that he was a long way from any major road or settlement save for the acolytes, who no longer had any interest in him. The fire he had set ablaze would be sure to keep away any visiting wolves or bears, and without Eva's trinket, he could be assured of no further magical interference, for now.

Jack awoke to a dying fire at first light. The morning dew and wet ground had tinged his mood somewhat but after a good night's sleep, he would not let that significantly dampen his spirits. He hung his lavish fur cloak that he had been using as a duvet on a nearby tree branch and whacked it a few times, hoping to dry it. He then prepared himself a breakfast of the berries he had foraged the previous day. That had been the only food the forest seemed to offer in abundance and for once, he was thankful for it; knowing he was probably eating better than those on the commune.

He gathered his things, fastened his cloak, and then checked his map. He should make it to the northern edge of the forest before lunchtime. A little after that he would reach a village called Klathin, just within the borders of the Duchy of Wylclyst, Lady Alice's domain. There would no doubt be an inn in Klathin. He had no idea how he would be able to get a bed and a meal for the night without any money but decided not to think of that now as he returned the map to his pocket and set off, checking his compass to see that he was on the north-westerly bearing. The idea of returning to some sort of civilisation before nightfall encouraged him greatly with every footstep.

As predicted, Jack reached the north-western edge of the forest before the sun had reached its highest point in the sky. His mild discomfort at being a little damp upon waking now waning. The warm summer sun and the brisk walk he had tramped from this morning to his current location had given him a new enthusiasm for his quest. He approached a footpath where a sign pointed the way to Klathin in four miles. He would be there long before nightfall.

The path was a small dirt track, not well trodden and not the cobbled and well-maintained route like the northeast road. That did not dampen Jack's spirits however. The notion that he would be entering the Duchy of Wylclyst within the next few hours gave his journey a sense of finality that he was all too eager to achieve.

He was punished for his eagerness almost immediately. There was a twinge in his ankle as it twisted. His foot had been caught in a dead tree root. He went down quickly, mercifully outstretching his hands for protection which grazed and cut as he scraped along the ground.

He tried to stand, but that made the pain worse, so he crawled to the side of the path and removed his boot and sock to examine his injury. It was sprained, not what he needed right now. Perhaps not the worst possible outcome but far from ideal. He had seen other guardsmen suffer sprains before. It usually meant at least a day's rest before being able to walk again with the aid of bandages and cold water, neither of which he had. Unbelievably, it only seemed ridiculous to him now that he had not thought to pack or even been provided with medical supplies for his journey.

He slithered a little further along the side of the path to the shade of a beech tree and placed his injured foot on a rock, elevating it and hoping that he perhaps possessed an extraordinary strength that allowed him to heal faster than most men. If not, he would have to rely on the kindness of a passing stranger. It could be a while before that might happen. This was not an often-used path and he doubted he would see another traveller for a while. Even if he did, he could not be sure that anyone he chanced upon would be trustworthy; they were more likely to be like Horace and his gang in a remote area like this.

He shifted his body a little so that he was able to keep his ankle elevated and prop his back against the tree. He then removed his resplendent fur coat and carefully draped it across his legs. He hoped that in displaying such a rich piece of clothing, it would encourage people to help him in the hope of a reward. It was just as likely someone would slit his throat and then help themselves to his fancy cloak but there was no way of concealing it and he had no choice but to take the risk.

Being killed or robbed was not Jack's biggest concern however. Though it was not yet midday, the sun would inevitably set tonight, and Jack had no way of preparing. There was no adequate wood nearby for a fire and even if there was, he was in no fit state to gather it and build one. A fire was the best way to drive away wild animals looking for a fresh kill and without its aid, he would be defending himself in the darkness without the ability to move quickly.

Perhaps it was the warm summer day and the shade of the tree. Perhaps it was the initial adrenaline release and shock of spraining his ankle. Perhaps it was the exhaustion he had acquired exerting himself since awakening this morning, but Jack felt his head droop as he drifted into an unwelcome sleep.

He resisted; as his head began to sink, Jack caught himself. *No!* he thought. He could not allow that to happen. Not when he was so close, he steeled himself and looked up and down the path waiting and hoping for a kindly traveller to notice his predicament and come to his aid. It was his only hope now.

An hour or several may have passed but he heard it eventually. The slow clopping of horse hooves. More than one and slowly coming from the direction he had come himself. A wagon that must have come from the great north road that connected to the path he was now using. Why a wagon would leave the well-built road to travel a more secluded one did not fill him with confidence towards his predicament, but he had no choice to try and barter his way onto it. He would not have the time to hide now and was in no state to run.

He breathed a sigh of relief when they came into view. They were men in uniform, petit-magistrates. They did not exist in the capital due to the presence of the Guard but more or less did the same job on their liege lords' land. There were four of them. Two driving the wagon and two either side, outriders and each armed with a musket and rapier. This was different to the Guard's pistol and cutlass, though Jack assumed that law enforcement in the countryside was a different challenge to that of the narrow streets of Graylenmouth.

Not believing his luck, Jack maniacally waved his hands at the men and shouted, trying to flag them down. He had no idea what was on that wagon but he knew he had to be in it, or he would not be leaving the shade of this beech tree for a while.

The wagon ground to a halt as the driver saw him and pointed Jack out to his colleagues. One of the outriders dismounted and handed his reins to the other before slowly making his way over to the trunk of the tree where Jack had propped himself up. He had a hand on his sword hilt but that did not bother Jack. He knew as a guardsman that one cannot be too careful when dealing with strangers. As soon as he realised Jack meant him no harm, the magistrate would do his civic duty and aid Jack in his quest.

The man crouched next to Jack, not too close, having taken stock of Jack's sword he had made sure to place himself at least far back enough to be out of range of an arm and sword's length. His uniform was a navy-blue tunic with polished silver buttons and yellow lapels, topped with an equally navy-blue bicorn hat, britches and black leather riding boots. He was staring at Jack with a mixture of curiosity and apprehension.

"Is everything alright?" He spoke.

"It is now. I was travelling to Wylclyst via Klathin but hurt myself," he gestured to his ankle. "I'd be grateful if you could take me the rest of the way or anywhere in between. I can't walk right now."

The petit-magistrate did not answer immediately but instead observed his surroundings. His eyes made a rhythm of taking in Jack and his dishevelled appearance juxtaposed with the rare and expensive ferramus sword and his fine fur cloak. "You're very expensively equipped and richly dressed but you don't strike me as an aristocrat or rich man?" He said finally.

Jack could not believe he had been so stupid as to not consider what his appearance portrayed to others. A dishevelled traveller with a rich man's sword and an equally rich man's cloak would inevitably raise eyebrows. Now Jack would need to explain himself quickly, and not truthfully. If he told them he acquired the sword from a Warlock whom he killed out of revenge, they would arrest him on the spot and he would be before the actual magistrate. If he told them he had obtained the cloak as a gift from a witch in the forest who ran a secret community of devoted acolytes, they would think him mad and take him to the nearest bedlam.

Jack quickly decided that his best option was to tell the truth and admit his secrecy. Only without certain details. "I'm a sergeant in the Graylenmouth Guard. I'm on a mission for the Prime Minister to deliver a message to Lady Alice in Wylclyst. As you can see, I'm injured and I need your help. Will you take me to Wylclyst? You serve Lady Alice, don't you?"

The outrider seemed shocked by that story. Jack was not sure he was convinced but he was certainly considering all he had just been told.

"Lady Alice is the lord we serve aye and I can tell by your accent, you're from Graylenmouth, but that's about all I believe!"

"It's true!" He did not know what else to say.

"You wouldn't mind showing us the message the Prime Minister has for her ladyship then?"

"I can't," Jack said. "It's not in ink and quill. I have to show Lady Alice's Warlock—"

The man interrupted Jack with a hollow laugh and a knowing smirk. "You'd be amazed how many criminals try to explain things away with magic."

Jack sighed in exasperation; as a seasoned member of the Guard, he had to agree with the man. He was now starting to wonder if he had perhaps unfairly arrested some people during his time in the Guard. He noticed the bitter irony and poetic justice as it appeared the same thing was about to happen to him.

The outrider drew his rapier and pointed it at Jack's chest. He then called over to his colleagues. "Fetch some irons, lads, and help me carry this man to the wagon. There'll be another guest in the barrack's cells when we reach Wylclyst." For a fleeting second, Jack thought he saw an expression of relief behind his arresting officer's eyes.

He wondered if there was any possibility that he could one day make a career writing a traveller's guide to the holding cells of Talamholean.

Chapter Twenty-Eight

Before taking a late Sunday lunch with her beloved that evening, Lyndsey handed a pre-written letter addressed to Adam Pluff to a messenger at her door. She had grown to like the little lord despite his naivety and wanted to warn him and to keep him safe. The letter warned that Victoria Lionsgate would probably acquire a new and scathing interest in him from tomorrow morning and he may wish to leave the capital for his own safety. After handing over the sealed envelope to her messenger and tipping him five shillings, she closed the front door and made her way to the dining room to join her husband.

Michael Carter was eager to declare how bloated and exhausted he was after finishing the Sunday lunch he and his wife shared that evening. Lunch at teatime was a frequent occurrence for the two of them as it was often the only way to fit it in around their work. Lyndsey was glad of this. Her husband usually slept like a baby after large meals, she would not need to come up with an excuse for where she was going or what she was about to do. The lack of needing to create a lie somehow felt less awful to her than actually doing so.

*

True to form, Michael fell quickly into a deep sleep that evening. Lyndsey crept from their bedroom and got changed downstairs. Black clothes, she did not want to be seen. She dressed herself in a black linen shirt and black britches, as well as a black woollen cloak and boots. The shirt belonged to her husband and was too baggy; not safe for climbing up the first floor of Lionsgate Hall but she owned nothing as dark. It would have to do.

Just as it had been on the Sunday night she and Jack had been called to Annabelle's, the streets of Graylenmouth were nearly as deserted on this night too. It was a warm summer's dusk yet Lyndsey pulled her cloak in tight and threw up her hood. She could have raced there safely given the empty streets, but she was in no rush and wanted to remain inconspicuous. If Victoria Lionsgate decided to inform the Guard tomorrow morning that her study had been broken into, it would be best if Lyndsey had not been spotted this night.

It was unlikely to Lyndsey that the gossip columnist would risk liaising with the Guard. The woman had too many secrets and people like that did not risk talking to law enforcement. Nonetheless, it would not hurt to keep herself unseen as she cautiously paced along through the dark city, avoiding the illumination of the streetlamps.

Lyndsey reached Lionsgate Hall quicker than she would have desired, but she would not turn back now. She stood across the road from the mansion, her eyes fixed on a window at the very end. It was next to the now boarded up one she had broken on her last visit.

Checking the street was empty and pricking her ears up for any possible nearby footsteps or the sound of horse and cart, she crossed the street while removing her thick woollen cloak. With another glance up and down the street, she threw it over the nearest lamp, plunging the nearby area into darkness.

She tucked her baggy shirt into her britches, as far as it would go, hoping it would mitigate the likelihood of it snagging and causing her to fall to the cobbles. She climbed slowly up the granite columns. The wealthy liked to build their houses with the aesthetic of the ancient temples to create an illusion of their great erudition. All the better for thieves wanting to reach the next story without having to use the front door. Lyndsey had arrested people for committing burglary in the same manner and could not believe she was now using that same modus operandi.

She arrived at the window ledge on the first floor and, once again, shimmied along until she reached the window of the study, stopping every so often to pull in her shirt lest it catch on a gargoyle. She reached the window of the study and withdrew the crowbar she had borrowed from Annabelle, six inches and tapered at the end. It had been concealed in her boot.

She placed the end in the small gap where the edge of the window met the frame. She took a deep breath. This could be loud and wake up anyone in the house, or any guardsmen who were nearby. It had to be done quickly so the noise did not last long, Lyndsey was beginning to wonder how criminals were able to cope with this level of stress.

She was forced to pause her plans and briefly prostrate herself against the window, hoping her shirt's dark colour would at least compensate for its impractical size. She gripped the crowbar tight as a drunk walked up the street singing a very loud drinking song. He was taking three steps to the side for every one he took forward. Lyndsey cursed the man internally and willed him to reach the end of the street and turn the corner.

He stopped. His singing ceased. Lyndsey awkwardly jerked her head and saw a befuddled drunk swaying side to side and staring curiously at the now inactive lamp with Lyndsey's cloak enveloping it. Lyndsey cursed herself for choosing secrecy over swiftness and how it may now give her away.

The drunken man lost interest and continued down the street, turning left as he reached the end. Lyndsey breathed again with relief and returned her attention to the window. She placed the crowbar back in the gap and grabbed it with both hands, stood side on to the wall and drove it away from her with one swift push.

There was a crack of splitting wood and the window swung open. She grabbed it while maintaining her balance before it swung all the way around, not wishing to carelessly risk another broken window at this house. She stepped down into the study, quietly and carefully. As she gently brought the window back in, she examined the frame. As the noise had revealed, the metal catch had cut a deep groove through the wood. Lyndsey knew Victoria would awake in the morning to the realisation she had been burgled. She was glad she had warned Adam to get out of town to save him from her potential wrath.

Lit dimly from the remaining outside streetlamps, Lyndsey could still see that this was the lavish study one would expect to be owned by someone like Victoria Lionsgate. There was a large bookshelf by the wall that housed a private library of science and philosophy books. Lyndsey doubted Victoria had read any of them and assumed those books were there for status. The chandelier in the ceiling looked as though it could house two dozen candles which would brighten every small nook of the room when lit.

The piece de la resistance was the beautifully carved table by the window. Perhaps eight feet long and five feet wide with ornate legs carved into mermaids and three large drawers with wood carvings of kelpies on each one.

Lyndsey did not have time to hesitate, there was a candle and a tinderbox on the desk. She opened the small metal box and with flint and steel gave flame to the wick on her third attempt. She hoped no one was in the hallway to notice.

She tried the top and middle desk drawers first; there was nothing in either of them of value. Receipts and financial reports of Victoria's expenditures and salary. Useful information to Mrs Lionsgate but mundane to Lyndsey who could discern nothing incriminating about the information.

She tried the third, final and bottom drawer; it was locked. Lyndsey did not hesitate to force it open. The broken window frame would be enough to alert Mrs Lionsgate she had suffered a break-in. There was nothing to be gained in caution now. She carefully placed the crowbar between it and the one above then pushed it forward like a lever. It sprang open with a soft click. Lyndsey stood motionless in the candlelight for a second, pricking her ears for signs of anyone being alerted to her presence.

Nothing, no footsteps or screams, and no panicked cries of 'Intruder!'. Lyndsey allowed herself another sigh before bringing herself and the candle to the floor and pulling out the drawer to its fullest extent.

There were many papers, enough to weigh down a tax collector's coffers. It was almost a miracle the bottom of the drawer had not fallen out due to the weight of it all. Lyndsey carefully pulled the top sheet of paper close to her face and squinted, gleaning what she could in the candlelight and wishing there had been a full moon behind her in the night sky.

It was a journal entry, dated recently but it did not reveal much. There was mention of Eva Valmarque and the dealings the gossip columnist has had with her. About how it made Victoria sick to her stomach to libel Bernard Crenshaw, the freedom writer.

Why does she care about that? Lyndsey was not overly familiar with Crenshaw's writings but agreed with what she was reading in Victoria's memoir. Chiefly, that it was wrong to print lies and smut about a man who had not done any serious harm to anyone. The possibility that Victoria Lionsgate might have a conscience was enough to grab Lyndsey and she read on. Squinting and straining her eyes, she pulled the next page from the pile, and the next.

It seemed that both Lyndsey and Victoria had a mutual fear and disdain for the red-headed Warlock and Victoria was only trying to gain her trust to obtain more information, but to what end?

Lyndsey kept reading page after page, almost forgetting she was an unwelcome guest in someone else's house who could be caught and arrested any moment now.

When she reached the end of the newest memoir, she had to cover her own mouth, remembering at the last moment she needed to be silent. *No!* She mouthed silently but with such dramaticism that if someone else were in the room, they would have heard the gasp without doubt. "It can't be," she whispered, barely audible at the realisation she had misjudged Victoria Lionsgate.

Lyndsey felt sick; she should be working with this woman, not against her. That would be harder than ever now. She had just broken into her house and rifled through her personal information. She would be lucky if Victoria ever so much as looked at her again, let alone trusted her.

Lyndsey resolved to leave immediately. Perhaps she could return first thing tomorrow as a visitor and explain herself. Victoria Lionsgate was a decent woman who had made more sacrifices and taken more risks in the last five years than half the sergeants, constables and captains in the Guard. Perhaps she would understand if Lyndsey explained herself and maybe she would forgive.

Whether or not returning first thing tomorrow was a good idea Lyndsey did not yet know. What she did know, with certainty, was that she had to get out of here and return home before she risked offending the venerable Mrs Lionsgate any further. She returned the papers to the drawer and the candle to the table then blew it out. She then crept to the window's edge, planning to leave as she had entered.

The way was barred, the drunk who had nearly caught her earlier was walking back up the street and with him, to Lyndsey's dismay, were two mounted members of the Graylenmouth Guard. They were fully armed and armoured, ready for any altercation.

Shit! thought Lyndsey desperately as she tried to suppress her panic. She only had her concealed derringers and knife. No good against well-equipped and armoured guardsmen with pistol and cutlass.

She could lie her way out of it. Say she was investigating a break-in she had witnessed in her capacity as a citizen. That would not work; it would raise questions as to why she had done so without alerting the homeowner and using the front door. She could say she was doing some secret undercover investigating, though a quick interview with Captain Thompson would soon reveal that Lyndsey had not been assigned such work. Her only option was to hide well and hide fast.

The house would soon be under search. She would hope to hide in a place they would not think to check then slip away quietly once they had gone. She ran to the study door. It was locked. *Double shit!*

"Up there. See! The window's been forced open. I know it looks like they just forgot to close it but look what they have done to the streetlamp. Could have sworn I saw someone hiding on the ledge there earlier too!" A man in a slurry voice said that made Lyndsey curse the proverbial faecal matter a third time.

"Thank you, Ned, we'll deal with this now," came a more authoritative voice from the dark street below.

Lyndsey was frantic as the bell to Lionsgate Hall rang. She ran back to the window sill and gently peered through. The other guardsman was waiting in the street below and had removed Lyndsey's cloak from the streetlamp. It was too bright; the way out was guarded. The bell rang a second time. To add to her stress, footsteps were racing down the hall and getting louder. Lyndsey ran to the door and stood at the side of the frame next to the hinges. She could hide behind it as it opened.

Lyndsey knew that would not work and went back to the desk to hide underneath it. She heard a key enter the lock. She froze, she should have dived for the desk but her fear would not allow any more movement save to slowly pivot to gaze upon her captor.

Daisy, the servant girl, moved around the open door with a loaded and cocked pistol in her hand, pointing it at Lyndsey's heart. Without order, Lyndsey raised her hands and bowed her head shamefully, disgusted at herself.

"We knew you'd be back," the serving maid declared looking strangely triumphant with her shaggy black bob and silk dressing gown. "Victoria *will* find this interesting." She threw a pair of heavy iron manacles at Lyndsey's feet. "Put those on," she ordered. Lyndsey obeyed.

Chapter Twenty-Nine

It was rare to be awakened on a Sunday night, but even more peculiar to be awakened by sergeants of the Guard on patrol duty. Lionsgate Hall was situated in a well to do area that criminals did not frequent. If they did, there were more ostentatious mansions to catch their eye.

The urgency with which the butler had roused Victoria immediately made her think of Adam Pluff and his harlot of a cat burglar. She immediately went to wake Daisy before greeting the guardsmen, with no more than a simple order. "Guardsmen at the door. Break-in maybe? Probably in the room where it would hurt us most. Check if it's safe. Now!"

Without any apparent confusion or words of query, Daisy made her way to the study. The fact she had been sleeping with a loaded pistol on her dresser told Victoria that she had seen the necessity for vigilance in the last few weeks.

Good servants were hard to come by, but Daisy was not a conventional servant. Victoria had found her five years ago. Daisy had come knocking on the door as an out of work actor; the patron of the theatre she had been working in had gone bankrupt which caused him to withdraw his sponsorship. Daisy, with all her acting skills, had thought the next most similar job was servitude. She had mentioned to Victoria in her interview about how servants, just like actors, feign respect and politeness by pretending to admire people.

She had taken a liking to the young actress and decided to hire her on a whim. She was grateful for that whim now as she had no idea how she could have accomplished all she had achieved in the last five years without her help.

In a dressing gown, bed hair and slippers, Victoria did not feel appropriately dressed to receive people. The reputation she had cultivated for herself as an extravagantly dressed female dandy made it all the harder to greet guests in night-time attire.

She met the guardsmen in the drawing room where she had previously entertained Adam. It was dimmer than one would expect at night as the servants had not had time to light the oil lamps. There were instead only two small candles lit on the coffee table in the centre of the room. The three shadows of Victoria and the guardsmen eerily danced on the oak panelled walls like silent observers who did not wish to be seen.

While Victoria held no animosity for the Guard, she knew having them around the house would do her no good. She would have to get rid of them as soon as she could and without causing offence or showing impatience. Either of those follies might raise suspicion which the guardsmen would pass on to their captain, who would pass it on to the mayor and so on. Eventually, the Warlocks would hear of it and Victoria was not willing to have them snooping around her study.

"Gentlemen, I trust my butler treated you well. To what do I owe this visit?" Victoria addressed the Guardsman politely yet formally as the protocol of her station demanded.

The two guardsmen looked at each other as though one was willing the other to start the conversation. With their zischagge's removed their youth did not escape Victoria's perception. Neither could have been older than around twenty-six. Had Victoria not had other matters on her mind, she may have devoted some of the present investigating whether it was a good idea to enlist the inexperience of youth to enforce the King's laws.

"We've had reports of a break-in, my lady," one of the guardsmen eventually said nervously, breaking the awkward silence. He had done a good job to keep his voice calm but Victoria noted his refusal to make eye contact with her.

"Mrs Lionsgate will do, I'm no lady I'm afraid. What makes you think there's been a break-in?"

"We were informed by a member of the public; we also noticed an attempt to extinguish the lantern outside your premises and there's an open window on the first floor."

Victoria immediately thought of the study and began to feel conflicted. She had sent Daisy there as a precaution, not really expecting actual danger. Now she was glad to have sent Daisy yet feared for her safety. She could probably handle herself against that young slut who had tried to break in previously, but what if young Pluff had sent someone else to rob her this time?

"An attempt to extinguish the lantern you say?" Victoria said, keeping her voice calm as her thoughts were on Daisy's wellbeing. "How so?"

"Someone put this," said the other guardsman, lifting a black cloak he had been carrying under his arm, "over the lantern. It almost made your house look invisible from the street. If I were a burglar, I'd probably do the same."

Victoria did not know what to say. The young guardsmen were right, she had an intruder. She now had another problem to deal with as soon as she could find a way to send these men on their way without raising further suspicion.

"May we search your house and make sure it's safe, Mrs Lionsgate?" The first guardsman asked, again just as eager to not make eye contact as he had been the first time he spoke.

She did not know how to proceed and left a lingering silence. If she refused them that would lead to suspicion as it would not be long before everyone knew she had something to hide. Why else would someone refuse their help?

If she accepted them, and they searched the house, they may come across all she was hiding. Victoria was trapped with nowhere to go and her only option now seemed to be to let this silence drag out for as long as she could while the guardsmen exchanged confused glances.

"Are you all right, Mrs Lionsgate?" The second guardsman asked after some time.

"Not really, I must say this is all a bit shocking," said Victoria who was not lying, though her reasons for that admission were kept secret from them.

"Mrs Lionsgate, I'm sorry to press you but you must give us permission to search your house before we can do anything," said the first guardsmen finally who seemed to have now learned how to make eye contact with another human being.

Victoria would have to allow it. She did not like sacrificing the last five years of work but Daisy's life might be at stake and that was more important. Victoria gave her permission and the guardsmen made for the drawing room door. Before they could leave, Daisy entered the room with a determined look on her face. She noticed the guardsmen and then the cloak under the second one's arm.

"There it is," she said like a reflex holding an outstretched arm towards the cloak. "I've been looking for it everywhere. Where did you find it?"

Daisy was a talented actress but Victoria had known her long enough to tell when she was lying. The guardsmen could not discern her dishonesty from her tone but clearly did not find her story convincing. "This is your cloak, Miss? What was it doing on the lamp post outside?"

Daisy looked nonchalant. "I was in the pub with some friends this afternoon, I must've forgotten it. It's been such a warm day, I didn't notice I'd lost my cloak. Someone must have dropped it off after closing time." The ability Daisy had to conjure convincing stories from thin air never ceased to amaze Victoria.

The guardsmen seemed more convinced than they had a moment ago but still needed more clarification. "Why did he leave it on the lantern? That wasn't very clever."

"It must have been late when he came by and he probably didn't want to wake anyone," shrugged Daisy.

"Not the wisest place to leave it," said the first guardsman again. "We thought someone might be trying to burgle the house."

"They still might." The second guardsman declared. "There's a window open upstairs that may have been forced."

"I'm afraid that's my fault as well, sorry, gentlemen. Sorry, Madam Lionsgate, you had been working so hard in your study all day and I thought it smelt strongly of candlewax, and it's been a hot day. I thought I had better leave the window open to air the room out." Daisy risked a knowing glance at her mistress at that very moment that the two men missed. Victoria knew there was more to explain, she had not set foot in the study once today.

Victoria and Daisy bid them good night with all the airs and graces etiquette demanded and Daisy showed them to the front door. Victoria waited with relief and trepidation for Daisy to return. She had dealt with the Guard and stopped them from snooping around without arousing suspicion as Victoria had hoped. She thanked her lucky stars for that theatre closing down all those years ago.

When Daisy returned to the drawing room, Victoria could not help herself. "What happened? Was it Adam Pluff? Was it his bimbo?"

Daisy looked at her employer with a mixture of pride and sympathy. "I think we may have overestimated young Adam Pluff after all, and I think we've underestimated…" she hesitated. "…the 'bimbo'!"

Victoria had no idea what to expect next from her servant.

Chapter Thirty

Lyndsey had been so sure of Victoria Lionsgate's guilt; that had been a mistake. Now she would suffer for her error of judgement. She knew that as she sat in the study with her hands in manacles, Daisy, the maid, staring at her triumphantly down the long barrel of a loaded pistol. She wanted to shout, she wanted to cry but a sudden movement would probably result in Daisy pulling the trigger. Lyndsey's guardsman senses told her that the serving maid lacked her own skills and experience with a firearm, but that would be irrelevant at point blank range.

Lyndsey risked a sigh and Daisy brought a finger of her gun-free hand to her lips, shushing aggressively. She had no idea what to make of Daisy but had in the last few moments acquired a newfound admiration for Victoria, she was adamant to make her amends.

She might have a chance to at least acquire Mrs Lionsgate's forgiveness, which might count for something. It would be one less thing to worry about in the face of what was to come. Any moment now her own colleagues would be escorting her back to the barracks in chains to spend the night in a cell. The humiliation to herself and the Graylenmouth Guard for the apparent corruption of one of their own committing burglaries would soon be known around the city. What that news would do to Michael alone was near destroying her but she could not do anything about that now. She could at least make amends with Victoria Lionsgate.

"I'm…I'm sorry," she said. "I was mistaken. I jumped to conclusions, about Mrs Lionsgate I mean."

"*What?*" Daisy said, confused and irked. She had probably been expecting an attempt from Lyndsey to talk her way out of her predicament and if she still suspected as such, was not used to this tactic.

"I thought she was corrupt, that's why I've been investigating her, but it appears," she gestured to the desk, "she's doing more than perhaps anyone in history to deal with corruption, *and* has made sacrifices to do so."

"*Investigating.* Who are you?" Daisy enquired and Lyndsey knew she was after further explanation.

"I was investigating possible corruption. In doing so, I discovered Victoria meeting with Eva Valmarque, that's why I sent Adam in to talk to her." Daisy now raised her eyebrows in surprise and leaned a little towards Lyndsey. "I thought she was collaborating with the Warlock. It never occurred to me that she was undertaking investigations of her own. She may be the bravest person in all Talamholean."

Daisy looked confused and lowered her gun. She opened her mouth as though she wanted to say something. Then she closed it. She opened it again and this time, graced Lyndsey with two words. "Wait here."

She left the room swiftly, no doubt to get the guardsmen. Lyndsey prepared herself for the disgrace she was about to endure when Daisy returned with the two of them and they recognised her.

She sighed a final time and looked down at her manacles. They were almost identical to the ones she had to carry in the Guard save for one difference. The cuffs were inlaid with black tourmaline and Lyndsey knew why. Black tourmaline could reportedly give one an immunity to magic as it suppressed the powers granted to those with it. Though Lyndsey had no magic, these cuffs would have been equally adequate to detain one who did. Victoria Lionsgate was, not only noble, but clever also and prepared for every potential outcome.

She heard footsteps in the corridor again. This time getting louder. Two people, Lyndsey steeled herself. The guardsmen were on their way to a surprise, a surprise for them that would also be to her disgrace.

Ironically, Lyndsey was surprised instead as the first pair of footsteps belonged to a returning Daisy and the second to her employer. "Well, young lady," said Victoria Lionsgate. "It appears we both have a great deal of explaining to do."

Chapter Thirty-One

Jack sat in the back of their wagon, his ankle in a bandage and his wrists manacled on a short chain. His sprain had at least afforded him the luxury of not having to walk as the petit-magistrates were likely to do so with other prisoners. Nevertheless, Jack could not believe he had been so naïve not to think these men would regard him suspiciously.

The sword and cloak that had given him away were now stored with the driver at the front of the wagon. If he could acquire his sword, then the ferramus metal would be strong enough to break his chains and afford him an escape. *If* he could reach it, even without his hands shackled, he was unlikely to get far with a sprained ankle, at least the petit-magistrates had believed him there and put him in the wagon.

These men followed a harsher code than those in the Graylenmouth Guard. They had arrested him, that much was certain, but on what charge? He had not been told. Judging by the suspicion the arresting lieutenant had shown, it was presumably theft of some kind.

When an arrest was made in the Guard, you were to make your quarry well aware of the reason for his arrest as a matter of legality, but none of the four men he was now in the company of had given him any.

The thundering wagon jumped as it went over a rock and Jack's whole body went up then down for a second. He came to the hard wooden floor with a thud and winced, the pain it caused shooting through his injured ankle. The swelling had gone down since they had placed him in the back of the wagon but he would still need more rest before he could walk.

As the afternoon sun made its way across the sky, the carriage slowed to a trot as the ground became smoother. Jack wondered if they were planning to stop in Klathin as he had. They had not stopped since his arrest a few hours ago but even on horseback it would have been impossible to make Wylclyst already before the sun had set.

He leaned slowly and involuntarily to the side as he felt the wagon turn a corner and travel a further few yards down the road to a stop. He heard the sound of horses being hitched beyond the canvas. One of them came into the wagon to speak to him.

"You're staying in here tonight," said the petit-magistrate clearly proud of his rank uniform and station.

"Where are we?" Jack enquired.

"Klathin," said the man in the blue uniform. "At an inn. Lady Alice won't permit her enforcers to spend money there, so we're all staying in the stables. There'll be one of us outside this wagon to guard you all night." The last statement was meant as a warning, Jack noted from his tone of voice, but his captors need not have been suspicious. Jack's ankle made an escape impossible and even without the injury, he was making use of a free ride to Wylclyst, his ultimate destination. He just would have preferred to make the journey as a passenger and not a prisoner.

A bucket was brought into the wagon for Jack's toilet, not an experience he wished to relive but he would make do. After eating the food they brought him, he carefully slid into an uncomfortable lying position and attempted to sleep.

Having a sprained ankle and one's hands chained made that difficult, making it harder still was the argument two of his captors were having just beyond the canvas. They were straining to keep their voices down over what seemed to be descending into a heated argument.

"We're to take anyone we find from the capital straight to Lady Alice or to Miss Emily, those are our orders," said one guard speaking quickly as though he did not have much time to get his point across.

"I think the lieutenant wants to question him before we do. He wants to know what this is all about," replied the other guard trying and failing to keep the tremble out of his voice, "and I don't blame him. Lady Alice ordering us out this far to pick up a traveller is one thing, but when we came across someone who fitted the description, I nearly lost my mind."

"If we don't take him straight to the manor when we reach Wylclyst and Lady Alice finds out, we'll be charged with treason," said the first man again with fear and urgency.

"...and if we disobey Lieutenant Bates' orders, it's mutiny," finished the second guard with an air of finality and defeatism.

That was a new development, and the new information did not make his situation any better. Not if this Lieutenant Bates got his way. If he did not, then perhaps Jack might be able to ride in this wagon all the way to Wylclyst and the completion of his mission. A preferable option despite the fact that he was currently under arrest.

Jack postponed the notion of sleep while contemplating ways in which he could convince Lieutenant Bates to take him straight to Lady Alice and not their cells. He would need to know the man's reasoning for not following her orders. Was he a stickler for the proper procedure? Perhaps, but not knowing the man very well, it was equally likely that he had his own, more sinister agenda and possibly one of a more political nature.

Without a blanket, mattress or pillow, and the lack of anything nearby to use as substitutes, Jack hopelessly tossed and turned upon the rough wooden floor of the wagon to find a comfortable position which would help him fall asleep. *I've slept on roadsides, in forests, and in ancient stone circles but this empty wagon is by far the worst and most uncomfortable!*

At that thought, Jack sprang up into a sitting position with such force, he was glad his ankle forbade him from standing as the noise would have alerted the guards. An *empty* wagon. Why was it empty? It had been since they had arrested him; they had been stopped here in Klathin for several hours now and made no attempt to load it with anything. They also intended to set off quickly at first light. No one goes to the trouble of carting a wagon around unless they mean to transport something. *Or someone; me perhaps?* Jack thought.

He had met these men, these official men, on a rare path that was not well used. A path that had led from Frostholme Forest. Had they been expecting him? How well did Lady Alice trust her own lawmen he wondered. Lieutenant Bates could not be trusted and nor could Jack risk an attempt to appeal to his sense of duty. Not while Jack was unsure if he had one. There were the two guards who he had just heard talking, he would have to hope to get one or both of them on their own tomorrow.

Fortunately, Jack had that opportunity in the morning when one of his guards came to take his piss pot. Jack greeted him good morning which he returned, upon which Jack recognised his voice as one of the men who had been talking last night. He had very short and shaved hair as all his captors did. Jack assumed that such a haircut was mandatory for Lady Alice's guard. Otherwise, it would

211

have been an incredible coincidence. Jack knew he would not be here for long and desperately seized the brief opportunity he had been given.

"What do you use this wagon for usually?" Jack asked. This wagon was far too small and flimsy to be used to transport prisoners. Jack knew that no answer to this question would help his situation, but he thought an attempt at small talk would probably be a wiser way to start before blindly leaping forward into more serious matters.

The guard paused and looked bemused. This was perhaps the last reaction Jack had expected from the man. He had been prepared for a stern request to be quiet or a complete refusal to acknowledge his existence altogether; Jack and Lyndsey would often react in one of those ways when a man they had arrested was in their custody. Instead, he hesitated and stared into the middle distance and paused himself, as though he was conflicted between following protocol and getting something off his chest which had been irking him.

"We travelled to the edge of Frostholme Forest with it," he eventually said, looking surprised at his current behaviour. "Bates said we had orders from Lady Alice herself to travel there and wait for someone. He said they might not want to come with us so we'd need the wagon," he finished abruptly, realising he had said too much. He looked straight at Jack with a great sense of fear in his eyes. He clearly found the whole situation unfathomable.

The young petit-magistrate clearly found his confusion to be too much and left promptly before saying another word. Jack was left to chastise himself for once again being so naïve. He had been desperate for help and aid with his injury, he had not thought to question the obvious convenience of meeting Lady Alice's own enforcers beyond her lands and jurisdiction. She had been expecting him, or at least hoping to expect him and sent an advance party. That is why they had orders to take him straight to Lady Alice.

His current predicament, while not ideal, did at least take him to the end of his quest. There was only one hurdle, which was Lieutenant Bates. He had his own motives. He was in charge of this advance party but only seemed to have been keen to follow his orders up to a point.

When Jack had unwittingly revealed upon their meeting by the side of the road that he was the one they were looking for, Bates knew he had his man and had no need to arrest him or put him in manacles, yet he had done so anyway. Why? Was Bates a curious man who just wanted to know more information or was he serving another plan? Or another individual? None of those scenarios seemed pleasant to Jack.

Jack knew he would be unlikely to deliver his message to Lady Alice without Bates being out of the way but had no idea how to do that. He needed to think of something, and he needed to do it quickly. Escape was not an option.

Though his ankle felt a little better after some sleep and he might be able to risk a walk, running would not yet be possible, and even if it were, he would be in the wilderness unarmed with no food and his hands chained together. He would have to talk the other three men into fleeing from their commander or, if it came to it, commit the mutiny they feared doing so.

He hoped it would not come to that but perhaps he could speak on their behalf when he reached Lady Alice and save them from the hangman. All three men would have to be united in their insubordination. Only then would they feel most confident to stand up to the lieutenant. It also had to be done quickly so that Bates would have no time to talk them out of it or fight back.

*

As the day went on and the wagon rolled forward, Jack thought he heard nervous whispers from beyond the canvas. He knew the men were scared at the prospect of disobeying their lady's orders at the behest of their commanding officer. Jack decided that this was probably the best thing he could work to his advantage. He would have to use this to create the opportunity he needed.

Not long after midday, the wagon and its guards stopped by a stream, his captors allowed him to sit outside. His ankle only allowed him to hobble slowly and they would have nothing to fear from an escape attempt, they would not need to watch him closely. Jack felt a little humiliated as he staggered and struggled to balance with his hands in manacles. He slowly moved from the back of the wagon to the side of the stream and lowered himself tentatively into a sitting position.

Lieutenant Bates was not nearby, apparently, he had wondered a little further along the stream and out of sight in order to give him some privacy for urinating. Jack assumed that he could not have been in the wild for very long, having been fending for himself long enough to know that after a few days, you did not care if others saw you pissing. Manners could hang when one was trying to survive in the wilderness.

One of the younger guards handed him bread which was accompanied by some fish that they had caught. He noticed that one of them was in the stream up to his waist, waiting patiently and catching a salmon out of the stream every so often, before throwing it to his companion on the riverbank who would gut and cook it over the fire. Jack wished he knew how to catch a fish like that, as well as prepare it for cooking. It would have made past events a good deal more pleasant.

Thoughts of gutting and catching fish would have to wait though. Bates was out of earshot and he may not have another opportunity. He swallowed a mouthful of salmon, cleared his throat and began to play his game. "How long have you served under the lieutenant?" He asked the Guard to whom he had spoken this morning, who was sitting nearest to him and to his right.

The young guard looked as nervous as he had done at daybreak. He did not want to answer but it seemed he was more troubled by not answering altogether. He eventually spoke, slowly and nervously. "Not that long, only three weeks or so. It's weird, he just arrived at the barracks, apparently on a transfer. Some of the older petit-magistrates were a bit annoyed, they'd been hoping for an opportunity to apply for promotion and then a new officer just arrived out of the blue." Reiterating this information seemed to be revelatory to the young man, who seemed to be becoming aware of how strange their current situation and orders were.

Though he did not show it to his captors, this revelation was more of a shock to Jack. Three weeks ago was when he had first met the Prime Minister and Eva Valmarque. That was the start of his quest, it had led him to this moment and all he had experienced since. The lieutenant had not only arrived among the petit-magistrates when his journey began, but he had also led the expedition to find Jack. He did not have a good feeling about Bates' motives. He had to act quickly. He could waste no more time – they would reach Wylclyst by nightfall.

"Don't take me to your barracks," he declared as though back in the Graylenmouth Guard and giving orders of his own to a constable. "Take me straight to Lady Alice's manor. I will ensure she is made aware of your bravery. Give me your names and I shall pass them on so she knows which men serve her loyally." Jack felt guilty at the hollow promise that he had delivered with such conviction. He had no idea what to expect from Lady Alice and whether she would care to reward those who were loyal.

He spoke with such authority that the man in the stream stood up straight, ignoring the countless salmon that leapt passed him in and out of the water. The three of them exchanged nervous glances, forgetting Jack's existence for a time as they all seemed to hesitate on the offer he had just made them.

Their ultimate decision would have to wait as the man by the fire gestured ahead, alerting them all that the lieutenant was returning, apparently having concluded his business. The men dropped their nervous glances and began to discuss their favourite ales and taverns in Wylclyst. Bates reached the area where they sat and ordered them to return Jack to the wagon. Jack had come close to convincing them, he had failed; he cursed Bates for not drinking more.

Stuck in the back of the wagon with no idea how much time was passing as it moved along the road to Wylclyst, Jack wiled away the hours wondering what fate awaited him once he reached the barracks.

Bates now seemed a mysterious individual. Was he a crazed loyalist like Leopold Braske or was he just a common criminal somehow abusing his power as a petit-magistrate for his own gains? Either way, Jack had no strength to fight and no means of bartering his way out.

He wondered if he would ever find out the contents of what Eva Valmarque had carved into his back and what his fate would have been once Lady Alice had received those words. Would she cast him aside or reward him, and which one would have been preferable to Jack? From what he had heard about Lady Alice, she was a spoiled aristocrat with little regard for others, be they commoner or gentry. Having the favour of someone like that could potentially be worse than their wrath. He would never know now.

*

The wagon hauled to a stop with a jolt an indeterminate amount of hours later. Two petit-magistrates helped him from the wagon and brought him before Lieutenant Bates. The sun was setting with an orange glow and they had stopped at a fork in the road. There was a sign where the lieutenant was standing, telling travellers that the town of Wylclyst was three miles along the road to the right and that Wylclyst Manor, the residence of Lady Alice, a mile to the left.

Something in the lieutenant's plan had changed. They were a good distance from either destination. Why stop here, and now?

Jack fell to his knees as the guards released him, his ankle unable to bear his weight for too long. Bates was plunging the ramrod into the barrel of his musket while the other three gathered around, surrounding him unnecessarily as escape could not be achieved by Jack.

Bates returned the ramrod to its holder before addressing his men. "I know you're scared, and I know you're suspicious of me." Jack had realised what the lieutenant was about to do the second he saw a musket being loaded. Receiving clarification only made him feel impatient as he willed Bates to shoot him in the head and grant him an instant death. "This man is in league with the Prime Minister," he continued with a point of the finger in Jack's direction. "He carries a message to Lady Alice, recruiting her to aid him in deposing our King. So I ask you, men, will you join me and defend King Wilfrid?" He cocked the musket. "Or will you stand against me and die a traitor?"

Jack had no idea why this man was staunchly loyal to the King, or if he was right about the contents of the message. He was probably a lunatic just like Leopold Braske or an idealogue like Rosie. Either way, Jack no longer had the patience. He waited for the others to buckle so that he could meet his fate.

"How...how do you know all of this?" said a voice from behind Jack. It was the nervous guard he had spoken to in the morning. His voice was full of confusion.

"I'm the King's spy, he placed me in the petit-magistrates when he suspected a plot against him," replied Bates. Jack knew that could not be right. As far as he was aware, his mission was known to none but himself, Eva Valmarque, the Prime Minister and Lady Alice. Even if the King had somehow been alerted to their plans he would not have been able to despatch a spy this quickly.

It mattered little. Informant or not, this man was clearly insane and not going to let Jack live.

"You turn up out of nowhere, recruit us for a sinister mission, then propose to kill a man without due process?" The guard said who had been catching the salmon earlier. "Are you mad?" He finished.

"Aye, I'm Lady Alice's man, not the King's and you've just shown me I'm right to make that choice," said the third guard. Jack felt bad for assuming they would cave as he had done a moment ago but knew it would not save him. They would not be able to overpower their commander before he pulled the trigger.

"Does he speak for all of you?" Bates said after some hesitation.

"Aye," replied the fisherman.

"Aye," replied the guard Jack had first spoken to.

If Lieutenant Bates was offended or shocked, he did not show it. Like many a madman, his face and body language showed nothing but indifference. "So be it," he declared as he gazed along the barrel of the musket that was pointed at Jack's forehead and pulled the trigger.

Chapter Thirty-Two

Jack flinched as white smoke filled the air and the bang pierced his eardrums, but he felt nothing. He did not appear to be harmed at all, save for the ringing in his ears. He looked up and saw Bates lowering the smoking musket that he had just fired over Jack's head. He then withdrew a sapphire from his pocket, closed his eyes in concentration as he grasped it and removed his shoes.

Bates' features were becoming more feminine and his hair was getting longer. A few moments later, a beautiful woman was standing there with long blonde hair and grey eyes. "Your loyalty has been noted, gentlemen," she declared to his captors. "Lady Alice will be informed that you three are to be trusted. You may return to your barracks. Leave the prisoner here."

The effect was jarring, seeing a woman in Bates' uniform and standing where he had stood a moment ago. The guards obeyed despite the fact they seemed as bemused as Jack and made their way back to the wagon, riding off in the direction of Wylclyst and leaving nothing except for Bates', or rather, the Lady Warlock's horse.

"Sergeant Sweep, my apologies for the deception. It is sometimes necessary to know who your enemies are," she said removing the key to the manacles from her pocket and throwing them to him. "Please lie down and I'll see to your ankle."

Jack removed his manacles then took off his boot and lay back on the grass as he was bid. He felt a soft woman's hand gently grasp his ankle and felt the muscle de-swelling, back to its normal size. He stood up and thanked the woman who then summoned her horse with a whistle. The mount trotted to her side obediently as she placed a bare foot in the stirrup and hoisted herself up.

She made a nod to the back of her saddle. "I hope you're not too proud to have a woman take the reins," she said with a feint grin. Jack was not, and he was even less willing to walk to their destination, wherever that may be, but every fibre of his being told him he should not ride with this woman. She had

218

manipulated him and played an elaborate mind game with both him and three others. To what end, he had no idea, but he could not refuse her. He may be free of the manacles and his injury but he was still unarmed and on foot.

He ascended the horse and put his arms around her waist. Despite his mistrust of her, doing that still felt bolder than when he faced Leopold Braske in single combat or fought Horace and his gang. To his satisfaction, she did not protest or resist his touch and she urged her horse into a slow walk.

Jack was not sure whether he could trust her and was even less certain of the fate into which he was blindly walking. A part of him did not care, even though she had just had a gun to his head. *That was not her,* he hoped to himself, *she was playing a part for Lady Alice.*

She had to be the Warlock who would reveal the message on his back and they could only be on their way to the manor now. Jack wanted to ask her this not only for clarification but also because he was desperate to talk to the woman he had just found himself alone with. Jack was a little shocked with himself. Only a few minutes ago, he had been preparing himself for what had seemed like an inevitable death. Now that felt like a lifetime ago as his mind seemed to be elsewhere and focussed on other matters!

"I adopted the identity of Bates when Eva Valmarque told me to expect you," she said eventually and relieving Jack of the burden to start a conversation. "I suspected you might be coming through the forest when you found a way to remove the tourmaline. I took those men to come and find you." She paused waiting for an acknowledgement from Jack who did not reply. He was not sure if this was out of his hatred for Eva or the effect this beautiful woman was unwittingly imposing on him.

Despite the nervousness he felt in her presence, Jack did eventually realise what needed saying. "Why the theatre? The petit-magistrates were as eager to take me to Lady Alice as you are. Why invent the story of taking me to Wylclyst and being the King's spy?"

She laughed and though she was mocking him, Jack found the sound to be a pleasant one; Holly had laughed like that. "Am I eager to take you to Lady Alice? How do you know I'm *not* the King's spy?"

"If you were, I doubt I would still be alive, and we're heading to Lady Alice's residence now, aren't we?" He concluded.

"You're an observant one, Sergeant Sweep. Eva may be a scheming harpy, but she knew what she was doing picking you," she said more to herself than him.

"She didn't pick me, I got in trouble for arresting the son of the Home Secretary and she took advantage."

She laughed again. "Do you really think that was a coincidence? Would you have accepted this quest if your circumstances were not dire? Eva must have knowledge of nearly everyone in the capital and how to manipulate them for her needs. Whatever situation you found yourself in when you met Eva, would have been her doing as well."

Jack felt he had been punched in the stomach and all his breath had gone out of him. He did not like that revelation but had to concede that the blonde woman was right. The bizarre state the man he had arrested had been in that night. The fact that Annabelle knew who he was despite never having met him. It had all been orchestrated.

"I'm Emily by the way, since you forgot to ask," she said cheerily and without offence that brought him out of his seething daydream. "...and you're right, Jack, I am here to get Eva's message from you and to Lady Alice."

"And the answer to my other question if you will?" Jack said, his thoughts now on his opinions of Warlocks with the memory of Eva's message carved into his back. "Why the theatre?"

"The petit-magistrates are the closest thing Lady Alice has to an army. An army she may have need of soon. Every now and then, it's a good idea to find out if there are any who are disloyal. Those men were young and their allegiances were uncertain. I recruited them to accompany me as it was the best way to test them. They passed."

Jack did not want to know what Emily would have done if the three young men had failed her test.

Chapter Thirty-Three

Jack and Emily reached Wylclyst Manor when night fell. Though it was now dark, Jack noted the sight of the building to be an underwhelming one for the residence of an aristocrat.

He had been expecting a grand sandstone or granite mansion like the buildings in which the higher classes resided in the capital. This was unpretentious in comparison with equally ordinary architecture. It was a red brick building, only two stories high and perhaps three rooms wide. The roof was thatched like a farmyard cottage. Jack thought this to be a larger version of a house that would usually be occupied by a rural commoner. Lady Alice was probably aware of her more meagre dwelling and perhaps embittered.

Emily and Jack dismounted before leading the horse to a paddock where other horses were roaming free amongst the grass. She then escorted Jack to the front door. "I'll show you to your room, Sergeant. Lady Alice has had a busy day and will no doubt want to wait until tomorrow before meeting you."

Jack could see no use in arguing, he was tired himself and desired to rest. Emily handed him over his sword then showed him to his room. It was as plain as one would expect from a house this size, but Jack would not complain. It still provided sufficiently more comfort than the wilderness or the back of a wagon.

He undressed himself and made his way to the bed immediately. His fatigue and his apprehension battled with one another before he could close his eyes. He did not know what tomorrow may bring. Lady Alice, for all he knew, may throw him in the dungeon or have him executed once he had delivered his message and no longer became useful to her. Jack tossed and turned until his exhaustion got the better of him and he fell asleep.

*

221

Neither Emily nor any of the servants woke him the next morning. The light of the morning summer sun penetrated the thin curtains and gently pried open his eyelids. Someone had laid some clean clothes out for him and he donned them accordingly before heading downstairs to where he assumed there would be someone waiting for him. Save the butler, there was not.

He was bid to sit down and await breakfast before being passed an envelope. It contained a message from Emily that informed him Lady Alice was holding court today and would not be receiving him until the evening. He was to make himself at home at the manor until attending upon them in the drawing room tonight.

The butler returned shortly with a generous plateful of bacon, sausages, eggs and black pudding. Jack enquired as to where Lady Alice kept court and was told it was convened in a disused barn four miles to the north of here. Four miles was not a long walk and Jack thought it might be a good idea to observe Lady Alice before actually meeting her tonight. He also wondered if holding court in a barn could embitter her further.

After breakfast, Jack made his way out the house and northwards up the footpath. By daylight, the residence of Lady Alice looked just as ordinary but certainly more resplendent as the morning sun bounced off the red bricks, cutting a striking figure against the rich green grass of the surrounding grounds. Towards the horizon, Jack saw a large black and white building which he assumed was the actual manor. For some reason, Lady Alice had chosen not to occupy it.

Unlike many aristocrats, Lady Alice seemed to put her grounds to good use, much of the grassy land had been dug up to accommodate vegetable patches where turnips, parsnips, and potatoes seemed to be thriving in preparation for the harvest in a few months' time. Fields were all being ploughed with oxen as seeds were being sown. He would pass wooden fenced paddocks of varying sizes in which cows, pigs, chickens, and sheep would be residing and grazing. Jack wondered who on Lady Alice's staff was a knowledgeable enough farmer to do all this.

Other than Emily and the butler, he had not taken note of any other employees; he assumed she did not have the space for anyone else, let alone the funds to employ someone who could run all of this.

He eventually reached the barn. A large wooden shack just off the path with thin wooden walls and an equally thin wooden roof. It had clearly been reopened hastily as a means of accommodating the lady's court. There was a large queue of people waiting to go in to petition Lady Alice with their grievances. Jack found his way in through a side entrance into an area where other members of the public were spectating.

Lady Alice was sitting on a grand wood-carved chair which itself was placed on a high wooden dais. Her clothes stood in contrast to the modesty of her accommodation. She wore a rich satin blue gown, flowing with golden embroidery. The stitching resembled hawks, her coat of arms no doubt. She wore so much jewellery on her wrists, neck and fingers, that it was a miracle she could sit up at all. Not that she was sitting in the proud and regal manner one had come to expect from nobles. She was slumped in her splendid chair at a slouch like a sullen child.

Her back was hunched halfway down the back wrest and her legs forward. Her long and curly black hair, which she wore down, was being played with by both of her hands as she fiddled with and twisted it at the end. She seemed more interested in her hair than her surroundings.

Emily was standing on the dais to the left of her lady looking every inch the regal one despite her bare feet. She was wearing a bright yellow dress to match her golden hair and had the posture Jack would have expected from Lady Alice. With her left hand she gently stroked a white stone set into a ring on the forefinger of her right.

"Next!" Lady Alice barked as the previous petitioner backed away from the dais in several bows.

"Mrs Tavish of Wattling Street," declared Emily as a young woman approached the dais. "She's here to plea for a lowering of taxes."

"Aren't they always," sneered Lady Alice not taking her eyes off her hair.

"Please, my lady," said Mrs Tavish, her hands clasped in front of her as though she were praying. "I run the local inn and customers are not showing up since a four-shilling levy was imposed on ale."

It appeared for a moment as though Lady Alice had not heard her, her attention on her hair before she eventually spoke. "When did I impose that tax, Emily?" She asked her Warlock, still refusing to look away from her curls.

"Six months ago, my lady," Emily replied clearly displaying enough dignity and poise for both her and her mistress.

"And has violent brawling been a problem since?"

"No, my lady," answered the Warlock.

"The tax still stands." She then took her right hand away from her hair momentarily to make a shoeing motion with her fingers towards Mrs Tavish as though she was an overly affectionate cat. Two guards had to help the innkeeper out as the bad news had not left the woman in a joyful state. She was sobbing like a grieving widow when she eventually left the building but it appeared that Lady Alice had not heard as she barked for the next petitioner.

Jack had seen enough; Lady Alice was no more a friend to the people than the Prime Minister. No wonder he wanted her in the capital, they had the same sneery disposition towards those they considered inferior. Jack decided to make his way back to the manor. A pleasant house that most people would consider themselves lucky to live in but had clearly turned Lady Alice sour. Jack's anger at the way she had treated the innkeeper was only matched by his fear at the realisation that she would probably throw him to the dogs later tonight after he had served his usefulness.

He thought about running again as he had done when he was in the back of the wagon but just as it had then, it seemed fruitless. He could walk now and he had his sword back but he did not know these lands which were Lady Alice's own domain and would not get far. It would not be long before he was found and brought back to her, which would make his ultimate fate worse than whatever Lady Alice had planned for him this evening.

Upon his return, Jack decided to attach his sword belt. He knew he would not be able to fight his way out, yet having it at his side emboldened him. He felt he was silently defying his hosts and showing them he would not be intimidated no matter his fate. He whiled away the hours until dinner exploring as much of the house and grounds as he was allowed before being received by Emily in the dining room at sunset.

Emily seemed to look more beautiful by candlelight than by daylight. Jack had noticed this, regardless of the heavy pit in his stomach he was feeling about his imminent end. She had joined him for supper but Lady Alice was nowhere to be seen. It felt as though he was a condemned man having his last meal before being sent to the gallows.

It was at least a decent meal; Jack ate roast chicken with an abundance of vegetables all roasted and served with gravy. "Is this all farmed on the grounds?" He asked Emily. Conversation with her now seemed less daunting to him as he assumed this would be his last night among the living.

"Well noticed." She smiled. "I see you did not waste your day in a tavern as many a visitor does. My lady will be pleased."

Jack doubted that would be enough to please Lady Alice so decided he would risk being brazen. "I have no money, and even if I did, it would have been hard to spend an entire day drinking with a four-shilling ale tax?" He widened his eyes at the last statement, hoping Emily would take his point.

Instead, Emily laughed. "I thought I saw you there among the public this afternoon. I must admit you probably did not get the best first impression of her ladyship. Try to forget it before you meet her."

Jack did not think forgetting his first impression of her would make much difference. He would meet her soon and Emily would have ways of revealing the message on his back, with or without his cooperation. Then she would have no further need of him.

They finished their meals and Emily led him into the drawing room. Lady Alice sat by the fire with her feet up on a pouffe and fanning herself like someone about to feint. Jack noticed she looked different by candlelight too, but not for the better. He had not seen her close up earlier today and now noticed many a crow's foot and blemish upon her skin. This afternoon, Jack would not have aged her over thirty, but seeing her in this light, it was impossible to put her at under forty-five.

Emily introduced him and she nodded, not taking her eyes off the fire. Jack was not certain how to react so gave an awkward bow before Emily offered him the chair opposite Lady Alice. He took it clumsily, not knowing how to sit. The noble lady was as slouching in her posture as she had been this afternoon. To mirror her may seem patronising but to sit properly may seem condescending. Jack, eventually, decided on an awkward slouch of his own which was similar but not identical to hers.

"I hear you have a message for me?" Alice eventually sighed with her attention still on the fire.

"Yes. Yes, my lady," Jack corrected himself nervously. "From the Prime Minister." He was more unsure than ever how to behave. She seemed to be the maddest person he had encountered so far. One wrong word, a wrong tone of voice or wrong gesture could seal his fate and not for the better. Unfortunately, he was none the wiser as to what those were.

Lady Alice finally withdrew her attention from the fire and smiled weakly at Jack. "The Prime Minister may have given you the impression it was his idea, and he may even believe that himself, but it's Eva Valmarque and the Warlocks' Council behind all of this, mark my words. Whatever they're offering me, it will not come without conditions I daresay. Isn't that right, Emily?"

"Yes, my lady. The Warlocks' Council weave their web in every aspect of governance, among the aristocracy and the wealthier of the commoners," Emily answered her mistress standing at her side like a loyal guardian.

Despite her weak smile and slouched posture, Lady Alice seemed to flip her entire personality around at that statement. There was a look in her eye and a spark in her voice that Jack had experienced before. A look and a tone of defiance, of disdain. Disdain for Eva Valmarque and the Warlocks.

Suddenly, Jack was wondering if he had misjudged Lady Alice. He still had no admiration for the way she treated her citizens but the fact that she shared his contempt for the Warlocks was at least something in her favour. He was also just as intrigued by Emily as he had been when they first met. It appeared that despite her power and station, she despised the Warlocks. That had to be a story worth knowing.

"Alas, thank you for making it all the way here alive and in one-piece, Sergeant," said Alice, who was now sitting up and appearing more in the present and less contemplative. "Now, the message if you please. I imagine we'll need Emily's help to read it?" Jack nodded, confirming the location of Eva's message on his back.

Emily bid Jack to remove his shirt and lie down on the leather sofa. She did not order or force him as Eva had done all those weeks ago, but he did as he was bid. Partly out of fear of offending Lady Alice but mostly, he had to admit to himself, he wanted to read it.

He had carried that message on pain of death and encountered fire spewing Warlocks, bullying ruffians, mad acolytes, and even bogus magistrates to get it here. He wanted to know what he had risked his life for.

Emily's hand against his back had a much softer touch than Eva's and Jack felt a strange tingle that he wondered might not be entirely due to the effects of magic. He then felt a short sharp pain across and between his shoulder blades, though instantaneous, it still made him wince.

"Sorry," said Emily with genuine sincerity as she ran to the desk to grab a quill and parchment to copy down the message. She bid Jack to stand up again and put on his shirt. Lady Alice did not take long to read the copied message Emily had just handed her before tutting and handing it to Jack. He wondered if she had meant to give it to him. Then, an encouraging gesture from Emily told him that she had. He looked down at it and read:

For the attention of Lady Alice, the government no longer functions. The King must be deposed. It is time to claim your birth right.

Jack was angry. That was barely three sentences. He had expected to be delivering a complex and comprehensive top-secret document. He could have memorised that; he could have carried that in a concealed scroll that could have been easily hidden or disposed of in the event of his capture. Molly, Simon, and Lucas had died for it. Three sentences that took less time to read and understand than one of Victoria Lionsgate's ridiculous articles. Did Eva Valmarque have such a sense of self-importance that she thought Jack and his ilk lacked the basic intelligence to memorise such a short request?

Neither Emily nor Lady Alice seemed surprised or felt the need to confirm anything to each other or to Jack. He began to feel a sense of frustration in the lingering silence. "Do you have a claim to the throne, my lady?" Jack said eventually unable to help himself.

"I am King Wilfrid's cousin. He never had any siblings which makes me his heir, after his sons that is. I imagine the Warlocks don't want them on the throne for fear that they are too much like their father. Making me the only available monarch they can crown. The fools." She sneered at the last two words but that was the last vestige Jack saw of her sluggish demeanour. She was now standing up straight by the fire, a determined look on her face like she had a mission to prepare for.

Her answer had given Jack more confusion than before. She was in the line of succession and an alternative to the King. The Prime Minister and the Warlocks wanted her as monarch. He had thought their plans may be of that nature the night he had received the back message, but he had not expected Lady Alice to respond with restraint, and perhaps reluctance.

"You…you don't want the throne then, my lady?" Jack said eventually, partly eager to understand her reasoning but mostly desperate to break the silence and keep her mind off the question of his usefulness to her.

"It's not a question of whether I want the throne. It's a matter of ethics, mine versus that of the Council." She looked at Jack enquiringly to see if he understood. Jack did not but he feared appearing stupid would not be wise. In the absence of his reply, she continued. "I have no children; I am not married and even if I was, I am past childbearing age. When I die, who becomes monarch then?"

"I imagine they've not thought of that," said Jack. "They're just desperate to end the gridlock between the Prime Minister and the King." Jack was unable to mask the uncertainty in his voice with that last statement. He was no scholar and he felt like a fraud discussing politics.

"Exactly. They *haven't* thought of it," said Lady Alice. "The petty fools are incapable of looking to the future and are prepared to potentially create a succession crisis one day just to solve a minor nuisance in the present." She was now working herself into a rage.

Jack's opinion on Lady Alice had changed a great deal since he had seen her this afternoon, but he still was not sure whether she was to be admired or feared. Nevertheless, he had to keep asking questions. This was all still a mystery to him, and he needed to understand. "Why do you think they would prefer you on the throne to your cousin?" He had hoped that did not sound condescending and he had taken a moment to think on his phrasing before asking the question. Desperate not to offend.

Jack was relieved to see that she did not appear slighted and instead seemed flattered. She fixed him with a grin and a glint in her eye. Jack had never seen a member of the aristocracy show their pride in such an unrestrained manner. "You saw me this afternoon dealing with the innkeeper. I stand by my decree, brawling is a curse that needs to be discouraged even if I had to beggar the old woman, but I do feel bad about my behaviour and the way I carried myself. That persona is an invention."

Lady Alice was cunning it seemed. Jack was not sure why she felt the need to adopt such a demeanour and did not think he would get an answer if he asked. The fact that she felt guilty about making Mrs Tavish cry but did not show remorse about taxing what little recreation the common man had, did not help to make his opinion of her any less conflicted.

He only had one more question to ask. "Will you do it, my lady? *Will you claim your birth right?*" Emily almost gasped. Jack had never been entirely sure how to behave in front of the upper classes, but he had clearly made a faux pas.

"I have been suspecting a request like this since news first reached us of the tensions between my cousin and the Prime Minister," she said. "Emily and I have discussed it. I could do a better job of ruling the country than many expect. I would have to remain as subversive as you saw me today. I could appoint an heir long before my death, and perhaps we could rid the nation of those irksome Warlocks." Emily smirked approvingly at the last comment and glanced down at the white stone in her ring.

Lady Alice now seemed resolute as she fixed him with an even more determined stare. "Yes, Sergeant, I will take my cousin's throne, but not for the Warlocks or their Prime Minister, but for Talamholean. Emily, inform the General and the Admiral; our forces sail for Graylenmouth as soon as we are able."

There was a pause. Perhaps she was waiting for a cheer or a clap from Jack and Emily. Jack did not know what that revelation meant for him. Probably nothing pleasant, he was a disgraced guardsman who had just delivered his message and given up his only thing to barter his life for. He was about as useful to Lady Alice as he now was to Eva Valmarque and the Prime Minister.

"Emily tells me you are clever, Jack." It did not escape his notice that she had used his first name for the first time this evening. "You also made it all the way here which tells me you are capable, perhaps you are loyal too? Will you aid me to take the throne? Will you swear your sword to me?"

Jack was shocked. He had not expected this, and it was a much better fate than he had been predicting for himself. He doubted that he could be much use to her, though he was not going to admit that to her here and now. He was hesitating, he still did not know what to make of her.

He did not like the way she regarded those without wealth and power but that made her no different from most of her class. On the other hand, she shared his disdain for the Warlocks and that was at least to be admired. Swearing an oath of allegiance to someone you were unsure of was unwise. So was refusing their offer when alone with them and their powerful sorceress. There was one option open to him. It was not the wisest course of action but perhaps it was the only honest one.

"With your permission, my lady, I would like to accompany you back to the capital and aid you any way I can, but with all due respect, I cannot swear you my sword until I have spent more time in your presence."

He had been foolish. It was not clever to tell aspiring royalty you were unsure of their character when face to face. Even Jack knew that. She would not allow him to live, she would have him flogged or imprisoned for what he had just said.

To his surprise, she smiled, and not a hollow or sarcastic one. "You appear to be wise as well," she said. "I hope in the coming weeks, I can prove to you that I am worthy of your sword."

*

Jack went to his room that night not entirely sure if he was lucky to be in this situation. Lady Alice seemed to have a bizarre and bipolar character about her. He wondered if being in her presence on their return to the capital would make him any safer than he had been on his journey up here.

It doesn't matter, he thought as he hung up his sword belt and dressed for bed. This was the situation he was in now. He would see how it played out as there was no wiser nor more practical option open to him.

He settled into bed and was about to blow out the candle when there was a knock at his bedroom door. He froze. It was late and a servant would probably announce himself instead of solely knocking.

It appeared he had frozen for too long. Emily entered the room without waiting for an answer and closed the door behind her. Without waiting for a reaction from him, she sat herself down at the foot of his bed. Jack would be lying to himself if he were not pleased to see her. He guessed, however, that the reason for her visit would not be the one that excited him the most.

"You've certainly gained her favour." She smiled, placing her hand affectionately on his knee. Although separated by the duvet, Jack could not deny the pleasure her touch gave him. He bravely made eye contact with her and almost got lost in her grey eyes. "You have made a good first impression," she continued.

"I know nothing of politics and war," he stated. Not wanting to offend Emily but not wanting to risk humiliating himself at a later date. "I'm effectively a *'brawler'*." He had hoped the emphasis on that last word would get his point across.

Emily understood his subtle meaning. "She is a little ignorant to the plight of the masses..." She admitted. "...but she has a good heart. She will rule well. Perhaps if you were at her side, you could help her understand the needs of the less fortunate. She does not confuse advice with insult."

Jack now knew the reason she was here. To convince him to swear his sword. Lady Alice may not have been offended by his reticence to show loyalty, but she was going to try every dirty trick to get him on her side. Either Lady Alice had seen something unique in him or she needed all the support she could muster. He would find out which soon enough.

"I'll admit, using taxation to force the poor into good behaviour is maybe not the worst thing a ruler has done, but I'm not sure I like it," he declared, knowing it was not wise to offer his opinions so openly to her, but she had played her game well. She was beautiful, and they were alone together in a bedroom with a very comfortable and accommodating feather bed.

"She would not dislike you if you told her. She may disagree but she would not make you regret challenging her. Is that not a queen worth serving if she rids us of the Warlocks' influence in the process?" If she had rehearsed that speech, Jack could not tell. Lady Alice inspired great loyalty in Emily and if what she had told him was true it was certainly a point in her favour.

There was however one logical flaw, which Jack could not help but point out: "Couldn't your magic deal with this, without the need for an army or even a long sail to the capital? Why not use pyrite and a score of sharp shooters to enter the Palace or the Warlocks' Tower and rid yourself of all your enemies in a single evening?" A violent suggestion that he would never have orchestrated or participated in, but Jack wanted to see what Emily's response would be.

"An interesting plan. Even if that were possible it would be unwise to seize the throne in such a manner; parliament would not give their support to a queen who began her reign with an act of barbarism."

Jack hoped political and practical reasons were not the only thing preventing her from avoidable bloodshed. "Why is it not possible?" he asked.

"Pyrite can only transport someone with magic and even then it can only be used once per lunar day. It would also require a huge amount to travel the distances you're suggesting. A small amulet will only transport the wearer a distance of about two-hundred yards. That's just one of many weaknesses the council have hidden from you for centuries." Her affectionate exterior was beginning to falter as she spoke the last sentence through gritted teeth, with an obvious scorn behind her eyes.

"It must be a rare thing to be a Warlock who despises the council," said Jack eventually after he had contemplated Emily's declaration.

"Just like a guardsman who doesn't like drunken brawling being discouraged." She grinned back at him as she regained her charming composure and reached behind her dress to unbutton it. "Are you tired?"

"That depends on what you're suggesting?" Jack said returning the grin with a wry smile and leaning towards her.

She returned his kiss with great passion and before too long, he was kissing her neck and removing the rest of her clothes. Jack knew she would be beautiful in her nakedness but that did not make the reveal any less pleasing to him.

This was probably the least wise course of action he had taken since leaving Graylenmouth but he did not care. He knew this was only happening so that Lady Alice could give him a compelling reason to remain and serve her, but tonight all his attention was on Emily. Only she mattered.

Chapter Thirty-Four

Lyndsey never thought she would get to wear a dress this expensive or eat in a restaurant so fancy. If this was Victoria Lionsgate's idea of undercover work, then Lyndsey had been doing it wrong up until now.

She had attempted to order one of the more affordable meals from the menu but Victoria had insisted she try the venison and ordered it for her at the Chronicle's expense. Not for ostentatious reasons but rather to stay convincingly in the role of the incredibly flamboyant and noble 'Lady Peel' that Victoria had assigned her.

The fictional socialite Lyndsey portrayed, was sitting in a booth at 'The Baroness Mermaid', Graylenmouth's most expensive and up-market restaurant. Victoria was sat at the same table with quill and paper, pretending to scribble down notes every now and then as she 'interviewed' Lyndsey. She would gasp hysterically every time a waiter came near with exclamations such as 'Oh how saucy!' and 'My, you never?' to keep up the pretence, but their time was otherwise spent in silence.

In the next booth, which was separated from them by a thin sheet of glass, sat Daisy. Looking ravishing in a dress not too dissimilar to the one Lyndsey had worn when she played Adam's servant. Though she appeared much more comfortable in such attire than Lyndsey had. She was unrecognisable in a red wig and the fake freckles she had painted on her face. She was checking her appearance in a small handheld mirror while she waited for Neil Monks. Lyndsey had been concerned that this man would trade the information to Daisy as though she were a prostitute, but Victoria had assured her it would not come to that.

The small bell at the top of the front door chimed softly and a middle-aged man walked in. He looked around, spotted Daisy, and made his way to the table. Daisy had made sure he would have to sit opposite her and near Victoria and Lyndsey, then they would hear him clearly without having to dodge his gaze.

Lyndsey knew it was better to hear him but looking at the back of the man's head felt awkward. Victoria had said it was probably for the best as they needed to appear as though they were not eavesdropping.

"I must say, I was thrilled to receive your letter, Miss Chavell," said the man enthusiastically. "I've always been an admirer of yours and I've read all your interviews in the Chronicle." Daisy gave the man a convincing sweet giggle then fluttered her eyelashes, equally convincingly. She was good at this; Lyndsey could not help but admire her.

"So kind. It's always nice to meet a fan." Daisy's voice seemed several octaves higher, and Lyndsey wondered how long her vocal cords would be able to keep up the act. "I must say you disappoint me," she added in playful tones that told the man her character was anything but disappointed. "When I heard you were a royal footman, I thought you would be dressed as one. I do so like a man in uniform."

"Maybe I'll wear the uniform at our next meeting," the man said lecherously and Lyndsey thought she might regurgitate her venison.

Lyndsey realised that such small talk would be necessary, especially if they wanted him to divulge the information they needed without raising suspicion but that did not make her feel any less impatient or revolted.

"Serving the King must make one feel so noble? If only by association," said Daisy. "I'd love to meet him but alas, he's no patron of the theatre. What's he like?" Daisy seemed to have the ability to ask the right question without alerting her subject that he was being interrogated.

"He is a noble man indeed and it is an honour to serve him," replied the footman this time with some trepidation. It seemed that despite Daisy's flirtations, he would not be easy to break.

Daisy was not deterred. "Such a loyal man. I hope the King knows how lucky he is to have you at his side, especially at a time when that awful Prime Minister is saying such nasty things about him." She added a tear to the end of her sentence which she wiped away gracefully with a handkerchief and a couple of short sniffs. "Forgive me, young man, loyalty is hard to come by in this day and age, and one cannot help but be touched on the rare occasions when one finds it."

Lyndsey would have stood up and applauded Daisy if it would not have given the whole act away. She had cried a real tear. The man responded by reaching across the table to grab Daisy's hand and bring it to his lips for a kiss. At least that is what she assumed was happening given that the man had his back to her.

Lyndsey tensed; she had her derringers concealed up her sleeves. A fight was not ideal and it would expose all they were trying to achieve but she was not willing to keep Daisy in danger. The girl was exercising her skills, she was doing it perfectly and Lyndsey would exercise her own if the necessity arose.

Noticing Lyndsey's sudden tenseness, Victoria calmly placed a hand on her forearm and gave her a reassuring look, telling her to trust Daisy.

"I could be loyal to you too, Marie," said the footman. "We are both unmarried, my footman's salary is not a small one and I have…other means of income. We could be happy in a maisonette here in the capital."

Lyndsey had to suppress a laugh this time. Her own husband had been a lot more romantic when he proposed, and they had been courting for longer than a few minutes when he bent the knee to her. Lyndsey assumed that famous actresses were perhaps more accustomed to this behaviour, especially when they were dressed as Daisy was.

"You're very kind," said Daisy after another sob. "But as you know, I will be forever married to the craft. Such is the life of a thespian."

"I'm sorry," said the man. "I shouldn't—"

"Not at all, not at all," Daisy interrupted, though Lyndsey agreed that he really 'shouldn't'. "It's always flattering to be admired and it may please you to know that I'm staying at the East Gate Inn while in the capital," she said with a playful wink. "Do you know it?"

"I do," said the footman, understanding Daisy's implication enthusiastically and completely oblivious to the fact that she had been sobbing only a moment ago.

"I fully understand that you cannot tell me all you do for the King, but maybe you can tell me something. What responsibilities do you have?" Daisy had now fully returned to a playful tone, subtly pushing her chest out and fluttering her eyelashes faster than what seemed humanly possible.

"My chief responsibility is to be the go between," said the man proudly.

Lyndsey, Victoria and Daisy all knew this but Daisy had managed to steer him towards the subject that interested them most. She had also leapt forward in the interrogation with great success. He may have only offered up a small revelation, but Lyndsey knew enough about royal protocol to know that he should not have said that.

When Lyndsey had reconciled with Victoria that night in her study and agreed to become her ally, she had been interested, though not surprised, to hear her tale of the missing trade bill at the hands of the Warlocks. Not long after that, Daisy's surveillance work had uncovered that the man responsible for the elusive bill, Neil Monks, was a fan of the popular actress 'Marie Chavell'. It did not take long before Victoria devised a plan.

"Forgive me," flirted Daisy. "An actress is so busy, that she often remains ignorant on some matters. What is a 'go between'?"

"When parliament passes a bill, and it arrives at the palace, I take the bills to the King and return the ones he vetoes to parliament."

"How exciting! You must be a well-trusted man, Neil, I imagine many an unscrupulous person would like to cosy up to you. For you hold so much responsibility. It's a good thing you can't be bought." Daisy had taken care not to sound accusatory, but it had sadly had that effect. Perhaps the fact that she had risked using his real name made it too much for him as he spilt his wine and swore loudly at his mistake.

Lyndsey thought she would definitely have a fight on her hands this time. However, rather than loudly plea his innocence or lash out and attack Daisy, he broke down into uncontrollable sobs of his own.

Daisy knew exactly what to do. She stood up, walked around the table and sat down next to him. She put an arm around him and kissed him softly on the cheek. "I'm sorry," she said apologetically. "We actresses have an affinity for the dramatic. I did not mean anything by it."

"I...I didn't want to do it." He sobbed. "I had gambling debts. They must have known. They approached me at home two years ago. They said if I made sure the occasional bill went missing and brought it their way, they would pay off my debts. But now I'm in debt to 'them'."

Lyndsey felt bad for wanting to laugh at the man earlier. She knew Eva and the Warlocks would not consider themselves above blackmailing a desperate man, but the revelation did not disgust her any less.

Though she did not require it, Neil had just confirmed all Victoria had told Lyndsey regarding the trade bill. She was not working as a guardsman at present, but she thought as one. She had the evidence in the form of a statement, the next step was to arrest, and if the suspect resisted arrest, Lyndsey would do her duty to uphold her protection oath.

Chapter Thirty-Five

"Excellent, Daisy," Victoria said as the three of them sat in the coach on the way back to Lionsgate Hall. "Another splendid performance, it's a pity I have no bouquet for you."

"It was incredible," said Lyndsey with genuine adulation before turning to Victoria, "but there are a few things worrying me."

"Yes?" Victoria said approvingly and with a curious smile. Since reconciling with the young Lyndsey Carter, she had grown to like her. She felt guilty for misjudging her after learning she was going above and beyond to find a missing friend. She had found her insight and skills most helpful. She and Daisy, between them, knew how to go about their investigations in secret but nothing of how to fight.

She had always worried what she and Daisy would do if the need arose and now Lyndsey was here to help in that regard. Mercifully, the need for the young guardsman to use her skills had not yet come, but Victoria was deeper into this investigation than she had been in any before. Lyndsey's presence could not have come at a better moment.

Lyndsey frowned. "Aren't you worried the Warlocks are going to find out Neil told Daisy what he's doing?"

"They may find out he's told someone and that could endanger him," she had to concede. "I'm not proud of that. Had I known he was going to break down so dramatically, I would have chosen somewhere more private for the meeting," Victoria spoke gravely. Men usually restrained themselves from such emotional displays in public, the burden of all the Warlocks had put him through had obviously taken its toll on the footman.

"I know the guardsmen who patrol near the palace. They're good men, I'll ask them to keep an eye on Neil," said Lyndsey. Victoria nodded approvingly. Lyndsey, it appeared, was well suited to the Guard as she took her protection oath seriously. "But aren't you worried they'll trace his confession back to you and Daisy?"

Lyndsey's selflessness was admirable. Afterall, she had been there too and could just as easily have the recent events traced back to her. Lyndsey had put herself in danger to no lesser extent, but she seemingly had not noticed.

"If anyone overheard that confession, they would have seen him say it to the actress 'Marie Chavell' and not one of us," said Victoria proudly.

"That's another thing," said Lyndsey. "What if Neil does go to the east gate inn looking for Chavell? Won't that look suspicious when he finds she's not there?"

Daisy chuckled. "She doesn't exist, apart from when I play her that is."

Lyndsey looked confused. "But he wrote to you, and he said he had read interviews with her."

"Both of which are true, we set up a fake postal address for her and Daisy collects the letters from the post office. A young actress will always be appealing to lonely men and it comes in handy more than you think when we're investigating. I only wish we could sift through all that fan mail quickly. Then we'd have found him a lot earlier and with much less hassle." Victoria took a long pause to admire the astonishment on Lyndsey's face.

"As for the interviews, which gossip columnist do you think conducted them?" Victoria added and Lyndsey seemed impressed. It reminded her that the grind of her usual day job could not always be a force for bad and sometimes made everything worthwhile.

Lyndsey said her goodbyes and departed the carriage as it passed through the City Centre, her own house being a short walk from there. They rolled on towards Lionsgate Hall and Daisy took off her red wig to look at it thoughtfully. "You know, I don't like myself as a redhead. I'll say this for Eva Valmarque, she pulls it off well." Victoria rolled her eyes affectionately. That was not enough to redeem the woman of her treasons.

Thinking now of the red-haired Warlock, Victoria believed it would soon be time to arrange another meeting. Confronting her was a possible folly, and perhaps the most dangerous course of action Victoria had ever taken. It would be prudent to plan thoroughly and mad not to involve Lyndsey.

Chapter Thirty-Six

Jack had never travelled by ship and it was not something for which he was made. He needed steady ground. He had often heard sailors at the ports in Graylenmouth sharing tall tales of exotic foreign lands and lusty Marailian girls who would swoon at the Talamholean accent, yet not one of them had warned him that one must fight to maintain his sense of balance aboard a ship. He would have preferred to stay at Wylclyst Manor. He had spent several days there before departing on Lady Alice's small fleet of fishing boats and had grown quite accustomed to the countryside. Now he was returning to his birthplace, but it did not feel like a fanfare of a homecoming.

He was standing at the helm with James, the captain of the trawler. James was a fisherman by trade, and Jack felt less awkward in this man's presence despite his rough nature and foul mouth. Not that his own company seemed required by Lady Alice or Emily of late. The two of them were locked away below decks most of the time, deliberating with the General and the Admiral regarding a strategy of how to take Graylenmouth.

Lady Alice had not pressed Jack about his oath but no longer showed him much hospitality either. Perhaps she had expected him to kneel before her after his night with Emily and swear his unending devotion to her cause. He had never promised such to Emily or her ladyship and was not bound by any sense of duty there.

Emily had become distant too since that night. She was not shunning him like Lady Alice, she would still smile and offer words of greeting when they passed each other on deck but her duty to her lady seemed to be taking priority.

Jack was not a military man but he hoped that the Admiral and General were. The titles were a little grandiose as Lady Alice did not have much of an army or navy to speak of. Around five hundred men, volunteers and a few eager members of the petit-magistrates had joined Alice's cause to put her on the throne. The

239

three small fishing trawlers they had piled onto to sail along the coast and then on to the capital, made up her navy.

This concerned Jack greatly. The Talamholean military was not a vast one but it was large enough and better equipped. They would not have much difficulty dealing with a small force of five hundred men and three fishing trawlers. It would only take one of the royal frigates to sink all three vessels in a heartbeat. If that did not happen, then these loyal and devoted men would be facing certain death when they reached the city walls.

Even if the garrison in Graylenmouth was unprepared for a siege, the Guard would be drafted into the city's defence. Lyndsey would no doubt be among them and that gave Jack grim thoughts. Lyndsey was more than capable of handling herself in a war, but Jack did not like the idea of potentially having to face his best friend on the battlefield. Honour stated that without an oath of allegiance, he would not have to fight, but given Lady Alice's grim situation, he doubted honour would matter to her.

He had to know what they were planning. He was afraid to find out and the idea of being involved made him feel ill. He had played his part as a pawn in Eva Valmarque's game and wanted no more of it, but it seemed that was a choice he no longer had. Whether he liked it or not, he had unwillingly instigated a revolution, and was now travelling with the invasion force of a woman who many would call a usurper.

He had to do something. It could still be many days until they reached the capital and he had no desire to while away the journey without taking action.

He bid James a good day who grunted back a farewell. He willed himself down to the lower deck and the captain's quarters, which James had given over to Lady Alice. He knocked on the door and Emily answered. A pleasant smile of surprise and curiosity spread across her face in an instant. "Yes?" She enquired. Jack was hesitant; he had been so determined just now, but he had not thought everything through. Wanting to come in might mean having to give his oath, which he was still reluctant to do.

"I was wondering if I could be of assistance. I know the capital well," Jack said thinking quickly.

"Please come in, Sergeant, your insight would be welcome," declared Lady Alice's voice from the corner of the room where she was sat at a table with two proud-looking men.

Emily led Jack to the table where he stood with her and the two men. These men were a bemusement to Jack. They spoke and carried themselves with the pride and refinement that military commanders are known for but were not dressed accordingly. They were wearing the rags and wool of a commoner. Jack now noted that everyone he had seen on the boat since boarding it yesterday in Wylclyst had also been dressed this way. The only exceptions were Lady Alice who wore her usual fine embroidered gowns and Emily in her bright yellow colours.

Lady Alice was the only one sitting. She sat up straight and alert in a high-backed chair, her eyes fixed on the maps in front of her. Maps of the capital and its surrounding area.

"Two royal frigates guard the mouth where the docks are at all times, my lady," said Admiral Nash, the proud man to Alice's left. "Thirty-six guns each and too much for our fleet. Therefore, I suggest we moor the trawlers here," he said, pointing to a bay on the coastline to the east of Graylenmouth. "And march the men the remaining ten miles."

"Very good," said Alice. "Any objections, Wallace?" She said looking at General Wallace, the man on her right. He shook his head. "Excellent, we will reach the mooring point in three days and the capital in four, if my navigational skills are not too patchy."

"They are not, my lady," said Emily with pride and admiration.

"Good! Anything to add, Sergeant Sweep?" Alice said looking up at him. Jack was unsure if she actually wanted his opinion. Perhaps she was daring him to challenge her. Better judgement told him that he should not ask what he wanted, but better judgement could hang right now.

"May I ask your plan, my lady? With regards to taking the capital." Once again, Jack was expecting Lady Alice to take offence but she did not.

"We have not the men for battle, but there are only two roads into the city, the east and the west. We will dig in and fortify ourselves there, cutting off supplies. They'll surrender within a month when the people are starving and rioting, my cousin will have no choice but to abdicate." Lady Alice seemed proud of herself, as though starving the masses for her cousin's throne was not even a necessary evil.

Jack was not sure the plan would work, "There is a port, my lady, which as your Admiral has just stated is guarded by two frigates. Food could be brought in that way." General Wallace turned a bright shade of red upon hearing that. He had obviously not considered this eventuality.

"Perhaps," conceded Lady Alice followed by a brief scowl in her General's direction, "but that will take time, time enough for the starving populace to cause unrest."

Jack had no idea how long it would take for food to be brought in through the ports and was not sure Lady Alice, nor her advisors, did either. There was also the fact that she probably did not have enough men to barricade the roads effectively. It would not be long before the defending force despatched a sortie to remove her small army, which would not last long against a cavalry charge. They had no cavalry of their own and no trained pikeman to withstand such a thing.

To Hell with her, was Jack's first thought. He had done enough. It was not his fight and this was not his war. He could slip away and disappear at dusk once they had moored, and she would be none the wiser. He could set off back into the countryside and start his life anew.

Jack felt shame. His willingness to run would put the lives of Lyndsey and Emily in certain danger. Lyndsey could be forced into the ensuing fight and even with Alice's minimal odds of victory, she could still be slain. When Alice inevitably lost, Emily would certainly be tried for treason, or worse if the Warlocks got to her first. Jack liked none of those outcomes and was not prepared to let them happen.

There was also the plight of the people to consider. He may no longer be a guardsman but he had still sworn an oath to protect the people of Graylenmouth. His conscience would not let him abandon them to a siege. Even a meagre one such as this would still see a rise in opportunism from the city's criminals.

He sighed. "I have another option, my lady."

"I'm all ears, Sergeant," she said encouragingly.

"Send word to your cousin and invoke Tarin Thal. I will stand as your champion." He could not believe what he had just said but he did not see another solution. It was the only way to save Emily, to save Lyndsey, and the lives of countless innocents both in the city and loyal to Alice.

"Am I to assume, Sergeant, this means I can expect your oath?" Lady Alice said curiously.

Jack hesitated; it would be impossible to stand as her champion without doing so.

"Yes, my lady," he said, trying to mask the defeatism in his voice.

Chapter Thirty-Seven

Lyndsey had sent message to the barracks that she had a fever and would not be able to report for patrol duty today. She felt guilty about malingering as she knew her colleagues would have to pick up the slack for her absence but Victoria's need was greater.

Daisy had shown up at her house yesterday to explain the plan and she had gasped with admiration at the genius of it all. That did not make the danger any less real. Victoria's strategy and the role she had assigned her within it gave her some anxiety, but she knew it was their best option now. Ever since Daisy had coaxed the crucial information out of Neil, she was beginning to wonder if the gossip columnist had cold feet. Now with Daisy's explanation, she knew nothing could be further from the truth and she swore never to doubt Victoria again.

If lying to her colleagues made her feel unpleasant; omitting the truth altogether from Michael made her feel nauseous. She checked the grandmother clock in the corner of the room. It was half past six. She would have to hurry. She had agonised over the note she was leaving for her husband who would not be home from his medical duties until dawn. If all went well, she would return home before he did and throw the note on the fire. If all did not go well then at least he would know that she loved him, that she was sorry for not explaining everything and only had not done so for his safety. She hoped he would understand.

He may still hate me but at least he'll know I valued him, thought Lyndsey gloomily before shaking the thought away. Notions like that were no help to anyone right now. She was going to live; she was going to save Jack and Talamholean from the vile Warlock and the influence of her council. She was going to return home to Michael's side to one day raise a family and grow old together.

Though it's good to prepare for all possible outcomes, she finally thought, sealing the letter and leaving it on the breakfast table for him.

243

She was dressed for combat, a loose silk fencing shirt, britches and her guardsmen's riding boots. She equipped herself with three pistols and a bag containing enough shot and powder to bring down a small company. She also brought her knife. Her skills with a sword were not equal to Jack's and a knife would work better in close quarters. Though she was more than skilled with a pistol, which would hopefully render the use of a knife superfluous. Her breast plate and zischagge were locked away in the barracks' armoury but she doubted they would be of much use when facing sorcery.

She donned her cloak, left through the front door and headed to the servants' entrance of Lionsgate Hall. Victoria had offered to send a coach, but she wanted to remain as inconspicuous as possible, and Lyndsey enjoyed the walk. A walk was a good way to clear one's head. A lot depended on tonight and she had to make sure her thoughts were unimpeded in order to play her part successfully.

She knew the streets of the capital so well that she had little need to pay attention as she made her way. Her mind was occupied on tonight and the mission. That was all that mattered right now, as though she was on patrol and chasing down a criminal. The rest of the world and all your other worries disappeared when the fight or the chase occurred and a miscreant had to be apprehended. The only thing that troubled her was the fact that Eva Valmarque, just like the criminals she dealt with, would probably not be caught willingly, she would probably put up a more challenging fight than anyone Lyndsey had ever dealt with before.

When she reached the servants' entrance, she knocked in a determined manner that those ignorant of the situation would have considered rude. Daisy let her in and led her to the room where tonight's proceedings would be taking place. Daisy was out of disguise and in a servant's uniform. Given her skills that was probably her biggest camouflage of all. They arrived in a secondary living room where Victoria was waiting for them.

This living room was the smallest room in Lionsgate Hall. Six square feet and windowless, many affluent people had a room like this in their mansions to conduct their immoral business dealings or cavort with their mistresses away from prying eyes. Lyndsey was relieved to see that Victoria's lounge did not contain a bed. The small room was barely larger than a broom cupboard. There were the oak wood panels that existed in many of the rooms here, but besides that there were just two armchairs, a coffee table and a wooden drinks cabinet.

"Good evening, Lyndsey." Victoria's tone was friendly yet urgent and Lyndsey understood there would be no time for pleasantries, of which she was relieved.

"Good evening," Lyndsey replied. She checked her watch. It was a quarter to seven. "We have half an hour before she arrives?" Victoria nodded in confirmation and the three of them went to their business.

Daisy thumped one of the wooden panels which triggered the spring mechanism and pushed the panel a few inches forward from where it had been previously. She then slid the panel to the side revealing a hidey hole; five feet tall, four feet deep and the same in width, created by someone having removed a section of the brick work. It had apparently been a creation of the previous owner, who often had the need to conceal one of his many mistresses from the eyes of his wife.

Within the hidey hole, Victoria had placed a small wooden chair and smaller bedside table as Lyndsey had requested. She sat down and carefully loaded her three pistols one after the other and placed them on the table. Daisy brought a jug of water. Lyndsey had refused the offer of a candle to Victoria's astonishment. It would not be wise to have a naked flame in a confined space with all the gunpowder she had brought.

"I had a servant clean the peephole," said Victoria. "Edward had one installed when we moved in. He thought it would make a good hiding place in case of a riot, but we never really used it." Lyndsey nodded in understanding. "I'm glad you're here, Lyndsey. Daisy and I are not experienced in combat, and I doubt Miss Valmarque will accept my offer without resistance."

Lyndsey had to admit: that troubled her as much as it seemed to trouble Victoria. Her last encounter with the sorceress had given her the impression that a Warlock's magic was neither as indestructible nor unbreakable as they claimed. Nevertheless, that did not give any of them cause to underestimate the redhead and how dangerous her powers made her, even if they were lesser than that of public perception.

"I feel compelled to tell you that it's not too late to back out of this if you want to," said Victoria anxiously. Lyndsey thought she saw her suppress a tremble.

"No, thank you," said Lyndsey abruptly. "She's threatened me, she's sent Jack into perilous exile, and now I find out that she and her kind are interfering in legislative matters illegally." Lyndsey did not want to appear rude to Victoria whom she respected greatly but neither did she want any favours. Stopping the woman was her duty, both as a guardsman and as Jack's friend.

Captain Thompson could not be informed as the Prime Minister had told her he was involved. Lyndsey did not want to appear self-righteous, but it seemed only she, Victoria and Daisy were in a position to see justice served tonight.

The doorbell rang and Daisy went to answer it. Lyndsey steeled herself as Victoria closed the oaken panel, clicking it back into place and plunging her into darkness. Lyndsey carefully dropped from the chair to her knees, crawled to the wall and put her eye to the peep hole. The room appeared as it had a moment ago, only now distorted as though it was a world contained within a glass sphere.

Victoria was sat in the chair nearest to Lyndsey with her back to her. Daisy returned with Eva Valmarque and showed her to the chair opposite before standing at her employer's left-hand side. Lyndsey had never seen the Warlock dress so modestly that it was almost a shock to her. Though still in black, the dress covered much of her, save her neck which was adorned with a single diamond set into a silver choker. Her red hair which usually flowed about her shoulders was now concealed in a black sequined bonnet. She had the appearance of an affluent nun. Perhaps it was the nature of what was to be discussed on this particular visit, or maybe she saw no need to dress like a harlot in the presence of only women.

"Given the contents of your letter, I would prefer it if we were alone, Mrs Lionsgate!" said Eva giving a command rather than a request.

"Daisy is my most trusted servant and undertakes a myriad of responsibilities. She is staying," replied Victoria, not bothering to affect her usual false persona.

Something about Eva's demeanour was making Lyndsey feel uneasy. Her sudden change in dress sense was not the only thing different about her. She seemed to have traded the arrogant and almost nonchalant persona for a steely one. The persona of a woman who had no time for anything other than the matter at hand. Lyndsey was not sure if this change in personality was down to impatience or fear. Either way, Eva would be more dangerous than usual like this.

There was something else as well, the diamond about her neck. It no doubt granted her certain powers, but what were they? Diamonds were rare in Talamholean, rarer than gold or magic users themselves.

"Very well," said Eva impatiently, wishing to get down to business. "Your servant will share the consequences of your actions. Do you know how many people have threatened a Warlock and lived to tell the tale?" Eva's green eyes could have illuminated the room as she opened them wide and held a rigid gaze upon Victoria.

"I imagine I shall be the first," said Victoria wryly. If Eva terrified her, Lyndsey could not tell now.

Though Eva did not appear fearful that Victoria had not buckled at her threat, it had clearly come as a shock. In the absence of an apology or an attempt to grovel, as she had no doubt expected, she frowned and narrowed her eyes quizzically before replying. "I'm somewhat surprised, Victoria."

Lyndsey noticed the sudden change in parlance, Eva had switched to using her first name and was trying to appear familial. That told Lyndsey that for whatever reason, she did not want to resort to violence. Not yet anyway. "I'm surprised that you wish to threaten me and jeopardise what could be a beneficial relationship with the council?"

Victoria laughed sarcastically which drew another frown from the Warlock. "I have written half a dozen articles libelling Bernard Crenshaw for you. Yet I'm yet to receive so much as a letter from the Warlocks. I wonder, Miss Valmarque, had my message inviting you here not revealed what I knew about the council's self-appointed veto power, would you have come at all?"

"I would like to know how you acquired that information and what you intend to do with it. That is the only reason you're still alive." With that declaration, she moved her right hand towards the diamond in her choker. Daisy began to move towards the Warlock and Lyndsey cocked the first of her pistols.

Victoria diffused the situation as she raised her hand to stop Daisy and, unknown to Eva, let Lyndsey know that she had things under control. "If you're now threatening me, Miss Valmarque, I should warn you that my latest column in the Chronicle is to be printed tomorrow. It will detail how I died at your hands after I discovered you were having a sordid affair with the Queen Consort."

Eva half laughed and half spluttered. "Even if that was true, no one would believe that absurd filth."

"Probably not, but you would be surprised how absurdity sells. Every literate person in Graylenmouth would be discussing what you get up to in the royal bed chamber by lunchtime. I wonder if the Prime Minister would still want you around." Victoria had a point. Reputation was the only thing more valuable to the powerful than money or magical abilities and even bizarre or libellous falsehoods could destroy them in a near instant.

Eva hesitated for a moment before shrugging. "Prime ministers change and so soon will the King." She raised her hands to the diamond on her neck and began to concentrate.

Daisy rushed at the Warlock but not before the diamond had granted her its power. She grabbed Daisy by the throat then stood and raised her in the air with a single hand.

Victoria screamed and stood up, standing only two feet away from Eva, she pleaded, "No! No, please." Eva struck Victoria across the mouth with her free hand and she fell to the floor with a scream.

Lyndsey, hoping that super strength did not make one's skin impervious to lead, threw her weight behind her shoulder at the panel which clicked forward. She slid the door open with one swift motion before pointing her pistol at the Warlock's head.

"Drop her!" Lyndsey ordered, her guardsman's instincts fully taking over.

Upon noticing Lyndsey, Eva fixed her with a malevolent stare and an unsettling glint in her green eyes. She squeezed her right hand, Daisy had time for one last fearful and silent wince before the Warlock crushed her windpipe and dropped the young girl; she fell to the floor like a marionette without strings.

Eva Valmarque opened her mouth and rounded on Lyndsey, about to offer a taunt, but Lyndsey would not allow it. Murdering Daisy had sealed her fate and Lyndsey would not permit her another second in this world. She pulled the trigger and an ear-splitting bang filled the room with white smoke. The shot landed in the forehead of Eva's skull. Brains and blood sprayed the wall behind.

Eva's corpse had barely hit the floor before Lyndsey was at Daisy's side. "I'm sorry, Daisy, I'm so sorry." Were it not for the shock, she would have wept. Were it not for a guardsman's instincts and a guardsman's training, she may have shot the sorceress without warning and Daisy may yet still live.

Chapter Thirty-Eight

Three days after Daisy's death, Victoria, Lyndsey, and many of the servants from Lionsgate Hall were in attendance at the young girl's funeral. Lyndsey was sobbing into her husband's shoulder which was to Victoria's approval. Not out of spite, she did not hold the young woman responsible for Daisy's death as she knew Lyndsey did herself. Though she had not known her long, she knew she was tough and had been worried she would not be able to grieve properly. The young woman's upbringing and time serving the Guard had hardened her. A hard exterior was more than necessary when one's occupation was law enforcement, but even the hardest shelled creatures possessed softer interiors.

Despite her own grief Victoria had wondered, more than once since Daisy's death, if Lyndsey's skills were being wasted in her current profession.

Gathered around the pyre on a hill just beyond the city walls, Daisy's lifeless body was wrapped tightly in linen and atop a wooden pyre. The flames were growing higher as they engulfed Daisy's embalmed body.

Victoria was wealthy enough to have brought her servant a burial in the cemetery, complete with a lavishly carved marble headstone. That would not have been what she wanted. With the exception of her employer, Daisy found the rich and the powerful to be profoundly boring company and would not have liked to spend eternity beside them. The theatre and the spectacle of a cremation would be a far more fitting farewell to an actress.

No one had given speeches at the funeral. For the first time in her life, neither the art of oratory nor penmanship had spoken to Victoria. She would always have excellent things to say about her former maid and friend, but her mind was a fog. A fog so thick, she could not see through it and out the other side. In the haze of that thick cloud was a fitting eulogy for Daisy but she would not find it until the mist had cleared.

I'll scatter her ashes on the stage of the theatre, thought Victoria, *and all the finest actors in Talamholean will read you their sonnets and poetry in your rest.* Daisy would like that.

She looked at Lyndsey who was still sobbing with her arms about her husband. There was at least one shining bright beacon amongst all the fog and that was Lyndsey. Daisy would have understood too. She knew that the search for truth was never over. If she did not, she would have returned to acting.

The funeral guests waited at the pyre until midday arrived. When the flames died down, they made the short walk back towards the east gate of the capital. The servants and Michael made their way to Lionsgate Hall for the wake. That would have to wait for Victoria, and for Lyndsey. She wanted to get the young woman on her own. It was her only opportunity.

As arranged, Victoria and Lyndsey made their way to a pub, 'The Stalwart Soldier'; it had been Daisy's favourite place to socialise. Her servants would prepare the house for a memorialising of their former colleague. Victoria bought them each an ale before acquiring a table in the corner.

Despite the upper classes claims about common men all being drunken and brawling brutes, the inn was secluded. It was one o'clock in the afternoon and the common man had to get about providing for his loved ones. There was no opportunity for drink and even less for violence.

"Thank you, Lyndsey," said Victoria handing her new friend a tankard. "My servants are amiable enough but I can't show weakness in front of them." With that last sentence, a tear ran down Victoria's cheek, grief finally having found a chink in her thick exterior, but it did not last long. Victoria wiped away the tear, cleared her throat, and steeled herself.

"My work has to continue," she went on. "Not just because it's what Daisy would have wanted but because it's my duty to the people," she said in a hoarse voice while using all her strength not to let her speech waver. Lyndsey nodded weakly in agreement, still appearing fragile herself after her own sobbing, the skin around her eyes was the colour of a blood orange. Victoria knew it would be cruel to wait for Lyndsey to find her voice, so she continued. "I think I've done all I can operating in the shadows. It's time I became more open about my doings, and operating in secrecy will be harder now without Daisy, but that means without my pseudonym, I'll be more in danger than ever. I'll need a bodyguard of sorts," she declared before concluding with, "The job is yours if you want it."

Despite her grief, the magnitude of the declaration was not lost on Lyndsey, who now widened her watery eyes in awe before meeting Victoria's gaze. "You mean...?" Lyndsey said followed by a long pause as her lower lip trembled.

"Yes," Victoria replied and then finished Lyndsey's sentence. "It's time for Bernard Crenshaw to cast off his, or rather *her*, anonymity."

The revelation appeared to fill Lyndsey with a great deal of surprise. She wondered if Lyndsey would attempt to talk her out of it. Not as a guardsman but as a friend. After all, Victoria's criticism of the establishment in the pamphlets she had published under the name 'Bernard Crenshaw' had not been a crime. There was no law prohibiting criticism of the powerful nor keeping one's true identity a secret, but when you are verbally assaulting the most powerful men in Talamholean, you in turn made enemies of them. Letting them know who you were was akin to parading yourself in front of them with a large target embroidered upon your gown.

However, there was only so much one could achieve operating in secrecy, and as she had said to Lyndsey, it would be a lot harder without Daisy's nigh irreplaceable skillset. Lyndsey's own skillset was vast but different to that of Daisy's and would serve her more effectively if she were writing as herself.

As her own employer, she could intimidate answers out of politicians and goad them with accusations of cowardice when they refused to speak to her, and Lyndsey would be more than adequate at shielding her from their threats.

"You don't have to decide now," said Victoria gently, hoping secretly and more than anything that Lyndsey would accept.

Before Lyndsey could even contemplate an answer, the city bells began to ring. The sound was as much a shock to Victoria and Lyndsey as it was to the inn keeper, who dropped the tankard he was cleaning with a thud. Those bells only clanged when celebration was to be called, but today was not a holiday and there were no festivities to honour.

Lyndsey and Victoria stood up and walked into the street, crowds were gathering densely before gradually parting for a man on a horse, resplendent in pearly white clothes and a purple silk sash as he strutted his mount down the cobbled streets towards the east gate. Behind him rode Alayna Strauss, the Chief Warlock looking both triumphant and apprehensive. The crowds were all joyfully chanting the same phrase. "Tarin Thal, Tarin Thal, Tarin Thal."

Tarin Thal? Victoria searched her memories but the closest answer she came to could not be right. Tarin Thal was an ancient custom that pre-dated the unification and had not happened for centuries, and as far as she was aware, never in a united Talamholean. It was an agreement that could be invoked by two people with a claim to the throne who could duel to the death for the right to rule. An honourable agreement used as a means of avoiding the mass bloodshed of their subjects.

This could not be applied in present day though. To Victoria's knowledge, only the King's sons had a claim to the throne besides Wilfrid himself. While it was not uncommon for a son to steal the throne from his father, the princes were infants and unlikely to be coveting the throne at an age when they were still crawling.

"I have to go!" Lyndsey said and she departed swiftly. Victoria did not try to stop her. She knew she took her responsibilities seriously and could not be swayed. In times of crisis, all guardsmen were expected to report for active duty. She was impressed at the speed with which Lyndsey had composed herself. She was a professional and kept a level head in moments of emergency. Victoria could not discern a single reason not to employ her.

Chapter Thirty-Nine

The fishing trawlers had moored one bright summer's morning in the small fishing village of Brixlen, only a day's march from the capital's east gate, when Lady Alice received her cousin's reply. He had accepted as all knew he would. To refuse a challenge of Tarin Thal would have made him look weak to his enemies and cruel to his supporters. Despite his overwhelming military advantage over Lady Alice, protocol and politics had forced him to accept.

Lady Alice and her meagre force of five hundred men marched along the coastal road to the capital. Jack, as the lady's champion, had been gifted a splendid white stallion as well as a silk cloak of blue and gold, the ceremonial colours of Lady Alice and her banners. He felt ridiculous on a lord's horse and in a lord's cloak. On occasion, he thought he caught Emily offering a smirk in his direction when she thought he was not looking her way.

Jack had found himself looking at Emily more often than he should in the last few days. He still had not been alone with her since that night at the manor. He doubted the witch returned his feelings and doubted even more he would see her alone again. He had agreed to be Lady Alice's champion and neither Emily nor Lady Alice herself would need to offer any more encouragement to him.

Jack rode near the front of the column that had disgorged itself from the fishing boats and headed west towards Graylenmouth with General Wallace still looking like a civilian and rather humbly dressed, which made Jack feel even more ridiculous in his silk.

Admiral Nash had rather conveniently asserted that an admiral's place was with his ships so stayed behind with his ragtag fleet. Just ahead of him and General Wallace rode Lady Alice, resplendent in a fine silk gown next to Emily, her most trusted adviser. Jack thought it was folly for Talamholean's potential queen to ride so frivolously and draw attention to herself where she could be shot at any time but did not protest as he knew she would be unlikely to listen.

253

"A queen must make herself known to her subjects," she had said to General Wallace before departing the boats, the General having had the same thoughts as Jack on the matter.

To the rear of Jack and the General was all of Lady Alice's fighting force. Five hundred men, all infantry, marching behind them. Although marching was not the right word. That was something trained and disciplined soldiers did. This was a volunteer army that was almost strolling while they carried their muskets as uncomfortably as a man may carry a cache of explosives with a lit fuse.

Most were younger than Jack and had looks of fear in their eyes. Jack had seen that same look amongst innocents in the capital who were violently threatened by robbers. Every time he dreaded his approaching duel, he would look back at the column and find the fearful face of one of these youths; it reminded him why he had agreed to be Alice's champion and allowed him to prepare himself for the approaching fight.

The column reached the grassy planes to the east of the capital by nightfall. Lady Alice ordered a camp to be established in an area picked by General Wallace. An area just out of cannonball range. Jack knew there was no artillery adorning the city walls but said nothing. He felt safer out of range whether the cannon was real or imaginary.

As Lady Alice's champion, he had been assigned a servant to set up his tent and cook his meals for him. It made him feel both relieved and peculiar. He never imagined he would have a valet. That was for rich people and eating food prepared by others felt somehow unfair, like he had not earned it. On the other hand, the fact that he would not have to tend to certain matters himself gave him more time for other things.

"Thank you, Nathan," he said to his valet upon noticing his tent had been set up. "What time will dinner be ready?" He asked not with the confidence of a lord but more with the hesitancy of someone who expected Nathan to turn around and aggressively tell him to cook his own dinner.

"In an hour, Sir. I'll build a fire now," replied Nathan politely. Jack was not used to being called sir. Even in the Guard, the title of sergeant was an affectation used by all those who participated in patrol duty.

"That's good, thank you, Nathan," he replied awkwardly. "I'm going for a walk. I shall return in an hour."

"Very good, Sir."

Jack departed. On his way, he asked several men to join him. Men who carried swords and men who looked like they could use them effectively. None of them protested or asked why. He was the would-be queen's champion now and to refuse him could mean dire reprimand.

He reached the edge of the camp with three new comrades, all armed with swords. No doubt family heirlooms or stolen from former opponents in previous fights.

There was a middle-aged man with a backsword like Jack's, though his sword was not of rare metal but ordinary steel and beginning to rust. He was of similar thin build and height to Jack, but his age probably gave him experience that Jack had not yet acquired.

There was a younger man, perhaps only a few years older than Jack, who carried what looked like a steel broadsword with two edges. Generally, a cavalry sword and used for swinging down at infantry, but the man was so muscular, it was unlikely that the sword's weight would hinder his attacks.

The final man was thinner than Jack and smaller too. He carried a rapier, like the one Jack had left Graylenmouth with. Three different opponents would hopefully give Jack all the training he required before his impending duel for the future of the monarchy.

Jack drew his sword and ordered the middle-aged man to come at him. The man was as experienced as Jack had expected. He knew where to aim his blows and knew how to parry Jack's effectively, but his footwork was not up to the standard of Jack's and it was not long before he had knocked him to the ground with an elbow to the ribs.

The bulky younger man with the broad sword had strength Jack had never seen before. Jack dared not risk a parry, his superior ferramus sword would easily absorb the blow, but his arm would not; the force would probably shatter half the bones he had there. Instead, Jack relied once again on footwork and speed. The man was strong but not fast. Jack ducked, weaved, and danced around the man and his broadsword; he eventually unwittingly turned his back on Jack and yielded a defeat at sword point.

His final opponent, the small young man with the rapier, proved to be the hardest. He was fast, faster than Jack. Jack had never been a muscular man so tended to rely more on speed than strength. Until now, he had never encountered an opponent faster than him. Jack was barely bringing his parries to the man's rapier in time. As Jack was beginning to feel exhaustion take hold at his fifth parry, he changed plan. When his opponent tried to bring the rapier down on Jack's head, he grabbed the man's wrist with his right hand, stopping him dead in his tracks. He forced and turned it clockwise until he dropped his sword and it fell to the ground, granting Jack a victory over his now unarmed adversary.

Jack took several deep breaths to get his strength back before saluting his three opponents. He thanked them for the warm-up. Now the real training would begin and he ordered all three of them to attack him at once.

He ducked, he danced, he spun, and he pivoted numerous times in this three against one training session. He acquired a few bruises and returned a few to each of them, then stopped as they all got their breath back before starting again. He had lost track of time and did not know how long they had been at it before Emily interrupted them.

"If you're quite finished, Sergeant?" The dance stopped and they all looked up. It had been so loud and taken all their attention that they had not noticed her approach. She was sitting there looking beautiful in the moonlight atop her mare in her usual yellows. She was leading Jack's stallion in her other hand and gesturing him to accompany.

Jack saluted his companions one last time and thanked them for the sword play, then mounted the horse and joined Emily. Emily seemed to be in a purely professional mood tonight as they rode back to the other end of the camp. "You won't get good training that way. You're my lady's champion now. If they harm you, they lose their heads."

"I know," Jack conceded. He had suspected that many of the bruises he had received could have been worse, and assumed his opponents were showing restraint, he had been too. He had no desire to kill someone in training, purposefully or by accident. "But training feels a lot better than doing nothing and just anticipating." Admitting that felt like cowardice but he wanted to explain himself.

Whether Emily agreed that his admission was one of cowardice he did not know, her mind seemed to be on other matters. They rode not to Lady Alice's tent, as Jack had first assumed, but to General Wallace's, where the General was awaiting them with ten members of the petit-magistrates. All were in shiny clean blue uniforms and the General now in a uniform of blue himself and a bicorn hat.

Without explanation, General Wallace handed a small white flag on a wooden pole to one of his men, a flag of parley, then joined Jack and Emily atop his own horse with a greeting.

Jack, Emily, General Wallace, and the ten men on foot now made their way towards the city across open green fields. There, Jack saw a tent bearing King Wilfrid's colours and a similar-sized entourage.

"Shouldn't Lady Alice be here?" Jack enquired.

"We are here to discuss the terms of your duel tomorrow," asserted Emily. "Protocol dictates that you, her champion, and I, her second, discuss details with our counterparts in the King's chosen people."

Formalities made no sense to Jack. Could he and the King's Champion not just fight to the death – the one still standing bringing victory to his liege? The pomp and ceremony made him feel that the aristocracy wanted to sugarcoat a brawl to make it feel more digestible. A woman was waiting for them at the front of the King's tent and Jack had attended enough witch burnings to know who she was, as well as the fact that she could only be the King's Second.

"Welcome," said Alayna Strauss. She was wearing a regal gown of the King's colours, red and bronze, with a rose quartz amulet about her neck and was as barefooted as Emily.

Alayna's entourage, who also flew a flag of parley, were the Palace Guard. All were dressed in leather buff coats and britches so pearly white that had it been daytime, it would almost blind people with the sunlight it reflected. They waited outside with General Wallace and the petit-magistrates as Jack and Emily entered the tent at the Chief Warlock's invitation.

Three others were within the tent besides Jack, Alayna, and Emily. A servant acting as a waiter, who was there to bring food and drink. A secretary to keep record of all that was said, and the King's Champion, a man dressed affluently in the pearly white uniform of the Palace Guard with a purple silk sash. He was sitting there at the rectangular table in the centre of the tent quaffing ale from a tankard. Jack noted this was unusual for a man who was presumably an aristocrat as they generally preferred to sip wine from goblets.

"Shall we begin?" Alayna said. Jack and Emily took a seat next to each other and across the table from her and the King's Champion, who now grinned at Jack unsettlingly as though they were old friends. He was older than Jack. Perhaps forty, he had shaggy greying hair and appeared beefier than any man Jack had fought before, which did not fill Jack with confidence. When he grinned, he revealed several missing teeth, which when paired with his off-centre and squashed nose, told Jack that he was the veteran of many a fight. He would have to be quicker than ever to best this man in the upcoming swordplay.

"First the formalities," said Alayna indicating to the secretary to begin the minutes. "Present at the parley before tomorrow's Tarin Thal are Alayna Strauss, the Chief Warlock and the King's Second. Sir Myles Grant, Captain of the Palace Guard and the King's Champion." She gestured to the man at her left sitting opposite Jack, who grinned again to show the many gaps in his teeth. "Emily Randall, *witch* and second to *Lady* Alice," the sarcastic emphasis she had put on the titles she gave Emily and Alice was not lost on him and he doubted they had escaped Emily's notice either.

"And finally, *Mr* Jack Sweep, Lady Alice's Champion." She had referred to him with the same level of disdain that she had shown Emily, but her eyes betrayed pure malice when they landed on Jack.

Many things were then discussed which neither Jack nor Sir Myles Grant had any involvement in; they both watched Emily and Alayna discuss the battleground. There was little disagreement there and they chose this very field just beyond the city. The time of the duel was to be at midday when the sun was highest which Jack assumed was purely for dramatic reasons. Then spectators; apparently the King would not be in attendance and neither would the rest of the Royal Family. Only the seconds, Lady Alice and ten other guests would be allowed to watch. Finally, the manner in which Jack and Sir Myles were to duel arrived on the agenda.

"As Lady Alice is the challenger, protocol dictates that the King, or in this case, his champion is given the choice of combat," said Alayna Strauss turning to Sir Myles.

"Swords or pistols?" Emily asked the Captain of the Palace Guard.

Sir Myles cleared his throat before speaking then took another sip of ale. From Jack's perspective, the man seemed to be taking decades to answer the question as Jack made every effort to control his anticipation.

"Pistols!" Sir Myles declared eventually.

Jack doubted he would live beyond tomorrow. True, Sir Myles was larger and no doubt stronger than Jack, but in a one-on-one sword duel, strength was not as useful as speed, and Jack had a ferramus sword that most other swords broke against after too much parrying. Jack had not used a pistol since his fight with Braske and doubted things could go well. The Captain of the Palace Guard was probably at the shooting range on a daily basis.

"If that is all then," declared the Chief Warlock clapping her hands together and badly affecting a yawn.

"Actually, it's not if you don't mind," said Jack to everyone's astonishment. Etiquette no doubt dictated that all the important matters had been discussed and it would be impolite to continue, but Jack cared little for etiquette. He would probably die tomorrow and he was not willing to do that without answers.

"Why are you here, Miss Strauss? Why are you acting as the King's Second when you and your kind seek to overthrow him and have put my life at great risk to do so?" He would look into her eyes and know once and for all what they wanted and why they opposed the King while making a display of supporting him.

At this, she agitatedly held a hand up to the secretary who put her quill down, apparently reluctant to have a historical record of his last comment. "Tradition dictates that the King's own Warlock, Leopold Braske, act as the King's second. Thanks to you, Mr Sweep, that is not possible. In his absence, I offered my services to the King." She smiled a sweet smile as she spoke.

Despite the hiccup in her grand machinations, she had been prepared for every possible outcome in order to save herself and all those who dwelt within the Warlocks' Tower. If Jack won tomorrow, Talamholean would have a monarch they themselves had chosen. If Jack lost, it would appear to the King as though Alayna and her Warlocks had stepped in and saved him at the last minute.

Jack thought he had significantly hindered their plans the night he freed himself from the tourmaline stone trinket, but he had barely inconvenienced them. The Warlocks' Council would retain their influence regardless of the outcome of the Tarin Thal.

Despite his reservations about Lady Alice, he now knew he had to win tomorrow. With her on the throne, the Warlocks would at least be unable to navigate the corridors of power without some obstacles. She and Emily would make sure of that and that seemed preferable to the status quo.

"Calm yourself, Sergeant," said Emily, placing a hand on his shoulder as he felt his tenseness disappear in a wave of serenity. Alayna smirked upon noticing Jack being brought to heel with magic. "Until tomorrow, Chief Warlock, Sir Myles." Emily bowed to each of them as she and Jack left the tent.

When returning to camp, Jack yearned for nothing more than to get Emily on her own. To speak to her, feel and caress her. He had hoped that she might visit his tent later to give him courage for tomorrow's fight but she never came. Jack faced what he hoped was not his last night in the world alone as he fell into a dreamless sleep.

Chapter Forty

Nathan awoke Jack the next morning with a hearty breakfast. The valet was an excellent cook, and in the absence of Emily's presence last night, he took some solace in the fact that his last meal was a good one.

He went straight to Lady Alice's tent after eating. He did not wish to spend time being idle today. He resolved to occupy the hours until the fight with as many things as he could. He was dressed resplendently. Nathan had laid out the clothes he was to fight in. A loose linen shirt and white and gold doublet with Lady Alice's hawk crest, wool britches, and walking boots. He would at least die better dressed than any of his ancestors, he assumed.

Lady Alice greeted him with a dramatic cry before holding out her left hand for him to kiss, which he did reluctantly. The humiliation of having to bow before someone was bad enough but the fact that it was one of the last things he might do made it worse. Emily had told him that Lady Alice may be worthy of his loyalty once he got to know her more. Perhaps she was right. Jack decided that if he lived, he would do all he could to make sure Lady Alice was a monarch he was proud to have placed on the throne.

Jack barely paid attention the rest of the morning as Lady Alice's guests approached him and thanked him for his courage. His mind was on the approaching duel, and if he was not lucky, his death. Jack wondered how history would remember him. As a fool who thought he could best the Captain of the Palace Guard no doubt. That would certainly be likely, but it mattered little now. Being a figure of mockery was of no concern if you were not around to receive it.

Shortly before noon, he made his way down to the duelling ground with Emily, Lady Alice, General Wallace, and the ten members of the petit-magistrates who had accompanied him and Emily yesterday. It was a short ride but seemed to take forever as Jack felt the lump in his throat and wondered if this were the last time he would ride a horse.

Upon arriving at the duelling ground, he and Emily met with Alayna Strauss and Sir Myles Grant. He shook hands with Sir Myles. "Best of luck to you." The King's Champion grinned through the many gaps in his teeth.

"And to you, Sir," replied Jack tentatively. He was not sure if he liked Sir Myles nor did he know if the man had accepted his own championship out of duty or glory. Yet, he did not regard his impending duel as a personal matter and held no ill will towards the man, even though at least one of them was about to die.

He stood back-to-back with Sir Myles then walked six paces on Emily and Alayna Strauss' command. He stopped and turned around to face his opponent.

For the first time in his life, twelve paces seemed more like twelve leagues as the Captain of the Palace Guard faced him, almost blinding him with his pearly white uniform. It was a bright summer's day and the blazing sun pierced Jack's retinas when he looked upon the man.

Emily brought Jack a pistol, powder, and shot. He observed Alayna do the same for Sir Myles from the corner of his eye. He primed and loaded the weapon before cocking it and holding it at his side. He did not have his hand on his heart or his finger on his pulse, yet he could feel his own heart rhythmically thudding so loud and fast, he thought it might burst his ribcage open.

Emily and Alayna walked to the centre of where the two champions stood. They then strode outwards until the four of them formed a diamond shape in the grass, surrounded by a ring of twenty or so spectators.

"The champions will take aim," barked Alayna Strauss and Jack raised his pistol, closed one eye and lined up Sir Myles' head in his sights.

"The champions will fire after the count of three," shouted Emily and Jack began to control his breathing. Lyndsey, who was a crack shot, had told Jack about the importance of breath control when aiming and firing. The trick was to fire halfway through an exhale to make your aim more accurate and Grant's head seemed the size of a walnut at this distance despite his size.

"One!" The Warlock and the witch shouted in unison as Jack expelled all the air from his chest. "Two!" They cried again and Jack refilled his lungs. He brought the trembling hand which contained his pistol under control. "Three! Fire!" Jack squeezed the trigger as he exhaled.

There was a cloud of white smoke and he felt a sharp jolt in his left shoulder. He looked down to see red stains spreading fast through his clothes and across the left side of his upper chest. He felt himself leaning forward as he tumbled to the floor before everything went black.

Chapter Forty-One

.

It was night-time, and in the gloom of the field where he had fought Sir Myles, Lyndsey and Emily were with Jack as he lay there helpless and dying. "You should have come with me to the shooting range more," said Lyndsey disapprovingly with a frown. "I told you your aim needed work and now Sir Myles has bested you. There's no escape now, Jack, not from this."

Jack tried to call out to Lyndsey, to apologise, both for his lack of skill in marksmanship and the fact that they would never patrol together again, but he could not speak. He tried to sit up but the pain in his shoulder shot through him every time he tried, leaving him helpless while he lay in the grass.

"You lost, Sergeant," said Emily. "You squandered Alice's claim to the throne. Now I will be executed for treason." Jack tried to apologise to her too. He had hoped that Emily had managed to somehow escape before the Warlocks had been able to arrest her, but it seemed she was now facing the hangman, or worse, the funeral pyre of Alayna Strauss.

Jack wanted to stand or sit but could do neither so he tried to shout and protest. He hoped to tell Emily he would defend her with his dying breath if he had to. His lover and his best friend just frowned disapprovingly as he groaned and grimaced, trying to form words of apology and words of affirmation but none came save for the feeble moans from his hoarse throat.

"It's OK, it's OK," said another voice. This one was a man's and one that Jack thought he knew. The field was slowly fading, a room was replacing it. White walls and white linen sheets along with a man in a brown leather apron pouring water into a jug. Jack recognised him though he was not sure why he was here.

"Michael?" Jack said, not fully understanding the situation but things now seemingly clearer than they had in the field.

"Yes, it's me," said Lyndsey's husband handing Jack a glass of water for his dry throat. Jack sat up and drank it in one long gulp, then massaged his head which felt it might split in two. "I had to give you a strong dose of opium before operating. You'll feel better when it wears off."

Jack clumsily rubbed his forehead with his right hand. His left arm was in a sling and there was a thick layer of bandages where his left shoulder met the top of his torso.

"Sir Myles' shot lodged itself in your collarbone and snapped it clean in two. It will take a few months to heal but you're actually quite lucky you know, not to have any arteries or organs damaged."

The pain was immense, Jack decided to say nothing. He did not necessarily agree he was lucky, but he was grateful to Michael Carter.

"Thank you, Michael," he said eventually. "How can I repay you for this?" Jack had no funds to pay for his surgery but did not want the man to work for free either.

"Don't worry about it. Lady Alice has already paid me three times my usual fee. All the royal physicians fled the city with the King it seems."

Jack suddenly realised why he was being treated for his wounds in the first place. "The King has fled?"

"He fled before your duel. I'm sure he would have come back had you lost. But as you've awoken and Sir Myles didn't, that would make Lady Alice our new Queen."

"Sir Myles is dead?"

"You shot him in the neck, severing his carotid artery; there's no coming back from that," Michael said with a pained wince.

Jack shuddered. He had been aiming for Sir Myles' head. That would at least have been a quick death. Being shot near the jugular must have made Grant's last moments unpleasant. He had been doing his duty to the people of Graylenmouth by offering himself for a Tarin Thal. Taking one life to save millions may have been the kinder option but that did not make Jack feel any better for killing the man.

"You know, I should probably give you a doctor's scolding for entering a duel but I'm sure Lyndsey will do a better job than me when she sees you," continued Michael.

Jack breathed a sigh of relief. "Lyndsey's safe? Lyndsey's OK?" He had a horrible feeling that the Tarin Thal may result in the criminal underworld taking advantage of the crisis and becoming bolder.

"Considerably safer and in better shape than you currently are," said Michael almost offended. "She's been on patrol since the Tarin Thal was announced but I'm sure she'll want to visit you once I tell her you're here. Mind you, she'll have to wait. Alice's Warlock has been stopping by here every half hour to check on you."

Just my luck, thought Jack. *She finally shows an interest in me again and I'm too weak to enjoy it.*

*

Michael had insisted that Jack needed more rest before even his own wife could pay him a visit. Jack was relieved as he assumed that although Lyndsey would be pleased to see him, her reprimands would require more strength on his part.

He spent the next two days doing little but eating, drinking and sleeping with no one but Michael for company. By the time of the next evening, he was starting to feel his strength coming back. His arm was still in a sling and would be for some time, but he was able to leave his bed and pace about.

Emily, at last, came to see him that night. Jack still noticed her beauty but was too preoccupied with his own injury to be mystified by it, or so he thought when she climbed into his bed next to him and kissed him immediately. "She sits on the throne thanks to you." She smiled.

"Why does that please you so much?" Jack asked her. He did not think that life under the new Queen Alice would be different from how it was under her cousin, at least for those like Jack who possessed neither wealth nor titles.

"You saw the way Alayna Strauss regarded me, the way she hordes magic and keeps it from those who need our help most. I may share their power but not their philosophies." Jack was beginning to understand. Alice shared common cause with Emily regarding the Warlocks. For that, the young witch was willing to overlook all her other foibles in order to bring down the council. Jack finally began to feel a small sense of righteousness for his victory in the Tarin Thal.

Jack was contemplating the irony of Talamholean's future political tension with a smirk. The Warlocks had arranged for Lady Alice to take the throne from her cousin as they disliked the tension between the King and Prime Minister, but it seemed they had replaced it with a new animosity with the very monarch they had chosen themselves. Alice had been correct back in Wylclyst, when she had warned about solving one political problem, only to create another. Jack would leave the capital and find a remote part of the countryside as soon as he could.

"Queen Alice would like you to take her side as the new Captain of the Palace Guard," stated Emily. He had no desire to do such a thing. Tradition demanded that he swore his oath of allegiance to the new queen after fighting a duel for her as he had promised, but tradition and promises were not binding legal stipulations.

Then Jack thought about all he had risked bringing Lady Alice back to the capital and all the innocent lives he had been thinking of when he suggested Tarin Thal. With more political tension in the future between the Crown and the Warlocks, could he really abandon those same innocents now?

In fighting and winning that duel, Jack himself had helped create this new political rivalry, albeit unwittingly. His conscience would not allow him to choose when he did and did not fight for the innocents, and he could not abandon them now. While no longer a guardsman, an oath of protection was still an oath of protection, and probably was legally binding if not strictly enforced.

"Tell the Queen I accept," said Jack, the tones of resignation in his voice were not subtle. Emily smiled and kissed him passionately. At least he would be seeing a lot more of her.

Chapter Forty-Two

Tomorrow, they will know, thought Victoria triumphantly as she finished Bernard Crenshaw's latest article, but not under the name 'Bernard Crenshaw'. This would be the first published writing under her own name that she would be able to take pride in.

It would also serve as protection for her and Lyndsey. The article contained the true account of how Eva Valmarque had died and how she had assaulted Victoria and killed Daisy. How she had intimidated Lyndsey with her magic and also abused the new Captain of the Palace Guard, the young man who had recently won Lady Alice the crown in the Tarin Thal and was rapidly becoming a symbol of heroism to the people. There was a great deal of this article devoted to the Warlock's illegal meddling in the corridors of power between parliament and monarch which included a personal plea to the new queen for vigilance on the matter.

Victoria hoped this would be enough to shield her and Lyndsey from the wrath of the Warlocks. If they sought revenge, they would appear petty, as well as guilty of all her accusations. Both her and Lyndsey would be safe from an open confrontation but they would have to be vigilant to more subtler forms of attack from Alayna Strauss from now on.

It felt good to no longer be writing gossip for the Chronicle; she had given Lord Bolingbroke her immediate resignation that morning. Her pamphlets would now be produced and sold solely by her and would be her main source of income. Victoria thought of Daisy, knowing she would be happy that she was no longer operating in the shadows.

Lyndsey arrived at Lionsgate Hall without being admitted by the servants, Victoria having given her a key shortly after the Tarin Thal. She was dressed as a bodyguard should be. A leather jerkin over a buff coat with sword and pistols adorning her belt. She hung her familiar black cloak up before joining Victoria.

"I made sure Neil and Adam were on the boat to Marailia and paid for their passage," said Lyndsey, confirming to Victoria that she had carried out her instructions. Victoria did not want anyone to suffer as a result of her published findings and had made sure everyone who may be endangered by her latest article was safely out of the capital. Neil and Adam were the last of them.

"Have you spoken to your friend about my proposal?" Victoria had been wanting to ask this since she last saw Lyndsey.

"Not yet, he's still in recovery but I doubt he'll have any objection. He has as much reason to hate the Warlocks as we do," said Lyndsey, who had previously suggested to Victoria that the young Captain of the queen's guard would be well positioned to report on any more bills that went missing, as well as how often the Warlocks were seen coming and going from the palace. "It's Captain Thompson that's angering me right now though. I can't prove anything but he's as corrupt as the rest of them."

"We'll catch him eventually. Truth will out," encouraged Victoria. Lyndsey nodded optimistically.

"Have your informants told you much about what's going on in the palace since Queen Alice took over?" Lyndsey asked, now removing her sword belt to allow her to lean back on the sofa with ease.

"Nothing I can confirm, but I would not be surprised if what I've heard is true," said Victoria grimly. She had bribed the occasional servant for information and the few that had been forthcoming did not tell her anything surprising.

Apparently, the expected tensions between Queen Alice and the Warlocks were only just beginning. With Leopold Braske gone, Alayna Strauss had apparently recommended herself to the Queen as her personal Warlock only to be refused.

She already had her own trusted magic user. The blonde woman who, if the rumours were true, was soon to become 'Lady Emily', and would be a huge affront to the council. The young woman flagrantly disobeyed the Warlocks' codes and guidance on the proper use of magic. Had Lyndsey's friend lost the duel, Alayna Strauss would have no doubt burnt her as a witch immediately and probably tied her to the stake herself.

Lyndsey was aware that her new employer was lost in thought, so instead chose another question, knowing that her first would not be definitively answered. "Do you think anything will get better under our new queen?"

"Difficult to say," mused Victoria at risk of becoming lost in thought again. They would certainly be different. Eva Valmarque would no longer be around to pull the Prime Minister's strings. The Warlocks would be unlikely to send him a replacement as he was known to have been fond of her. Left to his own devices, the capability as well as the allegiances of the man were very much up for debate.

The council had also unwittingly put a monarch on the throne of whom they did not approve. They had misjudged her as a foppish imbecile, more interested in expensive clothes than ruling. Only to discover that she was, in fact, a capable ruler, albeit one who possessed somewhat puritanical philosophies.

The previous animosity still existed. The only thing that had changed were those who held it and to whom it would be directed.